DEATH AT LA OSA

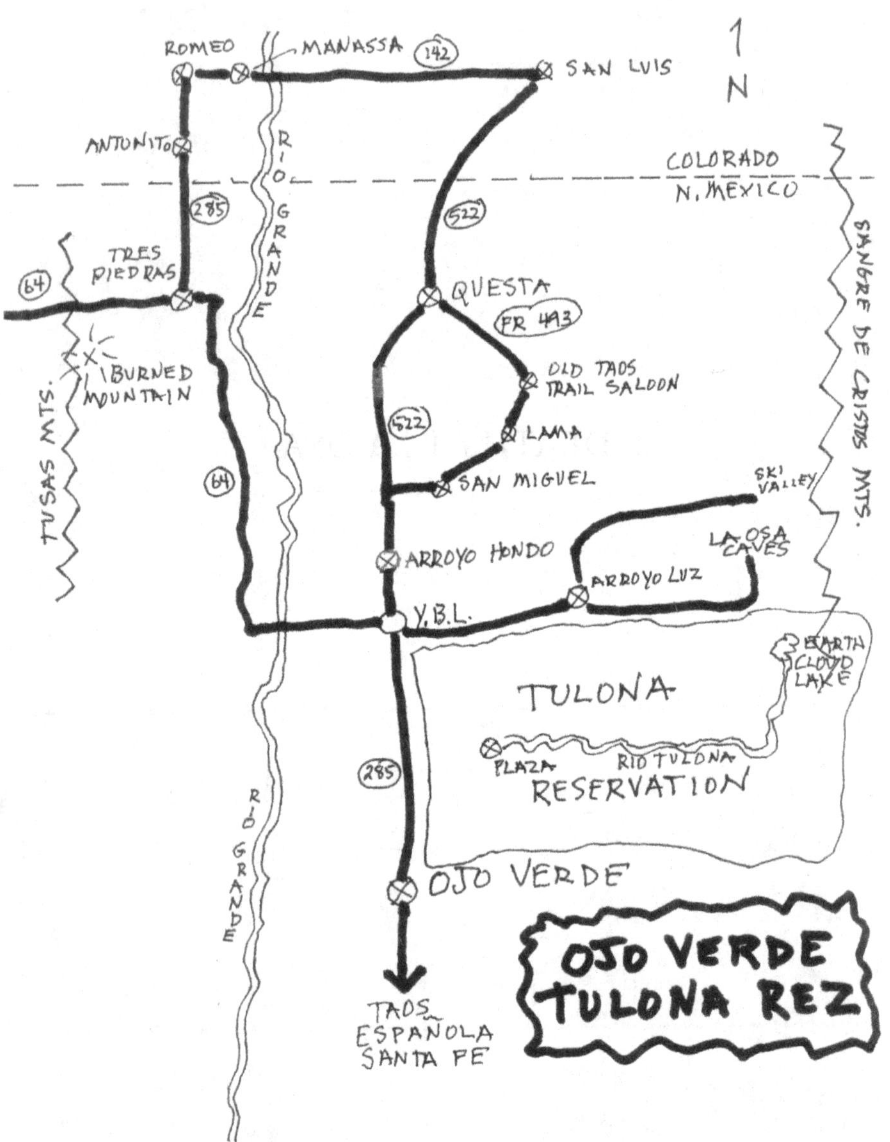

ROMEO
MANASSA
142
SAN LUIS
N
ANTONITO
RIO GRANDE
COLORADO
N. MEXICO
285
522
TRES PIEDRAS
64
QUESTA
FR 493
SANGRE DE CRISTOS MTS.
BURNED MOUNTAIN
OLD TAOS TRAIL SALOON
TUSAS MTS.
522
LAMA
64
SAN MIGUEL
SKI VALLEY
LA OSA CAVES
ARROYO HONDO
ARROYO LUZ
Y.B.L.
EARTH CLOUD LAKE
TULONA
PLAZA
RIO TULONA
RESERVATION
285
RIO GRANDE
OJO VERDE
OJO VERDE TULONA REZ
TAOS
ESPAÑOLA
SANTA FE

DEATH AT LA OSA

A Pueblo Tribal Police Mystery

A Novel

Jack Matthews

Santa Fe

Sunstone books may be purchased for educational, business, or sales promotional use.
For information please write: Special Markets Department, Sunstone Press,
P.O. Box 2321, Santa Fe, New Mexico 87504-2321.

eBook 978-1-61139-6232

Library of Congress Cataloging-in-Publication Data

Names: Matthews, Jack, 1942- author.
Title: Death at La Osa : a Pueblo tribal police mystery, a novel / Jack Matthews.
Description: Santa Fe, New Mexico : Sunstone Press, [2021] | Includes reader's guide. | Summary: "The search for a prehistoric turquoise mine, murder, pueblo ceremonialism, a bookshop, and sheepherders and horsemen form a contemporary novel set in the high country of the Sangre de Cristo Mountains of northern New Mexico"-- Provided by publisher.
Identifiers: LCCN 2021057873 | ISBN 9781632933300 (paperback) | ISBN 9781611396232 (epub) | ISBN 1632933306 (paperback)
Subjects: LCGFT: Detective and mystery fiction. | Novels.
Classification: LCC PS3613.A8483 D43 2021 | DDC 813/.6--dc23/eng/20211217

LC record available at https://lccn.loc.gov/2021057873

WWW.SUNSTONEPRESS.COM
SUNSTONE PRESS / POST OFFICE BOX 2321 / SANTA FE, NM 87504-2321 /USA
(505) 988-4418

I dedicate this book to sustainable Pueblo, Hispano, and Anglo agricultural communities of northern New Mexico.

Believe the wind.

—Charles Aranda, *Dichos: Proverbs and Sayings from the Spanish*

It is believed that certain Indian tribes of the Southwest still obtain stones from localities known only to themselves.

—Matilda Cox Stephenson, *Dress and Adornment of the Pueblo Indians*

PREFACE

This is a work of fiction and all characters are imaginary. The story is based on my field notes, ethnologies, and histories of northern New Mexico and the American Southwest. Most of the places in this story are real, but to respect the dignity of tribes, communities, and sacred spaces, I have fictionalized some locations. The overall landscape, however, in this story is real: the "very high and very cold" country of northern New Mexico as described by the Spanish explorer Hernando de Alvarado in the sixteenth century. I have neither sought nor used Indigenous informants in interpreting ceremonies that I consider living systems of spirituality. Furthermore, no Indigenous person has given me information, either freely or for payment. My Indigenous friends and I respect boundaries. I have written *Death at La Osa* by standards of Article 31, United Nations Declaration on the Rights of Indigenous Peoples, 2007.

1

Thursday, July 7, Day of Blessed Emmanuel Ruiz, Month of Sun House Moon

Since midmorning, two men hiked and searched terrain in the high altitude of the Sangre de Cristo Mountains of New Mexico. High mountain altitude diluted July summer temperatures to a chill. Direct sunlight heated the body like an oven, and if exposed too much, skin burned, despite the cold. As much as possible, they trekked in shade of aspens and spruce and conifers for the sky was dazzlingly clear, the sun hot. Shade was winter, clear spaces the summer. Their reconnaissance focused on two objectives: finding locations for deer hunting in late October and, second, unearth pots and projectile points at archaeological sites. Finding deer signs came first, pot hunting second. Their searching was military in style, though neither had served their country.

The older of the two broke trails. The younger followed behind and lateral to the older man's path. They called out, "deer pellets," to each other when they came across sign. They were on the southside of the mountain, crossing arroyos and small streams of water that fulfilled their need for fresh water at deer camp. As the older man crossed an arroyo, he noticed a blue-green rock that had washed down from higher up. He knew across the border in southern Colorado, the King's Manassa mine had yielded turquoise for decades, but it had played out like all mines eventually do. The earliest digging at King's Manassa and the Cerrillos district south of Santa Fe had occurred before the Spanish conquest. Natives had mined sites for centuries, for there was turquoise in New Mexico. "Are these the blue tears of heaven?" the older man gasped.

He pulled a geology hammer out of his backpack and struck a large conglomerate of rock with matrix like the smaller blue-green rock. The younger man stopped at the sound of rock breaking. The older man picked up the stone fragments, licked his fingers, and rubbed vigorously until dirt and debris disappeared from the surface. Brilliant blue-green turquoise reflected back into his widened eyes. A lapidary's sander and polishing would bring out the colors more vividly. His heart quickened and he grasped the arm of his younger friend.

"This is turquoise! Forget pot hunting! This is more valuable than any old arrowheads and pots! There must be more up the arroyo from this float!"

The two ascended the arroyo into the granite sides of a narrowing cleft. As they walked single file up the arroyo, they found three more matrices that upon polishing with their sweaty bandannas showed bluish-green turquoise. As they squeezed between two boulders, the passageway widened, the air cooled. They gazed upward into a hot sky. The sun's rays began to shine down into the crevice passageway. They suddenly stopped when they saw what lay on the ground.

Stone mauls, dozens of them, littered the ground with chipped debris. Several decaying wooden chisels and levers were stuck in crevices above the runoff of water. The work site looked like it had centuries ago. Whoever mined the cleft and cave had laid down their mauls and wooden chisels and walked away forever.

Over centuries, rain and snow had fallen, and the sun had shone down on exposed rock, providing the perfect chemistry for forming turquoise. The walls, wherever they looked, had large flecks of blue turquoise from the floor of the passageway to as far as they could see up the wall.

"Have you ever heard of the Blue Lady story, *amigo*?" the older man asked the younger.

"No, I never have."

"Well, we have found her."

Two years later
Friday, August 31, Day of Saint Nicodemus, Month of Lake Moon

In late summer, the Month of Lake Moon, the Tulona sang to Earth Cloud Lake. The Tulona, people of the Cottonwood Pueblo, danced and sang around evening fires. Sparks flew upward when fire tenders pitched wood they had gathered in nearby forests and along the pack trail from the Pueblo. In the high altitude of the Sangre de Cristo Mountains, the chill of late August enveloped the dancers. They moved closer to the fires, forcing cold away. Long had it been—decades ago—that the Tulona had demolished the U.S. Forest Service cabin nearby and thrown its timbers on Earth Cloud fires.

Close by, picketed horses whinnied to singing and dancing, even to silences between songs. Dancing expressed life. That was enough, but there was another urge—a duty. *They sang to kachinas in the worlds below Earth Cloud Lake and to the worlds and lakes the ancient ones left behind.* Prayers and songs reverberated in the sacred space, as cold air flowed down the slope of Tulona Mountain to Earth Cloud Lake. The ancient ones that came up to the new world long ago found open places of light. Even so, pain resided in the new world. And, so did evil.

Ben Lovato looked down upon Earth Cloud Lake and the dancers from a distance, not hiding, but not participating. He had sympathy with traditional ways and with his aged father and mother who shuffled to drumbeat, but he was not in the mood to dance, not even to please his mother, Snow Deer. Ben had ridden with Snow Deer and his father, Anton, to Earth Cloud Lake on tobiano paint horses of good stock several days before, and he was impatient to return to the Pueblo.

"Ho-o," he blew in frustration and impatience.

He heard horses whinning. The sixteenth-century Spaniards had brought the *kowena*—the horse—almost overriding their import of cruelty and religion. The *kowena* remained when the Spaniards fled in the Pueblo Revolt. Ben clenched his teeth, nodding affirmatively at the Spaniards being driven to Santa Fe, then to El Paso, over three centuries ago. But they returned; they reconquered. Ben shivered from the cold and the Legends of Black and White: Spanish cruelty, Spanish gifts of metal and horse.

Standing up and pulling his blanket more tightly around his body, Ben decided before dawn the next morning he would ride his gelding, Star, and Jess, his packhorse, down the Rio Pueblo de Tulona trail to the Pueblo. He would be criticized for leaving lake ceremonies prematurely, but he could handle that and make amends later in the Month of Corn Ripe Moon. He might have to toil additional hours of mending fence lines or repairing gates along the Arroyo Luz Road. It was toil for the common good, a slight punishment for leaving early.

For now, however, Ben imagined, I am like Magpie. I want to go back to the cottonwoods, the shelter of home, following the river downward to my village of tree-leaves-that-rattle-with-wind.

Magpie and Yellow Corn woman lived among cottonwoods. They had a child and when Yellow Corn woman went for water at the stream, the witches wanted her to become their lover. She refused and the witches killed her. Magpie mourned Yellow Corn woman and planned to throw the witches out of the cottonwoods. His child came under the care of Yellow Corn Woman's mother.

In gray light, before the sun rose the next morning, Ben saddled Star and loaded Jess to begin the trail ride of twenty-seven miles downhill to tree-leaves-that-rattle-with-wind Pueblo. Yes, he thought, my wife is pregnant, but she is careful in drawing water from the stream and will not be seduced by witches. He did not believe in witches. As he rode carefully on the pack trail, Ben saw the river flowing beside him. Ben clucked to his paint horse, Star, into a gentle pace away from Earth Cloud Lake. Jess followed dutifully behind in halter and lead rope.

Quail Looks Away had not gone with her husband to Earth Cloud Lake. She stayed close to her village and mother. Pregnant or not, she drew water from the stream that divided the Tulona Winter House from Summer House. She was strong in body and attractive, her unbraided hair, dark and shiny, falling gracefully below her shoulders. She did not like her weight gain with pregnancy, but that would go away. Quail Looks Away carried her empty Behrens pail and battered lard bucket to Rio Tulona and dipped the pails in fast-flowing water. Even in summer's August, water ran clear and cold. Neither cattle nor horses roamed upstream to pollute the water with urine and manure. The Tulona people kept their horses in a common *ciénega* pasture with corrals south of the Pueblo on the road to the town of Ojo Verde. The cattle and buffalo were tended in a pasture far away from the stream. Water flowing from the mountains stayed pure and clear. No sickness had ever come from Rio Tulona; the *acequias* were a different matter. You watered corn crops with *acequias*, not drink from them.

The buckets, tilted on their side, filled quickly with water. She lifted them out, set them on the ground to steady her grip, and walked back to her house near the Blue Stone People kiva on the south side of Rio Tulona, the Summer House side. As she strode by the kiva near her home, Quail Looks Away heard drum beat and singing from inside the kiva. The drum's sound was deep and resonating. The singer sang high in a warble that only an elder knew how to modulate.

"Hay yo—hay yo—hay yo—en-e-e-ya-a-a-a...en-e-e-ya-a-a-a."

Quail Looks Away set her pails down and attended the words as best she could understand. A sudden wind blew dust across the plaza and stirred the cottonwood trees along the river, the leaves rattling softly—green, luscious, and filled with moisture. Yellowed leaves fell with the wind. Soon all cottonwood leaves would turn yellow, falling in the stream and collecting along the banks. Quail would swish away the leaves with her hand to get un-leaved water for her kitchen. Rio Tulona was sometimes called Cottonwood River, for along its banks, leaves carpeted the ground.

She stood still until the elder's singing stopped. Quail Looks Away thought that by clock time, a quarter of an hour must have passed. By any estimation, clock time, Tulona time, it mattered not. Her traditional teachers had taught her that a person's attention in the moment was all that anyone ever had.

The present moment, "This! Now!" they had emphasized, "is all we have." Yet, incongruently, her teachers said, "The past is not gone, it relives again in our stories, our songs, the sacred places. The past relives in us."

Quail Looks Away had doubts about the past "reliving again," but she kept them to herself. One day, she would ask Bustamente, the cacique of the Tulona, to explain this circularity again, but she knew he would say, "Quail! You think too much and not *feel* enough!" And, to that, she would disagree.

"I'm thinking too much now," she chuckled, as she hefted the water pails back to her house.

Ben Lovato rode through the morning. In the afternoon, the sun bore down on him and his horses. The upslope wind had become warm, a natural occurrence, offset by the night's downslope of cold wind currents. He hoped for a thundershower to cool them off. The ride down the trail along the Rio Tulona had gone swiftly and without passing people. He felt lonely. Ben halted his horses, allowing them to blow and rest and drink from side streams that crossed his trail and fed into the river. He drank from his canteen. Soon, it was time to move on.

"Okay, let's go, *vamos, kowena*," he said.

"Vamos," was a much for himself as for his horses. He cinched up his packhorse, Jess, adjusted the bundles of gear under the packer's canvas manties, and started down the trail. Rio Tulona flowed on his left side. He rode slowly to keep his horses from overheating in the afternoon sun. He allowed Star to determine his own pace. Jess followed obediently with the lead rope secure, but untied from Star's saddle horn, so that Ben could throw off the rope in case they came between a mother bear and her cubs.

Ben was descending from Earth Cloud Lake, a journey of twenty-seven miles. A family could walk the trail or ride horses. The horse, the *kowena*, was the preferred method of travel. The current topographical maps had been altered to delete pack trails to Earth Cloud Lake and all other hiking or horse trails into the Tulona reservation from the National Forest. Tulona pathways and trails existed in the minds of the Tulona, not on hardcopy maps. Traditional knowledge remained oral. And, those that wrote down the knowledge had their manuscripts destroyed. Or worse, banished from the Pueblo.

Non-Native men and women were not allowed to travel the ceremonial trail, and Tulona guides supervised all fishing and hunting on reservation land. At one point in the 1920s, a federal government official, widely respected by the Tulona people, had initially been permitted to go with the people to the Earth Cloud Lake ceremony in the Month of Lake Moon. So much opposition was raised, however, against his accompanying the people, that after witnessing the overnight dancing at the first camping site, he was forced to turn around and blocked from completing the journey. The government official understood their reaction and wrote favorably of what he did witness at the first campground to Earth Cloud Lake. When he was a boy, Ben Lovato had heard stories of Wally Covington being turned around from his great-grandfather who had been one of the Tulona that protested.

By midafternoon Ben had ridden to the first rest stop, only ten miles away from Quail Looks Away. As he guided his horses onto a dirt road to the Pueblo, he saw an old, gray pickup under the trees just off the road. What caught his attention was the pickup appeared to have become stuck in a washed-out rut off the road.

The Tulona Tribal Police can handle this, he thought.

As he passed by, Ben thought he heard a cry of, "Help me!" He stopped his horse, saddled off, and ran up the slope to the pickup. Did an elder with a heart attack or stroke veer off the trail? The pickup had license plates from New Mexico—the new turquoise-colored plates—and black diamond stickers from the ski valley on the rear window. Whoever owned the pickup skied in the valley and was skilled enough to cheat death on black diamond slopes.

No elders I know of ski, he thought. Walking around to the driver's side, he saw a white man, a *fansaine* or snow-looks-like, prone on the ground, peering under the truck, looking at the underside.

"Hey, there, are you in trouble?" Ben asked. He would confront the *fansaine* later on being up the road to Earth Cloud Lake during ceremonial time. Ben looked around to see if the Anglo was alone. He saw no one else, just the snow-looks-like under the truck.

"I'm not in trouble, my pickup is. I tried to turn around and got stuck in this rut." Odd response, Ben thought.

The *fansaine* scooted out from under the truck and stood up, dusting his blue jeans off. Ben saw he was young, probably in his twenties, fit like an athlete, average height, blue eyes, and brownish-red hair. He appeared embarrassed. He held out his hand to shake Ben's hand.

"My name is Jason and I live in Ranchos, south of Ojo Verde."

Ben shook his hand and gave his name, "Ben Lovato, Tulona Pueblo, and you are trespassing, Jason. This is the Earth Cloud Lake ceremonial period and you are in big trouble up here on the road to the lake!" Ben thought this would define the situation, and maybe turn the guy around and get him off the reservation quickly without incident.

"Jeez! I really am in trouble," Jason quavered. "I had absolutely no idea this was a ceremonial period. It's beautiful here." He paused and looked around. "I was just out for a drive. Help me get out of the rut and I'll get back to Ranchos. Okay?"

"What were you really up here about, Jason?" Ben asked sternly. Suddenly, they heard distant thunder rolling from the north. Ben looked toward the sound, seeing trees sway at high altitude. A large thunderhead was building to the northwest, over the Chama-Tierra Amarilla region in the direction of the Jicarilla Apache reservation.

"What were you doing up here?" Ben repeated. The horses grew nervous from the wind and sound of thunder.

"I was driving down from the ski valley and took a road near the Chanson Restaurant. I followed the road till it narrowed...and I got nervous being this far up in the mountains. I was on the reservation before I realized it," Jason said apologetically. He reached over into his pickup bed and retrieved a shovel to move rocks from the back wheel where the truck had become stuck.

Innocent young man, Ben thought to himself. Yet, Jason had not answered his question. Ben wanted to get back on the trail to Quail Looks Away. He let his question drop for this was not an interrogation. Ben gave orders.

"Jason, you get in the truck and put it into forward, then reverse. Rock it back and forth with gear changing, and I'll see if I can give leverage with my body to push it out. You try and reverse your direction as I push from the front. Understood? Don't run over me!"

After a couple of rocking forwards and then reverses, the pickup came unstuck and rolled back on level ground. Ben threw Jason's shovel back in the bed and walked to the driver's side. He looked carefully in the pickup bed and saw only tools, odds and ends, nothing suspicious. Ben was thinking pot hunter or vandal. Jason was not a vandal.

"I recommend you leave quickly, and if you are stopped by the tribal police, you apologize and go with them quietly to their office. You may be able to get off the reservation without getting stopped." Ben figured it was a fifty-fifty chance that Jason could get off the reservation without incident.

"Many thanks, *amigo*," Jason said, "Drop by the Tablita Restaurant at the Ojo Verde Inn, and I'll complement your lunch for helping me.

I wait tables there and spend my wages skiing in the winter, up in the valley. Guess that's why I love mountains and got lost up here!"

Ben was put off by the "*amigo*," but let it go.

"Good, then. Be careful," Ben cautioned.

Ben waved him off, mounted Star, and proceeded down the road as the first raindrops fell. He saw gray sheets of rain falling down on ponderosa pines farther up Tulona Mountain to his right. To the north, low-hanging clouds and rain completely obscured Gallina, Lobo, and Flag Mountains. This rain would be heavy and hard on him and his horses.

Quail Looks Away stashed her water pails in the corner of the room inside her house alongside the Blue Stone People kiva. The drumming and singing had stopped; the mood lingered. She went back outside her home to look at the changing weather turning stormy and falling upon Ben in the mountains.

Quail's Summer House home was hers, different from most assumed ownerships that were male-dominated in the Pueblo. The council had approved of her co-ownership with her mother. They traced back ownership of the house to the generation of her great-great-grandparents, and she was the only surviving child of her parents. Ben had moved in with her from his father and mother's house on the Winter House side of the Pueblo, across Rio Tulona. Ben's parents had given him to Old Bow kiva when he was a boy. As a man, he returned to the Old Bow kiva on the Winter House side for ceremonial duties. Quail's parents had given her to the Blue Stone People's kiva on the Summer House side. Her ceremonial duties with the Blue Stone People kiva were not as extensive as Ben's with Old Bow. Nonetheless, she had privileges to enter the Blue Stone People kiva and assist when needed.

Quail Looks Away flinched at a streak of lightning and heard thunder from the black clouds to the northwest, toward Chama and Colorado. This was the day that Ben would return. She grew concerned about his safety and the horses, although she knew Star was sure-footed because she had ridden him on muddy trails when she collected herbs in the forest. Still, she was anxious. Quail Looks Away uttered a prayer—two prayers really—one prayer in Catholic sentiment, the other in the world of the Tulona people. Both prayers she believed were powerful and insured Ben's safe return, although she wondered if they would be heard—and by whom or what. Again, another question for Bustamente.

Lightning struck and hovered between cloud and trees. The afterimage of the lightning bolt stuck with Quail Looks Away for a few seconds. Then came thunder. The cold air of downdraft reddened her face;

in the distance, spruce and fir trees wavered violently back and forth in the wind. Nearby, in the cottonwoods along the river, the contrasting black-and-white feathers of magpies came sharply into focus. The birds held tightly on lower branches, chattering and griping about clouds obscuring the sun. Quail went inside her house and lit her propane stove to brew coffee. Because of the approaching storm, her mother would return soon from visiting her sister. She turned on gas lanterns that gave light to the room. Quail made coffee and got fry bread out of the breadbox. She spread butter and honey on the fry bread and poured herself fresh coffee, leaving enough for her mother if she returned hungry and thirsty. Fry bread with honey would sustain them both until Ben returned.

As rain began to fall, she looked out through her turquoise-framed screen door and saw two Tulona tribal police cars speed around the northern Pueblo ash pit and go up the road toward Earth Cloud Lake. Quail gasped, and uttered loudly, "*¡Mi Dios!*" The magpies abandoned the cottonwoods and flew across the plaza, disappearing behind the old adobe church steeple and cemetery. White burial crosses stood out against the dark clouds. The magpies took refuge from the storm under the collapsed roof of the old church. Quail Looks Away closed the door firmly against the wind and rain after her mother entered, wet and shaking from the cold. At the kitchen table, covered by red-and-white-checked oilcloth, she served her mother warm coffee and fry bread with honey and butter.

North of the Tulona Reservation near San Miguel, on the way to Questa, U.S. Forest Service biology specialist Janet Rael saw the sorrel horse entangled in fence wire off Forest Road 493. She stopped her green Suburban Forest Service vehicle and ran to the trapped horse. The horse lay still and had ceased kicking and thrashing the fence. Janet saw that there were no open gashes in its flesh—which was a miracle—and she ran back to the vehicle and retrieved a halter and lead rope from her field bag. Opening the Forest Service toolbox, she grabbed wire cutters.

Talking in a calming voice and not showing rapid movements, Janet slipped the halter and lead rope around the horse's head. Stroking his neck and working her way down to the gelding's hind leg that was caught, she cut the wire and carefully set it aside while continuing to talk softly, "Good boy, fine horse. You're a brave horse. Good fella."

After unwrapping the wire and freeing his hind leg, she coaxed the sorrel gelding to stand, holding firmly on to the lead rope. The sorrel stood free. She led him away from the fence, halted, and began to stroke his neck and withers. The sorrel looked back at her and nuzzled her shoulder in appreciation.

Up the road came a pickup and horse trailer. Luis Ortega from San Miguel stopped the pickup and ran to Janet and the sorrel. "Buck, how did you get this far away from the corral? You can't have opened the gate by yourself!" Janet continued to calm Buck as Luis switched halter and lead rope to his own tack. He loaded Buck into his trailer. They introduced themselves.

"He was a good horse to lie there and let me cut him loose," Janet said.

"How can I ever thank you, Ms. Rael?" Luis said.

"It's okay, no problem, Mr. Ortega. I'll stop by San Miguel someday, and maybe you'll let me ride Buck? And, have coffee with you and your family?"

"Of course, Ms. Rael. And, if ever the Forest Service needs me and Buck in search and rescue, call us, and Buck and I will be there."

Janet stepped up on a fender of the trailer and reaching between the panels, gave Buck a quick rub on his forehead. Softly, he neighed.

2

G. Armstrong Coe walked to the front window of his bookshop on Paseo del Pueblo Norte, two short blocks from the Ojo Verde Plaza, and saw tourists scurrying for cover as lightning flashed and rain fell. Coe's Bookshop was one of two bookstores in the Ojo Verde area. The other bookshop was on Cimarron Road—the so-called Ojo Verde Bookshop. Coe frowned at the name of his competitor: "Ojo Verde Bookshop." What gave them the blue nose to name themselves after the famed Ojo Verde Bookshop of Jennifer Arnold?

"After she went out of business, I'm sure they even tried to buy Jennifer's sign that now hangs in storage at the Wiggins Gallery," he grumbled aloud for the thousandth-time.

Jennifer Arnold had sold books in Ojo Verde for forty years and supported a local woodworker in her bookstore at the same time. Like many other Anglos, she had come to the mountains of New Mexico for a few days and wound up staying fifty years. She had found relative peace in the landscape and people and had put down roots. Maybe Wiggins will sell Jennifer's bookshop sign to me and I'll hang it in my place, he thought. He had already decided to hang it behind his front counter adjacent to a Dorothy Brett *Deer Dance* lithograph.

Coe's cell phone rang. He hated the thing. The phone interrupted natural flows of conversation and thinking processes, and the "infernal location application" could—if not turned off—keep track of where one was located or was supposed to be. Coe had compromised on buying a cell phone to please his daughter who lived in Santa Fe, and since he was sixty-five- years-old, she worried about him and begged him to get a cell phone for his travels to visit her. He bought one, and it had been nothing but a nuisance—but it had pleased his daughter. A landline was good enough for the Coe's Bookshop.

He looked at who was calling, but it only showed the number and Santa Fe as the call origin. "Robocall, I'll bet," he said aloud, punching the red circle to answer.

"Yes, Coe here," he answered impatiently. The cell signal rose and fell in strength like an AM radio wave at night.

"Just like the other calls," he muttered. Cell signals were digital, not analog, and the signals were either on or off, but not this sound. The sound rose and fell like it came across the seas.

Coe heard drums and singing, high-note vocals that he did not understand. The drumming and singing were Native American. It abruptly stopped.

"Who is this?" Coe said. "Is this some kind of a joke?" There was static; then the signal dropped out. Coe punched the phone for a callback and received a recording, "The number you have entered is not a working number. Please check your number and dial again." He checked recent calls and tried calling back, getting the same irritating recording. Coe scrolled down his recent calls and noticed his conversation two days before with his daughter in Santa Fe.

I need to call her today, he promised himself.

Outside the sky grew darker; rain poured down heavily, and grayish-white sheets on Paseo del Norte reflected headlights. Lightning flashed; the neon sign at The Ojo Verde Inn and Tablita Restaurant flickered and went out. The electricity all over Ojo Verde collapsed. City crews left their service depot and set up traffic signs at the major intersections in Ojo Verde to manage traffic. Dancing Rock Power Cooperative dispatched crews to reset pole switches and boxes. The crews checked for transformer blow-outs, but found none. Ojo Verdeans were accustomed to outages.

At Tulona Pueblo, gas lanterns continued to burn, shining light in houses along Cottonwood River. With thundershowers in the mountains, the river rose; the rush of water grew louder, but the stream did not threaten the Tulona. The storm tore yellow and green leaves from trees, as orphaned leaves formed clusters on the water, floating swiftly down the river.

Ben Lovato fell behind his schedule to arrive at tree-leaves-that-rattle-with-wind village by nightfall. He calculated he was five miles on bad road from the Pueblo, and the rain was not letting up. Ben decided to ride up into a stand of fir trees, shelter in place, and wait the storm out. By the time the rain stopped, Ben decided to stay the night in a stand of trees. He unsaddled Star and Jess, sheltering saddle and tack under a tarp to keep them dry.

After picketing the horses, Ben built a fire with some difficulty and set up his bivouac with sleeping bag. He double-checked that he and his horses were under green trees and not beneath dead trees, or those that leaned with roots showing. After a few minutes in the dry sleeping quarters of his bivouac, he fell asleep. He dreamt many things, but the dream he remembered when he woke was seeing Quail Looks Away standing by Cottonwood River, drawing water, and a stranger crossing the bridge walking in her direction. In the dream, Ben was far away, and he could not tell if the stranger meant well or was a threat. He woke before the dream ended.

Jason had entered the Tulona reservation by way of Fire Sleet Road that ran north-south from Pueblo Plaza. Rather than return the same way via Chanson Restaurant, he decided to follow Fire Sleet Road to the plaza and then back to town. If he was lucky, he might make it off the reservation without being seen. Jason's luck ran out.

Coming from Pueblo Plaza and Fire Sleet Road were two tribal police cars. When they saw his gray pickup, the lead car turned on its flash bar and blocked the road. Two policemen were in the front car, one young officer in the last wagon. Jason slid to a stop; the policemen motioned him to get out of the pickup. He complied and stood by his pickup. The thunderstorm enlarged to a dark mountain, and isolated rain drops fell. A few sleet pellets bounced off the ground, then stopped.

The three tribal policemen emerged from their vehicles, walking nonchalantly to Jason who had exhibited no threat, nor wore clothing that might have concealed a weapon. Sergeant Tony Romero asked Jason for his driver license. One of the officers looked in the bed of the pickup and shook his head, indicating there was nothing of interest.

"May we look inside your vehicle?" Romero asked.

"Go ahead and look," Jason replied, waiving his rights. Searching carefully, the officer found nothing of consequence.

"Why are you up here, Jason Taylor of Ranchos?" Sergeant Romero asked bluntly, after scanning the license through the database. Raindrops became larger, but still sparse.

"I was driving and looking at the scenery and mountains up here. Never been around here before. Usually, I'm over in the ski valley or down in Ojo Verde working. I'm really sorry to be a problem, Officer."

"How did you get around the barriers, Mr. Taylor?"

"I came by way of the road over by Chanson Restaurant, and I didn't see any barriers, Officer. I really didn't."

Sergeant Romero looked at his fellow officers, "We don't set up the barriers there at the entrance near Chanson?"

"No," one of the officers replied, "the entry gate is closed and locked. No need for barriers."

Romero turned to Jason. "How did you get through the gate? Open it? Break the lock?"

Jason blanched white. Even more snow-looks-like. "The big green gate with the yellow strip in the middle was open, sir. I didn't see any barriers, and the gate was wide open. I've seen it open before when I go up to the ski valley."

"We will see about that," Romero intoned. He turned to one of the officers. "Tafoya, you go now! Check the status of the gate before the storm rolls in! Larry and I will take young Jason back to the station and pursue our questioning. Larry, you drive Jason's car back to the office, and I'll take Jason in our wagon. Jason, you get in the back seat. First, let me give you a pat down. Hands on the hood of your pickup. Legs spread."

Jason felt guilty, really bad. Nothing had happened to him like this before. Sergeant Romero asked him to empty his pockets, finding nothing of consequence. Romero confiscated his Swiss pocketknife and cell phone, but said Jason could get them back after the investigation.

"You don't seem the type to handcuff, so get in backseat and be still. Your keys in the pickup?"

"Yes, sir. Am I in trouble?"

"You are trespassing on the Tulona reservation without a permit or guide, and this is August ceremonial time. Our sacred time. I'd say, Jason, you are in trouble, but let's go down to the tribal office and work this out. You're not the first *fansaine* to trespass and profane our land."

Jason was so shaken that he didn't even want a translation of the word, *fansaine*. It had to be bad. Raindrops grew larger and heavier. More sleet pellets fell, quickly melting. Romero drove Jason to the Tulona stationhouse and ushered him in quickly before the squall became fiercer.

Tribal policeman Richard Tafoya had turned around on Sergeant Romero's order and driven back to the Pueblo Plaza. From there he drove on Abalone Road past the Tulona Mountain Casino to the intersection of Paseo del Norte. He turned right on Paseo that was US Highway 64 and drove to the yellow blinking light intersection with the Arroyo Luz and ski valley highway. The blinking light had not blinked yellow for several years, but local Ojo Verdeans still referred to the intersection as the yellow blinking light intersection, even though it had been upgraded with red lights and pedestrian crosswalks. More than one tourist had to double back to Ojo Verde and ask for directions, again, when they found no yellow blinking light. A quick apology and accurate description of the intersection—red lights, turn lanes, no blinking light—directed the tourist correctly toward the ski valley and hiking trails in the National Forest. Policeman Tafoya turned eastward, toward Arroyo Luz, at the yellow blinking light—red light intersection—and drove to the first entrance of reservation. Through the rain he saw the gate closed, chained, and locked. He drove farther up the road to the second gate of Fire Sleet Road across from the Chanson Restaurant and stopped at the entry. Fire Sleet Road gate was wide open.

Tribal policeman Tafoya reached over to the passenger's seat to get his raincoat, stepped out of the police vehicle, walked up to the open gate, and looked closely at the chain and lock. Lightning struck up toward Tulona Peak; he flinched at the strike. Thunder soon followed. The chain and lock were hanging down from the big corner post. The lock was open and hanging on a chain link. He looked as far as he could down Fire Sleet Road toward the Pueblo Plaza. There were no cars on the road. A few outlier-Native homes—Pueblo-style with concrete-block construction—had cars parked in front and no lights in the windows.

Electricity out again. Dancing Rock Co-op has their hands full, Tafoya thought.

Tafoya grabbed his flashlight and shined it on the ground to highlight tracks and marks beside the gate. He saw distinctive tracks. A car or pickup had passed recently through the gate. Rain had not erased the tread marks. He took out his cell phone and snapped several pictures of the tread. Looking closer at the gateposts where the chain and lock hung loosely, he found footprints of a work boot, about a size ten. He took a picture of the footprints to compare with Jason's boots back at the office. Other than Jason, a *parciante* or *majordomo* of Acequia de Juan Leal may have opened the gate and forgotten to close it. That was not likely. Tafoya chained the gate and locked it, making a mental note to call the *majordomo* to see if he had opened the gate to check on the *acequias*. He ran back to the patrol car, glad to get out of the rain. He drove to the Pueblo by way of Fire Sleet, opting not to get back on pavement and go by the yellow blinking light, which was probably not blinking now, thanks to Dancing Rock Co-op.

When Tafoya arrived at the Tulona Pueblo stationhouse, he took a picture of Jason's truck tires and made a quick-and-dirty comparison: they were a match. Inside the office he grabbed a cup of coffee and asked Jason to show him the sole on his boot. Jason raised his foot, and Tafoya compared his photo at the Fire Sleet gate with Jason's boot tread—they were not even remotely close in comparison. Two different shoeprints. The tire treads, however, were a perfect match. Tafoya concluded Jason had come through the gate in his pickup, but had not been the person opening the gate.

He stepped to the front office. A call to the *majordomo* of Acequia de Juan Leal quickly answered the question if he was the person that opened the gate and forgot to close it. The *majordomo* stated he had been out checking on the *acequia* during the day and had a sudden family emergency.

"My wife called me in a panic. She badly cut her finger while slicing an avocado, and I rushed her to the emergency room. I failed to lock the gate as I went out to help her. I'm sorry, Officer." Tafoya told him not to worry about it and asked about his wife.

"She's fine, had to get six stiches. I'll be doing the cutting and chopping in the kitchen for a while," the *majordomo* said.

Tafoya walked back to the conference room where Romero and Jason sat. Larry, the other policeman on duty, sat in the corner sipping coffee and looking at his cell phone. Sergeant Romero asked Tafoya if he saw a warning sign near the gate about illegal entry onto reservation land. Tafoya said there were no warning signs, and informed him about the *majordomo's* wife and his failure to lock the gate. Romero asked Jason to explain in detail his activity before he drove through the gate opposite Chanson Restaurant.

"I had been up at the ski valley visiting with some friends that work at the new lodge. I finished lunch up there and decided to stop at the ice cream shop in Arroyo Luz. After having a chocolate ice cream cone, I headed back to Ojo Verde. I saw the open gate and thought I would drive down the road—see the scenery. The road had a street sign that read, 'Fire Sleet Road.' That far away from the Pueblo, I thought it was open country like around the Rio Grande Gorge or Arroyo Hondo."

Sergeant Romero believed Jason. An innocent, naïve twenty-something-years-old skier and hiker, a vagabond maybe, and a waiter at Tablita's. Ojo Verde and surrounding communities in northern New Mexico were full of young men and women like Jason—enraptured by mountains, climate, the illusory freedom of Ojo Verde until bills had to be paid and rent fell due. He had checked with the restaurant and confirmed his employment. Romero had a fifteen-year-old son that was eager to learn how to ski, and he could understand Jason's attachment to the mountains.

Romero stood up from his desk and pushed Jason's truck keys, Swiss knife, and cell phone across the desk to him.

"Jason! Don't drive on reservation land like this, ever again. Come by the tribal office and get a Tulona guide to hunt if that's your inclination or take photos. You are at a special time on our religious calendar to have been up that road. Fortunately, we had no ceremonies where you were. I am not going to give you a warning ticket or write this up."

He let his mini-lecture sink in. Jason smiled weakly, embarrassed, and said, "I'll never do that again. I want to be friends with you out here. Not an enemy." He stood there, facing Romero, waiting to be dismissed. Romero spoke.

"Human beings have innate curiosity, and, if treated properly, have desire to be harmonious with other human beings. Wisdom comes from observing nature like you were doing in gazing at mountains and losing the sense of self in a place of beauty. We Tulona people teach many things in the kiva and mountains that empower our tribe. I won't tell you any of our secrets, but one thing we teach and I learned it from my grandfather is, 'The people and the mountains are One. Lose nature, the mountains, the lake, the animals, and we will be scattered like people of other nations that have fractured. The deer, the Tulona people, the mountains are One.'"

Officers Tafoya and Larry turned their heads in surprise at Romero's words. They had never heard him speak like that before, and they had definitely not heard him quote at length his deceased, revered, cacique grandfather. Tafoya opened the palms of his hands and shrugged his shoulders to Larry as if, what's going on with Romero?

"Take your keys and cell phone and go back to Ranchos, and think about what has happened, and what I've said. Here's your Swiss Army knife, too," Romero ordered.

Jason took his keys and knife. He slipped his cell phone into his cargo pants pocket. "I will, Mr. Romero, I will."

As Jason started to open the door, Romero stopped him, "Oh, Jason, if you ever give lessons in skiing, talk to me. I have a son that likes to ski, but he needs an instructor. I think he could learn from you."

"Mr. Romero, I'd be honored to help teach your son all I know. Hopefully we will get great snow this winter!" Jason's step was lighter as he went out the door.

As Jason drove off in the pouring rain, Sergeant Romero spoke to Tafoya and Larry, "That snow-looks-like isn't so bad."

3

Saturday, September 1, Day of Saint Giles, Month of Corn Ripe Moon

The next morning, a Saturday, the first day of the Month of Corn Ripe Moon of September, Ben's dream world broke with the graying clear sky of dawn that soon turned turquoise blue. Ben released Star and Jess from their pickets. They seemed as impatient as he was to get back to Tulona Pueblo. He saddled his horses and rode carefully down the muddy road, slipping several times. Ben's kinsmen passed him by in four-wheel-drive pickups going up the road. Leaving their machines on the edge of the road, they walked into the forest to harvest windfall from yesterday's storm. A warchief in his pickup passed him on the road going in the direction of Earth Cloud Lake, then passed him again coming back down to the Pueblo a few minutes later.

Ben saw Tulona Pueblo below him and, in the distance, the deep rift of Rio Grande Gorge. Much farther on the southern horizon, he saw the flattop mountain, Cerro Pedernal, a source of agate for tools, although the 30.06 rifle with scope replaced agate points among today's deer hunters. Ben inhaled the perfumed scent of sagebrush blossoms, their purple petals standing out from dark trunks and pale-green leaves. Once, he had seen coyotes thrust their heads into sagebrush and come out smiling and yipping happily from the scent of its leaves and blossoms. When younger, like the coyote, he plunged his head in sagebrush and came away adorned with sage breath and blossom petals in his hair for the rest of the day.

Not stopping, Ben leaned down from the saddle, and with his knife cut several short sage stems bearing blossoms and tucked them inside his shirt.

As soon as the morning criers from Pueblo rooftops shouted orders and news, Quail Looks Away walked over to the tribal police headquarters and asked the officer on duty if all was balanced and good on Rio Tulona Road to Earth Cloud Lake.

"Were there problems yesterday afternoon? Ben was supposed to be back yesterday, and I have not heard from him."

"No. Nothing major, Quail. Nothing about Ben. Sergeant Romero and the guys came across a trespasser up the road, but nothing beyond that. They didn't even give the snow-looks-like a ticket," said the duty officer at the front desk.

She said thanks and asked about the health of the duty officer's parents, who she knew were elderly, and received a good report that they had gone to Earth Cloud. They are healthy to go that distance. Blessings fell their way, she thought. Quail Looks Away was relieved at the officer's reply, knowing Ben was returning.

As the sun rose higher, warming the morning, drying puddles of water on the road, Ben rode lower in elevation. He thought of his father, Anton, and his mother, Snow Deer, and hoped they had started back from the ceremonies. As he rode along Rio Tulona Road, he saw at a distance his village of tree-leaves-that-rattle-with-wind and heard magpies squawking, before he saw their black-and-white plumage and yellow bills. The breezes were light and next to the stream dividing Winter House from Summer House, he saw women and children carrying pails of water back to their houses. He smelled smoke from fireplaces and bread-making *hornos* long before he rode Star and Jess around the ashpit and onto the plaza.

He spurred Star across the stream to Quail Looks Away's house and dismounted to embrace his wife. She had come out of the house; her mother followed to greet him. From the inside of his shirt, he brought out the sage he had cut on the trail. Quail smiled and lightly brushed the sage under her nostrils. "Husband, I am glad you have returned safely." She placed the sage in her blouse pocket.

Ben untied the packer's canvas tarps and hefted his camping gear and clothing into the backroom along with the saddles and tack. He left the halters on Star and Jess and asked his cousin, who came out of a neighboring house, to lead them to the *ciénega* pasture and set them free with their horse brothers and sisters—other geldings, mare, colts, and fillies. His cousin, Lion Walks Night, gladly consented, for he knew Ben had been generous in allowing him to borrow Star for riding and checking fence lines for breaks.

Lion removed Star and Jess's halters at the pasture. Upon release, Star and Jess tossed their heads, widened their eyes, and galloped into the common field, turning one way and then another, joining up with the remuda who had been whinnying since they had come through the gate. Lion felt the ground shake as Star and Jess galloped to join their own kind. In celebration, the younger *kowena* ran to meet them. Then the remuda turned toward Lion and the entrance gate, galloping fast, stopping suddenly before the corrals, throwing up dirt clods. Mulling joyously, they turned quickly and ran, kicking, to the far end of the pasture.

"Aiiiie," Lion said quietly. "Acting like a bunch of kids."

The Churros knew their shepherds—Loretta and Armando Ortega of San Miguel. From the grazing meadows and high country of the Columbine-Hondo Wilderness, the Churro sheep slowly grazed and ambled down from higher altitudes, following an old road that led northward to the San Luis Valley of Colorado and southward to Ojo Verde and Taos. Hippie communes in the 1960s and a religious retreat near Lama had sprung up along the old road. In the evening, solitary figures walked for exercise along the narrow dirt road. The Churros, by habit, knew their final destination was San Miguel, a small village north of Ojo Verde. Loretta and Armando Ortega guided the flock of a hundred sheep down the slopes with the aid of Zeke, their border collie. The August monsoon thundershower the night before had drenched the forest. Moving as one ensemble, the Churros, Ortegas, and Zeke yearned for the first sunrays to strike them soon.

"Nothing is easy in this life, Armando," Loretta said, "but this morning is perfect in every way."

"Yes, my love. Although I wish we could move faster into warm air. Come sun! *¡Adelante!*" Armando looked possessively at the edges of the flock, making sure there were no upstart treks of young lambs into the forest. They had to stay together next to the road until they came to San Miguel where the Churro would be watered, examined, doctored, and fed for the day. Shearing was scheduled to commence tomorrow when their cousins from Tierra Amarilla arrived with shearing machines and noisy generators. Armando wanted shearing put off for a day.

"Tomorrow is Sunday, Loretta. We should put off shearing until Monday," Armando shouted.

"Yes, Armando," Loretta shouted back. That was good; she wanted to go to Mass.

Loretta and Armando Ortega had been in the sheep business since they married thirty years before. When they had married, Loretta and Armando had merged their flocks of Churros into one large flock. The lineage of their combined Churros traced back to their great-grandfathers and great-grandmothers. Beyond their families, the Churro breed was linked to Juan de Oñate's settlement in the early seventeenth century. So, when they came down from the Columbine-Hondo Wilderness grazing land, Loretta, Armando, and Zeke descended from a centuries-old agricultural pattern set in motion by the Spanish Oñate *entrada*.

Zeke barked in alarm. His bark was not a yip at errant sheep, but a bark of, "Strangers!"

"Uh-oh, Armando, look," Loretta said, "There is the pickup of the Game and Fish guys." She was referring to the New Mexico Department of Game and Fish who patrolled and checked permits for Wildlife Management Areas. The Columbine-Hondo Wilderness area came under their jurisdiction. Whatever warmth emanated from the sun evaporated. More often than not, the Game and Fish guys meant trouble, especially for sheepherders.

The New Mexico Department of Game and Fish was charged to oversee multiple-use of hunting, fishing, and grazing on public lands. Armando and Loretta had their grazing permits in order for Columbine-Hondo as well as the National Forest that encircled the Columbine-Hondo high country. Their permits allowed them to graze their own Churros and co-op sheep of the San Miguel Livestock Association.

The Game and Fish guys were equally protective of elk herds. In some cases, sheep forced elk herds of Columbine-Hondo to move from the high pasture meadows. A prejudice existed against sheep for it was said, "Sheep and elk just don't mix." The Churros came slowly down the road, milling around the two wardens. The sheep bleated, while Zeke monitored the edges of the band, eyeing the men suspiciously.

"Officers, what are up to on this perfect morning, as my wife just said?" Armando sensed no trouble, but who knows, he thought to himself.

The head officer spoke, "*Buenos días*. Yes, it's a good morning. A bit cold, but we've had a lot of coffee at the office." His partner nodded his head in agreement and adjusted his pistol belt to move the butt of his Glock out of the way.

"I'm Officer Frederick Peet and this is Officer Jose Naranjo of the New Mexico Game and Fish Department." The three men shook hands. Loretta, at the edge of the flock, nodded.

"I'm Armando Ortega and this is my wife, Loretta. That's Zeke the collie, and these are mainly my sheep with a few co-op ewes and lambs thrown in. We'd be glad to share some coffee with you," Armando replied, "as we have a big thermos of coffee left over from breakfast."

"Thanks," Frederick answered, "We're fine," dismissing the offer for coffee abruptly. "I need to ask you a few questions about the upland from where you came."

"Sure, Officer," Armando answered, trying not to sound nervous or hostile. Maintaining an equilibrium in face of the officials of the State of New Mexico, whoever they were, was difficult, if not downright impossible.

"I don't know a lot, Officer. My wife and I have been up with our Churros for only three days. My son had been managing before we came up and relieved him, giving us a chance to get out of town. He came down the road in his pickup early this morning. Maybe you saw him?"

"No, we didn't see him. Weren't looking for him. We were looking for sheepherders. We found you," Pete asserted.

Armando said nothing. He waited.

"We need to see your permit for grazing," Jose Naranjo spoke for the first time, a bit more forcefully than he had intended, quickly adding, "With your permission?" The addition of, with your permission, softened the request.

After handing grazing permits and attendant papers to Frederick, Armando glanced at Loretta who was walking through the flock, checking on the health and wellbeing of juvenile lambs. She nodded that all was okay with the lambs. They were nursing actively. No lambs were orphaned or rejected. She kept looking at the Game and Fish guys.

Frederick looked carefully at the permits, especially the dates for grazing and locations. He handed back the papers. "Your permits are in order." He hesitated, then said, "We have reports that a herd of elk were being displaced by a flock of sheep this side of Lobo Peak. The elk were spooked and moving toward Rio Hondo at a rapid pace. Did you come across any elk while up in the forest?"

"As I said, Officer, we've only been up here three days. Yes, we saw elk, and they were peacefully grazing and meandering toward Flag Mountain and Garrapata Canyon. They weren't spooked or anything. They appeared calm, and our sheep were browsing in scrub oak. Armando paused and then asked, "If you don't mind me asking, who filed that report?"

"A hunting guide from Valdez, down by Ojo Verde, called us two days ago. He had been up and around Columbine-Hondo and saw elk. And, said he saw sheep. Your sheep, the only flock in the forest." Frederick let the information hang thick in the air, waiting for Armando to respond.

Armando had to respond carefully.

"All I know to be true is what I have seen. My band of Churros, from the time I was up here in the forest, grazed away from the elk herd. I saw the elk. They were close, but they did not run away. In fact, the elk continued to feed in separate, but close areas, from my Churros. I saw the elk lie down and rest, while the sheep grazed nearby. There was a small herd of elk within a quarter-mile when we started down this morning."

The sheep began to lie down around the Game and Fish vehicle. A lamb came up to Jose and sniffed at his pants leg. "Hey, leave me alone!" he shouted.

Armando continued, "There's any number of things that could have spooked the elk, from cougars to bears to even the guide that saw them on the move. I know there's a prejudice against sheep being in the same grazing area of elk, but I've got to make a living and so does the co-op that sends ewes and lambs with me."

Loretta walked back to Armando and the Game and Fish guys. Armando looked at her and nodded in a way to ask her to comment. She intentionally chose her words less carefully than Armando.

"Officers, our grazing permits are in order. We didn't spook the elk nor did we come across any wildcat or bear on the mountain. Our son, Luis, did not mention any problems with elk."

Loretta continued. "I don't want to be rude, but we need to move our sheep to our pens at San Miguel and water them, feed them. You know, tend our flock." She looked at Frederick and Jose directly in the eyes and smiled broadly. Loretta was friendly, but prodded the inquiry to a conclusion.

Frederick looked at the flock lying down around his truck. Two lambs played in the shadows of a large ponderosa. He looked at Jose and shrugged.

"Okay. Be on your way. You know we will have to write a report on the guide's observations, and what you've answered here and now."

"That'll be good. Put it down for the official record, including our statements about the calm elk. And, we will log it into our field journal as well," Loretta said. She again offered to share their coffee with Frederick and Jose. They refused.

The Game and Fish guys turned their pickup around and started down the road. Zeke kept the sheep from trailing their pickup. Once the wardens were gone, the Ortega family and Zeke sheepherded the Churros to the Miguel pens. Water troughs were filled to the brim. Hay was thrown in bins and scattered at the far ends of the corral. The Ortega cousins arrived at noon. They set up their generators and shearing equipment to begin the next morning, but a discussion erupted about working on Sunday. Loretta was firm on not working on Sunday. The cousins decided to wait until Monday to begin shearing, allowing for Loretta's request and respect for Sunday.

"I don't think the village and the priest would like us firing up the generators on Sunday. Might disturb his prayers," one cousin joked.

The sky cleared through the day. Weather signs indicated a dry day after monsoon rains the night before. San Miguel villagers came by to visit the Ortegas and catch up on gossip, for they had seen the Game and Fish guys go up the road. Zeke settled into a favorite spot near the pens, a place where he could see the sheep and Armando and Loretta.

Zeke cocked his head in puzzlement when he heard Armando shout, "No!"

The San Miguel villagers said that early this morning a body had been found on the Tulona reservation, across the road and fence from Arroyo Luz, the village so peaceful and tranquil.

Tulona WarChief Juan Concha began his scouting of the perimeter of the reservation after a breakfast of scrambled eggs with green chile, fry bread, and coffee. Starting his reconnaissance at Abalone Road, he drove clockwise to the La Osa Falls Road, which would be his termination point. Concha made note of the Paseo del Norte fence line near Abalone. It needed repair after an eighteen-wheeler crashed through it two weeks before, killing the driver and stampeding the buffalo in the pasture. He checked the *acequias* that diverted water from Cottonwood River and Rio Arroyo Luz. Water still flowed, although shallow. Crops were already harvested by the ending of Month of Corn Ripe Moon, so water flow was not as critical. He passed by the gate near Chanson Restaurant and slowly made his way northward toward La Osa Falls.

He saw the red bandanna first, then the body.

Unholstering his phone from his belt, WarChief Concha called the Tulona Tribal Police Department. Warchiefs of the Pueblo were charged by the governor and council to patrol the Pueblo reservation boundaries, much like in centuries past to scout out approaching bands of Comanche, Ute, and Navajo. Warchiefs were powerful figures in olden days. They were still powerful and in charge of the scalps, although none had been taken in nearly two hundred years.

WarChief Concha initially thought the person might have passed out from drink or drugs, but when he saw the wound on the left side of the upper torso, he concluded foul play. The man was Native, perhaps Hispano, neither young nor old, and in good physical condition. Concha looked closer at the body. He noticed Red Feather work boots that were worn down on the soles, Levi pants, a blue flannel shirt, and t-shirt underneath. His hair was long—almost Pueblo-style, but not braided. A red bandanna, carefully folded, was tied firmly around his forehead and hair, like the wide-folded style of the Navajo with the knot on the side of the head, not in back.

It seemed to Concha the body had been positioned so that the head morbidly faced the homes across the road to Arroyo Luz. Why place the body in that direction? Why not toward the sacred Tulona Mountain? Arising out of a squatting position, WarChief Concha uttered a prayer.

Above you, the Star people have you,
Along the Star people road you go,
Along the flower path you and I shall go,
Beauty all around you may you go.

Concha knew he had blended Pueblo prayer with Navajo, but he had always liked, "Beauty all around," phrasing of the Navajo. It was the right prayer for the morning at this lonely place, the last place for Red Feather boot man.

Concha heard sirens. They would be arriving soon: The Taos County Sheriff's Office, New Mexico State Police, Tulona Tribal Police, *The Taos News* reporters, ambulances, and eventually the F.B.I. The F.B.I. would take jurisdiction since the body was on reservation land. As the sirens grew louder and closer, WarChief Concha carefully backed away from the body, placing his footprints in his tracks like when he first approached Red Feather boot man. With his cell phone, he took photos and video. To assist the tribal police, he wanted to preserve the evidence and show his entry and exit. Several people from across the road had come to the fence line. He yelled at them, "Get back on the other side of the road! Get away from the fence line!" The people complied with the warchief's orders, quickly retreating across the road.

New Mexico State Police had been parked at the yellow blinking light intersection, a mere four miles away, and they were the first to arrive. The state troopers blocked Arroyo Luz Road, allowing the ambulance and law enforcement vehicles to pass. The Tulona Tribal Police, in conjunction with the sheriff's department, methodically photographed and sketched the body's position. In concentric circles of scanning, they collected bits and pieces of unusual items. The coroner took the body's temperature and gave a simple preliminary cause of death as the entry wound on the left side. There were no blood pools beneath Red Feather boot man. He died elsewhere.

The Taos County ambulance service loaded Red Feather boot man into the ambulance and took him to the coroner's office for autopsy. WarChief Concha climbed into his pickup and continued to reconnoiter the reservation boundary. Concha felt oppressed—too many people that morning, too many law enforcement personnel, a dead body. He searched for sign of wildlife to alleviate the blackness of Red Feather boot man's death. He spotted several deer grazing at the edge of the forest in a stand of junipers. The deer raised their heads at the sound of his pickup. WarChief Concha stopped his pickup, killed the engine, and gazed at deer until they faded into forest shadows. Seeing them, healed him.

Santiago Majerus heard the siren coming in his direction from Ojo Verde as he lay in his bunk, recuperating from his ritual and hike from La Osa Falls. When one siren became two sirens, then three, then four, he pivoted out of his bunk, stood, and stretched. He put on his jacket and watch cap, opened the door to his trailer, and walked to the road in front of his home. He watched the New Mexico State Police vehicles slowing down, light bars flashing. Arroyo Luz residents in their pickups followed the police up the road. They were halted and ordered to turn around. Majerus walked past the idle vehicles and stood on the far side of the road with other curious onlookers. He saw the warchief and state troopers along with Taos County Deputy Sheriffs and the Tulona Tribal Police. Looking closer, he saw a body on the ground, clad in a blue shirt with a headband of brilliant red. The body, lying on its side, faced Majerus's home.

Strong colors that blue, that red, Majerus said to himself. Walking across the road, he peered at the boots on the body. Red Feather boots, he concluded.

"Hey! You there!" WarChief Concha shouted to Majerus. "Stay on the other side of the road!"

Majerus walked back across the road and stood still. He wondered where he had seen the warchief before. Then he remembered. He had seen the warchief at the Saint Francis Feast Day the year before. He was the Black Eye that set up the final clowning scene in pole climbing. His body painted in black-and-white concentric circles, the warchief had scratched sheep tracks in the dirt in a clockwise fashion around the pole. The rest of the Black Eyes had followed the tracks to the base of the pole. One of them had climbed the pole for the sheep, melons, and foodstuffs secured with rope at the top. Majerus was pleased with himself that he could still recall detail and recognize a face from months ago. So, perhaps, old age was not ravishing his body and mind as much as he feared.

Casting his fears of senility aside, Majerus thought about the night before when he trekked back from La Osa Falls. Did he see any blue-shirted, red-bandanna guy? No, he didn't see him, but there was rain, and it was dark. He didn't see anyone on the road. He was the only person walking. That was for sure. Something strange, however, did take place.

As Majerus had walked back home from La Osa, an old four-wheel-drive pickup drove slowly on the Tulona reservation side of the fence. He had thought nothing of it since the gates to the reservation were bent, decrepit, and damaged, offering opportunity to enter the reservation at several locations. Yet, something was odd. A flash of lightning had illuminated a faded corporate logo of the Culebra Mining Company on the door of the pickup. Santiago Majerus was not one to get involved, especially with law enforcement people, so he decided to keep what he saw to himself. Besides, a mining company truck on reservation, in the dark of the evening and in the rain, probably had nothing to do with the Red Feather boot man.

Yeah, sure, he thought to himself as he turned around and walked back to his house and orchard on the other side of the Tulona reservation.

Sometimes there was a day, but not often, when neither siren from the New Mexico State Police nor Ojo Verde firetrucks interrupted the quiet page turning of books at Coe Bookshop. This was not a morning of peace and quiet. This Saturday morning, squad cars and ambulances sped down Paseo de Pueblo Norte, heading north, and Coe's Bookshop windows vibrated with siren screams. Coe had come in earlier than usual to the bookshop to rearrange the local history section of his inventory. With power outage the day before, he had stopped his re-shelving and closed his shop early. He had gone home to an empty house. By battery light that evening, he read the newspaper and several chapters of Anne Hillerman's new novel. Coe's wife was visiting her aging parents out in Los Angeles, and he read more when she was away than when she was at home. Coe considered himself fortunate in his second marriage. Since he was sixty-five, if anything happened marriage-wise, he would not go back on the dating market. He would tend to the bookshop and socially circulate in book discussion groups that abounded in Ojo Verde.

And, feed the cat.

The cat. Fenster was a gray-tabby cat, like thousands of other gray-tabby cats in the county. One day two years ago, Fenster showed up at the Coe Bookshop front door when Coe opened for business. The month was November or December—during the holiday skiing season. Fenster was curled up in a tight ball, shielding herself from the cold and snow that had fallen the night before.

Waking from sleep, Fenster had rubbed up against Coe's leg as he opened the door that morning, and out of sympathy for her, Coe let her inside. Just for a few minutes. A few minutes ran into a couple of hours, and before lunchtime, Fenster had lain down under a table stacked with coffee-table books and watched customers come and go. When Coe closed temporarily for lunchtime, he let the gray tabby outside and gave her a few strokes, "Goodbye." Thinking that the tabby would go on about her way, Coe returned after lunch and his prediction was true; the cat was gone. He missed the cat that afternoon.

The next morning the gray tabby was at the front door, and Coe let her in again, speaking in soft tones, "Good kitty, nice kitty. Come on in for a spell." The "coming in for a spell" turned into the rest of the day, and by the end of the week, the cat had a name: Fenster. The name had come from a German history tome Coe was reading and was a derivation from the word, "defenestration." Fenster became a local cult-cat like the big poodle around the corner at the hardware store on the plaza. Coe had to put up a sign on his bookshop door, "Sorry, no dogs allowed inside. Cat encamped."

The sirens that Saturday morning alerted Coe and Fenster that something was happening out north, and when more law enforcement cars sped by, Coe turned on the radio to the local FM station and heard the bad news of a body discovered on the Tulona reservation next to the village of Arroyo Luz.

Coe knew that life was replete with bad, horrible events. Every week, the police blotter from the local newspaper carried the discordance of human communities. Someone steals a cell phone; the signal is tracked to the Indian casino. A fight breaks out on the plaza between two men, and the Ojo Verde policemen are called out to stop the bloodletting. The clerk at the nearby Native-run tourist shop runs out and shouts, "Those guys need less meth, more peace pipe! Ai!" Homeless people loiter on the Supermarket property and frighten customers away. At the Ojo Verde Children and Family Center, someone is reported standing on top of a car and screaming.

But the event of finding a dead body was more disturbing. What can be done? Coe thought. He called Fenster to his cash register, bent down, picked her up, and began stroking and petting her behind her ears. Coe put Fenster down and looked at the time: eight fifteen. Too early to call the wife in LA.

He walked to the front door, opened it, and stepped outside. Though the sun was out, it was chilly from last night's rain. Across the street in Ojo Verde City Park, the cottonwoods had begun to change color; he heard leaves rattle, brittle as they were. A wind from the mountains blew the scent of piñon wood burning in fireplaces to Coe. He inhaled deeply—so primal. With Priscilla gone from the house, he thought he might burn a smudge of piñon on the back porch that evening.

More sirens from the Taos direction became louder as they sped toward Ojo Verde town plaza. Coe walked back inside to get away from the approaching squad cars and closed the door to the paseo. As was his intention to come to the shop early, he began to rearrange the local history section. Fenster decided to jump up on the checkout desk and take a nap after cleaning her face with her paws. Coe looked out the window one more time before he stacked books. He saw magpies across the street waddle-walking on the ground, stabbing their yellow beaks in sidewalk crevices for bugs and morsels of food. He knew magpies ate carrion, but this morning, as far as he could see, they were vegans.

4

Later that Saturday afternoon, Dr. Eli Rosenbaum, Medical Examiner for Taos County, donned a surgical gown and protective face mask and strode to the porcelain table upon which rested Red Feather boot man. His assistant, equally dressed for protection and safety, walked to the opposite side of the examining table. The video camera activated at Rosenbaum's voice command; his assistant re-checked the battery power on the Nikon camera for still photographs. Three law enforcement officials, Tulona Policeman Richard Tafoya, Taos County Sheriff's Deputy Chris Cordova, and F.B.I. Special Agent in charge Diane Parker, stood apart from the autopsy scene, but close enough to see important details and ask questions. The leather gunbelts of Tafoya and Cordova squeaked as they shifted their stance.

Parker and her team of F.B.I. agents had arrived in the early afternoon from Albuquerque. Parker and her team were frustrated. The highway along the Rio Grande Gorge from Española twisted and turned and was under construction, so their arrival was an hour later than usual.

"Sorry we're late," Parker said. We ate burgers in the vehicles. We're not hungry. Let's get on with it."

Tafoya gave a sideward glance to Cordova, as if to say, Oh, no, a stickler for detail. Cordova looked straight ahead at the body on the morgue table.

An earlier search of the pockets of Red Feather boot man revealed nothing—neither driver license, credit cards, cash, nor papers. A fingerprint check turned up a blank in the data files of New Mexico and the federal government. A military-record check was still ongoing since the computers were down at the federal government's database for military records. Since Red Feather boot man was between thirty-five and forty-five years of age—so said Dr. Rosenbaum—the search for military records needed to go back twenty years or more.

Red Feather work boots were common footwear. A search of where they might have been purchased would be futile. The leather belt of the deceased offered more promise. The leather belt was harness leather, two inches in width. A custom-made buckle from a silversmith of Native origin, probably Navajo, exuded high value and careful crafting.

The center design on the buckle was a corn plant, surrounded by two large turquoise gems on either side of the corn plant. The source of turquoise was not identifiable. Cordova first thought the origin of the turquoise was King's Manassa found in southern Colorado. The vein of King's Manassa had been depleted for over twenty years and was evaluated as medium-to-high-grade turquoise, much like the Bisbee turquoise in southern Arizona.

"My first impression was King's Manassa, but a on second look, I'm not so sure, since the blue is approaching robin's egg blue, and that's not Manassa," Cordova said.

"I agree," Tafoya said. "Manassa tends toward green, this is blue, and the matrix is delicate. The silver is Navajo-made, I'm sure, but I'm not an expert on turquoise." Tafoya quickly thought of who he could turn to for assistance.

"Let me check out the evidence bag with the buckle, and I'll take it to Tony Rodarte on Paseo del Sur for further evaluation. We may get a lead on who made the buckle and find out the identity of Red Feather boot man," Tafoya said. He had known Tony Rodarte since childhood. The silversmith and jeweler had a reputation throughout the Southwest as the most knowledgeable jeweler of Indian crafts working in turquoise and coral. He was the co-author of *Southwest Turquoise Mines*, along with Steven Begay, published in 1985, that remained the standard encyclopedia for turquoise jewelry of the Southwest.

Tafoya turned to Parker and pleaded again, "Agent Parker, Rodarte knows turquoise. I'm sure he can help us. Rodarte wrote the textbook on turquoise mines back in the eighties."

"Go ahead," ordered Parker, "the speed with which we move on this, the faster we solve the case that looks like a homicide. At least we can start trying to identify the body by tracing the buckle."

Parker paused a moment, moving closer to look at the body. "What do we have here, Dr. Rosenbaum? The cause of death? Anything?" Tafoya waited for Rosenbaum's reply, evidence bag in hand with the buckle.

Rosenbaum began, dispassionately. "From the time I got out to the site where the body was found, the deceased male of approximately thirty-five to forty-five years of age had been dead twelve-to-eighteen hours. I can't be more precise than that because of rain and temperature changes Friday night. The cause of death was exsanguination from a large puncture wound to the upper torso, left side, that penetrated the rib cage and heart. The deceased bled out someplace else, not at the scene where he was found. The nature of the puncture wound is like a pick axe or rebar. Toxicology test results will indicate drug use, if any. The deceased was in good health, no cirrhosis. And there are no tattoos on his body, which is a surprise this day and age." Rosenbaum put down his cutting tools, walked to the deep wash basin against the wall, and began to scrub his hands.

As he washed his hands, he continued. "Whether this was an accident, homicide, or even suicide, we have no way of knowing. What we do know is that the bleeding-out occurred elsewhere, and he was dumped on the reservation. The placement of his body on the ground indicates a personal touch, perhaps one of respect. He was carefully placed on the ground, facing away from Tulona Mountain. Or so it seems. Again, the death scene took place somewhere else. That needs to be found. Someone conveyed the deceased to the reservation. He or she needs to be found. That's my first analysis. I'll write up a preliminary report and sign off later this afternoon, or in the morning. Expect a final report next week."

Deputy Cordova turned to Tafoya, "Richard, this is Saturday afternoon. Rodarte closes at noon."

"Oh, that's right." Tafoya turned to Parker, "I'll check out the buckle on Monday morning and see Rodarte then, Agent Parker." Her face got red.

"Will this investigation ever get off of square one! First, there's stupid construction from Española getting up here! Now it's a shop that closes at noon!" Parker raised her voice.

"It is what it is in *norte* Rio Grande," Tafoya replied. Parker glared at him.

Tafoya turned around, ignoring Parker's glare, and walked outside into the afternoon sun and near-cloudless sky, except for cirrus mare's tails high over Tusas Mountains to the west. He breathed deeply, forcing the formaldehyde smell of the morgue out of his lungs. He looked over at the vacant lot next to the medical examiner's office and saw ground squirrels perched on earthen mounds, looking for danger, chirping to their fellow kinsmen. A few fat ground squirrels loped between mounds. Tafoya had sympathy for the species, for he knew they took care of each other and stationed watch-squirrels throughout the daylight hours, chirping, "Danger, hawk!" when the shadow shrieked down from the sky. Tafoya thought of warchiefs patrolling reservation perimeters—just like watch-squirrels, only in pickups and ATVs.

After seeing Red Feather boot man across the road, Majerus walked back to his trailer house in Arroyo Luz. His trailer rested on a *suerte* or long lot. On the higher end of the long lot, an irrigation ditch derived from the Acequia de Luz watered his two-acre cultivated field. Majerus had inherited the trailer and *suerte* from his father who had been dead thirty years. His father had died of natural causes, but Majerus and his mother believed the stress of being a wage earner at odd jobs and cultivating the two-acre field of onions and garlic during the drought of the 1980s had hastened his death. Of the orchard, half of the peach trees had been saved through manual watering, yet, for two years, neither garlic nor onions matured to harvest. The Acequia de Luz had flowed so low during the drought that most of the microecology of the *acequia's* ditch had perished.

Majerus stepped off his porch and walked down one of the rows of garlic that had been harvested earlier in the summer, kicking the soil to determine moisture content and fertility. His soil needed more rain like the night before. He noticed peach tree leaves turning golden and falling. The sap was withdrawing from outer branches back to the roots, gearing down for the winter ahead. Finishing only half of his coffee, Majerus threw the rest of the brew away, gazing at the dark pool of coffee reflecting the sun on its surface as it soaked into the ground. I wish I could grow coffee trees here, he thought.

"Santiago! What's going on?" His neighbor shouted across the barbed wire fence and coyote fence, startling Majerus out of his reverie about coffee trees.

"Hey, Johnny Sisneros! Not much happening here. Just having a cup of coffee and wondering about the body up the road they found this morning. How are you, Johnny?"

"I'm okay, Santiago. Saw you contemplating your garden as I was stacking firewood. I probably know less than you about the body up the road. You know who it is?" Johnny asked.

"No, I have no idea." Santiago paused a moment and thought he would let the question slip by, but changed his mind and asked, "Did you see a pickup on the reservation side of the fence yesterday evening driving slowly along the fence line? An old, dark four-wheel drive with markings on the side door?"

After a few seconds of reflecting, Johnny answered, "You know, Majerus, I did see headlights on a pickup over there, but I couldn't tell anymore about it, other than it was a pickup and it was dark color. It was going slow to avoid slipping. I thought it was odd that late at night. You see it, too?"

"I did. I was out for a walk," Majerus said, "and thought it was strange, too. But, the warchiefs don't follow routine. It was probably one of them."

Since they did not know the Red Feather boot man had been killed elsewhere, Santiago and Johnny were more anxious than they should have been. Later, the evening news on the local radio station cleared up questions and comforted Arroyo Luz village, including Santiago and Johnny. The small comfort was that Red Feather boot man had been killed elsewhere—and not within their village limits.

Overhead, the sky streaked with cirrus clouds, and on the far horizon, mares' tails swished the turquoise blue of the New Mexico sky, giving a fragile background to the setting sun and the Pajarito Mountains near Los Alamos National Laboratory far to the south. The sky showed one jet contrail, and it was blurry, fading, dying. Quail Looks Away wished that she was lighter in weight to climb ladders to the top of Winter House across Cottonwood River to see colors at the end of day. Being pregnant blocked that wish, but she stood outside her home and saw most of the colors in the sky that ended the day with the return of her husband. Ben joined her, while Quail's mother walked to another row of homes to take food to an ailing cousin. Ben and Quail softly conversed about the returning congregants from Earth Cloud Lake, and how she was feeling physically, so close to the birthing. Slowly, but perceptively, the sun moved to rest for a moment on far mesas, then rolled downward below the horizon.

Several fires were lit outside homes on the Summer House side of the Pueblo. The tourists had been shooed away, and only Pueblo kinsmen and their guests visited among fires and gaslights inside their homes. Young men gathered on the bridge over Cottonwood River and sang love songs to young women about the plaza. As it grew darker, the Star People came out. Magpies and bluebirds roosted in trees and brush, waiting the night for sunrise. Tomorrow was Sunday, and Mass would be celebrated early in the Pueblo.

Ben and Quail Looks Away went back inside their home, spread blankets and bedrolls on their cots and floor, lit a piñon fire in the fireplace, and listened to their uncle tell stories of past victories and defeats, the bravery of the Tulano, and honorable deeds of their ancestors. The stories were not the traditional stories reserved for the Quiet Time of winter, but strong stories, nonetheless. It was a good evening, and all were full and happy with food and storied images of Pueblo past.

"Ai," Ben said, many times that evening, before he and Quail slept under Star People above, and the kachinas below.

5

Sunday, September 2, Day of Blessed John Francis Burté, Month of Corn Ripe Moon

At the altar rail of the Chapel of Nuestra Señora de los Delores in San Miguel, Loretta and Armando Ortega knelt together and received the Body of Christ from the Santa Fe visiting parish priest. Holding reverently the wafer, they ingested the symbol and walked back to their pew where they knelt and prayed. Their marriage had been sanctified in the chapel thirty years before, and they embraced communion rituals in the church once again. The hour of Mass was early in the morning, and propane heaters on either side of the chapel barely dispelled the chill of the morning. The popping of the heaters from expanding and contracting baffles, along with the slight smell of burning propane, was as comforting in a different way as the homily of the visiting priest. The *retabla* or backdrop of the altar held familiar symbols of Mary and Christ, but on the outer margins of the iconography, wildlife forms emerged: deer, elk, rabbit, hawks, and eagles in placement with sagebrush in the foreground and blue sky above. At the feet of Mary with her blue aura lay several sheep, Churro sheep from the shape of their horns and the soft fleece. The Chapel of Nuestra Señora de los Delores welcomed Anglo-amenity residents, wage earners, old hippies, ranchers, and sheepherders. And, far be it for the church to expel anyone for their vocation, for even the bartenders from Arroyo Hondo dance hall paid their weekly Sunday dues with bloodshot eyes and whiskey breath to Our Lady of Sorrows.

Mass concluded with the standard benediction, "The grace of the Lord Jesus Christ and the love of God and the fellowship of the Holy Spirit be with you all." Loretta and Armando exited the chapel and shook the hand of the Santa Fe priest, complementing him on his homily of forgiving one another's trespasses and driving to San Miguel to perform Mass.

Getting in their pickup to go up the road to their house, Armando leaned over and smiled at Loretta. "I always remember the day we got married in the chapel. You were so beautiful and I was so nervous. And, here we are thirty years later, in the same chapel, and I still get goose bumps sitting with you and remembering our life over these years. I would not have done anything different...oh, maybe a couple of things, but not the big picture. Wouldn't want even a day of it to be different," Armando said, as he drove slowly up the road to the house and corrals.

"Armando! What's gotten into you this morning? Are you getting sentimental on me?" Loretta said, as she laid her hand on his forearm. "I know what you are saying and I feel it, too. I love you, Armando, even in the days we wish to forget."

The morning sun had not risen above the mountains, but when they parked the pickup beside the trailers and corrals and turned west, Armando and Loretta looked off toward the Tusas Mountains and saw the sunlight brighten the deep conifer greens at the top of Burned Mountain. Beyond the Tusas, toward Navajo land, the hazy outline of the Jemez peaks emerged to the south. Between the Tusas and the Jemez, there were stratifications of flat plains, the Rio Grande rift, and mesas rising to the foothills of mountain ranges. The stratifications of sagebrush, the river gorge, and the dark green of cholla cacti, juniper, and piñon created a base to the Tusas like a layered cake, a natural holy bread.

Brunch service that Sunday morning at Ojo Verde Inn's Tablita Restaurant was busy. Jason Taylor sat down the tray of brunch breakfasts for a table of six in the middle of the dining room. Starting at position one at the table, he served to the right side of the client, Tablita's chile relleno and egg—a blend of Anaheim chile, pico de gallo, pumpkin seeds, chevre cream, rice and beans. Position one wanted his eggs scrambled over the ensemble. Jason complied with the order, although he recommended two eggs over-easy with the entrée. No accounting for taste, he thought to himself. The table of six was pleasant enough with orders of blue corn waffles, piñon-buttermilk pancakes, the Tulona entrée of poached eggs with yam biscuit, red chile, and cheese. Positions five and six rounded out the table with each having a bowl of New Mexico green chile stew with extra tortillas and pitcher of water. The table was further enlightened with orange juices, café lattes, and cappuccinos. Jason calculated in his head, before he had gone to the point-of-sale computer touch screen, a tip of at least twenty dollars. The ski season pass he saved for would cost him five hundred dollars, and a portion of the twenty-dollar tip would go to the season pass.

"May I get you anything else?" Jason asked, before he waited on an adjacent table.

The New-Mexico-green-chile-stew woman quickly answered, "How about two pitchers of margaritas and a pitcher of bellinis? That would make us all spend more at the shops when they open at ten!" Nearly all at the table laughed and nodded in agreement.

"Yes, Jennifer," said the Tablita-poached-egg man.

"Alllriiight, yes!" Said the blue-corn-waffle man.

Jason smiled as broad as he could and slightly genuflected in apology, "I am terribly sorry, but it is a Sunday, and we can't serve alcohol before eleven o'clock, even though this merry table would love our margaritas. Come back this afternoon, and I'll bring pitchers of spirits and more food." Jason calculated he lost twenty dollars because of the New Mexico drinking law.

"Well, over in Texas we can get drinks on a Sunday morning, if it is combined with food, pardner. And, I imagine in New York, the bars never close," grumbled the New Mexico green-chile-stew woman.

Jason wanted to respond that Tablita's Restaurant was located in New Mexico if he remembered his geography correctly, that Texas was five-and-a-half hours east of Ojo Verde, and by the time "y'll" got back to Texas to have your pitcher of margaritas, it would be past eleven in Ojo Verde where you could have ordered margaritas to your heart's content. Stay in Ojo Verde, shop and come back at eleven. Jason was polite, so his thoughts remained unsaid.

"I'm sorry for our antiquated law, but come back this afternoon, and I'll serve your drinks and complement your chips and salsa," he said instead.

The table of six began to eat their food, and those facing Paseo de Norte looked out of the windows and saw eighteen-wheelers carrying logs from fresh cuts up in the National Forest. Creeping along the Paseo de Norte, old pickups, Lexuses, BMWs, even a gasoline truck from Indian River Creek in Florida passed by Tablita's windows headed south to Española and Questa and Colorado to the north. Sitting at the table of six, those that faced away from the street looked at *vigas* in the ceiling and artwork for sale on the wall. The prices for the artwork of local Ojo Verdeans were priced to sell, and the piñon-buttermilk-pancake woman eyed the brilliantly-hued painting of the Church of St. Francis de Assisi on the wall above the serving order screen. The backside of the church had been photographed and painted hundreds of times, never failing to impress the viewer, especially when winter snows graced the adobe curves that implied feminine form. Georgia O'Keeffe and Paul Strand artfully rendered the backside of the church in the past, but the local Verdean artist amplified the lines with brilliant colors. The piñon-buttermilk-pancake woman kept gazing at the painting throughout her meal. Her next decision was deliberate and final.

I will buy that painting and make a place for it in my living room, the piñon-buttermilk-pancake woman said to herself. When brunch was over, she went to the front desk, pulled seven hundred dollars out of her purse, and bought the painting outright. As time went on, she never regretted the purchase, and her children rotated the painting among themselves after she died. Jason Taylor received an additional twenty dollars from her that Sunday morning at Tablita's. She slipped the additional tip to him, dissembling to the group as they left the inn that she had forgotten her scarf at the table. The piñon-buttermilk-pancake woman, by giving Jason the money, wanted to remember and enlarge her morning as a generous morning, a time reverently punctuated with giving and art.

The Blue Lady never appeared in his life. He had hoped and prayed for the Blue Lady to emerge from the mine pits where he worked, but she never showed herself. He had heard of her and believed she existed; the legends are true! He had read that beneath San Antonio, Texas, were numerous underground passageways inhabited by mysterious people, and on rare occasions the Blue Lady came from caverns beneath the surface and bestowed mercy and charity upon those in need. For example, the Jose Valdez family's daughter, Ursula, had been given a pouch of gold money, pearls, and diamonds, so that she could pay medical doctors to perform surgery on her father and restore him to health. A Puebloan Native told him that the Blue Lady appeared in New Mexico when the sky was deep blue, and wherever she stepped, blue flowers sprang up. He had asked the Native, "If you see her, will you not run to her and ask for charity and mercy? I will."

The Puebloan proclaimed in contempt, "The Blue Lady brings blessings and blue flowers wherever she walks. Why should I, or you, or anyone molest her with a request for charity? She brings blessings. Leave her be and attend her presence."

And he heard stories of the *La Señorita Azul* healing the sick and bringing out the North Star when hunters and travelers had become lost. Why then did she not come to him in his hours of travail that had stretched through his years? He had given up on the Blue Lady legend, until one day he and a friend were hiking in high country to find places for hunting camps in the fall, flint tools and pots to sell, when he noticed an arroyo outwash sprinkled with blue-green minerals—turquoise. The deer camps, arrowheads, and pots no longer mattered.

"Finally, she has come to me! Not in her ghostly form, but in blue turquoise! The Blue Lady has finally decided to drop a purse of gold coins, pearls, and diamonds into my hands. My wait is over!"

Yes, he had found the Blue Lady.

When Cortés first met Moctezuma at Tenochtitlan in 1519, Moctezuma asked him a question. "For what reason have you come here?"

Cortés is said to have replied, "We Spanish have sickness of the heart and its only cure is gold."

6

Monday, September 3, Day of Saint Gregory the Great, Month of Corn Ripe Moon

At the autopsy on late Saturday afternoon, Tulona policeman Richard Tafoya had started out the door with the Red Feather boot man's buckle. Deputy Sheriff Cordova advised him that Tony Rodarte's jewelry shop closed early on Saturdays. In response, he left behind the evidence bag with the F.B.I. team that had set up a secure evidence room at the National Forest headquarters on Camino Tecolote, across the street from the Taos County Sheriff's Department substation at Ojo Verde. Both the Forest Service headquarters and sheriff's substation had emergency generators that backed up Dancing Rock Co-op's inevitable outages. The Tulona Tribal Police occupied one room at the sheriff's substation with their major compound at the Pueblo.

Early Monday morning, upon entering the Forest Service headquarters, Tafoya greeted a khaki-clad woman behind the front counter who was sorting out maps and brochures for the display case near the front door. There seemed to be a never-ending stream of tourists, hikers, prospectors, woodcutters, and mountaineers asking for maps and guidance into the wild and not-so-wild forests. The khaki-clad woman's name tag read, "Janet Rael, MS, Biology Science Technician, U.S. Forest Service." Tafoya had not seen her before.

"Good morning, Ms. Rael. Can you direct me to the F.B.I. investigation room? I'm Officer Richard Tafoya of the Tulona Tribal Police."

Janet Rael set her filings of maps aside, stood up, and smiled. "I can do that, Officer Tafoya, but first I need to see some identification, strange as that sounds with you in uniform." Janet had the complexion of creamed coffee, and her hair was dark and cut medium length, tucked under a Forest Service cap that was not the cheap kind, but the tailored, heavily embroidered, serious business style. Her eyes were light brown with flecks of gold. She wore no makeup; her eyebrows carefully trimmed.

Around her neck, Janet had tied a red bandanna, tucked neatly beneath her shirt collar. Tafoya guessed she was five feet five, average weight. He wanted to know more about Janet Rael; but duty called.

Tafoya produced his creds. She read them, studied the photograph, and looked carefully at him. "You've lost weight, Officer Tafoya, from when the photograph was taken."

"Yes, I have," he replied. "I'm glad you noticed. That photograph was taken two years ago, and since that time I've gotten serious about keeping in shape. Also," he said laughingly, "I have cut back on the fried bread and Spam at the Pueblo."

Janet laughed; the laugh was melodious. "Well, I can see it's you, Officer, so let me call the investigation room and tell them you are coming."

She handed back his ID, and he made sure there was a slight touch of her fingers, as he took it back and tucked it in his pocket. Tafoya inwardly straightened his thinking toward the task at hand, rather than shifting into a mode of flirtation. He was single. He looked at her ring finger. Her finger was bare. That might not mean she wasn't married since jewelry in her line of work—and his—was dangerous in the line of duty. Still, no ring on her finger might mean she was single, unencumbered. He promised himself, on another day, hail stones or not, he was coming back to the Forest Service headquarters, even if it meant to pick up a map of which he already had dozens.

In the F.B.I. investigation room, Tafoya again presented his credentials, and after getting vetted that he was who he said he was, the agent on duty checked out the evidence bag of Red Feather boot man that contained the belt buckle. The buckle had been dusted for fingerprints on Saturday. The agent instructed Tafoya, "Don't let the buckle get out of your sight. Understand?"

Tafoya got miffed the F.B.I. agent reminded him of chain of evidence protocol. "I've handled evidence before. I know the rules. I'll have this back, probably before noon, and I'll submit a report on the jeweler's assessment. If you aren't here, you've probably gone to Starbucks for a latte, and I'll check the evidence bag into the sheriff's office across the street. Oh, I forgot! Ojo Verde doesn't have a Starbucks. What will you ever do, Agent?"

Tafoya waited for a comeback. The agent obliged.

"Guess I'll have to get some peyote from your brothers out there at the wigwam and smoke it," the agent shot back. "Or maybe I'll call Uber and have them port some latte up from Santa Fe. You know what Uber is, don't you, Chief?"

"Peyote is not smoked. It's chewed and...," Tafoya's back and forth with the agent was abruptly stopped by Diane Parker, the F.B.I. Special Agent in charge, who walked in the door. Tafoya and the agent stopped talking. Parker sensed some tension, but she was used to the tension that often rose up between the F.B.I. and tribal police. She had experienced it first hand from her tenure out on the Navajo reservation in Gallup and in Albuquerque with other Pueblos.

Tafoya and the agent looked at each other and laughed, shrugging their shoulders with body language that meant, "No hard feelings." Tafoya left the investigation room after paying respects to Parker, and once again stating to all concerned that he would comply with the rules of the chain of evidence. Much to his displeasure, Janet Rael was gone. She had been replaced by a snow-looks-like, and he was tall and thin.

Tulona policeman Tafoya opened the door to Tony Rodarte's jewelry store, The Silver Concho, on Paseo del Sur. The Silver Concho was smaller inside than what one imagined from the outside. The store had once been a private home; the living room and dining room had been remodeled into a display area and sales counter for commercial transactions. Directly behind the front counter, a double door had been removed, and one saw a large workroom with worktables, shelves, and cabinets. Two tall Case steel safes were flush against the back wall. Work lamps and magnifying lamps were placed at intervals throughout the backroom shop. A huge cottonwood trunk, two and a half feet tall by three feet in diameter sat on one side of the workroom. It showed heavy usage for stamping and hammering silver.

In the front transactional area of The Silver Concho, display cases offered rings, bracelets, necklaces, belt buckles, concho belts, and old pawn from the period 1890-1950. On the walls were hung Pueblo crafts: bows, arrows, papoose boards, shirts, and woven belts. In the corner, a conical shaped fireplace had been constructed and benches extended out on both sides from the fireplace, offering a sitting area for husbands whose wives were shopping. The shop had the look of a clean, bright trading post. Two Gray Hills rugs were draped from a *viga* against the wall. The jewelry was expensive. Not a cheap tourist trinket could be seen. Tony Rodarte's, The Silver Concho, emitted old silver wealth and gem-quality turquoise. Located two miles from the plaza, in the direction of Taos, The Silver Concho was a serious study of old Ojo Verde commerce and trade. Officer Richard Tafoya purchased gifts at Rodarte's for his family, and so had his father and grandfather before him.

"Hey, Richard," Tony said, greeting him with a smile, adjusting his glasses, and offering a two-handed shake.

"Mr. Rodarte, how are you?" Tafoya responded with a formality given to the old age of Rodarte and the rule of social exchange. Rodarte had worked with Navajo and New Mexico Pueblos throughout his life. He spent time going to trade fairs, fiestas, and trading posts throughout the Southwest to buy, sell, and learn the craft and skill of jewelry making. His book with Steven Begay, *Southwest Turquoise Mines*, was stated to be the companion of Joseph Pogue's, *The Turquoise: A Study of its History, Mineralogy, Geology, Ethnology, Archaeology, Mythology, Folklore, and Technology*, published in 1915. Pogue might have had a PhD, but Rodarte had fifty-plus years of experience in the New Mexico-Arizona jewelry business and turquoise mining. He had a scar on the left side of his face from a cave-in at the Los Cerrillos turquoise mines when he was a boy, attempting to shore up a section of the mine with his father. The scar gave him character; a chance to talk about turquoise.

"So, Richard, what do you have in your hand there? Looks like a silver buckle in a plastic evidence bag."

"What I have here," said Tafoya, "is the buckle from the body that was found Saturday morning out by Arroyo Luz on reservation land. I need for you to tell me as much about the buckle as you can. Who made it, where it might have come from, the quality of the turquoise stones, the approximate age of the buckle? If you know who the craftsman is, we need to get in contact with them, and see if he or she knows who bought it, or where it was sold. We have no identification on the body, and this is a starting point. Lots of questions, I know, but we need intelligence on this buckle in order to find a name."

"I see," said Rodarte. "May I take the buckle out of the bag? I need to examine it closer and magnify the stones and any hallmark of the artist."

"You can," said Tafoya, "but I have to be with the buckle and can't let it out of my sight. The rules of chain of evidence, you understand."

"I understand, Richard. Let's go back in the shop and put it under my magnifying lenses." Rodarte grabbed his cell phone off the counter and told his assistant to watch the front of the store while he and Richard went to the workshop tables.

Rodarte sat on a high stool and pulled another stool beside him for Tafoya. Tafoya took the buckle out of the evidence bag and laid it on a black-felt work board that was for display purposes. Rodarte looked closely. The turquoise was of a type he rarely had seen—if ever. Only fifteen percent of the turquoise on the market was natural, gemstone-grade turquoise, and this turquoise fell in the fifteen percent category. But this stone had another quality that made it stand apart from all other turquoise he had seen.

"Hmmm," Rodarte said

"What is it, Tony?" Tafoya asked.

"I'm not sure, Richard."

Rodarte focused light on the buckle. By the ruler, the buckle was five inches by three and a quarter inch. The silver was sterling. The designs were conventional symbols of Southwestern Native American artists. In the center of the buckle was a mature cornstalk. On either side of the cornstalk were turquoise stones.

"These turquoise stones are gemlike quality, not treated. They are oval shaped, significant in size. The brilliant color is blue with a tincture of green. What is so distinctive of these stones is the fern-like, moss-like matrices in the stone. It's called dendrite. Very rare, very valuable."

"Do you know the artist that made it?" Richard asked.

Rodarte turned the buckle over and focused a Led Loupe over a corner of the buckle and found three initials.

"I have three initials here on the back, RYz. I think I know who RYz is, but I am going to crosscheck it." Rodarte turned to Bille Hougart, *Native American and Southwestern Silver Hallmarks,* the artist initials guide for Southwestern craftsmen that he had on the edge of the worktable. It was the latest edition, essential to his business.

"The artist is Roger Yazzie, I think. He lives north of Sheep Springs, near Shiprock. I know him well." Rodarte thumbed through the guidebook until he found the identifying initials. "Yes, it's Roger Yazzie, the only RYz in the book. Sometimes he puts a hallmark, RY, but here it says he sometimes uses RYz."

"Can you call him and find out if we can send him a picture of this over the phone, so he can positively identify it, give us some information? I need to talk to him and ask him some questions," Richard said.

Rodarte replied that Yazzie only had a landline, not a cell phone. He brought up the contacts on his cell phone and called Yazzie. After ten rings, no answer. Rodarte redialed, and still, no answer. "I'll try again later, Richard." He scribbled the phone number and gave it to Tafoya.

Tafoya allowed Rodarte to take photos of the belt buckle with the cautionary note not to distribute the photos. After Rodarte snapped photos, Tafoya placed the buckle back in the evidence bag. Rodarte found one example of dendrite turquoise in his books and showed it to Tafoya. "You see how rare this type of stone is, Richard? I don't have an example of dendrite in my collection, and I've been collecting turquoise for half a century."

On the way out of The Silver Concho, Tafoya passed the Two Gray Hills rug and he wondered if Janet Rael liked Two Gray Hills themes over the Tec Nos Pos style. He preferred Tec Nos Pos, the Circle of Cottonwoods rug. Thinking he could find out which rug Janet preferred when he took the evidence bag back to the National Forest headquarters, he was disappointed, again. She was not at the front counter. She had gone to the Tusas Mountains for a game count. When he went into the evidence room, a different F.B.I. agent was on duty, so he did not have to quibble with the latte-drinking agent who had been fond of stating the obvious earlier that morning. But that did not make up for the disappointment of missing Janet.

Earlier, Forest Service officer Janet Rael walked out of the headquarters office in Ojo Verde and climbed into a light-colored forest green Chevrolet Suburban favored by the Forest Service. She checked the fuel level; it was full. The Suburban four-wheel drive was only a year old, so the fuel gauge was probably correct—probably. Not wanting to run out of fuel in the backcountry, she stopped by the fuel pump at the headquarters' fueling depot and topped off the tank. The tank took only half-gallon, so the fuel gauge was accurate, and whoever had the four-wheel drive before her was conscientious enough to top the tank before leaving the grounds. Janet's father had always cautioned her against faulty gauges. In flight school, her instructor taught her in preflight to check fuel tanks by untwisting the fuel cap and looking in the fuel tank to double-check fuel levels. "Gauges aren't the fuel tanks, Janet."

Janet steered onto Paseo del Sur, then took a locals' bypass around the Ojo Verde plaza and tourist traffic. Heading out on US Highway 64, she crossed the gorge bridge over the Rio Grande. Janet stopped at the Tres Piedras Ranger District and picked up Jeremy, another Bio Sciences Technician. They gathered their hardcopy forms for the field count and left notice where they would be going and when they would return. The military-grade laptop in the Forest Service vehicle had cell phone capability and an internal GPS. Radio communications included VHF, UHF, and a high-frequency band. Janet liked to take the laptop out of its cradle and work on a hood or tailgate.

How lucky I am, she thought, to be here in wide-open spaces and do science in *plein aire*.

From Tres Piedras, they continued on US 64 across the Tusas Ridge, turning north on Forest Road 421 toward Biscara Spring. Jeremy scanned for wildlife on both sides of the road. The drought had been hard on flora, land, and wildlife, but the monsoon of the July-August summer months had greened-up the meadows, for even the lupine varieties of plants looked like they might blossom again. Two springs for *norte* Rio Grande!

The ponderosa pine looked healthy; few trees in the count appeared wilted and decadent. The gambel and wavey-leaf oaks had prospered with the monsoon rains. Janet and Jeremy pulled off the road and, with binoculars, scanned for wildlife. Janet took the laptop out of its cradle, placed it on the hood, and began to enter data. Jeremy spotted a herd of mule deer, whose appearance was fat and healthy. Moving slowly on the road through the forest and counting for two hours, they stopped for lunch in a grove of aspens.

Janet unwrapped the aluminum foil from a Navajo burrito she had prepared early that morning at home. Her version of the Navajo burrito consisted of a large flour tortilla encasing diced boiled potatoes, scrambled eggs, and chopped Spam. Out of her cold lunch bag, she fetched a large container of green chile salsa she shared with Jeremy. As she bit into her Navajo burrito with diced Spam, she thought of Richard Tafoya and his losing weight from curtailing his Spam intake. He dressed so handsomely in the dark forest-green uniform of the tribal police.

Janet and Jeremy packed out their trash, leaving none behind. For afternoon field work, they drove forest roads by Turkey Lake, Blaze Tank, and Cunningham Gulch, checking on water tanks and the condition of grass and trees. They found mule deer track and mountain lion scat about Blaze Tank, and scared up another herd of deer near the corrals at Cunningham Gulch. They counted thirty deer in the herd. Janet was pleased the monsoon rains had alleviated most of the drought stress on the high parks and meadows. Their field work completed, Jeremy picked up the radio com, relaying to headquarters they were two miles from US 64 and ten miles from Tres Piedras.

Janet dropped Jeremy off at the Tres Piedras ranger station and drove a quarter mile from the ranger station to the Narrow Gauge Cafe. More of a quick-bite café, the Narrow Gauge Cafe had been a railroad stop on the historic Chile Line that ran from Antonito, Colorado, to Santa Fe, a route of 125.6 miles. It had shut down in the 1940s, but the café continued to throw hash and burgers and bake pies. Janet opened the door to the café and saw few customers at the tables. She wanted a large cup of coffee with double cream to drink on the trip back to Ojo Verde. Around tables sat cowboys, construction guys with whitened work boots, and a couple of isolates having soup and beer. She noticed a solitary middle-aged man finishing his soup and beer in the corner. After pouring her cup of coffee and looking at community notices on the bulletin board, Janet paid and walked out the door. The middle-aged man was holding the door open for her.

"Thanks," Janet said. "Have a good rest of the day."

"*De nada*," he said, "you, too."

Although he wore work clothes for rough tasks, he had a silver-polished belt buckle with a large turquoise stone set in the middle. Janet thought it strange to wear work clothes with a valuable buckle. She noticed that his hands were callused, and he was muscular in the arms and shoulders. He climbed into an old Ford pickup that had a faded logo of the Culebra Mine Company on the side. Since her Suburban was parked next to his, she glanced in the bed of his pickup and saw a new Bosch generator, shovels, pry bars, and pickaxes along with barbed wire and assorted tool boxes chained to the floor of the pickup. Despite the age of the Ford, the tires were new Goodyears for all-terrain, off-road travel. Five-gallon buckets contained smaller pry bars and chunks of granite, slate, and sandstone. He probably works with concrete, stone, masonry, she pondered.

Heading back to Ojo Verde, she drove to the intersection with US 64, turned east, and glanced in the rearview mirror. The Ford pickup had turned in the same direction as she, but was a quarter mile behind her. Not a threatening maneuver, she reasoned, but she would keep watch as she drove. Near Ojo Verde, at the yellow blinking light intersection, he turned northward toward San Miguel and Questa. She was relieved when he turned away from her. Janet continued on to the Forest Service headquarters in town and parked the vehicle with a freshly-filled, full tank of gas. The offices had closed, but she had a key to enter and leave the laptop and paperwork from the day's field work.

Janet climbed into her red Subaru and drove to her casita apartment on Zacate Verde. She lived on the second floor of the apartment complex and had taken the lease because it was cheap, close to the Forest Service headquarters, and the rear balcony faced Tulona Mountain. When the lease had come up for renewal a few months before, she had considered moving to a rent house with trees and grass of her own, but the rear balcony and windows looking out to the mountains was too good to let go. Most mornings, except when it was bitterly cold, Janet had coffee on the balcony and watched the sunrise. Besides, she was accustomed to apartments since her university days in Albuquerque; a home with trees and grass could wait.

After showering and washing her hair, Janet walked out on her rear balcony. She reflected on her day in the forest, the wildlife count, and full tanks of water from the monsoons. She thought of Richard Tafoya, the handsome man who made her chuckle and think of fry bread and Spam. "I wonder if his home on the Pueblo has trees and grass?"

7

Tuesday, September 4, Day of Saint Rose of Viterbo, Month of Corn Ripe Moon

To Ben Lovato, the Tulona were either finishing one ceremonial period or preparing for another ceremonial period; there was no in between. For his Pueblo, the annual pilgrimage up to Earth Cloud Lake was finished, and now a month of preparation began for the Tulona Saint Francis Feast Day that occurred on October 4. The Spanish under Alvarado in 1540 had entered the Tulona Pueblo on that day, the Saint Day of Francis. The Juan de Oñate *entrada* in 1598 reestablished a Spanish presence in northern New Mexico, sending Franciscans to the Tulona to establish a mission, the Mission San Francisco del Monte. From time to time, the black robes ran scared from the Pueblo, returning after uprisings were squashed.

The Tulona's Saint Francis festival on October 4 occurred four days after the San Geronimo festival at the Taos Pueblo. San Geronimo Feast Day was the preeminent Feast Day among all Eastern Pueblos along the Rio Grande. The approaching Saint Francis festival obligated Ben to dancing, racing, and pole climbing; and although their crowds were smaller and sales booths fewer than San Geronimo, Tulona Feast Day was popular, their races exciting.

Quail Looks Away lit a match to her propane stove and cracked eggs for scrambling, whisking vigorously. Boiled potatoes were diced, added to the eggs. Corn tortillas were heated to go with the breakfast, and red and green salsas spiced the food. Leftover beef fajitas added more protein to their meal. Quail's mother poured coffee and added dehydrated cream to the strong brew. The family sat down at the table covered with a red-and-white-checked oilcloth. The propane stove for cooking added heat to the room, and piñon wood crackled in the fireplace. The battery-charged radio played softly at one end of the table, but when the weather report came on, Ben turned up the volume.

"Temperature high today will be in the mid-seventies with temperature lower by ten degrees in higher elevations. Expect partly cloudy skies in the morning, clearing in the afternoon. Wind will be changing to the north with an approaching cold front coming into the area tonight. High temperatures tomorrow expected to be in the upper fifties. Warming on Thursday after tomorrow's temperatures in the fifties. Now a word from our sponsors." Ben turned down the volume.

"Quail, how are you this morning?" Ben asked.

"I am fine, Ben, but I am uncomfortable." Looking at her mother, "I don't know when the time will come."

"The child will come when he or she is ready. But I can tell you, it will be soon. Less than a week, I think."

Ben abruptly looked at his mother-in-law. "I am going to get the cacique and walk him over to say a blessing. I'm nervous about this, the festival, the ending of Lake Moon Month...all the changes taking place. Things seem...out of balance."

"Most of your balance, my dear Ben, can be restored once you begin your day," said Quail. She saw Ben's furrowed brow and felt his anxiety. "Perhaps a blessing and prayer from the cacique is a good thing. I would like him to come. But not for long. I have to go into Ojo Verde and get groceries. Go see if you can bring him now."

Ben wadded his napkin up and threw it in the waste bin. He stood up and walked out the door, gently closing the turquoise-framed door behind him. A few doors down, the Blue Stone People kiva rose impressively, its long ladder of spruce poles reaching into the sky, stretching for the next world. The cacique's house was next to the kiva. Ben knocked on his door. The cacique, Leonard Bustamente, opened the screen door. Smells of bacon and pancakes wafted through the screen.

"Grandfather," Ben asked, "is it too much to ask for you to come down to my house and give a blessing for Quail Looks Away and my child to be? Just a short visit. Right now, if you can," Ben said urgently.

Eighty-five-year-old Cacique Bustamente looked at Ben. Bustamente had recently had cataract surgery at Saint Luke Hospital, so he saw clearly Ben's anxiety.

"Yes. Let me get my coat. We'll walk together." Bustamente wrapped himself in his blanket rather than a coat. He walked back with Ben to his house. "You came back early from the dancing and singing at Earth Cloud Lake. Can you tell me why?"

"I was worried and concerned about Quail Looks Away, Grandfather. That's all."

Bustamente had another question for Ben. "I heard you helped a *fansaine* find his way back to his people from the lake road?"

"Yes, Grandfather, I did. He was an innocent snow-looks-like, I think. Just unaware of his surroundings...he was lost and got stuck. He came from the ski valley. He invited me to have lunch at his expense in the village." Happy to be walking with the cacique, Ben said, "We should go together, Grandfather."

The cacique replied, "I had a dream that you and I and a *fansaine* sat around a campfire. Maybe I should go with you." Pausing, Bustamente said, "Yes, let us do that, eat at his campfire at his expense. Oh, here we are at your door."

Ben suddenly got more nervous about going to the village with Bustamente to have lunch than he was nervous about Quail. Why did he invite the cacique in the first place? Ben inwardly groaned. He opened the door to his home and let the cacique enter first.

"Quail Looks Away, how are you?" the cacique asked. "And, Grandmother," referring to Quail's mother, "how are you?" They both expressed they were fine and how grateful they were that he had come to give a blessing. Ben stood to the side, observing.

Like a thin gauze of tissue shaved painlessly from the shoulder of the oldest living organism on earth, a mood, an atmosphere settled all around them, covering the walls and ceiling and floor, like a living, breathing lace. Enveloping, but not smothering. They felt a thin radiant blanket of a thousand years of continuous Pueblo mystical authority descend into the room. The words of Bustamente were his own, but not his own,

Hey ya, hey ya, hey ya, hey ya, ho!
Old Ones, I beg you hear me, in this moment!
Bring good! things upon this household and Quail Looks Away,
Bring good! things upon tree-leaves-that-rattle-with-wind People!
Old Ones! Make it so!

Finishing the song-prayer, Cacique Leonard Bustamente took blue corn meal from his medicine bag and threw it in the air with the strength of a young man, a young woman, and a joyful child. The corn meal floated down slowly onto the freshly-swept floor, while flecks of meal rested on their shoulders the remainder of the day.

Taos County Medical Examiner Rosenbaum submitted his final report to F.B.I. Agent Parker. She assembled Romero of the tribal police and Sheriff's Deputy Cordova at the Forest Service headquarters for a read-out and case update. As expected, Dr. Rosenbaum reported that the cause of death was the penetration of the upper body cavity with a large, moderately-sharp instrument like a drill or pick axe punctuating the heart. He reported neither drugs nor toxins in Red Feather boot man. Rosenbaum again stated that the circumstances of death could not be determined—accident, murder, suicide—although suicide was highly unlikely. The time of death was twelve to eighteen hours before the body was discovered on Saturday morning. Time of death was between two o'clock and eight o'clock, Friday afternoon.

Rosenbaum added a speculative notation to his report: "The cause of death was most likely murder, for if it was an accident there would be no need for taking the body from the scene. Leave the body in place, or rush the injured person to the hospital. There are more questions than answers at the present."

Agent Parker was frustrated and testy. "The timeline is the victim died between two o'clock and eight o'clock on Friday. That's last Friday! Here we are on Tuesday morning, four days later, and what do we have other than Dr. Rosenbaum's report?" Agent Parker asked. "Nothing!"

Romero interjected more information, "Tafoya has made inquiries with a local jeweler on the buckle, and he is returning to the jewelers this morning for more feedback. Preliminary analysis is that the turquoise is rare and gem-like. Rodarte, the shop owner, is making inquiries about the initials RYz. He thinks the craftsman's name is Roger Yazzie, north of Sheep Springs, on the Navajo reservation."

"Call Tafoya by cell now! See what he is doing on this," Parker ordered.

Romero punched in Tafoya's number, putting the cell phone on speaker.

"Hello, Tafoya here."

"Richard, this is Romero and I'm at the F.B.I. investigation room at the Forest Service, and I have you on speaker phone. Okay?"

"Sure, what's going on?" Richard knew that he must choose his words carefully because he didn't know who was listening. That bothered him, so, he asked, "Who's there with you, Sergeant?"

"Parker, Cordova, and me. That's it."

"Acknowledge. Go ahead. I'm in transit to The Silver Concho to talk with Rodarte."

"Call me back when you find out more, Tafoya. We are waiting." Romero looked at Parker, "No joy there—yet."

"What about the interviews of people living across the road from where the body was found? That's your responsibility," Parker asked Deputy Cordova.

Cordova cleared his throat, taking a sip of coffee to slow Parker down. "The victim was not from Arroyo Luz. We did strike some good intel from two *señores* living across the road, Santiago Majerus and Johnny Sisneros. I filed that report yesterday. You should have it in front of you."

Parker leafed through the case file. "Here it is, yes. You wrote, 'Majerus and Sisneros both state they saw a dark-colored pickup at about eight o'clock on the Tulona side of the reservation, going west to east slowly along the fence line. Sisneros thinks it was a late-nineties F-150. He saw some washed-out emblem on the side of the pickup, but couldn't decipher it. Majerus didn't see much, only a glance. They did not see who was driving. No one was on the passenger side of the vehicle. Since the pickup was on the Tulona reservation, they assumed it must have been a warchief patrolling.'"

"Was it the warchief?" Parker asked Romero.

"No, it was not a warchief," Romero told the team. "Warchief Concha planned a patrol the next morning. That's when he found Red Feather boot man."

"Well, then," Parker said, "we have an unknown person driving an old F-150 slowly on the Tulona reservation that was, or could be, the pickup or vehicle that carried the body."

"Nothing solid," Romero added, "but we do have tire tread photos of two vehicles, one the warchief who discovered the body the next morning, and, two, a vehicle possibly from the night before."

Talking paused. Romero doodled on a notepad. Then, Cordova spoke.

"I wonder why put the body there? They didn't want to leave Red Feather boot man where he bled to death for some reason. I wonder why?"

None of the three said anything. Parker broke the silence. "Get the identity of our victim. That's at the top of the list."

As Parker emphasized that point, Romero got a call from Tafoya.

"Tafoya, what do you have?" Romero asked.

Tafoya had walked into Rodarte's The Silver Concho and found the shop warm with a piñon fire blazing in the oval fireplace. The Two Gray Hills rug still hung from the *viga*. He walked over to see the price. Two thousand dollars, but well worth it, he thought. The clerk at the front counter shouted to the back of the shop that Tafoya had come in and was looking to buy the Two Gray Hills rug.

"No, I'm not, thank you. Just looking," he joked back.

"Come on back, Richard," shouted Rodarte. He rose from his work stool and shook Tafoya's hand.

"I started to call you last night when I heard from Yazzie out near Sheep Springs, but it was after dark and I didn't want to bother you," Rodarte said, apologetically.

"Did you find out if he made the buckle and for who?" Tafoya asked, sitting down on a stool across from Rodarte.

"I did find out some things for you, Richard. Yazzie said that he had met a fellow at a market show in Gallup. The man had two pieces of turquoise. Yazzie had never seen any turquoise like that and offered to buy all the man had, but the man said he just wanted Yazzie to work the stones into a belt buckle."

"What was the young man's name, Tony? Did Yazzie have a receipt of the transaction?" Tafoya interrupted.

"The man paid Yazzie in cash. He made sure he snapped photos of the turquoise before he let it out of his hands. Used a cell phone to take pictures. But as to a name? Yazzie can only remember that the man said he was from around Ojo Verde in the east, and his first name was Robert. Last name he can't remember. He wrote no receipt."

Tafoya sighed. "Well, that's more than we knew yesterday. I'll need Yazzie's address. Someone will have to meet with him and show him photos of the buckle and of 'Robert' to verify the identity. Robert may not be our victim. Yazzie's Robert might have given the buckle away or sold it to someone else."

"I'm sorry I can't provide you more information about Yazzie's work," Tony regretfully said. "I want to see the buckle and turquoise again, Richard. Perhaps I missed something the other day. Maybe I can pinpoint the mine it came from."

"I think I can do that. First, let me step outside and call Romero and tell him what you found out about Robert and Yazzie. Give me the phone number again and address of Yazzie, so I can give that to them. I'll be right back."

When Tafoya returned to Rodarte's workroom, Tony had poured him a cup of coffee.

"Sit down for a couple of minutes, Richard, I want to give you a quick lesson on turquoise."

Richard complied, for he knew Rodarte was the expert on turquoise, and it seemed that turquoise was a critical element of getting at the truth. Tony Rodarte explained that turquoise color ranges from a sky-blue color to pale green. The sky-blue color or robin's-egg color is the preferred choice of color, but the color of blue is not absolutely the chosen color of all cultures. The matrix or lines within the worked stone is also a desirable attribute in turquoise. The four qualities of turquoise are density, color and clarity, matrix, and rarity.

Tafoya noticed the scar on Rodarte's face from the Cerrillos mine cave-in when he was a boy. Rodarte continued on with his lesson.

"Richard, the allure of turquoise stretches across time and the world. From Persia and Egypt to the American Southwest to China, this blue stone has been considered magical in power and, definitely, attractive in adornment for kings, queens, and the laity. In the Southwest, turquoise blue is considered the Father Sky stone, the male gem. Green turquoise is believed to be the Mother Earth stone, the female gem. Apache hunters and warriors, in their belief of turquoise's power, attached pieces of turquoise to their bows, so that arrows flew unerringly straight to their target. Here in New Mexico and the Southwest, some of the richest and most abundant mines of turquoise in the world have been discovered and exploited. Some of the mines are still active today, but a number have been mined to extinction, such as the Cerrillos Mines. You know, Richard, I worked with my father in the 1940s at Cerrillos and the Tiffany Mine." He touched the scar on his face.

"What was that like?" Tafoya asked.

"I was a boy and enchanted by mines. Even today I am. The mines about Mount Chalchihuitl in the Cerrillos district were huge! The main pit of Chalchihuitl plunged two hundred feet in depth and extended maybe three hundrred feet across. The debris from the quarry covered as much as twenty acres and amounted to a hundred thousand tons of waste rock. We didn't find much there, but we did at the Tiffany Mine, nearby. At both places, potsherds and ancient stone mauls, chisels, and picks lay about the ground. I picked some up and brought them back to the house. Here, let me show you."

Rodarte stood up from the working stool and walked over to the corner of the workroom to a large steel armoire, pulled out a key chain, and unlocked the door. Tools, burlap sacks, steel pans, lanterns, and a Dutch oven were on display. On the bottom shelf was an old wooden box; Rodarte pulled it out and set it on the workbench. Well-worn stone mauls that had been worked down to smoothness and monochrome potsherds filled the large box. Rodarte lifted out a stone maul; Tafoya held it in his hand. It was heavy.

"How old do you think this is, Tony?" Tafoya asked.

"The experts say the Cerrillos Mines were excavated as early as AD 900. Legend has it that Moctezuma proudly wore pendants and necklaces from the Cerrillos. So, these mauls could have come from as early as that. Maybe earlier," Rodarte answered.

Tafoya enjoyed the science and history lesson, but he needed to move on to the station. He had one more question: "Tony, take me through steps of making Robert Red Feather's buckle. Maybe there's a step I can dig deeper into."

"Sure, Richard, it's pretty simple and straightforward. First, you find a source of turquoise. That's the mine. Then you extract the turquoise with its mother matrix, the surrounding material about the turquoise. Second, you take the unrefined turquoise and matrix to a lapidary, the shop that cuts, grinds, and polishes the turquoise. Finally, once you have a polished stone of turquoise, you take it to a jeweler, or maybe the lapidary has a jeweler that will set the stone in a bezel. A bezel is a setting for the stone, and that can be attached to a buckle, pendant, earring, bolo item. Hundreds of ways to show it off."

"So, Tony, we have a miner, lapidary worker, and a jeweler?"

"Correct, but one person can be all three. In the case of Robert Red Feather, it seems, we only know the jeweler: Roger Yazzie of Sheep Springs. But neither miner nor lapidarist."

"Well, maybe we know one miner or lapidarist among many other prospectors and lapidarists," added Tafoya. "Our poor Robert Red Feather."

Cacique Leonard Bustamente of the Blue Stone People kiva sat on the bench, stemming out from his conical fireplace, and rubbed his forehead. The inner room of his Pueblo home buffered sounds from the plaza to indecipherable muffles. Bustamente's wall displayed a buckskin medicine bundle, calendar, and a small piñon-wood Christian cross—different lineaments of his long life. He had fashioned his life as a servant to the Tulona people. The well-being of the Tulona people depended on his being aware of the change of seasons, and the work associated with spring, summer, fall, and winter. And, as important, the time of ceremony linked with the seasons. He was a keeper of traditional knowledge. Tulona stories—the narratives—must be told and become embedded in the Tulona. Their well-being, whether Winter House or Summer House, white corn meal or blue corn meal, depended on keeping the stories alive. Bustamente rubbed his forehead. Was there an imbalance, a cross-purpose, arising in the Tulona Pueblo with Red Feather boot man? He pondered the question and breathed easier when he arrived at an answer for the Tulona.

"Tafoya and Romero know what to do. They are our special guardians in cases like this."

Bustamente walked out of his quiet interior room. He opened the turquoise-painted door to the outside and gazed at the Pueblo Plaza spread out before him. Late in the day, daylight faded as the sun slowly arced downward in the west, becoming more southwesterly as fall progressed to late December and winter, the Quiet Time. Bustamente reflected that earlier that morning a request had been made of him. He had visited Ben Lovato and Quail Looks Away's home to give a prayer, a Tulona blessing for the family and the Pueblo. That gesture was good, very good, for the prayer found rest in the adobe walls of the room and the hearts of those that heard: Ben Lovato, Quail Looks Away, and Quail's mother, Deer Rain Looking. Bustamente felt the words lodge in each of them. Even the adobe walls of their home recorded his words and seemed to be capable—yes, the walls—of singing them back forever to the village of tree-leaves-that-rattle-with-wind.

Bustamente climbed ladders to the topmost roof on the Summer House Pueblo. The climb taxed his muscles, but he had strength enough. As he climbed from rooftop to ladders to rooftops, he passed his kinsmen, gazing out toward the setting sun that fell on Mt. Pedernal, the flat iron mountain that drew people for obsidian and its shrine on the apex. His kinsmen spoke, "Alo, Grandfather." Others nodded, as he climbed to the topmost roof on Summer House side. It was as if he stood at the top of the world. He acknowledged the height he stood upon, looking at the setting sun. Bustamente spoke.

I am here, Sun.

8

Wednesday, September 5, Day of Saint Teresa of Calcutta, Month of Corn Ripe Moon

G. Armstrong Coe drove to the Santa Fe Airport to pick up his wife who had been visiting her parents in Los Angeles. New Mexico State Highway 68 to Santa Fe, challenged him. From Ojo Verde to Velarde it was two lanes, some of the worst miles in the state. Once past Velarde, the road broadened to four lanes all the way to Santa Fe Airport. Before Velarde, however, the road wound along the Rio Grande for twenty miles. Coe saw a good running river, not the best he had seen; but the river was running moderately high, making for good rafting—an activity he would never do. SH 68 cut basalt cliffs on the east side of the Rio. On the west bank, a narrow, unpaved, road had been cleared. Whoever uses that? he thought.

Coe breathed easier and relaxed, as he drove his car out of the Rio Grande SH 68 chute at Velarde and onto a four-lane highway. He saw green long lots of irrigated land to his right, fed by diversion irrigation ditches: the Chisos Ditch, the Riconada Acequia. Coe wondered if any of those long lots or *suertes* ever came up for sale. Surely, he thought to himself, a family gets tired of working the orchards and Hatch chili pepper gardens—the *chile del norte.* The thought of Hatch chili peppers triggered the smell of roasting Hatch peppers in the large tumbling cylinders at the Railyard Farmers Market in Santa Fe. Even in ice cream, Hatch was added. Coe had Hatch-peppered ice cream at Tablita's down the street from his bookshop. Jason, his preferred waiter at Tablita's, had insisted he have just a taste, and when he had a sample, he double ordered a bowl of it.

He glanced at the digital clock in his Toyota Corolla that read, eleven fifteen a.m. Priscilla's plane would touch down at noon. Coe slowed down to pass an old pickup truck in front of him. The pickup—a Chevy, maybe as old as the 1980s—had several colors of replaced doors and fenders. The driver was an older Hispano male with a woman, most likely his wife.

The male was wearing a felt cowboy hat that was sweat-stained and had a hawk feather stuck on the left side of the hat under the hatband. Wooden side rails kept in check a large load of firewood. Even though Coe's passenger window was rolled up, the cowboy waved in acknowledgement. Coe waved back. The cowboy's window was rolled down; the hawk feather fluttered in the wind. Coe thought of hawks that killed and danced on their prey. When he first settled in Ojo Verde, he had seen a hawk dance on a vole it had killed in a meadow along the Chama River near Abiquiu. Happy, playing? but why dance on the kill? Coe thought.

As Coe drove past the cowboy, he noticed the Northern Rio Grande Heritage Area in Alcalde. Coe looked over to the heritage area and saw the large bronze statue of Juan de Oñate on a horse. He looked close at the statue, set amidst four flagpoles displaying flags of New Mexico, Rio Arriba County, the U.S., and the adjacent Pueblo of Ohkay Owingeh, known in other times as the San Juan Pueblo.

"Yep, Oñate still has both of his feet," Coe uttered aloud.

Oñate having both of his feet on the honorary statue had not always been so. In 1997, in the dead of the night, Oñate's right foot was sawed off, amputated, stolen. Twenty years later, in a secret meeting in northern New Mexico, a *New York Times* reporter had met with the man that had severed the statue's right foot. Coe remembered reading the article, and how the *Times* reporter held the severed foot in his hand—a large and heavy bronze casting. The "foot surgeons" had amputated the appendage after hiking miles to Alcalde during a December winter's night. The whole act was to protest the four-hundred-year anniversary and celebration of Spanish conquest in New Mexico. Oñate's nephew and several Spaniards had been killed in an Acoma Pueblo ambush in 1598. Acoma was overrun in retaliation, and captured Acoma males over twenty-four years of age were to have a foot cut off as punishment. Neither of the two protestors who severed Oñate's foot were Acoma Pueblo Natives. One of the "surgeons" was of Iroquois ancestry, the other a native New Mexican. The Friends of Acoma protested the celebration of four hundred years of Spanish conquest and supported the "surgery." The act split Hispano communities for they had intermarried and lived side-by-side with Native Americans, yet they were proud of Spanish heritage.

Coe wondered how the Tulona felt about the Oñate surgery for they, too, had intermarried and lived beside Hispano communities. He did not remember any protest in 1997 when the "surgery" occurred. The Tulona and Ojo Verdeans—Puebloan, Hispano, Anglo—continued cordial relations, so far as he could recollect. The Oñate "surgery" illustrated, he thought, the complexity of ethnic relations throughout the Southwest.

Coe's reflection dissolved, as he came into Española's traffic; low riders cruised beside him. Española, New Mexico, was famous for the customizing of automobiles that drove inches off the ground. Low riders had suspensions that bucked and rolled the chassis two or three feet or higher off the ground. "This is exciting," Coe thought. A few low-rider cars drove past him, and he passed a beautiful, yellow-painted, flame-striped Chevy pickup with the driver and his wife or girlfriend on the bench seat, close beside him. As he had read, most wives and girlfriends supported their guy's habits of low riding, and some women built their own low riders for fun and sport. Coe made a mental note to bring Priscilla to one of Española's Saturday low-rider rallies.

With Priscilla on his mind, Coe sped up, took the new loop around Santa Fe, and parked in the Santa Fe short-term parking lot. Looking at his watch, he entered the parking lot when Priscilla's American Airlines Flight 330 from Phoenix was on final approach. Coe was eager to embrace his wife whom he had not seen for a month. When she walked out of the entryway, he broke into smiles. Priscilla beamed, hugged him close, and said she was eager to settle back into high country and the familiar routines of Ojo Verde. When Coe and Priscilla arrived home, both worked together cooking a green chili stew and settling back in with local vegetables and cool mountain air. For dessert, Coe had brought home from Tablita's a half-gallon tub of Hatch ice cream.

An hour before Coe embraced Priscilla in Santa Fe, Tulona policeman Tafoya turned into the parking lot of the Forest Service headquarters. He pulled alongside a green Forest Service van and turned his ignition off. Tafoya unholstered his cell phone and brought up his contact list, scrolling down to the "S's." The contact list alphabet on the right side of the cell phone page was troublesome to pinpoint A's, B's, C's, and S's. Tafoya's fingers were large, and the alphabet list at the side of the page must have been set up for children. He scrolled down the S's to The Silver Concho and tapped in the number for Tony Rodarte. Tony answered the phone on the first ring, and said he was staying at the shop until dark. If Tafoya brought the turquoise by for him to look at a second time, he might be able to shed light on the origin mine of the dendrite matrix. Tafoya replied he would be over within the hour.

Tafoya climbed out of his police car, painted in a slightly different shade of green than the Forest Service vehicle next to him. It was a darker green with bold black lettering, flash bar on top, radio antennas sprouting in four places—including high frequency for deep reservation activity where there was no line-of-sight (LoS) connections—and reflective tape all around. He straightened his belt and Sig Sauer P226 pistol on his waist. Tafoya wore no hat, and his half inch length of dark, burr-cut hair gave him a younger look than his thirty-three years.

Tafoya opened the front door of the Forest Service headquarters, hoping to see Janet Rael. And, there she was, seated behind the greeting console. Tafoya walked up to the front counter, as Janet looked up from her work.

"Officer Tafoya, how good to see you again! How can I help you?" she asked, smilingly.

Tafoya thought, that's nice, but I wish she would have been more effusive, and said something like, "I've been waiting for you to come back, and what are you doing for lunch?"

Quit thinking so much, he reprimanded himself.

"Call me, Richard," he said, politely.

"I will, Richard. And, you can call me, 'Janet,'" she responded, smiling.

"Yes, I will, Janet. Thanks," said Richard. He stood there looking at her, not remembering what he came inside for. Then, he got his bearings back again.

"Janet, I need to go back to the F.B.I. room and retrieve some evidence. Can you call back and tell them I'm coming?"

Janet rang the F.B.I. room, looking up at Richard, "Officer Tafoya of the Tulona Tribal Police is here and needs to see you." She paused, and added, "The agent said, 'come on back,' Richard," acknowledging his first name. Richard smiled and spoke.

"I grew up at the Pueblo, kiva instructed and all that, and went to Ojo Verde High School. That was fifteen years ago, Janet. I don't remember seeing you around. You go to school at Ojo Verde?"

"No, I didn't attend public schools here. I grew up in Albuquerque, went to college at Eastern New Mexico State, studying biology, and then got a job with the U.S. Forest Service. I transferred to Carson two years ago. I really like it here. Cooler than Burq by a long shot. Where did you go to college, Richard?"

"I went to the community college in Española, studied sociology and criminal justice, then joined the military."

"What branch?"

"The Army. Served a tour in Afghanistan and came back to the Pueblo, and the tribal police department hired me. The Pueblo is my life. Probably won't ever leave," Tafoya said. "Do you have any Pueblo family in New Mexico?"

"I do," Janet said, haply. "On my mother's side she is one-half Isleta.

I know a little of the language and customs from visiting my aunts and uncles there. I am on the rolls, but haven't lived there in a long time."

"Well, what do you know! We have the Tiwa connection between us. I think Isleta, Sandia, Picuris, Taos Pueblo, and my Tulona communities are related. Your last name, Rael, is not Isleta?"

"No," Janet said, "Rael is Spanish on my father's side."

Plans swirled in Tafoya's head: invite Janet to dances and ceremonies at Tulona, they go to Isleta to visit, take Janet on a hike on the Tulona reservation, play the flute for her, ask her to dinner, ask her to marry him. Whoa! Too much thinking, slow down, he thought.

"Are you all right, Richard?" Janet inquired, when Tafoya grew quiet for a few seconds.

"Yes, yes, I'm fine. Just thinking if I knew any Raels. I don't. You are the first."

The door down the hallway opened, and the F.B.I. agent stepped out and shouted, "Are you coming or not, Tafoya?"

Tafoya shrugged his shoulders at Janet and said, "We will have to catch up on more of our life stories at another time."

"I would like that, Richard. For sure."

Ever since Tony Rodarte, owner of The Silver Concho, had talked with Richard Tafoya and seen the turquoise on Robert Red Feather's death buckle, he had researched deeply his files and books. Dendrite within any turquoise was formed by the crystallization of foreign material, most likely an oxide of manganese, said the experts. It looked like miniature ferns had been fossilized in the stone. Rodarte was frustrated that he did not know the mine from which the turquoise came. There were slightly less than three dozen active mines for turquoise in the United States, but there were amateur prospectors that found small deposits and exploited them without benefit of legal claims. Those finds would not be registered as active mining operations. That's probably what happened here, he thought. Still, I need to look through my collection.

He went to a steel cabinet in the corner of his shop and opened its large doors. His collection of turquoise rivaled the Smithsonian. He pulled out one tray after the other. Each item had provenance numbers attached; he consulted his checklist he had composed for over thirty years. Rodarte's cabinet collection offered up stones for his jewelry making, but it was also for reference and history. His earliest acquisitions came from the Cerrillos mines when he was a boy. He took out trays that referenced King's Manassa in Colorado, Hachita, and Santa Rita mines in New Mexico. When he lifted the tray from Cerrillos mines near Santa

Fe, he touched the scar on his head and cheek from injury at the cave-in at Cerrillos in the 1940s. He thought of his father who cried at the blood flowing from the wounds on his son's head. They became closer after that accident.

He heard the door open in the front display room, and the bell ring. "Mr. Rodarte, the policeman is here," shouted Maria.

"Come on back, Richard," Rodarte said. "I still have fresh coffee on the stove."

Tafoya declined coffee for it was late in the day. Settling down on the stool next to Rodarte, he pulled the evidence bag with turquoise out of his leather carrying pouch and placed it on the worktable. Rodarte adjusted the magnifying lens above the turquoise and turned on its light.

Rodarte talked as he looked through the lens. "What makes provenance difficult is that a mine may have many different hues and matrixes. The Cerrillos mines, which Ancestral Puebloans worked, have over seventy-five different hues. The same can be said of the Kingman mine, or the Number Eight of Arizona. Yet, on the other hand, take the Mojave mine in Montana. It produces a distinctive green turquoise called Green Apple turquoise. It's unmistakable turquoise, but some Royston turquoise out of Nevada resembles the Mojave Green Apple. I've been dealing with turquoise for over fifty years, and I still can't tell the provenance of some turquoise."

"So, are you saying you're not able to pinpoint the mine this turquoise came from? Even on the second look today?"

"I'm sorry, Richard, I can't identify the mine with one hundred percent accuracy. I can tell you, that if you take *out* the dendrite matrix from this turquoise, it would be turquoise from four locations. Factoring *in* the dendrite matrix, however, I don't know where it comes from exactly. I don't even have the dendrite matrix pattern in any of my inventory stones. It's that rare."

Tafoya had thought that if the provenance could be found, it might lead to the identity of Robert Red Feather and some other person involved in his death. That angle now seemed a dead end.

"I can say this, Richard," Martinez said, looking at his notes. "In my factor analysis of this stone, and without using molecular testing, this turquoise is derived from a King's Manassa-like mine. The mine is probably in northern New Mexico, southern Colorado area. But even that conclusion is debatable."

Disappointed, Tafoya drove away from The Silver Concho. When he entered the Forest Service headquarters to return the turquoise, Janet Rael was not behind the counter. He took the evidence bag back to the

F.B.I. storage safe and signed the register for the agent on duty. On the way out, he asked the Forest Ranger behind the front counter as to how mining claims were filed on federal land in New Mexico.

"The federal Bureau of Land Management is where the process starts. Then the State of New Mexico has a say-so in claims." The Forest Ranger added, "We run into mining hobbyists and weekend prospectors all the time on forest property. They don't file claims. They just take the rock."

9

Friday, September 7, Day of Blessed Frederic Ozanam, Month of Corn Ripe Moon

F.B.I. Special Agent in charge Diane Parker called an inter-agency meeting of Tulona Tribal Police, Taos County Sheriff's Department, and the F.B.I. team in Ojo Verde. They would meet at Forest Service headquarters on Camino Tecolate. The Friday morning meeting started at nine o'clock. The Tulona officers attending were Romero and Tafoya. Once again, Tafoya was disappointed when he entered the Forest Service building; Janet was not behind the front counter. Romero and Tafoya ambled back to a seminar room and found Parker and one of her agents at the table going over memorandums. Chris Cordova, the Deputy Sheriff from Taos County, stood in the corner, his back to the group, talking on his cell phone. When Parker cleared her throat and stated that all the principals were there, Cordova hung up and holstered his cell phone.

Parker tapped her pen against a lectern she had set on the seminar table.

"We have new information. Not enough, but more than we had two days ago. And, I think Tafoya has something about the turquoise," Parker said, opening up the meeting. "Before we hear from Tafoya, let me bring this case with Robert, the Red Feather boot man, up to speed."

Tafoya had his notebook out, pen ready. He looked around the table. The other F.B.I. agent had taken his coat off, his Glock pistol resting snugly against his hip. The agent was left-handed, as his Glock rested on his left side. The agent brought out a Cross ballpoint pen from his front, non-buttoning, pocket. Romero leaned back in his chair and stretched, scooting forward to the table and unzipping a small notebook to jot down Parker's mini-lecture that was sure to come over the next half hour. Tafoya lapsed back to a few days ago when he last saw Janet Rael. He hoped she would be at the front when the briefing concluded.

"This is what we have so far," Parker began. "Ah, let me correct that.

Maybe it's better to say what we don't have. There have been no hits on fingerprints on any of the databases: state, nearby states, or the federal database. The computers came back online a few days ago, but since there were no results in the search, I did not feel it necessary to inform you by email that we had no hits. We have canvassed Arroyo Luz, across the road from where Robert Red Feather was found, and all we have is that two men saw an old pickup going slow along the fence line the night before he was discovered. One of the men reported a logo on the side of the pickup, but could not provide any details." She paused, then, "Cordova, what about missing-person bulletins filed in Taos County? Anything come up there? I guess we'd heard if there were."

Cordova shook his head, "No, nothing there either. We had a missing person notice filed a couple of days ago, but it was one of those Silver Alert issues. An old man in his eighties had taken off in his Volkswagen, and hadn't been seen in two days. Alzheimer's, I think. Tragic."

"Agent Parker," Sergeant Romero spoke up, "I've circulated the sketch we made of the Red Feather man among the Tulona, and posted the sketch on the bulletin board out front of our office on the reservation, but no one has come forward to identify. We have a good rumor tree out there, but no new data."

"We published a sketch in *The Taos News*," Parker added, "and it was out yesterday. Those street vendors will be selling papers again today, I think. Okay, this brings me to the next point. I notified the F.B.I. out in Gallup to interview Roger Yazzie at his home near Sheep Springs. I faxed them the photograph we had of Red Feather boot man to show Yazzie. They went to his home, interviewed him, and showed him the photograph. Yazzie positively identified him and remembered his first name as Robert from the Ojo Verde area. Robert did tell Yazzie that he discovered the turquoise by chance, while scouting for deer-hunting camps in a National Forest. Robert admitted he first noticed the turquoise in an outflow from a mountain, and he had followed the float trail up into a crevice where he found more turquoise. He was close-mouthed about the location of the mine, of course."

"I'll bet he was," Cordova snorted.

"Anyway, Yazzie asked Robert, 'Who did the preparation and polishing of the stone?' Robert stated he had friend that had a private lapidary finishing the stones. Yazzie said, in his own professional opinion, the person that polished the stones was a skilled craftsman. Not a hobbyist," Parker paused. No one had any comment.

She continued, summarizing, "We have Robert Red Feather and a person or persons that dumped his body. The person that dumped his body may have killed him, or might not have killed him. And, the person that dumped his body may be a skilled craftsman with a lapidary. Or not."

Tulona policeman Tafoya waited his turn to speak.

Finally, Parker said, "Mr. Tafoya, what do you have from Rodarte? Any more information on the turquoise?" Tafoya straightened up in his chair.

"Mr. Rodarte could not precisely identify the mine that the turquoise came from, although the blue and greenish cast of the stones with dendritic matrix has attributes from the Hachita mine in southern New Mexico and the King's Manassa just over the border in Colorado. Rodarte said there may be other sources. He said we could analyze the turquoise by isotope ratios of hydrogen and copper, but that would require taking a sample, and the cost of testing runs into the hundreds of dollars. There's a database of twenty-two resource areas in the U.S. and Mexico that can be correlated. Rodarte did conclude that the turquoise probably came from a mine in northern New Mexico or southern Colorado"

"As to isotope analysis, I don't think we want to do that just yet," Parker responded. "Go on, Tafoya."

"Basically, that's it. The turquoise is gem-quality, skillfully cut and polished, and he has not seen any turquoise like it.

No one said anything for a moment. Parker's F.B.I. agent continued to jot, Romero stretched his back again, Cordova pulled out his phone when it vibrated, then sett it down when he looked at the caller's identity. Parker then spoke.

"I have some other information. The tire tracks of the pickup that may have carried the body were blurred from the rain, but we were able to get an identification. They are new Goodyear tires, but hundreds of stations and shops sell them in Taos County and adjacent counties. The tires are the most popular brand for trucks that Goodyear makes."

"That's no help," Cordova said.

"Right," Parker replied.

"The F.B.I. is going to run DNA tests on Robert Red Feather, but is there another line of investigation we need to follow? Some angle we haven't taken? I'm at a loss to do anything else other than canvass the Arroyo Luz residents again," Parker asked.

Sergeant Romero held up his hand.

"You don't have to hold up your hand, Sergeant. This isn't a classroom. What is it?" Parker asked impatiently.

"In the interview your agents had with Yazzie, did they ask Yazzie if Robert Red Feather had a certain way of speaking, or have an accent that might indicate Hispano, Indian, Anglo? We know from skin color that

Robert Red Feather is not Anglo, but is he Hispano, Indian, or mixed? Or what? Did Yazzie and Robert Red Feather speak English? How was his English? Did they speak Spanish? How was his Spanish? Did your guys ask that of Yazzie?"

"Let me look at the notes," Parker said. She quickly scanned the notes. "No, they made no mention of anything like that."

Tafoya piped up. "I know the Navajo are big on lineage and clan affiliation. That's usually a starter for conversation between clans, but also among strangers they encounter. Did Yazzie begin the conversation with a clan announcement, his family clan, mother's side, father's side? Robert Red Feather might have volunteered clan affiliation, if Yazzie did."

Parker expressed frustration with both Romero and Tafoya's questions, but she looked over the interview notes again. Again, she found nothing in the interview notes that Yazzie had started his conversation with Robert Red Feather by Navajo clan announcement.

"Sorry, nothing in the notes regarding clan affiliation."

Tafoya thought to himself, what *did* they find out in the interview? Sounds like sloppy procedure. Yazzie needs to be interviewed again—by a Native American. He might open up and feel more comfortable talking with a Tulona rather than an imposing, brash F.B.I. agent. He started to suggest a Native American interview with Yazzie, but stopped himself.

Abruptly, the other F.B.I. agent spoke up. "How long is Robert Red Feather going to stay on ice? Shouldn't we bury him soon?"

Tafoya thought, what a weird question. He looked at Romero who was shaking his head. Cordova looked straight ahead at posters pinned to the bulletin board in the room: "Smokey the Bear says the fire danger today is 'Severe.'" Tafoya knew the fire danger was "Low" because of last weekend's rain. Smokey's needle poster was out of sync with the recent rain.

Parker replied that Robert Red Feather would remain in the morgue for thirty more days. Then, hopefully, a kinsman will appear, claim the body and give the investigative team vital information. "We are not in a hurry to put Robert Red Feather away."

Agent Parker stated next that she and her partner were going back to Albuquerque that afternoon. The evidence of Robert Red Feather would be relocated in the Taos County sheriff's substation across the street, and the investigative room closed down at the National Forest headquarters.

"I'll be coming back in a couple of weeks, or sooner if any solid information breaks the case. Deputy Sheriff Cordova will be in charge of the case," Parker said, authoritatively.

"All due respect, Agent Parker," Sergeant Romero spoke up, "Robert

Red Feather was found on the Tulona reservation, and that makes it the Tulona Tribal Police next in charge of the case, I believe. Jurisdictionally, we are the authorities in the second instance behind the F.B.I. in these kinds of cases. I have no problem working with you, Cordova, but I think the tribal police should have next oversight." Sergeant Romero couched his objection in respectful tones, although his face had darkened. Tafoya wondered where this jurisdictional flap was going. The answer came quickly.

"Thank you, Sergeant Romero, for raising that question," Parker responded. "In cases that rise to this level, the F.B.I. has primary jurisdiction on Indian land, uh, reservations, I mean. That's indisputable. Tribal policemen, be they Pine Ridge or Tulona, have jurisdiction only on their reservations, not outside tribal land. However, by extension the tribal policemen can range outside tribal land for reasons of...," Parker trailed off when Tafoya raised his hand.

"Yes, Officer Tafoya. What now?"

Tafoya took a deep breath, and proceeded, "We have a Cross Deputization Agreement with Taos County, Mora County, and Rio Arriba, Agent Parker, as well as the Navajo reservation. We can pursue leads and investigate in those jurisdictions, with notice and presentation of credentials to appropriate law enforcement offices. I'm not saying that we Tulona Tribal Police won't work with Deputy Cordova. We will. But, we, the Tulona, can pursue leads off the reservation without worrying about jurisdiction. Why, we even have CDAs with Ohkay Owingeh and Isleta."

Parker responded testily, "Well, if I can't get some agreement here, or cordiality, I can always throw the directorship of the case to the Bureau of Indian Affairs law enforcement division out of Ohkay Owingeh. How about that, Officer Tafoya?"

Tafoya pushed back, "Who directs the investigation does not affect the ODA the Tulona has with other entities, Agent Parker. For your information, the BIA is understaffed at Ohkay Owingeh, and they don't even have a head person for the law enforcement position filled down there," Tafoya responded with even temper, almost cordial, since Parker had inserted the word, "cordiality."

Before Parker could answer, Sergeant Romero spoke up, "The Tulona Tribal Police will be happy to work with the Taos County Sheriff's Department and have Deputy Cordova coordinate the case. The CDAs will permit we Tulonas to pursue multiple leads off the reservation, if necessary."

Romero turned to Tafoya and nodded as if, "Do you agree?" Tafoya smiled and nodded in assent.

"That settles it, then," Parker concluded. She went on to say how she hoped the case could be cracked open soon, and that she would answer emails and voicemails from Taos County and the Tulona policemen as promptly as she could from her office in Albuquerque. Parker shook hands with Cordova, Romero, and Tafoya, and then asked her fellow agent to unlock the evidence locker and go with Cordova across the street to deposit the evidence in the sheriff's substation department.

As Romero and Tafoya left the investigation room, Tafoya saw Janet Rael behind the front desk. "I have something I want to say to Janet, so you go on ahead. I'll catch up with you later, Tony." Tony looked at Tafoya and raised his eyebrows as if, oh, I see what you're doing.

Tafoya took a deep breath. He thought, how can I best approach Janet? And, what do I want from her? Maybe, better yet, what do I want to give her? What should I say first?

Tafoya did not have to initiate anything because Janet had seen him go into the investigation room at nine o'clock. She had come out of the supervisor's office and had seen the back of Tafoya in his dull-green uniform, as he entered the F.B.I. room. She prolonged her tasks behind the desk, so that she might be present when Tafoya's meeting was over. She did not know when the morning briefing would conclude, but she was determined to be there when Tafoya exited. She was rewarded with her perseverance. The F.B.I. briefing was short. Strange, she wondered, why such a brief meeting? Nonetheless, here he came down the hall, and Tafoya looked very nice, very straight, and very handsome in his dull-green uniform.

"Hey, there, Richard! Good to see you again," she opened the exchange. Another Forest Service employee, a ranger assigned to the Peñasco area, glanced up at her, and then Tafoya, wondering what prompted Janet to speak. She was usually taciturn, not verbose. None of his business, the ranger thought, and turned back to his paperwork he was behind in filing.

"Hi, Janet, good to see you, *amiga*." Tafoya wanted to use his Spanish now and then with her, out of respect for her background and family, and also to show his fluency in addition to English and Tiwa. "How are you? *¿Como esta?* I was hoping you would be here when I got out of the meeting," he said warmly.

"I'm glad I'm here, Richard. We had to cut short our last conversation because of your work back there." What should I say next? she thought. Maybe business? Yes, that was the tack to take. "How's it going with Robert Red Feather?"

"It's not going very good, Janet. Robert Red Feather has not even been identified. How'd you know his first name?"

"Oh, Parker was talking to me the other day."

"I see, no problem, just curious. We don't have an identity and don't even know if it was murder, although it likely was. We don't have the scene of the murder. And, between you and me, I think the F.B.I. botched an interview out on the Navajo reservation near Sheep Springs. I may have to take a trip out there to question the interviewee, again. Just very frustrating, Janet."

"You want a cup of coffee, Richard?" Janet asked. "We have a breakroom, and the coffee is decent enough."

"That sounds good. After the meeting I've been in, I need coffee."

"Come around the front counter and follow me."

In the breakroom, Janet poured Tafoya a cup and one for herself. Neither took cream nor sugar. Just black—for today. With a slight gesture, Janet raised her cup of coffee in a non-verbal toast. Tafoya reciprocated.

"Why don't we go outside, Richard, I know you've been stuck in the conference room, and I'm needing some fresh air."

There was an east portico outside Forest Service headquarters. The sun had come up over the Sangre de Cristo range of mountains shielding Ojo Verde. Where Janet and Tafoya stood, the sun beamed down, warmed them. Tafoya was relaxed and curiously at ease with Janet. Janet breathed slowly—it was a conscious effort to do so, because she was nervous. Nervous about wanting to keep a conversation going, nervous about extending herself and being open—for she had been hurt before. That was one of the reasons she relocated from Albuquerque to the Forest Service in northern New Mexico. As they talked, Janet relaxed, and by the time they finished their coffee, she was laughing.

Much earlier than Parker's inter-agency meeting, Ben Lovato arose before sunup, feeling a slight plunge in morning temperature. Temperatures were falling each night, heading into winter and the time of silence. The adobe and stone in the fireplace continued to radiate heat from the night before. It was not time to begin storytelling this early in September, but that time would come after the snows fell around Christmas and the Deer Dances.

Quail Looks Away had been the Deer Mother in a Deer Dance, but this year the Deer Mother would be someone from the Winter House Pueblo, across Cottonwood River. Squatting down in front of the fireplace, Ben arranged split logs in an upright, leaning angle—like a teepee, some said—and put tinder under the wood, and lit it with a match struck on the side of the Diamond Strike Anywhere matchbox. He preferred to strike the match on the box, not the edge of the fireplace that would leave a mark. He blew on the fire.; it flamed. As the fire grew, the room lost its chill. Quail Looks Away stirred from the bed and sat upright, running her hands through her hair to straighten out the night's sleep. Ben had lit the gaslight; a soft glow fell on Quail. Quail's mother, Deer Rain Looking, entered from the backroom and began making coffee.

Ben turned on the battery-powered radio to the hear the weather forecast. He kept the volume low to avoid hearing the hawking of commercial products. When the news came on, he turned up the volume. He ignored the world news, but paid attention to an update on the identification of the body that had been found one week ago on the Tulona reservation.

"The victim's first name was Robert, believed to have resided in our area. His death was suspicious, and any information that the public possesses needs to be reported to law enforcement officers in the Ojo Verde vicinity, or call nine-one-one."

What worried Ben about the victim was the failure of anyone to come forward and say that a member of their family had been missing. Perhaps Robert had been in the habit of disappearing for long periods of time, and the family would not think anything unusual about his disappearance. Ben was puzzled. Why would Robert's body be placed on the Tulona reservation? He could have been dropped off at ten thousand other places. Why here? What sort of statement was being made to put Robert on the reservation?

"What are you so deep in thought about, husband, before your coffee in the morning?" Quail Looks Away asked.

"I was just thinking about that body that was found last week. That's all."

"The gossip at the stream is that witches killed him and flew his body to the reservation as a curse."

"I don't believe in witches, and neither do you. Curse for what?"

"A curse on the Tulonas to spark division and conflict."

"Aii! There is no such thing as witches! There's always conflict. Nothing new there. Just the gossip of idle people," said Ben. "You shouldn't dwell on the dead body or witch curses, Quail. Not good for you or the baby." Deer Rain Looking nodded in approval of Ben's admonition.

The coffee perked, filling the room with intense aroma—the aroma of a new, fresh day beginning. The piñon fire crackled; scent from burning logs filled the room as smoke exited the chimney. Conversation stopped, then began again.

"How are you feeling this morning, Quail? Ben asked.

"Aii, I'm very uncomfortable, Ben. I don't think it will long before I have our baby."

Deer Rain Looking turned around from the propane stove where she was boiling water for oatmeal and stared at Quail. "Do you think we need to take you to the Indian Health Clinic up the road this morning? At least for a look-see, a checkup?"

"No," Quail said, emphatically. "I'll be fine. I wish my sister did not live so far away. I would like to have Flowers Dancing with me when the baby comes." Quail paused, then said, "Maybe I'll give her a call today."

"I'll take you to the clinic," Ben said.

Quail interrupted Ben, "I'll be fine, husband." She paused, then said, "Ben, you go do what you have to do today and don't worry. Okay?"

"Okay, Quail. All of this is strange to me. You to be uncomfortable and a child on the way. Do we have everything we need for this big change?" Ben spoke to Quail and Deer Rain Looking.

"Yes, yes, yes, yes," replied Deer Rain Looking, rapidly. "The midwife is close by, and she knows Quail is due soon. The Indian Health Clinic is up the road, and Saint Luke's Hospital in Taos is only fifteen minutes away. Besides, I'm not leaving Quail's side."

Ben sighed loudly, "Aii," and resigned himself to the natural flow of events.

What else could he do? He threw another split log on the fire, got a bowl of oatmeal and cup of coffee, sat down, and ate his breakfast. While spooning his oatmeal, Ben planned his day. First, he would check the level of propane in the fuel tank behind the coyote fence outside the house as his first chore. Later in the morning, he would ask his cousin, Lion Walks Night, to go with him into Ojo Verde to get a load of wood. Then he remembered that Cacique Bustamente and the warchiefs had called a meeting of Old Bow kiva to plan the Saint Francis Feast Day activities. That was after lunch; he would be back in time from purchasing wood in the village. Ben hoped his duties as a ceremonial participant would be minimal. He was going to have his first son or daughter, and he wanted to be with them as much as he could. His communal obligations, however, came first, and he would do as he was told. He might protest—but not too much.

"The Tulona must help the sun rise and cross the sky," Ben thought. "My child will gain strength with the Tulona and the sun's rays. I'll do what the council says."

10

Saturday, September 8, Day of Nativity of the Blessed Virgin Mary, Month of Corn Ripe Moon

Tribal policeman Tafoya drove fast to the reservation gate across from Chanson Restaurant, where Jason Taylor had entered on a self-promoted, sight-seeing tour of the reservation, allegedly not knowing he was on Native land when he drove through the gate a week ago Friday. The next morning Robert Red Feather was found dead across from Arroyo Luz.

"That was a week ago!" Tafoya said aloud, giving a fist-thump to the dashboard.

As he sped to the reservation gate, Tafoya thought about his coffee break with Janet Rael the day before. They had talked about their families. Her mother was an enrolled Isleta tribal member, who had met her father when she had tagged along with a group of Isleta young women to Albuquerque to see a movie. Janet's future father and friends had gone to a café across from the movie theater, and when her mother and friends went to the café, they had sat at a nearby table and struck up a conversation. The two groups, who were familiar with a dance hall a few miles away, decided after the meal to go dancing. That was back in the 1970s, and the music was rock and roll and Mexican fast-dance tunes. Janet said her mother and father only danced with each other that night—no slow dancing—and he asked if he could come and see her the next weekend in Isleta. She had said, "No," to the next weekend since she had plans, but two weekends in the future she would see him. From that chance meeting in Albuquerque, they fell in love and married the next year. Tafoya had listened carefully to Janet's family narrative, envisioning dancing with Janet at Old Maria's Hall in Ranchos de Ojo Verde.

Tafoya looked through his windshield at Tulona Peak; then, scanning northwest toward Colorado, he saw the approaching squall line. The alpine life zone at Tulona Peak disappeared in fog and cloud. He calculated that it would be a couple of hours before the rains came down and halt his investigation—until then, he would focus.

Tafoya liked being a tribal policeman. He liked solving puzzles and cases to resolve the irritation of doubt. He believed he was a sentinel that kept bad guys from hurting others. He was a protector, a centurion for the safety and good of the Tulona, and the community-at-large. Tafoya kept fit physically, studied the latest techniques of investigation, and scored the highest marks at the pistol range. The Tulona Council stood behind him. They considered tribal policemen protectors of Pueblo life and customs. Yes, the tribal policemen delved into drug issues, drunkenness, the terrible domestic violence, but the Tulona Council of elders saw them as the embodiment of historic warriorhood. All men and women of the Tulona Pueblo were, in a sense, warriors, but the tribal policemen carried the lance and were empowered to throw it at chaos and violent behavior.

Tafoya was frustrated. Robert Red Feather lay in the morgue. One week had passed since he was discovered on reservation land. Among all other cases and issues that he had investigated and defused over the past week, no progress had been made on Robert Red Feather. That irresolution was stopping today, now, *¡este momentito!* He was going to scratch and dig until something turned up that would start resolving the mystery.

Tafoya opened the reservation gate across from Chanson Restaurant. The late-lunch crowd was climbing into BMWs and Ford pickups, heading elsewhere. He thought about Jason Taylor at Tablita's, wondering if he was working today. Tafoya turned eastward, following the fence line. The Chanson gate was one and a half miles due west of where the body was found. Other gates were in between the Chanson gate and where the body was discovered, some firmly and tightly locked, others not so much. Deep, eroded gullies lay in front of some gates, making it impossible to drive through. Tafoya noticed the elevation gradually rose from Chanson gate to the spot where Robert Red Feather was found. He stopped his vehicle where Robert Red Feather had been dumped.

Tafoya left the motor running on his Explorer and parked it away from where the body had been found. He walked to the spot where the body had lain, about ten yards from the fence line. Over the fence line and across the road were several homes and long lots within the Arroyo Luz village limits. He counted three houses he could see, and behind plum thickets and willows along the Arroyo Luz *acequia*, he counted several more homes, some highly gentrified—definitely not trailer houses. Tafoya made a note to interview every house across the road in Arroyo Luz within sight of where the body was found. On his notepad, he sketched the position of the houses across the road.

Then, he turned around and faced southward, looking into the reservation. His Explorer was in the way, so he moved it, gaining a broader view looking southward from Arroyo Luz. Fog and rain obscured the mountains. From where he stood, the reservation was a level plain of three miles to the Pueblo. In the distance, Tafoya saw and sketched in his notebook the location of several concrete-block houses that had been built. Within a mile of where Robert Red Feather was found, he counted six homes. The Tulona Council approved the houses to be built away from the Pueblo Plaza, each having electricity from Dancing Rock Co-op. Each of the homes had tall woodpiles and corrals for horses. "Ah, the horse," Tafoya said aloud. Nothing struck Tafoya out of the ordinary about the concrete-block homes. Nonetheless, he was going to stop and interview the residents. He turned back around and faced the homes in Arroyo Luz.

Between the Tulona Reservation and Arroyo Luz was La Osa Cave Road, running east-west. The road began in Arroyo Luz and ran eastward two miles, turning sharply to the north and running for a half mile before it ended. A hiking trail at that point took people to the La Osa caves and waterfalls. Before La Osa Cave Road, in Arroyo Luz, the highway from Ojo Verde and Chanson Restaurant turned northward and linked up with other roads leading to the ski valley. Tafoya reasoned that the pickup carrying Robert Red Feather probably came from the Chanson Restaurant-Ojo Verde direction. The only feasible entry gate, it seemed, was across from Chanson, about a mile and a half away. But that might not be the case, I'm presuming too much, he cautioned himself. Tafoya made a note to investigate other gate entrances along the eastern fence line. There might be another entry gate farther toward the La Osa caves, he reasoned. As he looked up from his notepad, he saw someone across the road in the direction of the Arroyo Luz houses.

Through a canopy and stand of cottonwoods and willows, Tafoya saw a man sitting on his porch, looking back at him. The home sat at the back of a long lot that had been harvested for onions and garlic. Fruit trees, scattered in the garden, yielded peach and plum.

That's the old Santiago Majerus place, Tafoya said to himself. He made a note to interview Santiago, and whoever else lived there. He knew Santiago had been interviewed by the F.B.I., but maybe he would be more forthcoming with him.

Tafoya went over to the precise spot where Robert Red Feather had been laid down. Dozens of law enforcement people had surveyed the spot; a hundred photos had been taken. The ground had been walked over by investigators, so there would be no new clues discovered. Anything remotely of value had been picked up and placed in the evidence box. Tafoya stood and looked carefully at the ground where the body had lain. Robert Red Feather, when put down, had his head facing where? Tafoya unholstered his cell phone, entered a password to get into the F.B.I. server that held the case file, and scrolled down to the photo of Robert Red Feather on the ground. He stared closely at the photographs.

It was clear. Robert Red Feather was definitely facing in the direction of Santiago Majerus's home and *suerte*. He was not facing any other house. In his death, Robert Red Feather stared at Santiago Majerus, the old rumored-to-be witch, a Sleep Maker. Yet, despite the body's placement, Tafoya reasoned that there was no evidence to prove that Robert Red Feather was intentionally placed to face Santiago. And, as far as he knew, Santiago's practice of sorcery was merely a rumor. Majerus was just a normal old *parciante* cultivating his garden and orchard, as his father and grandfather had done before him. Still, he wanted to interview him.

As Tafoya stood there, he saw the man on the porch rise from his chair, wave at him, and start walking in his direction. As the man came closer, Tafoya identified him as Santiago. Tafoya climbed through the loose barbed wire fence, crossed a gully to the other side of the road, and met Santiago. He took his radio out of the belt holster and communicated to headquarters that he was away from his vehicle on La Osa Cave Road and was going to interview Santiago Majerus. Tafoya would have preferred to have driven to Santiago's home in his Explorer and conduct a more formal questioning, but this chance encounter would have to do. Besides, Santiago came to him.

Santiago appeared enthusiastic. "Officer Tafoya, so good to see you! I remember you as a boy growing up on the reservation when I used to visit my cousins and friends at Tulona during holidays and ceremonial times."

"Santiago Majerus! I haven't seen you in many years. *¿Cómo está usted?*" Tafoya used the formal address, not the informal *tú*. He wanted the conversation to be on a plane higher than a friendly catch-up on news and old times.

"I'm good, *poco más o menos*, a little more, a little less by the day," Santiago said, laughingly. "If it's any of my business, what has been going on with the case? I saw an article in *The Taos News* about the unfortunate fellow."

"We are still investigating, but no new leads, Santiago."

Santiago paused and contemplated whether he should tell Tafoya about the Culebra Mining logo on the side of the pickup truck. He would be asked why he didn't tell the F.B.I. in the first place; he had a ready answer. Still, should he disclose? He made up his mind quickly.

"Perhaps I can help, Officer Tafoya. I remembered a couple of days ago that the pickup I saw that Friday had a faded logo on the side. The logo was the Culebra Mining Company. You know, the place up in Colorado."

"You didn't say anything to the F.B.I. about this?" Tafoya shot back.

"No, *perdón*, Richard. I just didn't recollect the logo when they questioned me. They're pretty intimidating. Besides, my memory isn't what it used to be," Santiago said.

Tafoya saw the thinning body of Santiago, a much older man than when he saw him at the Pueblo, years ago. He remembered Santiago as robust and muscular, his arms displayed pridefully in short-sleeve shirts. How much longer does he have? Tafoya thought, pressing on with his queries.

"I have a question, Santiago. Do you have anyone that might wish to do you harm? Say, someone that has threatened you recently, or in your past? Extraordinary arguments over land, water, whatever?"

"No, of course not, Richard. I may have had conflicts, but nothing that would cause me to be really worried about my life or getting hurt. Why? Have you stumbled on something that may cause me trouble?"

"No, Santiago, I haven't. We are still trying to figure out if there is a reason the body was placed here rather than elsewhere. Don't worry, I'm still trying to reason this out."

Tafoya instructed Santiago if he remembered anything important to get in touch with him. They parted ways after a few minutes, catching up on the news, and whether or not the squall line, just a few miles away, was going to rain on Santiago's trees. As Tafoya climbed back through the barbed wire fence, the wind picked up, bringing a downburst of cold air and rain. He quickly turned around and drove eastward down the fence line, turning on Fire Sleet Road back to the Pueblo.

Santiago walked back to his long lot and trailer, getting wet, causing him to shiver from the cold. He quickly changed his shirt and put on a sweater to go back out and sit on the porch. As the rain intensified and the thundercloud moved to block the sun, lightning struck in the mountains and sharp cracks, like the air broke apart, resounded from Arroyo Luz to Ojo Verde.

Santiago knew of two people that had—long ago—wished to do him harm. The long arm of the past touched him on his shoulder; he shook his head in futility to ward off his past. He knew what he must do: "Tomorrow is Sunday. I need to go to Mass."

11

Sunday, September 9, Day of Saint Peter Claver, Month of Corn Ripe Moon

On Sunday, the Roman Catholic Church celebrated the Saints Day of Peter Claver. Like many other black robes, Jesuit Peter Claver came to the New World as a missionary, landing in Cartagena on the northern coast of South America in 1610, the same year Don Pedro de Peralta was appointed governor of New Mexico and moved the capital to Santa Fe. Claver attained sainthood by administering to the thousands of slaves that entered the New World through Cartagena. The priests' homilies, intoned at the Church of Our Lady of Assumption in Ojo Verde, the Mission of San Francisco del Monte at the Tulona Pueblo, and St. Mary's in Arroyo Luz, strained to interpret Saint Claver's heroic and unselfish behavior as an example for daily life in northern New Mexico.

It was a stretch, but the priest at Ojo Verde achieved an analogy: "The homeless, loafing on plazas and using opioid drugs, need a loving hand like Saint Claver to wipe their brows—figuratively speaking, of course. Donate to homeless shelters and give to the church's coffers as a way to alleviate suffering."

Santiago Majerus and his neighbor, Johnny Sisneros, walked the half mile to the village of Arroyo Luz to attend Mass. They had not started out together, but when Sisneros saw Majerus walking ahead of him, he shouted, "Wait up!" Finding that Majerus was going to Mass, and not to get breakfast or ice cream at the Calico Cow Café, Sisneros and Majerus strode side-by-side to the Church of St. Mary's. Sisneros was able to take the Eucharist since he had been to confession, while Majerus prayed and genuflected in conformity to the rites. He had not been to confession in several years. As Majerus sat during the homily on Saint Peter Claver, he reflected upon his seventy-six years. He had been given a good life with a family that cared for him. He had acquired a decent education and skill set that enabled him to sustain himself on his two acres at Arroyo Luz.

But yesterday's questioning by Tafoya stirred darker corners of his life that were not good.

Majerus had repressed events of his past, but two enemies now arose in front of him. Both enemies were dead, but their descendants knew the bad-blood stories. In the 1950s, when he was attending Ojo Verde High School, one of his classmates had become involved in a cheating scandal on the admissions exam to the University of New Mexico. The cheater was a braggart and had told his classmates, including Majerus, how he was going to ace the test. He was going to put his study notes under the boys' bathroom trashcan near the testing room. Then, claiming a need to go to the restroom when the test was being conducted, he would go and look at his notes hidden under the trashcan, gaining the advantage by looking up answers. On exam day, the cheat worked.

Passing the exam with high marks and gaining entrance into the university, the young man bragged day in, day out, about his going to UNM the next year. Majerus finally got tired of hearing him boast and told him that he could not have passed the exam without cheating. The young man accosted Majerus. They had a fistfight off-campus after school. The principal heard about the fight and dragged them in for discipline. Majerus never told the principal what started the fight, but other students informed the principal about events leading up to bloody noses. The upshot was the young man lost his admission status to the university and was expelled from high school the rest of the year, causing him to graduate a year later than his cohorts. He never attended the university. The young man, Lester Yablano, threatened to get even with Majerus. Lester was eventually drafted into the Vietnam War and killed in a bar fight in Saigon. Majerus considered the threats of Yablano vanished with his death, but a brother of Yablano accused him of "ruining my brother's life." That was thirty years ago.

The more serious shadow in Majerus's life emerged when he was in his fifties, during his tutelage under a Navajo medicine man. Majerus was Navajo on his mother's side. The Navajo connection shaped Majerus, bringing him in contact with his second enemy.

When he was a boy, Majerus traveled west with his mother once or twice a year to the Navajo reservation, so that she could visit her maternal relatives at Dibe bito, a place translated, "Grassy-field-blowing-in-the-wind." Two other names identified Dibe bito: Tooh' Haltsooi, the Navajo House name, meaning, "Verdant Springs," and the English postal name, Sheep Springs, more commonly used. A clan relative of his mother would drive them 275 miles in an old Chevy, a trip lasting over five hours from Ojo Verde, to visit her family. As was Navajo custom, Majerus was of the same clan as his mother, The Bitter Water. Since his father was not Navajo, there was not an immediate affiliation, "born for" clan, of his father. Majerus, however, at the urging of his mother, affiliated with the clan of *her* father: The Yellow House People. That clan was his "born for" clan.

His mother's father, of the Yellow House People, was sixty years old when Majerus met him at a Blessingway Ceremony near Tohatchi, south on US 491 from Sheep Springs. The healing ceremony was held west of Tohatchi near the Chuska Mountains. His mother had driven from Sheep Springs to see her father on a courtesy visit, but when she arrived at his trailer house in Tohatchi, he was not there. His neighbors said he had gone to a Blessingway Ceremony to help with tending fires and managing food preparation for the two-night ceremony at Betty Kirk's house, some twenty miles toward the Chuskas. She decided to drive to Betty Kirk's.

The road to Betty Kirk's house was washboard and rocky. Majerus's mother had a hard time navigating, but managed to find the Kirk place by faithfully following the turns near Red Willow Wash and the dead cottonwoods at the high rocky knoll. Her clan relative sat in the back seat and complained all the way there, especially since she did not like the Yellow House People in the first place. Majerus heard that there was stolen horse somewhere in the aggravation his mother's clan kin had against the Yellow House People.

When they arrived, his mother's father embraced them all, including the complaining Bitter Water woman who had sat in the back seat. His name was Jonah Chee. He was a helper for the singer of the Blessingway. Betty Kirk and her family had requested the two-night ceremony to bless their new hogan. Their family had moved a quarter-mile away from their previous home where Kirk's mother had died unexpectedly in the hogan. Rather than live in a hogan where someone had died and whose ghost may be present, they built a new home and wanted it blessed with a chantway—the Blessingway.

Jonah Chee was a close friend of Betty Kirk's husband, Laughing Horse, and had helped construct the hogan and large brush arbor near the home. Grandfather Jonah Chee took six-year-old Majerus by the hand and introduced him to the dozens of families camping out for the ceremony. The ceremony began about sundown, lasted through the night to the dawn of the second day. Majerus observed the dry paintings and heard songs and prayers. He saw his grandfather tend fires, and held, reverently, the Blessingway singer's mountain-soil bundle, containing soil from the summits of Navajo sacred mountains. The mountain-soil bundle fascinated Majerus, along with colored corn meals and crushed flower petals for dry paintings. He made friends with several boys, especially a cousin of his from the Yellow House People. His name was Steven Begay.

Majerus's reverie about his enemies was interrupted. He was at Mass, not the Chuskas.

The priest at St. Mary's intoned the introduction to communion and invited the worshipful to participate. Majerus sat back and bowed his head while Sisneros went to the front and had Holy Communion. Perhaps he would go to confession this week and fully enjoin the rites next Sunday. At the end, announcements were made about marriages, catechism classes, and a bazaar the next Saturday. Lunch was to be served after Mass in the parish hall with live music. Sisneros stayed, but Majerus decided to walk back to his *suerte* and ruminate about the enemy he did not deserve, who arose from the earth near Sheep Springs, the place of Grassy-field-blowing-in-the-wind.

Majerus walked slowly to his long-lot home on La Osa Cave Road. Before he walked up his driveway, he stopped, and looked across La Osa to where Red Feather boot man had his last repose. He sighed heavily and shook his head. "Are you a part of my past, *hombre muerto*?" He went into his kitchen and fixed a tuna salad sandwich. Sitting down at his dining table that looked out on his orchard, he opened a coke carefully, making sure he did not let it spew over his oilcloth. "I'm going to confession this week."

Steven Begay was not the enemy. Majerus and Begay had kept in touch by mail and telephone. Both still had landlines. Cell phones were terribly expensive, and neither one of them wanted to be on a short leash. Steven Begay had co-authored a book on turquoise with Tony Rodarte. Majerus had checked out the book at the Ojo Verde Public Library and read the words of his Yellow House People cousin with clanship pride.

As Majerus ate his sandwich, looking out on his orchard whose leaves were turning yellow and brown, he remembered meeting the Navajo medicine man, Niesmith Saltwater of the One-walks-around clan. It was when he had taken his mother to Sheep Springs to spend her last days with her family and clan. Majerus was in his fifties at the time. His mother insisted on residing with her niece and family who had a trailer, hogan, and brush arbor near Grassy-field-blowing-in-the-wind. It was there she wanted to spend her final years; then, be buried in a mountain canyon. Reluctantly, Majerus agreed to take her.

When they had arrived at the niece's home, Niesmith Saltwater was visiting with the family. Saltwater was in his seventies, medium height, and dressed in baggy gray-white pants, a long purple velveteen-like shirt, concho belt, moccasins, and a red bandanna tied over his head. About his neck he wore three long strands of turquoise and coral with a fetish at the end and a short-leather choker. When Majerus was outside under the arbor to get away from the heat of the trailer, his niece told him that Saltwater was a medicine man, and was the last surviving Navajo that knew the Big Godway chantway. But, she said, "He is more famous for the Red Antway ceremony."

Later that evening, Saltwater and Majerus talked. Majerus became entranced at Saltwater's Navajo view of the cosmos and the land. "Every element in the universe is filled with power and can be grouped with similar elements that the Navajo call, *people*," Saltwater began. As Saltwater explained to Majerus, there are Corn people, Cactus people, Mountain people, and so on. "Every element, even insects, are people."

Majerus saw this as creating personification—an anthropomorphic signature about non-human things in the universe. This personification, if believed fervently, compelled the believer to care for all things as if they were *people*. Saltwater asserted that human beings fell out of balance and harmony if they mistreated the people—people being the Corn people, Cactus people, Chipmunk people, and on and on. Each people have deities, gods and goddesses, supernatural beings that care for their well-being. Majerus had knowledge of the Pueblo supernatural world, and he saw Saltwater's teachings that evening as supplementary to what he believed. Being a Catholic from infancy and into adulthood, he now had three views that made up his spiritual world, Catholicism, Puebloan, and now, Navajo.

By the end of the conversation, going into early hours of the morning, Saltwater and Majerus formed a friendship and bond that deepened as Majerus returned to visit his mother. On his third visit to Sheep Springs, Saltwater introduced Majerus into the Red Antway songs and narrative, seeing him as a possible acolyte that would carry the chantway into the future. Saltwater was careful to let Majerus make up his mind. When Majerus asked if Saltwater would teach him the Red Antway ceremony in its entirety, Saltwater said yes, but there were conditions upon accepting him.

"You are Navajo enough, being one-half, born into the Bitter Water clan of your mother and assuming your mother's father's Yellow House clan," Saltwater said. "But know this. You will have to move here to the Navajo reservation, staying with your cousin's family if you gain their permission. You have to live here because the instruction will take several years. Do you think you can do that?"

Majerus was willing; the teacher had appeared. "I will," he said. "I know my niece well enough, and since my mother is here, I can be with her. I'll find, or build, a hogan if necessary. I know farming and cattle tending, so I can piece together wages. I can get on the Navajo roll for benefits." All was set.

Saltwater looked kindly upon Majerus. "But that is not all, Santiago. You are required to pay me for my teaching," Saltwater said, laying down conditions. "Not necessarily money, but in foodstuffs, tobacco, hay for horses. You will know how much to give for the knowledge and time I spend with you. Do you agree to this, in exchange for being taught the Red Antway?"

Majerus agreed to the conditions that evening, and immediately began to plan for the move to Sheep Springs from Ojo Verde. Not long after settling in with his cousin and mother in Sheep Springs, his second enemy appeared.

Soon after settling into a routine at Sheep Springs, Majerus went with Saltwater to assist him with the Antway at Newcomb, north of Sheep Springs. At the ceremony, he met Saltwater's son, Roger Saltwater, who worked at the Red Mesa Power Company and coal firing plant. Majerus immediately sensed from the son, a standoffishness and hostility. During the evening, he and the son crossed paths outside the ceremonial hogan.

"So, you are my father's student of the Antway?" Roger Saltwater pointedly said.

"Yes, I am, I'm glad he took me on," Majerus replied.

"Those ceremonies are all superstition and worthless," the son said, dismissively. "I don't see why he goes on and on about them. I think he does it because it brings him money. And, you're having to pay to get the songs and paintings, aren't you?"

"Well, I am having to pay for his time, but it's worth it. It's what I have to do to learn the Antway," Majerus shot back.

Roger Saltwater spat on the ground to the side of Majerus's boot, and stalked off to his pickup. Majerus saw him reach in his cooler in the bed of his truck and pop open a can of beer. Being away from the hogan and around several other GMC pickups, Roger Saltwater guzzled beer without arousing notice.

Majerus walked back to the hogan and began to sweep clean the hogan for another part of the ceremony that night. He was puzzled at the hostility from the son. A few days later, he asked Saltwater, "What is your son's problem with me?" Saltwater shook his head, bit his lip.

"Many years ago, my son asked me to teach him the Red Antway. I refused. He was interested in learning, but I had raised him and knew he was not in harmony with the 'people' for me to teach him. He had a cruel side to him that I was unable to cure. He trained the horse people, not joining up with them, but forcing them with the spur and whip. When I refused and explained to him about his not being in harmony with horse people, he implored that I teach his son, when he matured, to become a medicine man. I put him off about teaching his son and made no promises. Roger and his son lived far away from Sheep Springs. Over the years we saw each other, but were never close. He keeps his son, my grandson, away from me. I think he does it for spite. That's the story, Santiago, and since I have taken you to teach, he is probably jealous."

Majerus finished his tuna fish sandwich and rinsed his plate in the sink, setting it aside to be washed later. His ruminations about Saltwater and his jealous son, depressed him. Seeking to break the mood, he opened the door to his trailer house and walked out on the wooden porch to breath the fresh afternoon air of Sunday. He stood and gazed at his orchard and the mountains toward the east. More leaves had fallen from his peach trees; the cottonwood leaves had begun to change color, turn brittle. He heard rattling sounds of cottonwood leaves. A flock of piñon jays flew noisily across his property. The magpies he had seen and heard griping earlier had flown the orchard, to return again in the morning. He wondered who was the kachina in Navajo cosmology that protected magpie people?

The memories of Roger Saltwater began to fade with his contemplating magpie kachinas. But the story of Roger refused to stay down; he was killed in a power plant accident at Red Mesa Power Company, no longer an enemy to confront. But his son? Where was he? And was Roger's son, now an enemy?

Ben Lovato and his cousin, Lion Walks Night, had driven up the road alongside Rio Tulona to gather firewood to supplement a small amount of piñon they had purchased the day before in Ojo Verde. The day before, firewood vendors near the yellow blinking light had sold all their wood by the time Ben and Lion Walks Night stopped to purchase. From another highway vendor, Lion Walks Night purchased elk antlers that were seasoned from years in the sun. He planned to craft knife handles that fit buffalo-horn blades. Deer antlers made durable handles, too, and they were in high demand, but none were for sale.

Ben and Lion parked their pickup by the side of the road and walked up a trail into the forest. The mid-morning sun began to bear down on their wood gathering. They picked up windfall wood from the weekend before, each carrying five loads of deadwood from the forest floor to their truck. Ben pointed out to his cousin where he had slept the night after encountering Jason Taylor, the *fansaine* whose pickup became stuck on the road to Earth Cloud Lake.

"I put down my bivouac right over there, cousin. I picketed Star and Jess and covered their saddles and tack with tarp. I wish I had ridden all the way in to the Pueblo, but I didn't."

"I understand, cousin. That was a hard rain, and you had miles to ride before you got to the Summer House. You were right to stop."

Lion Walks Night walked farther into the forest, continuing to gather wood. As he stepped off the main trail, he came to flatter ground and a clearing with granite boulders on the northeast side. Soot-blackened boulders loomed in front of him, indicating many fires, many camps. He stopped. Ben came up behind him and halted. Except for wind in the trees, all was quiet.

"This is one of the places I was tested when I was a kiva initiate," Lion Walks Night said, solemnly. "That was long ago. I had forgotten precisely where my ordeal took place."

Ben and Lion Walks Night stood still, lost in thought and remembrance of those months of instruction and testing of powers under their fathers and grandfathers. Ben had been given to the Winter House Old Bow kiva. Lion Walks Night had withstood the ordeals meted out by the Summer House Blue Stone People kiva. They were boys when they learned; their kiva teaching stretched out for eighteen months, two times the human gestation period.

"We were down there a long time, cousin," said Ben, referring to the underground kivas.

Lion Walks Night started to say something, but then stopped. He walked away from the smoke-stained boulders and said, "Let us go away from here, Ben. We should not talk of such things here. This is different ground. This is sacred ground."

Ben nodded in agreement and said, "We have enough wood. Let's head back to the Pueblo. I feel like Quail Looks Away may need us, cousin."

Ben drove faster than usual back to the Summer House side Pueblo. As they turned onto the plaza from their gathering windfall, a covey of Gambel's quail flew up suddenly in front of the pickup. Normally, quail roamed in the desert zone, 500 feet lower in altitude. But like many animals and plants, they did not see the imaginary lines of life zones when scouring for food. Quail stuck together in coveys.

"Quail! A family grouping. Up here. This high, Lion!" Ben exclaimed.

"The quail people have come to visit their sister—your wife, my cousin," Lion responded.

As they entered the plaza, they looked across to the Summer House side and saw a gathering of people outside Quail Looks Away's home. The people were happy.

Ben Lovato, husband of Quail Looks Away, felt sick at his stomach. In a happy, nervous way.

On Sundays, such as this Day of Saint Peter Claver, G. Armstrong Coe invariably felt guilty about opening his shop while church bells rang at Ojo Verde's Church of Our Lady of Assumption, three blocks away. As bells rang, Coe unlocked his bookshop door, bent down and scooped up his cat, Fenster, and went to the backroom to turn up the thermostat to take the chill out of the shop. Thinking of weather, he turned on the radio to get a short weather forecast that broadcast on fifteen-minute intervals. Once the music stopped and the disc jockey quit blathering on about crossover country and rock music, the forecast was given.

"Weather today, Sunday, is forecast to be mild, temperatures in the seventies during the day, and tonight's low for Ojo Verde and vicinity is forty degrees. There will be increasing clouds as an early season cold front is moving in tomorrow. In addition, fall foliage alert! Up near Wheeler Peak and in the Truchas Mountains, aspen trees have started turning. And now, back to music!"

Trees turning in the fall brought tourists to town, and they shopped for books after seeing the colors in the mountains. Coe's Bookshop carried new books, but most of the items he had for sale were used. He focused on New Mexico history, the Taos Art Colony, Pueblo Indians, and Southwest fiction including the new Chicanx writers. The one area of printed sources he kept off his shelves was the ethnological and anthropological studies of the Tulona, dating back to the nineteenth century. Those books had created deep controversy in the Pueblo. Coe shelved them in back of his shop where Fenster chomped her kibbles. Only to serious scholars and writers did he show those studies.

The Tulona, like many Eastern Pueblos, were secretive and closed to inquires of their traditional ways, particularly religious knowledge. In the past, Native informants were shamed and cut off from the community, even banished from the Pueblo, who cooperated with scholars. The Red Willow People in Taos had gone through a horrific period in their history when the anthropologist, E. C. Parsons, published her work on the Pueblo in 1936 that identified the names of the kivas and other information they had wanted to keep secret. The Tulona and Red Willow people encased, shielded, and protected traditional ways. If customers insisted on a book about Puebloan ways, Coe sold them Alfonso Ortiz's *The Tewa World: Space, Time, Being, and Becoming in a Pueblo Society*, knowing full-well the reader would not make it past the first two chapters because of its complexity.

"Try understanding 'Made People' and 'Dry Food People!'," Coe said behind their back.

A man opened his shop door. Coe had never seen him before, but that was not unusual because tourists from around the world stopped in, most he had never seen. The man walked down one of the book aisles, looking quickly at titles, searching for a specific section or book. He was not browsing; he was on a mission.

"Can I help you find something?" Coe asked politely. The customer was in his fifties, but it was hard to tell. He had the physique of a man in good shape. Whether Native or Hispano, Coe could not discern; but he was not Anglo. Or, maybe there was some Anglo in his makeup. Coe did not like to stereotype physical, ethnic traits, but it often gave him a clue as to how to start a conversation. The man wore work clothes: Levi's, western work shirt, and work boots that were well-broken in. A broad, wide-brimmed straw hat, not entirely western in fashion, was sweat-stained. He wore a wide leather belt with a silver belt buckle with a large turquoise stone. When the man spoke, Coe picked up a hint of Spanish and, perhaps, Navajo. His hair was long, tied in a chignon.

"No, not right now," the man said curtly, as he continued to mission-search for something.

"Well, let me know if I can help you," Coe answered.

The man strode down another aisle and encountered Fenster who was sitting on her haunches in the middle of the aisle. She looked up at him and did not move, blinking once.

Instead of remarking on Fenster as, "Nice, kitty," or "Pretty kitty," the man side-stepped her without speaking. The man looked back at Coe as if to say, "You've got a cat in here." It was not a pleasant expression he shot Coe.

Coe couldn't resist saying, "Our feline section of books is near the front of the store."

"I'm not looking for cat books. I'm looking for the rock section, geology."

Coe told the man that the geology section was on the bottom shelf, under the New Mexico natural history section, over by the music. Coe pointed to the location.

The man bent down and looked at the geology section and pulled out Tony Rodarte and Steven Begay, *Southwest Turquoise Mines*. He thumbed through the book quickly and tucked it under his arm, most likely for purchase, Coe thought.

"Are there any other books like this?" the man asked.

"Well, there's *New Mexico* magazine's *The Allure of Turquoise* which is a beautiful and popular book we sell a lot of." Coe walked from behind the front counter and pulled the book for the man who looked at it, then handed it back to Coe.

"Not interested in that book," the man said abruptly. "I'll take the Begay book."

Coe calculated the tax on the book and began to write out a receipt.

"I'm paying cash and I don't need a receipt," the man said, as he handed him a fifty-dollar bill.

"Very well, then," Coe said, as he opened the drawer to his cash box and gave the man his change. It was a strange sale, an even stranger man, Coe thought, as he started to put the book in a sack. But the stranger took the book without a sack. He did say thanks and walked out the front door. Coe noticed that as the man handed him the fifty-dollar bill, he brushed Coe's hand. The man's fingers were rough, callused. Not the hands of a full-time accountant, Coe thought.

As the man walked to the parking lot and opened the door to his pickup, he admired the new paint job he had put on the door, obscuring the logo of the Culebra Mining Company that had been mentioned in connection with Robert Red Feather on late-night FM radio news.

12

Monday, September 10, Day of Saint Thomas of Villanova, Month of Corn Ripe Moon

The cold front descended during the night, shaking the shutters on Loretta and Armando Ortega's adobe home in San Miguel. By morning, a thin sheet of ice, like a carapace, covered water in the troughs. The Churro broke the thin sheet of ice with their muzzles. Nonetheless, at first light, Armando shattered the remainder of the ice with the blunt side of a hatchet.

"The fall is coming, and I need to get used to the early morning routine. *¡Dios mio!*"

The Churro flock in San Miguel would be well-tended during winter. The fences were tight, corrals repaired, and enough hay had been put aside for one flock of thirty head. The second and third flocks, about thirty-five head each flock, were to be transported in the next few days over Palo Flechado Pass to grassland near Cimarron, on the edge of the plains. Armando planned to drive the trailer loads of sheep over the pass to his cousins. It was a two-hour trip eastward on US 64 over Flechado, and he was nervous driving the narrow highway through the canyons. Yet, there was no other choice. Grazing land, during winter, had to be found for their sheep.

"Armando, breakfast is ready!" he heard his wife call from the house.

He gave one more glance at the thirty sheep in his care and walked back to the house. He pulled the wind breaker tighter around his body; he noticed few people stirring about the village. He looked up into the sky and saw clouds, passing fast. The top of Lucero Peak was obscured, and he imagined frost gripping the aspen at higher altitudes. The turning of leaves might come earlier than expected. Before he walked in the house, he picked up an armload of firewood and brought it inside to start a fire. Although the propane tanks were full, and stoves turned high in the house, Armando wanted a fire in the hearth to hear crackle of wood and resin bubbles whistling. Besides, once the woodfire was going strong, he could turn his back to the fire, warming his body. Sure, you could warm your body by the propane stove, he thought, but by woodfire, heat radiated to the body differently, and it cast lambent light in the room.

At the stove, warming in a different way, Loretta cooked bacon and, in a flurry of creativity for a Monday morning, prepared an omelet from one of her numerous cookbooks she shelved in the hallway bookcase. This morning, she prepared the roasted corn omelet with goat cheese and wild mushrooms from a New Mexican recipe book, Gordon Grayback and John Montoya's, *La Casa Buena: The Cuisine of Santa Fe*. She and Armando had never been to La Casa Buena Restaurant in the capital city, but she had bought the used cookbook at Coe's Bookshop for a good price. The goat cheese she had purchased at the small store in Rio Hondo, but the wild mushrooms she had gathered in the forest near Cimarron. Her grandmother had taught her the difference between bad and good button mushrooms. Although her cousins wanted her to tell them where she found the family of mushrooms, she had refused, but since they were going to shepherd their sheep in Cimarron through the winter, she was going to reveal her forest secret, with strict orders to leave mushrooms behind for future meals. "Help sustain *that* family," Loretta said.

Loretta eased the omelet out of the cast iron skillet onto three plates—one for herself, one for Armando, and a plate for Luis who had come in for breakfast. Zeke stayed with Luis the night before, alternating his visits each night with the family. Zeke padded to the window overlooking the corrals to check on the sheep. Satisfied with the sheep munching hay, he went to the fireplace and, keeping a short distance away from the flames, he laid down, putting his head between his paws, and looked at the Ortega family give the blessing. Luis leaned back in his chair and looked through the door into the living room to check on Zeke in front of the fire. The roasted corn omelet tasted fresh; Luis and Armando lavishly complimented Loretta on her dish. Tortillas and strawberry jam filled out the breakfast, and when it was over, the two men washed dishes, as Loretta helped put things away in their proper place. Armando, ever since they were married, washed the dishes, and Luis adopted the habit, vowing silently that if he ever married, he would treat his wife as he had seen Armando treat his mother. And, that included washing the dishes and pans after meals.

Once the breakfast dishes were stashed away, the three Ortegas poured themselves another cup of coffee and discussed their plans for the day. Loretta was going to tend to washing clothes and light housekeeping and, if time permitted, visit a friend two houses down who was a widow and needed company. Armando asked Luis to help him doctor a few sheep and cut the mud dabs sticking to the wool. Luis consented to help, but said he wanted to go to the Tulona Pueblo in the afternoon to see one of his friends, who had asked him to help trim hooves on several horses. Zeke would stay behind in San Miguel, while Luis went to the Pueblo.

Even though clouds obscured the sun, the sun by mid-morning had warmed San Miguel to above freezing. All ice had melted except for water troughs in the shade, and that would be gone by mid-afternoon. The wind out of the northwest persisted in blowing steadily, as Luis and Armando put on their work bibs to doctor and cut dabs off sheep.

Anticipating Luis Ortega trimming the hooves of Star, Jess, and Sweet Hija—the mare owned by the cacique—Lion Walks Night haltered the three horses in the communal pasture south of the Pueblo. He led Star and Jess, walking between them, as Sweet Hija, whose lead rope was dropped over her withers, followed the three of them. Sweet Hija was thirteen years old and had bonded with Lion Walks Night; when prompted, she followed him and Star and Jess.

"Come on, Hija," Lion Walks Night said, clicking his tongue for emphasis.

Hija fell in line behind Star, while several other horses tagged along in concert. Lion thought to himself that maybe it was not such a good thing to bring them in trail-ride mode to the Pueblo corral. When one of the horses, a sorrel, attempted to nip Hija on the flank, she turned and bared her teeth. Such an aggressive display shooed the sorrel gelding away, and he ran back to the center of the pasture. Lion led each horse across the dirt road to the Pueblo corrals close to the plaza, giving them protection from the wind, as he and Luis worked on hooves. The stables had a coyote fence on the north side, blocking the wind, and a thatched brush roof.

A flock of eight crows alighted on the corral fence panel, gripping, chattering.

"Aii," said Lion Walks Night, in a greeting to the crows. "Where are your cousins, the magpies?" He received no response, chuckling to himself, "The magpies are hiding in the red willow trees and don't want to socialize with you guys."

He heard the short beep of a pickup horn. Lion looked up and saw Luis drive into the Pueblo compound and park. He let Star's front hoof down, dusted his hands, and pocketed the hoof pick. He walked out of the corral to where Luis was unloading a small duffel full of trimming tools. He grabbed his farrier chaps from the backseat.

"Hey, Lion!" said Luis.

"Hey, yourself, bro," Lion replied. Luis and Lion shook hands, giving each other a fist bump in greeting. They had known each other since high school. Luis was a grade ahead of Lion Walks Night, and they had run track in the 400-meter run and relay. Lion had consistently beat Luis in the 400-meter run; Luis insisted that Lion had a Pueblo spirit guide boosting him. Every year, Luis attended the Saint Francis Feast Day races and watched Lion run from the cottonwoods in the east to the priest's bower in the Pueblo Plaza.

"Are you running again this year, Lion? Luis asked, knowing that Lion never missed a race for his Pueblo.

"Of course, brother. You coming to watch the Summer House win?" Lion replied.

"Yes, Lion. I'll help pick you up when you run out of breath and stumble!"

As Luis started to put on his farrier chaps, Lion stopped him.

"Before we get started, brother, I want to take you to my cousin's house and show you something."

"What is it? Why can't you just tell me?" asked Luis.

"I want you to see and know this thing," Lion said, mysteriously.

Luis started to put his chaps back in the pickup.

"No, Luis. Put your chaps on. I want you to wear them to see this thing."

Luis slipped his chaps on, buckling them tightly around his legs. The chaps were smooth and worn with thousands of hoof trimmings and shoeing; he had picked up the trade in his twenties. The smell of leather, stained with sweat and horse, rose from the chaps.

Lion Walks Night and Luis Ortega walked to the home of Ben Lovato and Quail Looks Away on the Summer House side of the Pueblo. The sky remained overcast in the afternoon; the wind in the high altitudes blew clouds quickly away. The top of Tulona Mountain remained obscured, and dust blew across the bare, dry plaza. Wind Old Woman found it difficult to pick up dust in the plaza, but she had more success stirring the water's surface on Cottonwood River, dividing Summer House from Winter House.

Lion opened the screen door and knocked on the solid turquoise door. Ben opened the door a quarter-way, then fully when he saw Lion.

Lion spoke first. "Hello, cousin. Is it all right if I come in? I want to make an introduction. You remember Luis Ortega, don't you?"

"Ah, yes, you always lost to him in the track meets," he joked. "Come in."

Luis walked in behind Lion; the scent of sweetness and flowers filled his nostrils. The room was warm. The overhead skylight allowed sunlight, although muted by cold-weather clouds. Luis saw several people in the room he did not know.

He nodded in greeting, and when they saw him dressed in chaps, they choired, "Heyyyyy," in low tones.

Luis inhaled more than a sweet, floral scent; he could not identify it. The scent was fresh and new, like a sudden waft of wildflowers in spring meadows in high country. Or, the scent he knew well—the sweet breath of a newborn lamb.

"Come here, Luis, meet our first child, a girl, born yesterday," Ben said.

Luis looked at Lion. Lion nodded. This was the "thing" he wanted Luis to see. Quail Looks Away held the baby and adjusted the blanket, so that Luis could see the baby's face. The baby was awake, wide-eyed, squinting toward the skylight. As Luis came close, the baby turned her head to him and opened her mouth slightly.

Luis sat down in the empty chair next to Quail. Quail looked at Ben, and Ben nodded his assent.

"*Luis, hold her in your lap, so that she comes close to the leather and smell of horse and life in the world*," Quail said, giving the baby to Luis.

Luis took the baby girl in his arms. She squirmed, then settled on his chaps, in his lap.

"We have not named her yet," Ben said. "She'll have a Tulona name and a Christian name. The Tulona name will come later."

Luis held her for another minute, then Quail took her from him. Lion Walks Night bent over to get closer to the baby girl. "One day, I hope you will ride horses with me."

"You will see us all dance one day, little one. We will teach you our steps," spoke a young woman that Luis did not know. The room fell quiet. The people looked at Quail and the baby, their faces somber but with the slightest of smile at the corner of their mouths. Ben spoke and broke the nativity reverie.

"You have work to be done with my horses, Lion?" Ben said, indicating it was time to go.

Luis and Lion left Ben's home and walked back to the corral. Luis was curious and asked Lion who the young woman was that said, "We will teach you our dance steps."

"That was Flowers Dancing. She is Quail's sister from Española. She came up to be with Quail. And, now, to be with her niece."

"Is she married?" Luis asked. "I saw no ring on her finger."

Lion glanced at Luis, as they reached the corral and opened the gate to begin work.

"No, my brother, she is not married."

Luis culled Sweet Hija from the stable and gave the lead rope to Lion, so that he could hold her as he began to trim. He lifted Hija's right-front leg, as she shifted her body for trimming. He put her leg between his legs and chaps and began to pick the hoof clean. Then he cut away the inner frog tissue with his sharp knife. Holstering the knife, he took the hoof clippers and began to trim the hoof, like trimming fingernails.

"That's good," Luis said.

"Yes," Lion replied, "Hija always holds still and helps as you trim."

"I wasn't talking about Hija. I was referring to Flowers Dancing. Very good that she's not married," Luis said.

Jason Taylor had the day off. The day before, Sunday, had been busy for Ojo Verde Inn and Tablita's. The tourist traffic should have slacked off with school and colleges starting fall classes, but it had not. He had worked a double shift at noon and in the evening, making good tips, a large portion of which he set aside to purchase a season pass that the ski valley had been raised to $550 for the approaching winter. Since he had the day off, he decided to go out to the Tulona Pueblo and visit Romero. He thought he might chat with the tribal policeman about his son who liked to ski. Perhaps he could meet his son.

Jason turned into the parking lot in front of tribal headquarters where the police department was located. He noticed in the corral a couple of cowboys that were tending horses. Looking closer, he saw one of them trimming hooves. As he walked to the tribal police station, his stomach felt queasy when he thought of being detained last week. I've come this far, I'll go ahead, he said to himself, as he let out a long breath, he had been holding in.

Opening the door to the station, he smelled gun oil. At the front desk, Tafoya was cleaning one of his pistols, the Sig Sauer. Tafoya continued ramming a clean white patch of cloth down into the barrel with a ram rod as he looked up, "Hey, Jason, what can I do for you?" He set the disassembled pistol down on the desk, wiped his hands on a red work rag, and stood up.

It was hard for Jason to read Tafoya's mood. "I wanted to see Officer Romero, if I could?"

"He's gone for the day, Jason. Won't be back in till Wednesday. He's at a conference in Albuquerque looking at powerpoints on new procedures. Unlucky him. Can I do anything to help you?" Tafoya smiled, putting Jason at ease.

"No, thanks," Jason answered. "I was looking to talk to him about his son who likes to ski. Thought I might chat with him about giving the son lessons, come the winter. Talk to his father first, though."

"Well, sorry," Tafoya said, "Romero is gone, and his son is in school this afternoon. So, you are out of luck all the way around."

"Thanks, anyway," Jason shrugged. "I'll catch him another day."

Jason walked out of the station, back to his pickup. Again, he saw the two cowboys working on the horses. He stopped to observe. The Tulona holding the horse by a lead rope glanced over at him and nodded. The other man trimming the hooves was engrossed in his work and did not look up. Jason felt a bit out of place, dressed as he was without work boots or cowboy boots. He had on his good hiking boots and outdoor apparel, but still incongruent to the scene. Despite being self-conscious, he stood and watched.

Jason leaned on the corral panels. He began to relax in a strange way. What he was looking at was a centuries-old pattern of keeping horses in shape. Preceding that came the taming of the horse. They were large—very large—and could do lots of hurt to a human. The training of a horse to civility must be complex, Jason pondered, but gratifying to the breaker of horses. Breaking horses? Jason thought the phrase horrific, even cruel. Breaking? That wasn't the phrase he thought described the taming process. As he looked at the scene in front of him, he concluded that the horses weren't broke; they were getting along with their human companions. They were not "broke."

I may not be tough enough to fit into cowboying, if I ever had the chance, Jason thought, regretfully.... He continued to gaze at the corral tableau—horses, men working with *kowena*.

"You ever go riding?" A voice said behind him.

Jason turned around and saw a Tulona. He had a thin blanket wrapped about him, blue jeans, work boots—not cowboy boots. He looked familiar.

"No, I never have. Just looking at what's going on," Jason replied.

"They are trimming horses' hooves. Two of the horses I own, Star and Jess, the two paints. The brown horse is owned by someone else. Her name is Sweet Hija, the Sweet Daughter."

Jason recognized the Tulona. "You are Ben! You helped me get unstuck back up there," pointing with his chin toward Tulona Mountain.

"Yes, I am," said Ben, the wind blowing his broad-striped brown blanket, exposing a knife in a customized leather sheath, branded with Tulona symbols.

Turning to the corral, Ben said, "How's it going, Lion?"

“Doing fine, we’re just about through with Hija, then we’ll trim Star and Jess.”

“Lion?” Jason said. “Lion?”

“Yes, that’s part of his Tulona name. Lion, like the mountain lion,” Ben answered.

“Do you have a Tulona name?” Jason asked, then thought better. “Sorry, that’s none of my business.”

Ben leaned on the corral panel, watching Lion and Luis trim. He thought about Jason. This Jason, this snow-looks-like, is young, respectful. He is not selling anything or trying to buy anything. He wears hiking boots, nice ones, look used. He has no liquor on his breath. Ben decided to reveal himself to the *fansaine*.

Ben stood back from the corral panel, folded his arms across his chest, and turned to face Jason. He adjusted his blanket tightly about his body. Jason stood apart from the corral and faced Ben, the wind blowing a whorl on the dirt road in back of Ben. The crows that had been feeding on refuse in the corral rose as group and flew toward the old church. Ben spoke forcefully, in certitude.

“I am Medicine Wind, of Old Bow Kiva, of the Tulona Winter House people, a fast racer with eagle down blowing, husband of Quails Looks Away, a new father, and friend of Star and Jess. I am Medicine Wind.” Jason transfixed, nodded almost imperceptibly.

Lion Walks Night and Luis Ortega heard Medicine Wind; they stopped attending Sweet Hija. They stared at Medicine Wind, expecting more words, an oration on the incomprehensible-spirit-that-moves-in-all-things. None came.

After several seconds, Ben turned to them and said, “You better finish the cacique’s horse because you have Star and Jess to work on.”

“No long speeches today, Luis,” Lion said with a grin. They resumed working on Hija. Luis had not known Ben’s Tulona name, until he spoke to Jason.

Jason felt stuck in two worlds, one world of the Tulona, Medicine Wind, and horses. The other world, Anglo from San Antonio, Texas, ski bum, and a waiter at Tablita Restaurant—a *fansaine*. One world he came from, the other world he desired to enter.

13

Tuesday, September 11, Day of Saint Cyprian, Month of Corn Ripe Moon

By the seasonal count of the Tulona, established by centuries of experience in desert and mountains, it was *already* autumn in northern New Mexico along Rios Grande and Tulona. Autumn, or harvest, came in August. Tribal policeman Tafoya knew this, yet he had to reckon the season by other standards—Gregorian calendar, science. He held both constructs without dissonance, preferring the Tulona way of reckoning time. It was autumn, the Ripe Time; it was September, the Month of Corn Ripe Moon. Regardless, Tulona time or Gregorian time, it was time to get to work and solve the mystery of Robert Red Feather.

Tafoya rose early. He lived in a concrete-block house on the southeast side of the reservation, built with the approval of the Tribal Council thirty years before. Residing there gave him space and distance from the Winter and Summer Houses of the Pueblo. His small house had electricity, a well, and septic system. Tafoya was adjacent to roads leading into Ojo Verde where the tribal police had a substation across from the National Forest headquarters.

Tafoya drove to the tribal police substation in Ojo Verde. Once parked, he looked across the street to the Forest Service to see if Janet Rael was exiting a vehicle. She was not to be seen. He needed to find out what car she drove, so he could at least know if she was there. Then, he would find some reason to go see her. Inside the substation, Tafoya greeted the sheriff's administrative assistant, walked to the breakroom, and poured a cup of tasteless coffee. He retrieved a duplicate hardcopy file on Robert Red Feather in the evidence locker and walked to the tribal office room.

Finally seated at his desk, Tafoya looked at three components of data in front of him. One file was the hardcopy file that contained interview reports, photographs, and the field notes of where the body was found. The second component of the data was his private digital file subsumed and encrypted in the Tulona Tribal Police Department server—wherever that was located. A cloud somewhere with Google, Amazon, he guessed. Within it were jottings, notes, maps, and diagrams of intersecting places, events, people, and anything else in the Robert Red Feather case that might show a connection, or intersection, with people, places, things, chronology. The third component of data was the F.B.I. computer file of the case.

He entered his password on the computer for the Robert Red Feather case on the tribal server, split his screen, brought up a new window for the F.B.I. file, and entered his password for the agency. New information popped up.

"Finally," he said aloud. A DNA test had been run on Robert Red Feather, revealing ancestry tangents. He was 56% Native American, 36% Spanish-Mexican, 4% Germanic, and 4% Norwegian. There was no DNA match with known DNA registers, but the sample had revealed he was more Native American than Spanish-Mexican. The other two percentages could be discounted. Unfortunately, there was no detail as to what Native American tribe his DNA connected. Probably several hundred Native American samples were in a universal panel somewhere in the ether, but a Google search gave him no answers.

Tafoya retrieved his letter-sized yellow pad from the desk and listed the valuable pieces of evidence. Victim, first name Robert, was about thirty-five years of age, dying by large puncture wound to chest inflicted elsewhere from where he was found. He wore work boots, work clothes, belt buckle with turquoise stone of unknown mining source, red bandanna tied around head. Victim placed carefully on ground facing Arroyo Luz, perhaps in the direction of Santiago Majerus. Dark four-wheel-drive pickup with Culebra Mining Company logo on side associated with body. Pickup had new Goodyear tires and had not entered area before four o'clock on Friday afternoon, August 31. That was the day he had taken photographs of the Chanson gate entrance to the Pueblo, the same day he worked the Jason Taylor trespass case. Santiago Majerus and Johnny had seen a pickup on the Tulona Reservation at about eight o'clock that evening.

Tafoya continued to list facts on his yellow tablet. Robert, last name unknown, had been identified by Yazzie of Sheep Springs as the person that gave him turquoise to mount. Tony Rodarte of The Silver Concho could not identify the turquoise, but he did point the way to Yazzie. The F.B.I. interview of Yazzie was thin. The search for who purchased the pickup truck from Culebra Mining Company had gone nowhere. The company had sold their trucks to various auto auction houses in the Four

Corners area, and the sales records of the auction companies enlarged the scope of inquiry to thousands who bought trucks through car dealers. The public service announcements about the Culebra logo, in *The Taos News* and on local radio stations, had dredged up one pickup with the logo, located in Ranchos de Ojo Verde. The truck had been parked for ten years in the backyard of an abandoned adobe home, and it was overrun with wild vines and chipmunks. And finally, no one had come forward filing a missing person report matching Robert Red Feather.

Tafoya leaned back in his chair, took a sip of coffee, and then went back over the list of facts and cold trails. He saw two leads he needed to follow. One direction was to go and interview Yazzie at Sheep Springs, making it a Tulona-to-Navajo conversation. The other direction was to question Santiago Majerus again for information on where he had lived and possible enemies in his background. This time, make it a more formal interview, so that coincidences might surface as to Majerus, Robert Red Feather, and his killer.

"I'm doing the Majerus angle right now!" Tafoya grabbed the telephone directory. "Thank goodness they still print these things!"

Tafoya picked up the landline telephone from its cradle and punched in Majerus's phone number for his residence in Arroyo Luz. The number rang and rang. He allowed it to ring beyond a normal four or five times because Majerus might be out on his porch or in the orchard. On the tenth ring, just as Tafoya was about to hang up, Majerus answered. Tafoya asked to come out within the hour to ask more questions about the Robert Red Feather case, and go over what Majerus saw on the evening of August 31. Majerus consented and said he would make a fresh pot of coffee. He had sweet rolls from Calico Cow ice cream parlor he would warm up as well. "I look forward to your company," Majerus said.

As Tafoya drove out of the substation's parking lot, he glanced over at the Forest Service. He saw Janet get out of a car she parked under a steel-roofed arbor that doubled as a structure for solar panels. He was too far away to honk. And, bad form, he thought. Besides, he needed to see Majerus, move the case off high center. He made a mental note Janet was driving an old red Subaru with wind erosion on the front of the hood. I knew it would be a Subaru, he thought.

At the yellow blinking light, Tafoya turned eastward toward Arroyo Luz. Driving in that direction placed the mountains directly in front of him, filling his windshield. The clouds from yesterday had vanished with dry, cold temperatures during the night. The turquoise-blue sky sharply outlined Tulona Peak and Lucero Mountain. The north wind buffeted his patrol car, and when he pulled into Majerus's *suerte* and trailer house property, the cottonwood trees swayed back and forth with wind gusts, altering shadow patterns, dappling the ground. Tafoya liked to think shadows moving gave vitality to the day—visible motion of wind, like tall grasses swaying.

Majerus was seated on the porch, waiting, and stood up when Tafoya turned into his driveway. They greeted and went inside for coffee and sweet rolls. Tafoya noted the house was swept clean, the dishes washed and draining on the side board. The trailer house had withstood the elements and seasons reasonably well, but it was a trailer house, and would probably fall apart in another ten years. Majerus might be dead by then, Tafoya thought. Wouldn't matter. The smell of the house was of soap and disinfectant and cleanliness. The curtains were all drawn to let in the sun, and, most likely, drawn back across the windows at night for privacy, Tafoya surmized. His overall impression was that Majerus was taking care of himself and his home in a better manner than most bachelors.

After they had finished a cup of coffee, and a sweet roll that Tafoya ate out of courtesy, Tafoya opened the interview. He told Majerus that he was in no way under suspicion of being involved in Robert Red Feather's death. Majerus asked him why he was being questioned again, since he had been interviewed by the F.B.I., and Tafoya had talked to him a couple of days ago?

Tafoya answered, "I suspect Robert was placed across the road for some reason involving you. I want to know more about your past, so that I might be able to connect dots, see coincidences with Robert Red Feather, the killer, and you." Majerus understood. He said he would help anyway he could, and that he had given lots of thought to enemies he might have made in the past.

"I remember two people I have crossed with," Majerus admitted.

Tafoya opened up his notebook and took out a pen. Majerus told him about the Yablano kid back in high school that had cheated, but Yablano had died in Viet Nam. His brother had accused Majerus of ruining Yablano's life but it came to nothing. He heard that the Yablano family had moved to Truth or Consequences; the Yablano angle was a dead end.

"The other conflict," Majerus said, "is a long story. It began when I studied to become a medicine man on the Navajo Reservation, twenty-five years ago. In learning the Red Antway Chant ritual, I made an enemy of my teacher's son who had wanted to study under his father, but his father had refused. The son died in a power plant accident, but he had an offspring, a male, that may have carried his father's anger toward me." Tafoya was aware of clanships and Navajo culture, so he pressed for information.

"Who are these Navajos you talk about, and what are their clans and locations, Majerus?"

Tafoya told Majerus he was turning on a voice recorder. Majerus began his story with his kinships. He told Tafoya that he was born to the Bitter Water clan of his mother. Many of her relatives lived at Sheep Springs, New Mexico, also known in the Navajo as Dibe bito and Tooh' Haltsooi. Since his father was Hispano, he had no immediate "born for" clan. His mother, however, insisted he claim the "born for" clan of her father, The Yellow House People. Her father, Jonah Chee, Majerus's grandfather, lived south of Sheep Springs at Tohatchi, where he met his teacher.

His teacher was born to the One-walks-around clan. His name was Niesmith Saltwater and his son, who became the jealous rival, was Roger Saltwater. Majerus explained the father's rejection of his son to teach him the ritual of Red Antway, and how the son was killed in a Red Mesa Power Company accident. Tafoya thought that he was going to need a couple of pages of graph paper to get all the clan relationships established. Sketching and graphing would come later; he still had questions.

"What evidence you do you have that Roger Saltwater's son might have carried anger against you, Majerus?"

Majerus replied that he had no evidence. He didn't even know Roger Saltwater's son's name. His teacher, Niesmith, had wanted to be close to his grandson, but Roger had not permitted it. Pushing further, Tafoya asked if he knew Roger Saltwater's "born to" clan, and Majerus replied he had no idea, but it wouldn't be hard to find out because Niesmith was a well-known singer of the Red Antway, and intended to revitalize the Godway Chant that was becoming extinct.

Tafoya asked Majerus where he had lived over his years. Majerus told the family narrative. His father had met his mother at a festival, the San Geronimo Festival in Taos. They courted and married and moved to Arroyo Luz where his father owned a small farm. There were three children of the marriage, "I am the only survivor." His father died of a stroke, and he and his mother continued to live in Arroyo Luz. He drove his mother frequently to visit her relatives at Sheep Springs, until finally he took her back for the last time, twenty-six years ago, to end her days under a Navajo arbor. In his teens and twenties, he went to school in Ojo Verde and learned to tend and manage cattle on big ranches around Ojo Verde, particularly toward the Tusas Mountains.

"You never married?" Tafoya asked.

"No, I never found another."

"What do you mean, 'I never found another'?"

Majerus explained that he had fallen in love in his twenties to a beautiful girl in Questa. They had courted, and he had visited her family in the old, formal way. He had even gone to church with her and the family in Questa. His mother and father liked her as well, but the Questa girl's parents were prejudiced against his Navajo lineage. One Saturday afternoon, when he went to visit, the father of the Questa girl met him as he stepped out of his pickup in front of their house. Politely, but firmly, the father told him that he was not welcome in his home anymore, and that he wanted him to go away and never come back.

"Go find someone of your own kind. We will stay with our kind, Santiago! Now, go!"

Majerus said he asked what his daughter thought about this? The father told him that she agreed and did not want to see him again. Majerus said he got back in his pickup, broken-hearted, and returned to Arroyo Luz, confused, hurt, angry, and without the Questa girl. A few weeks later, a letter arrived from her at his post office box in Arroyo Luz. She said she still loved him, but she could not go against her parents' wishes, and that he should find love in another place. She respected his heritage and was sorry her parents did not.

"I never found another, Officer Tafoya. Never did and never wanted to look very hard, either."

Tafoya turned off the voice recorder.

"I'm sorry, Mr. Majerus, I truly am." They sat in silence, sipping coffee.

Majerus stood up and walked to the window, looking out. The wind persisted in blowing. "When I mastered the Red Antway, years later, I thought about using my ritual knowledge to get her out of Questa and come be with me," Majerus whispered. "But in the end, I decided against that. It's a misuse of traditional Navajo knowledge, and I would have never known if she really wanted me."

Tafoya did not write Majerus's last comments down. He changed direction of questioning.

"What else can you tell me about the pickup you saw that Friday evening, the day before Robert Red Feather was discovered, Mr. Majerus?"

Majerus told him that it was a four-wheel-drive Ford pickup, dark color, maybe dark blue or black, had faded wooden siderails. The precise year was hard to determine, but probably in the 1990s models. "It had the Culebra logo, as I told you before." Majerus continued standing, looking out the window. Tafoya began to put away his pen, but then he thought of another question that might open up a new angle of motivation for someone to antagonize Majerus.

“I have one more question and I’ll be gone. I have heard that you practice sorcery. That you are known as Sleep Maker. Are the stories true?”

Majerus turned around from the window, his expression hurtful, yet resigned. Tafoya did not take his eyes off of Majerus as he came over, sat down, and slumped in the kitchen chair. Straightening up, he placed his elbows on the table and talked slowly. Yes, he had been known, maybe still was known, as Sleep Maker. The name had been applied to him by a few people in Arroyo Luz. His neighbor, Johnny Sisneros, had told him many years ago that some people in the Arroyo Luz community had found out he was Navajo medicine man, had seen him going alone up to the La Osa Caves and Lucero Peak, and returning with herbs and spruce branches. That was coupled with the fact he lived alone and did not attend the Catholic church as much as he used to.

“Sleep Maker is a Tulano name, maybe even Ancestral Puebloan. I lived alone after my mother died and wanted to stay here with the old home place, tending the garden and orchard, working as a ranch hand. Yeah, I lived alone because my mother died. I had no surviving siblings, and as I told you, I never found another. The witchcraft accusations came from a few people in the village who had bad luck, failed marriages, and sickness. So superstitious and ignorant were they, that they blamed their own failings and misfortunes on an outside malevolent force, a Sleep Maker in their midst. Anyone but themselves. So far as I know, no Puebloans see me that way. In fact, I have many friends on the Winter and Summer House sides that come see me for herbs and curative prayers. In my shed out back and my spare bedroom, I keep herbs and spruce and other plants. Surely, Officer Tafoya, you know the power of spruce?” Tafoya nodded his head because he saw it in the corner of the kivas.

Majerus stood up and opened the door to his spare bedroom, and through the door, Tafoya saw spruce branches and herbs hanging from the ceiling. Tafoya was impressed, but also thought, “That’s a fire hazard.”

Majerus continued. “My hair is white and long and it hangs down sometimes in front of my face like a Sleep Maker. My medicine bag contains powerful elements of the four mountains and earth colors of both the Puebloan and Navajo ceremonies. I have no other name other than Santiago Majerus, born to the Bitter Water and born for The Yellow People of my mother’s father. I sing the Red Antway, but I haven’t performed a chantway in over five years. No, Officer Tafoya, I’m not a sorcerer or witch or malevolent force. I work the other side of the street, the other side of the road—The Good Road. I am true to my teacher of the One-walks-around clan.”

A strong wind gust buffeted the trailer house, causing a washtub to bang against the outside wall.

"Ah, the Wind," Majerus said. "The Winds flow through our bodies and give us life, give us the motions of our day and night. The hair whorl in our heads and the whorls in our fingertips and toes are the residual traces of the Winds when our ancestors were created. The breath out of our mouth and lungs are Winds that give us life."

Tafoya turned his hand over and looked at the circle-whorl in one of his fingers and loop-whorls in other fingertips. He knew that such patterns, idiopathic and particular to every person, connected people to crimes—or not. The resonance of winds leaving whorls in flesh seemed haunting. This interview with Majerus had taken a mystical turn; Tafoya was uncomfortable.

Majerus looked at Tafoya, waiting for another question. None came.

Tafoya expressed his gratitude for the additional information, and that he needed to get back to the office to write up a report. Majerus saw him to the porch and told him to come back anytime, "You are always welcome." The Tulona reservation was just across the road, so they were neighbors of sorts. As Tafoya stepped off the porch, Majerus asked him, "Are you going to be racing on Saint Francis Feast Day in October?" Tafoya replied he was not, but some of his cousins were. Majerus said he hoped to go to the festival and see Tafoya's cousins run.

Tafoya started his patrol car, and before he turned right on La Osa Road, he radioed headquarters, asking for an APB to be sent out again for a dark blue or black, four-wheel- drive Ford 1990s pickup, wooden side boards, with a Culebra Mining logo on the doors. "Be sure you add the Culebra logo to the APB, or we'll be stopping every pickup in the county."

Tafoya turned right on La Osa, and began to make plans to drive to Sheep Springs to interview Roger Yazzie, Tulona-to-Navajo.

In late afternoon, the wind lessened. Above Tulona Pueblo, the sky cleared, the mountains seeming less mysterious without clouds passing rapidly in the alpine altitudes. After he had conducted the interview with Majerus that morning, Tafoya wrote and uploaded his interview notes to the sheriff's department and F.B.I. servers. He called F.B.I. Agent Diane Parker, requesting permission to travel to Sheep Springs to interview Yazzie. She gave no resistance to his request. He was surprised Parker so quickly agreed. She did state that the costs of going to Sheep Springs and lodgings, if he stayed overnight in a motel, must be borne by the Tulona Tribal Police, not the federal government. The rest of his day was spent helping the Taos County Sheriff's Department serve two warrants for court appearances concerning child support. Tafoya helped direct traffic at the yellow blinking light intersection because of an accident. By the time he finished paperwork at the station, it was late afternoon, and he decided to go home, fix a sandwich, watch TV, and go to bed early.

Tafoya drove to his territorial style concrete-block home near the edge of the reservation, adjacent to Ojo Verde city limits. Sagebrush and creosote bushes surrounded his home except for a fifty-foot cleared space, getting narrower by the year. He parked under a portico, backing in and facing outward to the driveway and road, so that he could make a fast exit in case of trouble on the reservation. He hoped the night crew for the tribal police and sheriff's department could handle the accidents and bad guys—without calling him.

Living alone, a half-mile from Pueblo Plaza, suited him. Sleeping away from his kinsmen stopped their knocking on his door at all hours for help with a domestic disturbance or rebellious runaway teenager. Yet, Tafoya often went back to the Pueblo in the evening to visit his mother and father and cousins. In the early evening, he might stay and listen, even join in the singing of songs on Cottonwood River bridges. During the Being Still time in the winter, Tafoya spent nights listening and telling stories of Magpie, Coyote, giants, and deer of the forest. He would fall asleep listening to his uncles tell stories deep into the night; then in the morning, Tafoya would go back to his territorial home, dress in uniform, and catch the bad guys.

Tafoya's contented balance, of having a home apart from the Pueblo and peaceful traditional activity on the plaza, was disturbed. The "disturbance" was Forest Service biology specialist, Janet Rael. She was not trying to make life miserable for Tafoya. He wanted to spend time with her but was unsure on how to proceed. Should he ask her to lunch or dinner? Should he bring her to the Pueblo to meet his family, and what exactly would be the excuse to do that? There was the Saint Francis Feast Day coming up on October 4, less than a month away. Then, there was the grand San Geronimo Day festival in Taos on September 30. Aii! What to do?

Tafoya decided to go the Pueblo, not stew about Janet. He walked into his mother's and father's house on the northside of the Pueblo, his mother thrusting a bowl of green chili stew into his hands with blue corn tortillas. Although he had already eaten, he consumed the stew quickly and asked for a second bowl. He washed it down with a glass of sweet tea poured from a gallon jug of Lipton's pre-sweetened tea. Sitting outside under an arbor after the bowls of stew, he talked with a cousin who said the cacique's horse, Sweet Hija, was a fine mount to ride, and that he had ridden her up the Rio Tulona to the first campground toward Earth Cloud Lake. Looking across the stream toward the southside house, Tafoya saw

Quail Looks Away and her mother with the newborn baby girl.

"Have they named her yet, cousin?" he asked.

His cousin did not know, but Tafoya's mother who overheard the question said, "Yes, they have. Her name is Dezba Lovato. Her Tulona name is Blue Flowers Springing, like the Blue Lady legend."

The sun's last rays inflamed the tops of Tulona Mountain and Lucero Peak, turning the alpine spruce and fir near timberline into golden-red trees. Tafoya looked toward the east and the chain of mountains that gave rise in the distance to the Truchas Peaks. He saw the change in the mountains that indicated a midpoint of fall, the Ripe Time. Blurry at first, the splashes of color against the dark conifer green came into his focus.

"Look! There are streaks of yellow and red on the mountain! The aspens are turning!" Tafoya exclaimed. The love songs of the Tulona young men, singing on the bridge nearby, rose in volume, as if to acknowledge Tafoya's discovery.

To himself and no longer miserable, he said, "Tomorrow I will show the red aspens to Janet Rael, the Isleta."

14

Wednesday, September 12, Day of Holy Name of Virgin Mary, Month of Corn Ripe Moon

At the Ojo Verde tribal police substation, Officer Tafoya greeted the administrative assistant as he walked into the office. Sergeant Romero was in the coffee lounge with sheriff's deputies, and when he saw Tafoya, he broke off the conversation to talk to Tafoya. After Tafoya got a cup of coffee, they went back to Romero's desk.

"I hear you got authorization to go to Sheep Springs to interview Yazzie again, do it right this time, as Tulona-to-Navajo. That true?" Romero asked.

"Yes, that's true, Tony, but the tribal department has got to pay for it."

"No problem. I noticed the budget has funds, and the supervisor wants this case to get traction. You going alone?"

"Yes," Tafoya answered, then sipped his coffee, "I have no plans to take anyone. I shouldn't be gone more than two days if I leave early Friday morning and start asking questions of Yazzie when I get there. I'll come back Saturday. Probably drive in late that evening. It's just under three hundred miles to get there." Tafoya had not thought about driving alone till now. There's no one he wanted to go with him. Janet? He shook that off, for the moment.

"Think you can hold down the Pueblo, until I get back, Romero?"

"Of course. Be back by Saturday night so you can help me handle the weekend tourists and Saturday-night fights at the bars!" Romero said.

Tafoya went back to his office and opened up his emails to scan the Robert Red Feather case for new information. Nothing of importance had been added to the case. The emails were merely announcements for workshops and a notice for him to get a performance test for pistol proficiency in the next sixty days. No problem there, he thought. He made a list of things to prepare for his trip to Sheep Springs. He realized he needed maps, detailed maps of the Navajo reservation. With that thought, he quickly stood up, walked out the front door of the substation, saw the red Subaru was there, trotted across the street to get maps from Janet Rael, and show her the red and yellow aspen slashes in the mountains.

Tafoya jogged across the street to the Forest Service headquarters. He opened the door to the front office. Janet was not behind the front counter. Without pausing, he went to the coffee breakroom and found Janet pouring a cup of coffee. Several other Forest Service employees were lounging around and looked suspiciously at Tafoya, dressed in tribal policeman's uniform with pistol, mace, handcuffs, and radio-comm instruments attached to his black belt. He nodded, relaxing the group. Janet turned around and smiled, her eyes softening at the sight of Tafoya.

"Hi, Janet, you have a minute or two to step outside, so I can show you something?"

"Sure, Richard. Let me pour you some coffee, and we'll go outside."

One of the Forest Service rangers said, "Watch out, Janet, don't waive any of your rights!"

"Oh, shoot, Janet, I forgot my warrant to take you in!" Tafoya said, going along with the tease. Janet blushed, thinking to herself that he did not need a warrant to take her in. Outside, they stepped to the northeast side of the headquarters, facing the sun for warmth, to see the mountains—as Tafoya intended. The temperature was cool, pleasant. The day seemed young, new, abundant with opportunity.

"I'm leaving Friday for Sheep Springs, out on the Navajo Reservation, Janet."

"How long will you be gone?" Janet asked, secretly hoping his absence would be short.

"Not long, two days, probably back before I have to spend two nights out there. I've got to conduct an interview with an artist at Sheep Springs about our unidentified Red Feather boot man. I don't think the F.B.I. got as much information as they could have. I'll speak to him as Tulona to Navajo, not F.B.I. to Navajo."

"Going by yourself, Richard?"

"Yes, it's about a five-hour trip. One of the reasons I wanted to see you was to get maps, highway maps, reservation maps, or Bureau of Land Management maps."

"We have maps I can give you when we go back in. Most of our maps are related to the Sangre de Cristo, but we may have some for the northwestern quadrant, detailing the Chuska Mountains. That's close to Sheep Springs."

"Good, Janet. That's just what I wanted. Thanks."

Janet took another sip of coffee that had finally cooled down enough so it would not burn the tip of her tongue. She hated to burn the tip of her tongue because it would stay with her all day long. She looked at Tafoya, "What did you want to show me, Richard?"

Tafoya sat his coffee down on the ground next to the wall of the headquarters.

Placing his right hand gently on Janet's left shoulder, Tafoya pointed with his left hand toward the Sangre de Cristo. He pointed with his whole hand, not a forefinger starkly pointing at mountains and trees. That would embarrass the mountains. He took his right hand off of Janet's shoulder, as she focused at the area he pointed out with the fullness of his hand.

"Do you see the yellow slash of aspens about three-quarters of the way up the mountain? There is the yellow-gold splash, maybe the first you've seen this month of the Corn Ripe Moon?" Tafoya lapsed back into Tulona time reckoning.

"I see the splash of yellow-gold, Richard! Yes, it is my first sighting! I had my head down in paperwork all day yesterday and did not look up there."

"Okay, Janet, now look to the left of the largest yellow-gold splash." Again, Tafoya pointed with the fullness of his hand. "You see the red aspen?"

Janet looked closely. "Yes, Richard, I do! The red! That's so cool, beautiful!"

Tafoya looked closely at Janet as she looked at the red aspens. He saw her long, dark hair, clean and shiny, tied in pony tail, like the cacique's horse, Sweet Hija. Her skin was bronzed, a beautiful composite of Isleta and Spanish. Her teeth were nicely formed and white, not the blaring white of TV commercials, but a healthy, well-brushed whiteness. Her nails were well-trimmed, short and tailored for activity, not lounging. She was neither short nor tall, just three or four inches shorter than he.

Janet turned and looked at Tafoya looking at her. Embarrassed, he stooped down, picking up his cup of coffee, breaking his stare. His black belt squeaked as he stood erect. He glanced momentarily at her as she softly smiled back. Tafoya spoke.

"Ay, the aspens of Feast Days. The People at Red Willow place bring them to their Feast Day like we do for our feast of Saint Francis. We cover bowers to shelter the priest and our elders on racing days, and once the races are over, the aspen bower is taken down, the aspen branches distributed to Puebloans that wish to have them in their homes. The aspen trees greeted us when we emerged from the last world." Janet, being

Isleta, knew the spiritual narratives of emergence. She felt no need to speak of aspens and previous worlds to Tafoya.

Three magpies flew into the cottonwoods across the road in front of the Tulona substation, one chattering fiercely. The magpie calmed down. Two flew away.

"Have you run at the Tulona relays, Richard? Janet asked. She would like to see him run.

"Yes, I've run. Nowadays, I am obligated to keep the peace at the ceremonies, so I don't run. Have you ever been to the Tulona ceremonies?"

Janet replied that she had not gone to Tulona Feast Day and races, but had attended the Deer Dance and Buffalo Dance at the Taos Pueblo and wanted to go again. The Christmas Eve procession at the Taos Pueblo was a spectacular event, she added, despite the loud report of rifles fired in the air for celebration and the pungent smoke from the pyres that stung her eyes. Tafoya wanted to ask her to the Tulona Feast Day of Saint Francis on October 4, but since he would be on duty, he did not. I'll do more thinking on an invite, he promised himself.

Finishing their coffee, Janet and Tafoya went back inside the headquarters. Janet brought up three routes to Sheep Springs on Google maps. The computer was extremely fast in the Forest Service headquarters, Tafoya noticed. Much faster than the cranky servers at the Pueblo, or wherever they were in the cloud.

They worked together, planning three routes to Sheep Springs. Route 1, Tafoya designated the Chama route. Route 2 was the Grants-Gallup route, and Route 3 was Gallina-Cuba. Janet fetched and gave Tafoya all the relevant maps she had. Most were highway maps. She did find an old map of the Navajo reservation and a detailed map of the Chuska Mountains. Janet unfolded the detailed map of the Chuskas and nearby Sheep Springs, looking at the Sheep Springs region closely.

"Thirty-five hundred by five hundred feet, dirt," Janet intoned.

"What are you talking about, Janet?"

"Sanostee Airport runway, Richard. It's about fifteen miles or so from Sheep Springs. The Gallup airport is farther, but in any case, once we landed, there are no wheels to get around in."

"I don't know how to fly, Janet, and the Tulona police department doesn't have money to charter," Tafoya replied.

"I know how to fly, Richard, instrument rated, lots of hours in the air. I was just curious about the area you are traveling to. We could be there and back in one day," Janet said, with a gleam in her eye.

Tafoya stuttered, "I-I-I'm impressed. A pilot? Wow!" What next, he thought, is she opening an art show in Santa Fe?

Janet said she could rent a plane at the Taos Airport, but it was only a lark she thought about it in the first place. "There would be no rental car at the Sanostee Airport. Besides, it's a private field. They don't even have a windsock there." She folded the map and handed the stack of maps to him. She came from behind the front counter and walked with him out the door. The sun had risen farther in the sky, the heat forcing a haze in the mountains, partially blurring the yellow-gold, the red of aspen. Janet turned to Tafoya.

"Thank you, Richard, for showing me my first changing aspens of the season.... I hope you have a safe trip out there and find the identity of Red Feather boot man. I know you must be anxious to resolve the case."

"Yes, I am. We all are. It's a pity no one has come forward to claim him. Very sad." He paused. "Janet, we've only known each other for a little over a week, but I really do enjoy seeing you, talking to you." He thought he sounded lame. Maybe he should have gotten her a Hallmark card from Walgreens. Aii, but he forged ahead.

"When I return from Sheep Springs and get resituated, I'd like to give you a call, maybe we can go out to lunch or something." Tafoya thought this would be the time for her to say, I'm married, or, I'm committed. Sorry, Officer Tafoya.

Janet said nothing of the sort, but reached in her left breast pocket and brought out a business card. She reached over to take Tafoya's pen, "May I." He said yes, and let her take it out of his pocket. On the back of her Forest Service business card, she wrote her personal phone number, gave it to him along with his pen. Tafoya reached in his billfold and pulled out a business card as well. Taking his pen, he wrote down two phone numbers; one was his personal cell phone and the other his landline number, telling Janet his cell phone had spotty service at his home on the reservation.

"I live in a weird spot where the cell towers don't always triangulate. I wouldn't want to miss a call from you."

In parting, they shook hands firmly and gave each other a half-hug. Saying their take cares to each other, they looked up in the mountains at the red swipe of quaking aspens. Then turning to one another, Tafoya and Janet simply nodded, smiled, and went their separate ways.

The Old Taos Trail—one of several—from Questa to Ojo Verde and Taos, ran north-south, paralleling the east side of State Highway 522. The old unpaved road had a new designation: Forest Road 493 or FR 493. The road was suitable for passenger vehicles, went close by Lama, and directly transected San Miguel where the Ortegas lived. At San Miguel, the old road joined SH 522 and disappeared under asphalt. Modern traffic stayed on SH 522. In the old days, before SH 522, or its previous designation SH 3, the Old Taos Trail took Natives, traders, freighters, and packers north into southern Colorado and east to Bent's Fort, and that in turn, linked up with trails to Missouri and places east. Along the Old Taos Trail, now FR 493, settlements of small property owners, ranchers, old hippies, and even a spiritual compound had residential niches of houses, yurts, corrals, and bunkhouses back among juniper and piñon brush. Lobo Mountain rose 12,000 feet toward the east.

Between Denver and Taos, for a long period of time, the only saloon and store was on the road north of Lama and San Miguel—the Taos Trail Saloon. The store had closed down, and private owners over the years had remodeled and added on to the structure. In its heyday, the saloon had corrals, a general store, rooms to rent, and adjacent space to camp, water livestock, and rest for the final leg of travel into Ojo Verde and Taos. A graphic of a large whiskey jug, ten feet high and six feet wide, had been painted on the side of the saloon, lest any sojourners gallop their horses and mules straight on to Ojo Verde bars. The large whiskey-jug painting had been retouched dozens of times. In the last thirty years, sadly, the whiskey-jug painting and house had fallen into disrepair, a window broken, shingles missing, tree branches cluttering the premises, and corral panels flat on the ground.

Such disrepair and inattention fitted the present renter. Inside his house, the Old Taos Trail Saloon, he kept his turquoise, raw and unrefined as it was, hidden under a secret floorboard that in the past had served as a secret cache for the saloonkeeper. Prohibition in the 1920s did not stop the cash flow of the saloon from selling Taos Lightning, beer, and whiskey. Other caches of bootleg whiskey were stored in the adjoining forest. Renting the old saloon house gave him the solitude he wanted. He could do wage work in the county, go up for a few weeks to the mining corporation in San Luis Valley, and chisel away for turquoise at the Blue Lady. He parked his pickup truck behind the saloon or in the barn, hidden from the old trail road.

On occasions through the years, he met neighbors as they fought wildfires with wet burlap sacks and shovels. They joked with him, and he took their teasing reluctantly.

"Hey, saloonkeeper, the fire is spreading your way! We need help!"

He shortened his nickname to, "Keeper," and his neighbors adopted the sobriquet. His days and nights before finding the Blue Lady had been stale and empty, few good times arising. Since the turquoise of Blue Lady, his life gained meaning, and he thought of his younger days near the

Chuskas and the chantways droning into the early morning hours.

"Yes, some call me Keeper, but I am Andreas Saltwater, born to the Bead People and born for the Black Streak Wood People."

Andreas Saltwater hammered his chisel into rock and extracted a large chunk of turquoise in mother matrix. He was mining back into a narrow gulch, the entrance hidden by rockfalls and boulders, undisturbed for centuries. Around his feet, debris from Ancient Puebloans who hammered with rock mauls littered the ground, a foot deep in places. Rotten wood levers, carved by Pueblo workers, stuck up from the chips, and a few levers were still embedded in the walls. Here and there remnants of pottery broke into smaller pieces as he stepped on them. His objective that day was to fill two small knapsacks with mother rock and Blue Lady turquoise. By noontime, when he took a break, Saltwater had filled one of the knapsacks.

The touching and disposing of Robert's body gave him the shakes. His reaction came from his phobia of touching the dead. Saltwater had been reared as Navajo, and his mother and father had warned him about ghosts and touching dead bodies. Even the speaking of a dead person's name was taboo, opening up one's spirit to ghost sickness. Saltwater tried to beat back his apprehension with shrugs, trying to convince himself there were no such things as ghosts.

Robert had deserved what happened to him. There was no going back and changing what happened or why. Saltwater took a hasp and filed down the point of his chisel, then applied a finer file to sharpen the chisel. He hammered farther into the mother rock, extracting turquoise. With Robert working with him since their accidental discovery, they had extracted five-hundred pounds. They used two lapidaries, one on the Zuni Reservation, the other in Colorado. Most of the turquoise they extracted lay in an unrefined state back at the Old Taos Trail Saloon, hidden in the bootlegger's cache and buried in earthen caches in the forest.

Saltwater finished his extractions by mid-afternoon. A slant of sunshine fell into the narrow crevice as he buckled his second knapsack. It was a productive day. Then he heard a voice, a wavering voice, barely above a whisper, calling his name, "Andreas...Andreas...." He recognized the voice. It was Robert. He shook uncontrollably. Saltwater knew it was his imagination playing tricks on him. But the voice was there again, "Andreas...Andreas...."

Andreas was tired, depressed: "There are no such things as ghosts. Superstition."

Lifting the knapsacks, one on each shoulder, Saltwater turned sideways through fallen boulders, walking out of the mine. With a broom-piece of brush, he erased his tracks and scattered debris and limbs on the trail. He looked back as he eased himself down the gulch. The entry to the crevice was hidden, and unless you knew where it was, no one would see it. Andreas had put the Blue Lady mine to bed for the night and locked the door to her bedroom.

15

Thursday, September 13, Day of Saint John Chrysostom, Month of Corn Ripe Moon

Slight in force, the wind came as a zephyr from the south. In Ojo Verde, if one did not listen to weather forecasts from Albuquerque TV stations or Ojo Verde FM, a person looked outside in two directions for indicators of weather change: northeast, up into the mountains to see if clouds covered the peaks, for what was up there usually came down to the villages and Pueblo. The other direction was looking at cottonwoods. They swayed with winds, from a gentle back-and-forth to a harsh, violent, waving of large branches. In spring and summer, cottonseeds floated, ending their snowfall by July. The tree leaves remained attached until autumn frosts descended. Whether zephyr or gale, wind rattled leaves, sending a song from ancient time, leaving whorls etched in the audience's fingers and toes. Cottonwoods grew high, as much as 150 feet, within an average life span of fifty years. During their lifetimes, cottonwoods danced and waved and rattled, forecasting change. Believe the wind and cottonwood.

Coe and his wife, Priscilla, sat on their back patio early in the morning before he opened the bookshop on Paseo del Norte, sipping coffee, eating orange marmalade on toast, and looking at cottonwoods at the back of their property. Upper branches of the trees gently swayed. They faintly heard the bells of the Church of Our Lady of Assumption near the plaza, ringing the first time at eight o'clock. The wind was light from the south, not pushing bell sounds away. Their backyard was full of activity. Hummingbirds had begun to drink nectar from the feeders, chickadees manically moved up and down tree branches to peck at seed feeders, and magpies, large and fully-tailed in black and white, flew in twos and threes from tree to tree. Some hummingbirds emitted the sound of a bull-roarer by the quick beat of their wings; others squeaked in protest if driven away or challenged.

Coe and Priscilla exchanged plans for the day. Priscilla had a book club meeting in Taos. This month the club would meet in Taos; in October they would come to Ojo Verde, and Priscilla would host the discussion group in their home. Coe had plans to work all day at the bookshop. He would leave the shop at five o'clock and go across the street to Tablita's and have a drink or two before he came home. Magpies flew down—three of them—from the backyard fence and began to hunt for bugs and worms and small carrion.

"Look, Prissy. Look at how the magpies walk around looking for food. It's like walking on the ground is as natural as flying to them. They don't spend as much time walking around as quail, but pretty close to it." Prissy had heard that observation a hundred times and yawned.

Prissy looked up from her plate of toast and marmalade at the magpies. She remembered from fall of last year when a magpie flew to the front porch, perching on her rocking chair each morning at the same time. For whatever reason the magpie stayed perched for five or ten minutes, then flew off to join the rest of the flock, chatting loudly midway up the cottonwood trees, overhanging the street in front of them. For several weeks, the magpie returned at the same time, perching on her chair. It would turn around and look into the front window, perhaps seeing its reflection, or seeing her look out at him, or her, from the living room. Might the magpie return this fall? she questioned.

Our Lady of the Assumption church bell rang the half-hour. Prissy drove their only car to Taos for the book discussion group. Coe had no choice but to walk to his shop on Paseo de Norte. Ojo Verde village was quiet. Schools had opened in the county, and colleges and universities throughout the state were holding classes. The Ojo Verde Inn had vacancies in the middle of September, even on the weekend. The vacancy sign was lit. A few Tulona walked to the plaza. Coe noticed they were looking at car traffic circling the plaza and reading newspapers on benches. Ojo Verde kept the old New Mexico atmosphere of the land of "pretty soon" or *poco tiempo*.

Coe unlocked the door to his shop, and was greeted by Fenster who got a rub and then walked out and around the building. Coe opened his hardcopy calendar and looked at the Feast Days for the Tulona and Taos Pueblos. Double checking his hardcopy calendar against the websites of the Red Willow and Cottonwood Peoples, Coe saw that the Taos Pueblo Feast Day was on September 30, and the Tulona Feast Day of Saint Francis on October 4. Although the Taos Pueblo San Geronimo Feast Day was one of the most spectacular feast and dance days of all Pueblos, eastern as well as western, the Tulona Feast Day drew large crowds as well. The

Hopi, Navajo, Apache, Zuni, and nearly all the Rio Grande Pueblos had attendees and artistic booths of jewelry, pottery, and dry goods at Tulona's Saint Francis Feast Day. Coe planned to take Priscilla to both feast days, leaving his shop clerk in charge of sales for those days. Coe heard Fenster at the door. He walked over and let the cat in. Walking up the sidewalk and turning into his store, Lion Walks Night came in the door.

"Hey, Coe," he said, "and, good kitty to you, little cat." Fenster came over to Lion Walks Night, got a rub, mewed, and then sauntered to the back of the store for kibbles.

Lion asked Coe if he had any technical books on horses, dealing with farriering and veterinary medicine. Coe had a good-sized section on horses, including technical books.

"I thought you knew all there was to know about horses, Lion?" Coe said.

Lion replied that he wanted to look at some old techniques of training and books on tying halters and hackamores. Coe pointed out the equine section. Lion began to go through the books on horses when Coe's cell phone rang.

Coe was prepared to find out more about the strange drum beating and singing that had come through, mysteriously, on his cell phone. From under the front counter, he pulled out a mini-portable voice recorder and turned it on. Then, Coe answered the phone, placing it near the voice recorder. Like other times, the same rhythmic beat of the drum and high-pitched singing came strangely out of the phone, varying in amplitude like the old analog AM radio stations late at night.

Lion, who was squatting looking at the bottom shelf of horse books, stood up and turned to stare at the front counter where Coe had his recorder on and his cell phone speaker at high volume. "Do you understand and know this music, Lion?" Coe asked above the drumbeat. Lion walked around a table of books and stood next to the phone and recorder.

"Yes, I do, Coe. I think that's from our Buffalo Dance. That's Bustamente singing and Lujan drumming. That's in the middle of the dance. Who is sending this to you, Coe?"

The music and drumming rose and fell in volume, fading in, fading out. This time the music lasted nearly thirty seconds as Coe raised his voice to the phone, "Who are you? Why are you doing this? Speak up!"

No one answered. Just music and drumming. Then, it stopped. Coe backed up his recorder to make sure he recorded the music. The recorder played back thirty seconds of drumming and singing. Coe did not know Tiwa as the Tulona spoke it; he could not translate or understand the words.

Lion Walks Night stood silent, his concentration far away from horses and hackamores. "I think we should take this to the cacique. Right now, Coe!"

Coe told Lion that he did not have a car to drive three miles out to the reservation, but Lion replied they could start walking, and one of his innumerable cousins would come by in a pickup and give them a ride. Earlier, Lion had come into Ojo Verde by hitching a ride with one of his kinsmen. Same way back. Coe's assistant came in to take over the shop while Coe and Lion began walking to the Pueblo. They walked one block toward the Pueblo when one of Lion's cousins offered them a ride to Leonard Bustamente's home on the Summer House side of the Pueblo. "I told you so, Coe," Lion chuckled.

Coe had seen the cacique at Pueblo dances and his photograph in the newspaper, but had never met him. He was aware of the cacique's role as spiritual leader of both sides of the Pueblo, and that the cacique held the title for life. Lion introduced the two of them. Bustamente shook Coe's hand, just like the custom in any other social situation. Coe sensed in Bustamente a thoughtful man, one whose emotions were held in check by an ancient code, unknown to outsiders. He wished that he had met Bustamente under different circumstances.

Coe summarized the five phone calls over the past three months. The drumming and music were the same. There were no threats or speaking and, until the last phone call, all calls had lasted fifteen seconds or less. This last phone call was over half a minute. Coe said he had recorded the music, allowing a Tulona identify it. Lion had happened to be there shopping for a book on horses when the call came in.

"I saw it as very important to come see you at once, Bustamente," Lion said, "so that you might know that someone has been recording our sacred songs and using them to...," he paused, "I don't know what they are trying to do."

"Let me listen to the drumming," Bustamente said. Coe turned on the recording from the beginning. The cacique cocked his ear to listen carefully and bent over for a closer hearing. When the singing stopped, Bustamente said he wanted to hear it again. Coe rewound the recorder and played it again, this time turning up the volume even louder. The cacique listened carefully, tapping his foot to the beat. When the drumming finished the second time, he inhaled and exhaled before speaking, "Uh-huh, that's it."

"What do you mean, Grandfather, 'that's it'?" Lion asked.

"That singing is the Buffalo Dance recorded at a rehearsal, not the actual dance. And, I remember that rehearsal; several Pueblo boys, teenagers, were there. One of them either accidentally or intentionally made the recording. May have been done intentionally to learn the song and drumming."

Lion and Coe did not know what to say. Lion merely said, "Hmm."

Cacique Bustamente continued, "I remember the boys that were there. Our men would not record. They know the songs by heart and pass them down orally, not by recording. We have a number of musicians from the Pueblo that record drumming and singing; they make discs for selling. It's a part of making a living with our traditions, but the council watches over the compositions carefully. We don't allow our traditions, like this, to be put down on paper or recorded. I remember who was there and I'll have a talk with them."

"You think they called me as a prank, a joke?" Coe asked. "I'm not that concerned, but it was a little eerie to hear."

"I'll talk to the boys, Mr. Coe. You know how teenagers are. Silly games and stupid behavior occur with the Tulona, just like with the Anglo or Hispano," the cacique responded.

The three of them laughed, remembering their youth as well. Coe left behind his micro-recorder and said he would pick it up, or have Lion Walks Night bring it by the shop when the cacique finished lecturing those responsible. Lion and Coe caught a ride back to the bookshop, and Lion bought a book on horsemanship that included technical chapters on making halters and farriering. In a couple of weeks, Lion brought back the recorder, and two Tulona teenagers came to Coe and apologized. Coe accepted their apologies and asked them, what were their interests in school? They both liked sports. Coe rummaged around the store and gave them paperbacks on football and basketball.

"No charge. Come back and see me anytime." The teenagers did come back again. Coe never received any more phone calls projecting drumming and singing. Ever.

16

Friday, September 14, Day of Exaltation of the Holy Cross, Month of Corn Ripe Moon

In Ojo Verde, the padre at the Church of Our Lady of the Assumption walked to the lectern in front of a small congregation for early morning Mass at seven o'clock. The faithful sat back from the kneeling rail to listen. Sunday's early morning Mass occurred the same time as Friday's, but usually pews were full on that day. The padre scanned forty or fifty souls in attendance. Not bad, for a Friday, he thought. He opened his leather-bound, loose-leaf notebook to his homily. The padre wished to inspire, not admonish—or, so he hoped.

"Reflect if you will. At the gravesites of our kinsmen, here in Ojo Verde, out at Saint Jerome of the Tuah-Tah Pueblo, and at San Francisco del Monte of the Tulona Pueblo, we put crosses at graves, inscribing names and birthdates and death dates. For our poor faithful who have died in traffic accidents, we see beside the roadway the *descansos* with candles, some even solar-powered, and plastic flowers. The cross is there. The cross is the universal image of our belief in Christ and precepts emanating from his sacrifice and resurrection. Today, September fourteenth, the Day of Exaltation of the Holy Cross, we focus on not only the cross's history, but what it stands for. In the fourth century, Saint Helena, mother of the Roman Emperor Constantine, went to Jerusalem and ordered an archaeological dig for the tomb of Jesus. In the course of building the Basilica of the Holy Secular over the tomb, workers found three crosses, one of which was touched by a dying woman; she was healed. In the seventh century, Emperor Heraclius fought the Persians and regained the cross that had been stolen. When he sought to carry it back to Jerusalem, the story is that he had to take off his imperial clothes and put on pilgrim's clothing in order to move the cross. The cross has become a symbol of beauty in art and of the story of resurrection in our church. The *descansos* we see beside the road attest to a place of death, but also the cross of resurrection." The padre paused and took a sip of water from a glass placed on the first shelf under the ambo. Thirst quenched, he continued.

"Just yesterday, I went to visit an ill member of our church at Arroyo Luz and I saw three *descansos* alongside the road, as well as a new *descanso* at the spot where a body was discovered Saturday, a week ago. Even that poor, unidentified soul deserves a cross to help rest his soul." The padre crossed himself.

Jason Taylor came out of his reverie when the heard the padre mention the body found on the Tulona Reservation. He had been out there wandering around on the Friday before that Saturday. Not knowing he had come through the open gate onto the reservation, he had become stuck on the road to Earth Cloud Lake, arrested, and detained by the Tulona Tribal Police. Did he see anything that Friday afternoon? The gate was open. The weather was threatening storm. But there was nothing odd. I just pulled a stupid stunt by going up the mountain in an area he should not have been, he thought.

Jason, by attending Mass early Friday morning, had met his religious obligation for the week. He drew a regular shift for brunch on Friday most of the time, and the weekend work usually prevented him from attending on Sunday. So, the early morning Friday Mass fit his schedule. He was not a devout Catholic, not even practicing a rigorous confessional time, but his early boyhood and attendance at St. Mary's University in San Antonio propelled him to be observant. He walked to Tablita's, a quarter mile away, donned his apron, and began to serve tables becoming crowded at Friday brunch.

Sergeant Romero hasn't come by to get a free meal, he thought. I wonder if he heard I stopped by to see him? He'll probably show up when I least expect it. No sooner than he expressed those thoughts, Sergeant Romero came to the maître d's console. A teenager accompanied him.

Jason went up to greet the sergeant. The maître d' stepped aside.

"Jason, meet my son, Alexander" Romero said. "Alexander, meet Jason, your ski instructor."

"Never begin a voyage on Friday." Where had he heard that? Tafoya worried he was starting his investigative trip to Sheep Springs on Friday. What was the source of that piece of advice? How was a Friday any different from any other day of the week? Friday was the name of a day. Just a day, an arbitrary name given to a span of time between two other arbitrary names, Thursday and Saturday. "Never begin a voyage on Friday." At his concrete-block house on the southeastern edge of the Tulona reservation, Tafoya had set up a desktop computer with superfast internet connection via

Dancing Rock Internet. A satellite dish connected him with a stationary satellite in the southern sky, above the Truchas Peaks—or so he liked to imagine. Early this Friday morning, before he departed for Sheep Springs, Tafoya fired up the desktop and googled, "Never begin a voyage on Friday." The results of his Google search were mixed.

The first link, "Old sailors' superstitions came up, 'Never start a sea voyage on Friday! It will end badly!'" I'm not on a sea voyage, Tafoya thought. As he read down the website page, it turned out to be an advertisement for a Caribbean cruise ship line. The second link for information was just as bad. "Cruisers Clearing House Forum answers questions about cruising. Sign up for membership."

"Yeah, right, I'm not going to another commercialized site," he said aloud.

Finally, on the third link he opened, the answer was found against starting a voyage on Friday, as well as a few other days of the year. Sailors predominated the folklore, the superstitions arising out of Biblical stories. "Don't start a voyage on any Friday. Christ was crucified on Friday. Don't start a voyage on December 31, because Judas Iscariot hanged himself on that day. Don't voyage out on first Monday in April—Cain murdered Abel. Avoid starting on the second Monday in August because Sodom and Gomorrah were obliterated on that day." Tafoya wondered how the *specific* dates of Abel's murder, Judas's suicide, and the destruction of Sodom and Gomorrah were determined? There was even a reference that ancient Romans did not start a voyage at sea on Friday. Tafoya found his answer, satisfying his curiosity. Since he was not *that* superstitious, he packed his duffle bags and threw them in the tribal police vehicle. To be prepared, he also packed in water, a grub box, and tent. Sheep Springs did not have a motel.

I'm leaving today, Friday. I will be extra careful—just in case old mariners were correct about bad days to start a voyage, he said to himself. Tafoya commenced to do a walkaround his vehicle to check on the condition of tires. That was not part of his habit pattern, but he walked around, nonetheless, just to be sure.

Deciding on Route 1 that he and Janet had named, Tafoya began the Chama way to Sheep Springs—Friday, it was. Following US 64, he crossed the gorge, drove through the Tusas Mountain range and on toward Dulce. In Dulce, the Jicarilla Apache Nation operated the Wild Horse Casino and Hotel. Tafoya glanced over at the casino as he drove by. Before the noon hour, the parking lot was full; casino LED lights were burning bright. Tafoya turned south at Dulce, then headed west to Bloomfield. On state highways and Indian service routes, he eventually drove through the Navajo Mesa Farms, arriving at Sheep Springs by two o'clock. It had taken him four hours and forty-five minutes travel time. To the west of Sheep Springs arose the Chuska Mountains. Roger Yazzie's trailer house, hogan, and arbor lay five miles toward the Chuskas from Sheep Springs. Before heading out to Yazzie's, Tafoya stopped at the Sheepsprings Express Mart to refuel and get a cup of coffee. He checked his cell phone before he exited the car; he had a strong four-bar signal.

Tafoya called Yazzie—no answer. That did not concern him because Yazzie told him that he and his wife ignored most of their calls. Tafoya called the tribal station in Ojo Verde. Romero was delivering an arrest warrant of a man wanted in a domestic abuse case. He had enlisted two Taos County sheriff deputies to assist him in delivering the warrant. Tafoya felt guilty for not being there. He would redouble his focus to interview Yazzie, hopefully not wasting the department's money and avoiding Romero's blowback when he returned.

He looked up from his phone and saw Navajos inside the Sheepsprings Express staring out the windows at him. Tafoya realized that he was facing the store directly, so he backed out of the space, turned his vehicle around so that he faced outward. He glanced in the rearview mirror and saw the Navajos were still staring at him, although a couple had drifted away from the window. Tafoya wondered for a second if it had been a mistake to drive the police car and wear his uniform.

Tafoya went inside the Sheep Springs mart, and a cheery, friendly, male clerk greeted him, "Hey, Officer, welcome to Tooh' Haltsooi! How can I help you?"

A line of shoppers stood looking at Tafoya, their handbaskets full of sodas, chips, canned tomatoes, canned peaches, bread, and milk. Another clerk behind the counter began to ring up the products, speaking Navajo. Tafoya did not understand Navajo and he wondered if they were talking about him.

"Hey, back at you! I need gas, but first I need to get some coffee," said Tafoya.

"It's over there against the backwall, past the chips and crackers. Help yourself, it's on Tooh' Haltsooi!"

Tafoya walked past the dogfood and automobile aisle, found the drinks counter, and poured a large cup of coffee. It was too hot to sip, but it was freshly made and smelled rich. Shoppers in the coffee aisle stood aside, flush against the shelves, as he walked back to the counter. Tafoya said, "Excuse me."

As he started to walk out the door, the clerk mentioned that he had a cousin living at Tulona and another cousin employed at the Harwood Museum in Taos. Tafoya knew the male cousin that lived in Tulona, and he would pass along he had seen his Navajo cousin at Tooh' Haltsooi Sheep Springs mart. As he walked out the door, two Mormons—so he surmised by their Anglo clothing and beards—walked in the store. They had a large church next door to the mart. Tafoya filled up his gas tank. After refueling, he sat in the car and spread Janet Rael's maps in front of him. His inboard computer had maintained a secure connection with its internal GPS all day long, but he wanted a hardcopy backup for navigation as he turned west toward the Chuskas to interview Yazzie.

Tafoya drove southwest out of Tooh' Haltsooi on paved Indian Service Route 134 for four miles. He then turned off the paved road onto the unpaved ISR 5006 that began to rise in elevation to the lower foothills of the Chuskas. The road remained passable and well-maintained, until he came to Yazzie's place. What the condition of the road beyond Yazzie's was not an issue for him—or so he hoped. The GPS worked, but Tafoya noticed his cell phone and the phone within his inboard computer was spotty in service, yet still within the one-to-two-bar signal strength range. He was glad to see power poles, erected all the way to Yazzie's and beyond, carrying the industrial age into Navajo backcountry.

Roger Yazzie, Navajo silversmith, was also a stockman. His manufactured home was surrounded by rectangular corrals, several barns and outbuildings, and a round pen for training horses. By Tafoya's quick count, three other residences were associated with Yazzie's compound. Each residence had a hogan and outdoor arbor. Yazzie had given Tafoya instruction to drive to the manufactured home with a new red-roofed barn in back of the residence. He drove his car to the front of the home. Two Australian shepherd dogs and an older blue heeler barked at his car. Yazzie came out the front door and whistled the dogs to silence. He wore a work apron and had a frayed Dallas Cowboy baseball cap on backwards. He was slightly overweight, but agile, his smile unforced and happy. Tafoya was relieved with this first impression of Yazzie—no overt demeanors of aggression, apprehension, or pathology.

"Hey, Officer! I saw you coming up the road. From my elevation here at the compound, I see far, almost to the Rio Grande," Yazzie laughed. "My name is Roger Yazzie, born to Near the Mountain clan, born for the Meadow People. Welcome to my home!" Yazzie gestured broadly with both arms. Tafoya liked him.

Yazzie stepped off the porch onto the driveway and vigorously shook Tafoya's hand. At Yazzie's door appeared his wife; she invited Tafoya in for iced tea. "This is my wife, Pauline," Yazzie said. Greeting her warmly, Tafoya entered her well-kept house. A television was turned on low volume, a soap opera episode flickered on the screen. The living room had a leather sofa and two reclining chairs upholstered in cloth. The concrete floor had been stained a light-bronzed color. A tall bookcase, standing next to the television, held a set of World Book encyclopedias, paperback novels, and a few hardbound copies of equine behavior and training horses. The living room, dining room, and kitchen all fit together in a great-room concept of spatial arrangement. Tafoya concluded that being a Navajo silversmith of Yazzie's skill and reputation paid well. He had horses, and *kowena* were expensive to manage and feed. Yazzie's wife offered to warm up a bowl of mutton stew that they had for lunch; Tafoya accepted a bowl and a second helping when it was offered.

Tafoya looked at his field watch and noted the time when he finished the second bowl of mutton stew. It was two thirty. "Roger, I have to retrieve my briefcase from the vehicle, and we need to get started." Yazzie suggested that they go to his shop in the barn at the back of the house. Tafoya thanked Pauline for the stew, and getting his briefcase out of the car, he and Yazzie walked behind the house to his barn and workshop.

Yazzie's workshop reminded him of Rodarte's The Silver Concho in Ojo Verde equipped with sturdy worktables, grinders, small tools, power saws, the cottonwood log for stamping and striking, multiple desk lamps, and magnifying lenses. An exhaust vent set above one of the worktables. A steel Remington safe stood in the corner, its door locked. Through an open door, he saw a backroom with additional tables, a large refrigerator, and propane cooking stove. Another door was open to a well-lit barn with fresh alfalfa hay stacked against the walls. The workshop area was insulated; the barn was not. Yazzie directed Tafoya to a long partially-cleared table. Two stools with backrests were drawn up. While Yazzie fetched hot coffee from the backroom, Tafoya pulled files from his briefcase, a micro recorder, notepad and pen. He began his interrogation slowly.

"As I told you on the phone, I wanted to go over the contact you had with Robert, our murder victim found on the Tulona reservation. I know the F.B.I. interviewed you, but I have additional questions," Tafoya opened. Yazzie said he understood. Tafoya showed Yazzie photographs of Robert and the belt buckle.

Yazzie identified Robert and the belt buckle once more. "Those were gem-quality stones I mounted in the buckle," Yazzie added.

"When you conversed with Robert, did you notice any accent or inflections in his voice that might suggest his family or mother tongue?" Tafoya asked.

"What do you mean, 'mother tongue'?"

"The language of his childhood or first language that he is familiar with. Did you converse entirely in English?"

"We conversed mainly in English, but he sprinkled his English with Navajo and Spanish, mostly Navajo."

"You think he may have been fluent in Navajo?" Tafoya asked.

"Fluent? I don't know about that, but he seemed comfortable with the Navajo words I used."

"Did the F.B.I. ask you about his clan affiliations?"

"No," Yazzie answered, "they did not, but I couldn't have told them what his born to clan was, because I didn't find out until last night."

Tafoya jerked his head up from his notetaking and said, excitedly, "What do you mean, 'you didn't know until last night'?"

"I only found out last night from Pauline, my wife. It was like this: When Robert came to pick up his buckle in July—I had worked on it for a week—Pauline met him at the front door. I was in the workshop in back of the house, here in the barn. She greeted him at the door, and he casually mentioned his name was Robert, born to the Two Rocks-Sit clan, and he then asked where I was. So, last night when I told Pauline you were coming today, she said, 'Oh, is it about Robert born to the Two Rocks-Sit clan?' I said yes, and that's how I found out."

Tafoya nodded he understood. Facts are falling my way, finally, he thought. He sifted among his files and retrieved a chart of clans. So far in this case, he had been told about: One-walks-around, Bead People, Black Streak Wood People, The Yellow People, Bitter Water, and just today, Two Rocks-Sit, Near the Mountain, and Meadow People. "And, that's not even determining born to and born for," he said aloud.

"What did you say?" Yazzie asked.

"Oh, nothing, Yazzie. I'm dealing with a lot of Navajo genealogy. Not used to it."

"Yeah, I know, Tafoya. I am full-Navajo and lived here on the reservation my whole life, and I still get confused about clans and kinship," he said, laughingly. "I noticed on your charts there that you have in large letters, the Bitter Water clan. Where did that come from?"

"Oh, you can read upside down," Tafoya smiled. "That's from a man I've been interviewing at Arroyo Luz, near Tulona. His name is Majerus, Santiago Majerus."

"Santiago Majerus?" Yazzie repeated.

"You know him?"

"I do," said Yazzie haply. "Majerus worked for my dad several years ago off-and-on, while he studied with the medicine man, Niesmith Saltwater.

He trained horses. He could work with a horse for a couple of hours and mount the horse with no bucking or violence by mid-afternoon. A lot of Navajo came here just to watch him train. He also helped with cattle. How is he doing?"

In his line of work, Tafoya was graced with coincidental discoveries, intersections of people and events that just happen to fall out of the sky, or letters that drop from the pages of a book one searched through. He now knew Robert's clan affiliation and Majerus's work location that might lead to the Saltwater families and Majerus's possible enemy.

"Majerus is healthy and collecting medicine herbs." Changing directions, Tafoya asked, "Have you come up with Robert of Two Rocks-Sit's last name?"

"No, I'm sorry, Officer. My wife and I have racked our brains...we can't remember. It was like, Bijda...Zeta...started with a 'D' or 'Z,' I think."

"Are there any Two Rocks-Sit clan people living in the area?" Tafoya said, pursuing another tack.

"Yes, there is a family of Two Rocks-Sit back up near Sheep Springs. I can give you directions. It's the old house, the first house on your left-hand side on ISR 32, as you turn into Sheep Springs village. Their family has another house next door. The Two Rocks-Sit have been there for years, having moved from the Chuskas many years before." Tafoya noted down the directions.

Tafoya asked if there were any family of Saltwaters living nearby. "Not here in Sheep Springs. Majerus had to go south, toward Tohatchi, to meet up with Niesmith, the medicine man. You might inquire at the chapter house here in Sheep Springs for Saltwater residences."

Tafoya glanced at his watch; it read three thirty. He wanted to investigate the Two Rock-Sits in Sheep Springs as soon as possible. He began shuffling his papers and putting them back in his briefcase when Yazzie spoke up.

"There's one more thing, Tafoya. On the back of the gemstones, there were two large letters, a 'B' and an 'L'. The surfaces were flat on the reverse of the stones; the stone on the right-hand side was the 'B' and the left-hand side was the 'L'. They had been carefully carved in the stones."

"Did Robert say what the letters stood for?"

"He did. The 'B' was for blue, the 'L' was for lady. Blue lady. He said it was the name of a saint of good fortune, a Catholic saint of some sort."

Yazzie offered to put Tafoya up for the night in one of their unoccupied bunkhouses. Tafoya said he appreciated that, but he was going to try and make his way to Tohatchi for the night and get a motel room there. He might have to take him up on the offer to sleep in the bunkhouse, and, if so, he would give him a call. "No need to call me," Yazzie said, "the latch key is on the outside, and I'll know it's you from your police car. Stay over for breakfast if you do sleep in the bunkhouse. Besides, there are no motels in Tohatchi."

Fred Nez and his wife, Christine, saw the green patrol car of the Tulona Tribal Police turn into their driveway and park in front. A police car never bore a messenger of good news. When they saw the young Richard Tafoya get out of the car, carrying a letter-sized pouch, their fears lessened somewhat, but not much. He was hatless with a burr haircut, youthful, almost high-schoolish. And, he was alone, so it couldn't be bad, could it? Tafoya knocked on the door, but before he gave the last rap, Fred opened the door. Tafoya explained that he was investigating a case involving a Two Rocks-Sit clan member at the Tulona Pueblo. "Would you mind answering a few questions?" They agreed to help. When Tafoya came in, Christine offered him a tea or soda, but he said, "No, I'm not going to be long, but thanks."

Fred Nez called the Catholic priest in Tohatchi for the consolation of his wife, Christine, born to the Two Rock-Sits clan. The priest would arrive an hour after Tafoya left the Nez's home that had become crowded with family. At first, the priest balked at driving up to Sheep Springs because of impending weekend Masses. "After all, it is a Friday, Mr. Nez." But when told of the circumstances, the priest said he would come immediately.

Tafoya decided to spend the night at the Yazzie bunkhouse and start out for Tohatchi and Tulona early the next morning. Tafoya managed the Nez interview reasonably well, he thought, despite the number of voices speaking softly in Navajo. At Yazzie's bunkhouse, he had called Romero about the case and had written a report on the laptop brought in from his vehicle. The signal strength was weak, but the laptop finally loaded up.

At the interview with the Nez family, Christine was the clan member of Two Rocks-Sit. Both she and her husband, Fred, were asked if there were any Two Rocks-Sit kinsmen living, or had lived in the Tulona, Ojo Verde, Taos area. Both of them had several kinsmen, some Two Rocks-Sit, some not, that had resided in the northern New Mexico. Christine mentioned that her older sister, who lived in Gallup, had an older son that had worked at the Culebra Mining Company in southern Colorado and lived for a time in Questa, but not Ojo Verde. She thought that inconsequential, but had mentioned it anyway.

Tafoya asked her if she had seen her nephew lately? She said she had seen him back in the summer for a few minutes, as he stopped by on the way to Gallup to attend a jewelry market show and visit his mother.

Christine said his full name was Robert Dihyja, born to the Two Rocks-Sit clan.

"I have an ink sketch of a person whose identity we are trying to find. Would you look at the sketch and tell me if you identify the person in the sketch? Maybe you, Fred, would take a look at it first, then Christine?" Tafoya took the sketch out of his leather pouch and handed it to Fred. He looked closely at the ink drawing, and, without a word, handed the sketch to his wife.

"Yes, that's Robert, my nephew, I think," Christine said. Her husband nodded in agreement.

The knot in Tafoya's stomach tightened as he took his next step, bringing out the photo of deceased, Robert Dihyja. The photo was of Robert on the mortician's slab, sheet pulled up to his neck. No embalming marks could be seen for the sheet had been pulled up to obscure the carotid incisions near his clavicles. As an object of relief to the scene, the red bandanna he had worn was neatly folded and placed beside his head.

Tafoya stood up and asked Fred to stand beside him. He drew the photo out of his leather pouch, kept it in his hand, and asked Fred to look at it. Fred gently shook his head, faintly, side-to-side, "It's Robert." Tafoya asked Christine to corroborate. She saw the photo and began to tear up. She crossed herself and cried. The priest in Tohatchi arrived an hour later. He had to travel on Friday, even if it was the day of crucifixtion.

By the time Tafoya parked, facing outward in front of Yazzie's bunkhouse, the stars, the Night People, were beginning to come out and look over their worlds, this world. He saw the evening star and the faint beginnings of the Milky Way. Yazzie's compound had outdoor lights, but they were turned off. Tafoya knew why. To look fully at night sky, you need to embrace the dark, and to embrace the dark, lights need to be off; even campfires need extinguishing. To the west, the silhouetted Chuskas cut the alpenglow light, squarely away. Gold and red colors turned darker. The sky cloudless, contrail-less. Tafoya saw the Night People begin to sparkle, begin to dance.

Tafoya's Friday was coming to an informative end—for a change. He had acquired Two Rocks-Sit knowledge from Yazzie's remembrance prompted by Pauline. He had obtained knowledge from Christine Nez's tears. Tafoya silently promised to find out how Robert Red Feather boot man, now Robert Dihyja, born to the Two Rocks-Sit clan, met his terrible death, his head swathed by a red bandanna, now folded neatly, next to his shroud.

17

Sunday, September 16, Day of Saint Cornelius, Month of Corn Ripe Moon

Morning broke, the sun's rays appeared high in the sky. The mountains shadowed the plains as dawn gave way to a bright atmosphere, the turquoise sky shimmering. The rosy fingers of dawn, as someone once told a story, touched New Mexico blue. Miles below Ojo Verde and San Miguel, a zephyr of wind circulated counterclockwise on the Jornada de Muerte below Albuquerque, gaining strength to a forceful, but not destructive, power spinning north. The southern breeze was unseasonably warm. The visiting priest at San Miguel scurried from the parish home to the chapel, his frock tight against his body. The wind from Jornada de Muerte stirred dust in front of the chapel. The padre unlocked the two massive French doors that had been carved in the nineteenth century and restored in the twenty-first millennium by Peñasco woodcrafters. The Ortega family had paid for all the restoration work, and on the holiest days, such as Easter and Christmas Eve, they gazed and walked slowly beside the doors as they entered Mass. The padre wondered how the Ortegas, mere sheepherders with little ownership of land, could afford the restoration work. His questioning was not out of criticism, but out of gentle curiosity, a belief he had about the mystery of God's grace to the Ortegas, and to Holy Mother Church. As he swung back the door, the wind from Jornada del Muerte flowed into the chapel, forcing altar candles to flicker, yet, none went dark.

Loretta and Armando Ortega attended the ten o'clock Mass, enjoying the warmer temperatures of mid-September. Seated in their regular pew midway to the altar, they liked the breeze that came down the aisle. The padre had left the front doors open and two windows raised near the front of the auditorium. Older parish members grumbled, so eventually Armando stood up from his genuflections, closed the front doors and lowered the windows. The padre nodded in assent. Fortunately, the priest gave a short homily and, after Holy Communion, turned the laity's attention to the approaching festivals of San Geronimo at the Taos Pueblo and the Saint Francis at Tulona. He stated he would be in attendance at both festivals and a special Mass would be given at vespers, the night before, at Mission San Francisco del Monte. He urged the parish members to attend the Tulona festivities and participate in the special Mass before Feast Day.

"May the Lord be with you," he said in dismissal.

Richard Tafoya slept in. The drive to Sheep Springs on Friday and the interviewing of Yazzie and the Nez family was draining, stressful. That day was followed by Saturday at Tohatchi Navajo House, obtaining information about Saltwater families living in the area. The House secretary in Tohatchi, after establishing Tafoya's credentials, told him there were three Saltwater families living around Tohatchi, and that a number of Saltwaters had relocated in Gallup. He interviewed one family of Saltwaters living in Tohatchi, and all they said was that the medicine man, Niesmith Saltwater, had passed away.

"Oh, he passed in about, maybe, I dunno, maybe 2006?" That's not a lot to go on, Tafoya groused.

But they did know he had been buried in the old way, carried up into the mountains and covered with stones—the "old way, you know." As he finished the interview that Saturday morning, he received a call from Romero, who ordered him to return to the Pueblo and terminate his meanderings in Navajo country. Romero relayed that Robert Dihyja's mother and assorted relatives had driven to Ojo Verde and positively identified Robert. He had interviewed the mother, and she provided information the tribal police needed to sift through and act upon. Romero told him to drive back to Tulona; he could take the next day off, which was Sunday.

Tafoya slept in on Sunday morning and felt guilty when he looked at the clock: nine-thirty. I'm off work today, so what does it matter? he thought. He dressed in mufti, drove to the tribal police station, parking the police car facing outward. An admin sat at the front desk—no one else in the station. He hung the car keys on the wall hook behind the front desk, walked outside, and strode to his parents' home on the Winter House side, promising himself to think of anything but Robert Dihyja.

The day was unseasonably warm with a wind out of the south. The wind was not even strong enough to stir up dust. Alongside the stream that divided Summer House from Winter House, a few people had spread blankets for an early Sunday picnic. Mass was ongoing in the church;

tourists were beginning to walk about the plaza and shop at the few stores open before noon on a Sunday. Tafoya walked to his parents' home, knocked on the door, "It's me, Richard, your son."

The living room was cool, but not cold; the smell of the propane stove wafted in the room. Tafoya's father had gone to visit a cousin on the Summer House side, but his mother was there, sitting in her upholstered armchair. "Richard, so good to see you, my son." They had brief hug, and she offered him coffee. He said he was hungry, so his mother brought out chokecherry jelly, biscuits, and margarine. He sat at the table while she warmed the biscuits in a freshly-washed, oiled Dutch oven, cutting the biscuits in half. "No fry breads this morning, son. Besides, the chokecherry goes better with biscuits."

The church bell of San Francisco del Monte rang, indicating Mass was over. A few tourists had come early to attend Mass, and they lingered, like many Tulonas, at the mission door to chat with the priest. Tafoya poured himself another cup of coffee and walked to the screen door, staring at the faithful and tourists shopping. He looked farther into the distance, skyward to the mountains. He saw slashes of red aspen in the higher altitudes; Tafoya wanted his mother to know his heart.

"I've met someone, a woman. Her name is Janet Rael," he said to his mother. "She works for the Forest Service as a biology specialist. She is Isleta."

Tafoya's mother asked him how he met Janet and if he had dated her. He answered he had not dated her, but was probably going to ask her out—soon. She commented, "It is good she has a job with the Forest Service. Those last a long time. We know several Tulona that have worked all their lives for the Forest Service, and they have good benefits. How old is this Janet Rael, of the Isleta?"

"Younger than me, I don't really know, probably late twenties." That's good, thought his mother. She is young and within child-bearing age, and she has benefits, like my son.

Quail Looks Away carried Dezba as she and Ben walked upstream along Cottonwood River. The warm air from the south had prompted them to hike beyond the old wall of the Pueblo and picnic under cottonwoods. The spot they unfolded their falsa blankets was the starting line of the races on the Feast Day. From where they picnicked, one saw the entire racecourse from starting line to the Pueblo bower, faintly in the distance. In a few days, males of the Pueblo would run fast and earnestly—for the people, the sun, the whole world.

"Will you be running this year, Ben?" Quail Looks Away asked, as they settled onto maroon and gold-striped Mexican falsa blankets.

Ben had thrown a pack saddle on Star, enabling Star to carry food, drink, and baby paraphernalia in panniers. Star had been hayed and fed that morning, so Ben tied him by halter rope on a low-hanging cottonwood limb in the shade. No need to hobble the horse since he was full and happy. Star turned himself so he could hear family talk and see Dezba nurse. His flanks relaxed, one back leg resting, then the other; peaceful and content was he, under cottonwoods dappling the ground.

"Yes, I will run, Quail," Ben replied, and nodded in the direction of his newborn daughter. "I'll be running for Dezba especially this year."

"And I'll make sure I'll be standing on the roof with Dezba, so she can see you run fast," said Quail. "She won't know it's you, but I'll point you out anyway and ululate at the top of my voice. But next year, she will know and remember."

"Wear that bright yellow Pendleton blanket to make you stand out to me as I run," Ben asked.

Star heard a whinny and jerked his head up. He saw Lion Walks Night riding Jess along the race track from the Pueblo. He whinnied in response. Along the stream, magpies were chattering, and in shallow eddies of the stream; they bathed quickly and flew into the lower branches of the cottonwoods and willows to dry off and preen. The arrival of Lion on Jess brought magpie bathing to a quick end.

Ben's back was to the racecourse, and he turned around to see Lion and Jess. Quail looked up from nursing Dezba and waved, saying nothing as Dezba was falling asleep in the warm air and sounds of flowing water. Lion tied Jess next to Star, using a slip knot on another low-hanging branch.

"Come, eat, Lion. We have turkey and ham sandwiches, chips, ice tea," said Ben, as he stood up from the blankets and went to the panniers Star had ported, retrieving a reusable plastic glass for Lion's tea. Lion ate a turkey sandwich, double-loaded with mayonnaise.

"This is really good," Lion said, chomping, smacking his lips. He volunteered he had ridden Jess upstream to their picnic site for exercise, but also to ask if Quail and the baby needed a ride back to the plaza. "Quail and Dezba can ride Jess as I lead him." She accepted the offer since the hike from the Pueblo had been tiring. As they finished their sandwiches and rested, Lion brought up the latest news.

"Have you heard the police identified the body out at Arroyo Luz?" They had not heard. "His name is Robert Dihyja. He's Navajo, born to a clan called the Two Rocks-Sit, out near Sheep Springs. His mother lives in Gallup, and the family came yesterday to make arrangements to take him back out to Gallup to be buried."

"What was he doing here?" Ben asked.

"I don't know, but he used to work for the Culebra Mining Company up in Colorado."

"Who killed him?" Quail asked.

"The tribal police have no suspects. They don't even know where he died," replied Lion.

The four of them finished lunch. "I'll put the bit on Jess and ride him back," Quail said. "You can carry Dezba back to the plaza since she is asleep and full of milk, can't you, Ben?" she asked. "It's not that far."

"Of course, you feel up to riding Jess?" Ben replied.

"Yes, Ben," Quail laughed. "You feel like carrying Dezba?" she asked, smilingly.

Quail put the bit on Jess, adjusting the halter out of the way, checking there were no tight spots to chaff him. Lion folded blankets and put away food and plastic glasses in the panniers, hoisting them to Star's pack saddle. Ben took Dezba from Quail, nestling her in the crook of his left arm. The racecourse was the way back home. Racecourse soil had become soft from barefoot-run contests, decade after decade. But in places, stones protruded, the track hard-packed, dried-out by the sun. No mind, Pueblo racers still ran barefoot, strong and fast, fiercely balanced upon the earth.

Lion Walks Night stood beside Jess to help Quail mount. She waved him off. Jess was a small horse, thirteen hands at the withers. Quail had on Ariat hiking shoes as did Ben. She put her foot in the stirrup, stopped, and took her foot out of the stirrup. Flat-footed, she grabbed the saddle horn, and in one swift motion without using the stirrup, mounted Jess. Lion and Ben knew she was strong and prideful, not excessively so, as they uttered in unison, "Ay! Quail!" They started back to the Pueblo: Quail on Jess in front, Ben and Dezba to one side, and Lion leading Star.

"Let's go, Jess, let's go, boy!" Quail ordered. She gave a firm kick with her Ariats to the sides of Jess, and he reacted exactly like she wanted. Quail rose in the stirrups to stay in rhythm and looked back at her family.

"I'll see all of you back at the plaza. Bye, Dezba. Love you, girl!" she shouted.

Ben and Lion looked at each other and shook their heads. "A strong woman, that Quail," Ben proudly said to Lion, as he nestled Dezba closer to his chest.

18

Monday, September 17, Day of Saint Robert Bellarmine, Month of Corn Ripe Moon

Tulona policeman Tafoya drove to the to the Taos County Sheriff's Department substation in Ojo Verde. He drove slowly, agonizing over the called meeting about Robert Dihyja, hoping it would be cancelled. Tafoya was determined to truncate the meeting. Because of the new information, F.B.I. Agent Diane Parker had driven from Albuquerque the night before. He dreaded meetings with powerpoints, especially those that had paragraphs of data aside, under, over, and hovering at each bullet point. Arriving at eight o'clock, before most officers were present, he looked across the street and saw Janet Rael's red Subaru at the Forest Service. I'm calling her today, he promised himself. Grabbing a cup of coffee in the breakroom, he went to a desk assigned to the tribal police, pulled up the data on Dihyja, and sat there until the meeting began.

He saw Parker go into the conference room. "Here we go," he said under his breath, as he trudged to the meeting. Tafoya sat down at the far end of the table from Parker. The lead Deputy Sheriff, Chris Cordova, holstered his cell phone and sat down. Another deputy sheriff was present, but Tafoya did not know him. Sergeant Romero sat near the front of the seminar table. A secretary with the tribal police pulled her notebook out of her briefcase to take notes. A New Mexico state trooper, a lieutenant, appeared bored with the proceedings, but perked up when the secretary sat down beside him. Tafoya looked up at the ceiling and noticed an overhead projector light up as Parker tapped keys on her portable laptop. Oh, no, a powerpoint, Tafoya grimaced.

The projection screen to the side of Parker lit up with bullet points that had several lines of data beneath each point. Tafoya prayed a storm would come up and cut the power off, and the Dancing Rock Co-op would not be able to find the blown transformer for hours. Sergeant Romero turned slightly to face Tafoya and grinned. Parker tapped her pen against the lectern like a school teacher.

Parker droned on for fifteen minutes, which seemed like an hour to Tafoya. When she came to the interview of Dihyja's mother on Saturday, Tafoya listened up.

"Dihyja's mother told Sergeant Romero that Robert was a fine son and had never been in trouble with the law. We ran a check on him. She told the truth. He had graduated from Tohatchi High School in 1996. He stayed close to his family and lived with them after high school when they moved to Gallup. He worked at different jobs, went to the community college in Gallup but did not graduate, majoring in business and going to night school as he worked during the day. In 2006, he moved to Manassa, Colorado, taking a job with the Culebra Mining Company. He made good money, sending some of it home to his mother by Western Union every two weeks. He visited his mother in Gallup and traveled to the reservation for ceremonies and see friends. The recession in 2008 laid him off for a few months, but he stayed in Manassa with a male roommate until the mine picked up in activity in 2009. His mother never did meet the roommate."

Tafoya scribbled a note, "Find the roommate!"

Parker continued, "He worked for Culebra until he was laid off a final time in 2015. The mining operations at Culebra were coming under environmental scrutiny, and some of the major sources of precious metals were playing out. The company continues mining operations we found out, but on a very limited budget."

"I bet all she did was google 'Culebra Mining Company,'" Tafoya whispered to the trooper beside him.

"What was that you said, Officer Tafoya?" Parker asked pointedly. She always noticed Tafoya's behavior over any others. "I couldn't hear you."

"Did anyone personally interview Culebra company officials?" Tafoya asked, thinking quickly.

"No, Officer. That's on our 'to-do list.' Whomever conducts the Culebra part of the investigation will check that out, as well his roomate's identtity."

"Thanks, Agent," Tafoya said, hoping to close the exchange with Parker. She had covered one bullet point.

"Continuing on," Parker droned, "we ran a Colorado driver license check and a New Mexico check, too. His New Mexico license was invalid from 2008, never renewed, and his Colorado license went defunct in 2016. He got his Colorado license in 2007. The address in Manassa for Dihyja was checked out yesterday. Two people, that never heard of him, have been living at his listed address since 2015. We have run deep searches on Dihyja for military, federal firearms, concealed carry license, criminal, civil, and found nothing." The second bullet point of the death-defying powerpoint ended.

Surprisingly, Parker turned the powerpoint off as well as the projector. Thank goodness, she isn't going to an electronic sketch pad, Tafoya opined quietly.

Parker brought up possible directions the case should follow. She asserted the tangent to follow was to get information from the Culebra Mining Company. That offered the best route to get a connection to Dihyja, suspects, and more information.

"Who should go to Culebra and follow up? Any volunteers?" Parker asked.

Parker looked at Tafoya, and the whole group turned around and looked at Tafoya. He turned around to see if anyone was in back of him. No one sat in back of him.

Turning back around, facing the group, smiling faintly, Tafoya said, "I'll take that vector to southern Colorado. It's not that far away...so, are we finished here?"

Tafoya and Romero decided to have lunch at Maria's Café on the way back to the Tulona Pueblo. Romero was hungry for the enchiladas his chef-cousin cooked at the café. Tafoya delayed calling Janet until later in the day. They sat at the rear of the dining room that had a laminate floor and Poncho Villa posters on the wall. Sitting with their backs to the wall, they conversed before their tacos and enchiladas arrived.

"You are headed to Culebra company," Romero stated. "I am going to drive along the fence line on the reservation side, across from Arroyo Luz, and look for entrances we might have missed. You locked the Chanson gate back after we detained Jason. We know the *mayordomo* forgot to lock it originally, giving Jason the opportunity to come on the reservation. I'm going to check the fence line again." Their enchiladas came, smothered in fresh green chile sauce. They ate, attenuating their conversation until they were half-full.

Tafoya ate quickly and asked, "Romero, when you interviewed Dihyja's mother, did you ask about any relatives at the Tulona Pueblo?"

"I did. She absolutely knew of no kinship to the Tulona. Matter of fact, she exhibited a hostility to Puebloan people."

"How so?" Tafoya inquired, scooting back in his chair, surveying the dining room.

"It had something to do with Kit Carson of Taos rounding up the Navajo in the 1860s for the "Long Walk" and cutting down peach trees. I told her, 'He didn't cut the peach trees. It was Captain John Thompson.' Since Carson was associated with Pueblo people, she didn't like the Tulona. History like that doesn't fade away, Tafoya."

Simultaneously, their radio coms went off. A major accident had occurred at the yellow blinking light. Their assistance was mandatory. They already heard sirens in the distance. Their check had already been put on the table—the staff was very attentive—and they placed cash on the table plus a twenty-percent tip. Romero and Tafoya ran out of Maria's Café, jumped in their vehicles and entered, with light bars flashing, the highway to the yellow blinking light.

Time went fast for Janet as she wrote field reports from her surveys in the Santa Barbara River area, near Peñasco. The Santa Barbara River always flowed. Its flow came from Jicarita Peak and Chimayos Mountains. She liked going up the forest road to the Santa Barbara campground, for the area was cool and green, even on the hottest days. Janet finished her reports late in the afternoon. Now it was six o'clock, and she had worked an hour overtime with still no message from Tafoya. She said, "Goodbye for now," to her coworkers and walked outside, not anxious to drive home to an empty apartment, but neither compelled to meet her friends at a bar for drinks. The beauty of the mountains fell upon her like cold, down-sloping winds, pushing all other senses aside. She saw the sharp outline of Tulona Peak against the sky. She was lonely. She felt lonely because no one was sharing with her, just then, the beauty of the montane landscape. Janet saw more yellow and red aspen slashing through green conifers than yesterday, a turning of season before her eyes in plain sight. Sadly, missing him, she thought of Tafoya.

At the Pueblo, there was a chill in the back room of his home; Cacique Leonard Bustamente shivered. In the next room, he heard the soft, melodious tones of Tulona speech, his wife and friend talking, laughing. Although it was mid-September, Bustamente started a piñon fire in the conical fireplace. He warmed himself, pulling his blanket tight around his body. He noticed the lessening of the sun's glow through the skylight, stirring his memory, his life. He stood up quickly, abruptly walking out of his home, leaving his wife and piñon fire behind. He climbed the ladders carefully and stood on top of Summer House.

High clouds and jet contrails pervaded the southern sky; to the north, cumulus clouds erupted ferociously over southern Colorado. He had failed to check the weather forecast on the radio and wondered if a change of weather was coming. The clouds appeared heavy, cobalt blue in places with the bottom edges clean-cut, un-ragged, crisp, as sharp as an obsidian knife. Several of his kinsmen joined him looking westward toward the setting sun. Burbles of conversation, in hushed tones, arose.

Gentle laughter, chuckles, and "Ays" evoked harmony for the moment. Bustamente drew his blanket tighter around himself and canopied his head, wondering how many more arcs of the sun he would see.

Janet's cell phone rang, her ringtone being Taos Pueblo music. She thought the Isleta needed their own ringtone, and the Forest Service deserved a ringtone of elk bellowing over at Eagle Nest Lake. She looked down—Tafoya! She had already entered his name into her contacts.

"Hello," she answered, nervously.

"Hi, Janet, this is Richard. How are you doing?"

"I could not be better, hearing from you now that you've come back from Navajo land," she replied haply. "I kept thinking that I might have to fly out to Sanostee Airport, if you were surrounded and under attack."

Tafoya really liked her, this biology specialist, pilot. He laughed, "I hadn't gone out to plunder, just investigate, so I was okay, but I would have called had I been in trouble."

"That's good. I would have come. How was Sheep Springs?" Janet asked.

"It was productive. I found out the true identity of our victim and some other things, so it was worth the drive." Tafoya paused. "Would you go out to dinner with me tomorrow, after work, say six o'clock? My schedule is subject to change, so if I can't make it, I'll call. And, I have Thursday, all-day off, so we could have dinner then, if I had to cancel." Tafoya made sure that they were going to get together, so he had the backup plan for Thursday. Come hail stones or storm, he was determined to see Janet.

"Yes, Richard, I'd love to have dinner with you." She thought to herself that she could do the morrow and Thursday, too.

They agreed to meet at Tablita's Restaurant at six o'clock in the lobby of the hotel. Tafoya was excited at seeing her in a dinner setting; Janet was warmed by the first move Tafoya made. If he hadn't called, she thought, I would have, Isleta-to-Tulona, biology specialist-to-tribal policeman, woman-to-man. Strangely, despite being by herself at the apartment, Janet no longer felt alone.

19

Tuesday, September 18, Day of Saint Joseph of Cupertino, Month of Corn Ripe Moon

Tulona policeman Tafoya made an appointment with the manager of the Culebra Mining Company in San Luis, Colorado for nine o'clock. The trip took an hour from Ojo Verde, going up NM SH 522, then changing to CO SH 159 at the state line. The manager was in his fifties, bald, a pot-belly, and moderate height, neither short nor tall. His face was round and red at the cheeks, a holdover from bourbon. He was a manager of the business end of the company; other personnel directed mining technology. The manager was the numbers guy: how much gold, silver, precious metals, even turquoise, were extracted? What's the cost of extraction? Market value? Tafoya was ushered into a large office with whiteboards of numbers, maps, and several filing cabinets, all of which bore substantial locks. Tafoya, after pleasantries, wasted no time in asking questions.

The manager had already pulled Dihyja's personnel file. "How long did Robert work here at Culebra?" Tafoya asked.

The manager looked down at the file, "Robert Dihyja was with the company from September 2006, laid off because of the recession two years later, rehired in March of 2009, then laid off with lots of other workers in 2015. Currently, we are way down in production and shutter our doors for weeks, depending on the value of metals in the markets." Tafoya sensed a permanent closing in the near future. The manager answered further questions about Robert. "He had a good employment record, few sick days taken, and had been elevated to crew chief because of his seniority and ability to lead." The manager gave Tafoya the residential address in Manassa and the address in San Luis.

"He lived in San Luis?" Tafoya asked.

"Yes, he and his friend, who also worked here, lived in San Luis for the last couple of years before the big layoff."

“What was the name of his friend?” Tafoya quickly asked.

“Andreas Saltwater, Andy for short. Let me get his personnel file.” The manager went to one of his filing cabinets, dialed in the combination, and pulled out Saltwater’s file. Andreas Saltwater had been hired in 2009, and his address corresponded to Robert’s, both in Manassa and in San Luis. He was laid off the same time as Robert. The manager said that Saltwater was also a good worker, no trouble noted in his file. There were no photographs of either of them.

“Did either of them leave a forwarding address when they were laid off?” Tafoya asked.

“They didn’t leave a forwarding address at the time of their termination, but a month after they left San Luis, each one of them sent the same post office box address to our front office in order to receive their yearly benefit information. We have a good retirement program,” the manager bragged.

Tafoya wrote down the post office box address. It was in Questa, New Mexico, about thirty minutes north from Ojo Verde, on SH 522. He would stop there on his way back to Ojo Verde.

As soon as he climbed back in the patrol car, Tafoya typed in the new information on the laptop, and added that he was going by the San Luis address, although he believed that Andreas had moved from the Colorado residence. Tafoya informed the stationhouse, in a separate email, that he was stopping at the Questa Post Office on the way back to Ojo Verde. He requested a copy of the Colorado driver license that would have a photo of Andreas Saltwater.

Tafoya found the San Luis residence unoccupied. He walked around the house and peeked in the windows where he saw only trash in the house—no furniture. The back door was unlocked, and he went in to look around. The bathroom’s mirrored cabinet, in its interior, smelled of men’s cologne. He couldn’t identify it, but it was definitely leathery and musky. The bathroom needed a thorough cleaning, as did the kitchen. Bedroom closets were empty, except for lonely coathangers. The living room hosted a satiliette dish, removed from the roof of the house. Tafoya wrote down the rental sign information and called the rental agency. The residence had not been leased out since Robert and Saltwater had left in 2015. The woman at the agency had the same forwarding post office box address in Questa as the Culebra Mining Company. She had mailed the deposit check to the Questa POB. “Do you want to rent the house?” the rental agency asked.

Pushing the rules of operating a patrol car as he crossed the Colorado-New Mexico border, Tafoya switched on the emergency flash bar and sped to the Questa Post Office, turning off the bar before he entered the city limits. The Questa Post Office smelled of paper—letters, magazines, manila envelopes, stamps. And Lysol soap. He asked to see the postmaster and was ushered in behind the counter to the postmaster's office. The postmaster was postmistress, Venessa Gonzalas. Showing his credentials to Gonzalas, he asked about the post office box of Dihyja and Saltwater. She went to a filing cabinet and pulled out the card for the post office box number.

"I see Andreas Saltwater was the name under which the box was rented in 2015. Robert Dihyja was a designated person to get the mail and receive mail. It was closed by Andreas Saltwater a couple of weeks ago, September 4. No forwarding addresses. Only one key was turned in. He had to pay for losing the second key."

Tafoya thought for a second, then asked, "In order to get a box number, you require some identification, don't you?" The postmistress replied in the affirmative and pulled up on her computer screen the full application. She replied that the identification Saltwater presented was a Colorado driver license. The address on the driver license was the same address in San Luis he had checked out. Tafoya asked if she remembered who came in to collect the mail and how often? She chuckled and said that it was impossible to know who collected the mail and how often. "I'm sorry," she said, apologetically. "People check their mail at all hours—day and night."

When Tafoya settled in the driver's seat of the patrol car to drive back to Ojo Verde, he looked at the laptop and opened the new message that had a link to Saltwater's Colorado driver license. Good! More facts!

The license data read, "Andreas Niesmith Saltwater. Born: 10.04.1962. Address: 112 Red River Road, San Luis, CO 81152. Height: 6 ft. 0 in. Weight: 180 lbs. Eye color: Brown. Hair: Dark Brown. Race: Native American."

Saltwater's photograph showed an oval face, long hair, a slightly large nose but not out of proportion. He had a non-descript look on his face, not grimacing, seemingly uncomfortable in having his photograph taken. Saltwater had no facial hair as expected. Tafoya looked closer at the photograph. There was a horizonal scar under his right eye. He was wearing a dark calico shirt, reminiscent of Navajo style, and hanging out of his left-side shirt pocket, there appeared to be a crumpled red bandanna, as if he had been wearing the bandanna and had stuffed it in his pocket for the driver license photograph. On the whole, Tafoya thought, he was neither handsome, nor toward the ugly. He was fifty-five years old. He would have a birthday in sixteen days, on the Feast Day of Saint Francis.

Tafoya looked at his watch: three o'clock. He drove fast to the Tulona

Pueblo police station. On the highway from San Luis and Questa, he sidestepped the thundershowers, but at the Pueblo, showers began to fall. The higher reaches of Tulona Mountain were hidden by clouds and fog, the yellow and red aspen trees obscured. Sergeant Romero met him at the station door, staring at the rain coming down on the plaza.

"Did you read my report on reconnoitering the boundary line between Arroyo Luz and the reservation?" Romero asked.

"No, I didn't scroll down for case updates," Tafoya replied.

Romero went on to explain that he had carefully driven the boundary line that morning before the rains came. He counted ten gates between the Chanson Restaurant gate and the last gate near the La Osa Road turnoff. "Every gate had been rammed at some time or another. All of gates were damaged, some of them really bad to the point that panel rails were broken," Romero explained. Further, he added that the last two northeastern gates, those closest to La Osa, were bent in a "V," and the last gate showed signs of multiple entries and exits.

"The chain and lock around the posts could be bypassed by simply unhooking a snap-latch, like that kind of latch used on a horse's lead rope. Unsnap the latch, unwind the chain, leave the lock in place, open the gate. That simple. There's been traffic through there recently," Romero said.

"So, the conveyor of Robert Dihyja's body probably came through a gate at the upper end of the fence line" Tafoya surmised. "I locked the Chanson gate on the afternoon of Jason Taylor's detention. All other roads were blocked because of ceremonial activities. Dihyja's conveyor, probably the murderer, came through the far gate near La Osa. He could have gone back out again the same way, or driven through the Pueblo since it was dark and rainy."

Romero nodded in agreement, then adding, "We still haven't found the kill site." They both shook their heads in frustration.

"Is there coffee made?" Tafoya asked. He was dragging and tired of driving.

"There's not a fresh pot, but I made some after lunch," Romero answered. Tafoya went back to the breakroom. Thunder crashed, the lights dimmed, went out, then came back on. He poured himself and Romero a cup and went back to the window, looking out over the plaza, and watched the cottonwood trees sway in the wind. Magpies flew back up the stream, finding shelter among thick brush and tree groves. Lightning flashed, then came the roll of thunder. The lights flickered again, and this time, went out and stayed off.

"Well, the Dancing Rock Co-op guys are going to be resetting the breakers all over the place with this storm," Sergeant Romero chuckled.

The Tulona tribal police station's backup electric generator started up, and the offices became bright again. Tafoya sat down at the front desk and began writing his notes for the day's investigation in the computer. Romero continued to look out the window at the rain coming down. Once Tafoya had finished his report, he fetched a yellow pad, standard letter size, and began to jot down pieces of information on the pad, drawing lines and arrows between pieces of disparate information, hoping to see relationships. He knew that what he knew was *not* all there was to know about Robert Dihyja.

On his yellow pad, Tafoya wrote, "Robert Dihyja—friend and roommate of Andreas Saltwater. Saltwater's whereabouts unknown. Questa POB for both Robert and Andreas. Both employed at Culebra Mining Company. Turquoise belt buckle—mine source unknown, lapidary unknown. Initials 'B' and 'L' on back, stand for Blue Lady. Pickup with Culebra logo—location unknown, seen near body."

Tafoya looked at the discrete bits of information. He suddenly realized he might make a connection to the case. He unholstered his cell phone and called the manager at the Culebra Mining Company. The manager answered on the second ring. Tafoya asked him if the company had sold their used pickups to employees—to Dihija and Saltwater in particular. The manager said, "Yes." He would look up the information and call him back. Within fifteen minutes, the manager called Tafoya back.

"I do keep good records, if I do say so, myself," the manager boasted. "The company sold a pickup to Andreas Saltwater in 2007. It was a black Ford 1996 pickup. We sold a blue Ford 1995 pickup to Robert Dihyja the same year. The rest of our used pickups we sold to used car lots all over the Four Corners area, and some car lots in Texas."

"Did you leave the Culebra Mining logo on the pickups?" Tafoya asked. The manager replied that the logo was scrubbed on pickups sold to used car dealers, but those cars sold to employees, they left the logo on the vehicles. Tafoya asked for the VIN numbers. The manager took a picture of the VIN numbers and other vehicle sale information on his cell phone and sent it to Tafoya. Tafoya did not hang up until the photos came through, clear and readable. Unfortunately, when he entered the information for a search on the New Mexico car registration site, the addresses that came up were the POB in Questa that was no longer used.

The license plate registrations, along with a description of the pickups, were sent out in a bulletin to law enforcement officials in New Mexico and the surrounding region. Tafoya felt he was getting warmer in finding Saltwater, and that might just lead him to solving Dihyja's death. Tafoya put away his yellow pad, stood up and stretched, and informed Romero he was taking off and going home. He was finished working as tribal policeman for the day. "I'm meeting Janet Rael for dinner at the Tablita's Restaurant at six o'clock."

Not wanting to pry, Romero said, "Well, have fun, brother. Say, 'hello,' to our snow-looks-like buddy, Jason Taylor, if he is on duty. He is going to be the ski instructor for my son, come the snow this winter." Tafoya said he would convey Romero's words. He ran in the rain to his pickup and looked up at the mountain and through the mists saw slashes of red and yellow aspen.

Earlier in the day, G. Armstrong Coe began a new habit pattern—walking to and from work. If necessary, Prissy, his wife, could come by and pick him up if the weather was bad, or if he was simply fatigued from the day's work. The weather forecast had indicated rain showers, so he had brought along a poncho. Coe's walk was invigorating, and as he opened the door to his bookshop, Fenster greeted him—faithful feline security guard. He let Fenster out for her morning constitutional, turned up the heat, cleaned the litter box, and made sure kibbles were fresh in Fenster's food bowl. Fenster soon came back to the front door, mewing to be let in. Coe complied with his security guard.

Shop business that morning was slow. He closed for lunch and walked to a sandwich shop on the plaza, having a tuna salad sandwich and iced tea. Returning after a forty-five-minute lunch break, he scanned his bookshelves, finding empty spaces and making notes about restocking. Coe noticed in the biology and geology section that Rodarte and Begay's, *Turquoise Mining in the American Southwest*, had sold out. He remembered the unsocial customer that had come in and paid cash for the Rodarte book. After taking inventory for an hour and waiting on customers, Coe pulled up his stool behind the front counter, sat down, and began to reorder books, using the website of each publisher. When it came to replacing Rodarte and Begay, *Turquoise Mining in the American Southwest*, he decided to call Tony Rodarte at The Silver Concho to see if he had additional books on *Turquoise Mining* that he might buy to replace his inventory.

Rodarte's counter clerk answered the telephone, patching him through to Rodarte. "Hey, Coe, how are you doing?" They exchanged pleasantries, and Coe asked him if he had extra copies of his book on turquoise mining. He needed to restock his geology section. Rodarte said he did, and he would take them out of stock; Coe could come and get them in the next couple of days.

"I'll autograph them and slip my business card in the book. Get some sales!" Rodarte said.

As Coe was about to hang up, Rodarte stopped him, "I had a guy come in a couple of days ago that wanted to talk about turquoise mining. He brought in my book and asked me to sign it. He said he had just purchased it from you."

"Tall, Indigenous-looking fellow, well-built?" Coe asked.

"Yeah, he was well-built, about fifty years old, I think. Fairly friendly, knowledgeable about mining. Asked about the La Osa Falls area bearing turquoise."

"I remember him. He wasn't very sociable with me," Coe said. "Is there turquoise up there at La Osa?"

"No, not any more. It's been pretty well mined out, and it's now under a protective association and they don't permit any prospecting. There are several stair-step falls up there, each of which is significant. One or two areas are, or used to be, sacred sites for the Tulona and Red Willow Pueblos. Anyway, he was interested in turquoise in the area, and I indulged his curiosity to a point. He asked me to sign my book, 'To Andreas, Best wishes with the Blue Lady, Tony Rodarte.'"

"Blue Lady? What's that about?" Coe inquired.

"He didn't answer, murmured something about a rich lady. I let it go."

"Thanks, Tony, I'll be by in the next couple of days to pick the copies up. You need to get more copies of your book printed. Take care."

Rain showers kept the dinner crowd thin at Tablita Restaurant. Jason Taylor served three tables in the main dining area. His coworker served two—not the best of days for waiters. The wind associated with rainfall blew softly, gusting quickly, then diminishing. Rain and wind stripped leaves from the cottonwoods, the leaves puddling in clumps at drain holes. Rainwater gave a sheen to the streets. Dancing Rock crews reset the breakers, and the streetlights came on, reflecting off the pavement into Tablita's front dining room on Paseo del Norte. The five o'clock early-crowd for dinner produced only two more table servings. Both servers would remain on duty until nine, regardless of the number of clients, because you never knew about drop-ins. Jason looked at the reservation logbook: Richard Tafoya, party of two, six o'clock. "Is that the tribal officer?" he started to say, as Tafoya and Rael walked up to the maître d' standing desk. "Yes, the very same," he said quietly.

Tafoya and Rael were seated in a small, open alcove that looked onto Ojo Verde Inn's inner patio. The patio was a courtyard for seven casita units built away from the main hotel. Two of the casita units were permanently occupied; one by an elderly rich heiress from New York, the other by a well-known, retired Hollywood actor who had played in crime films since the 1950s. Their table—Jason serving attentively, but not cloyingly—provided Tafoya and Rael a private space away from the windows facing Paseo del Norte and rain sheen from the street.

Tafoya and Rael looked out into the courtyard that had several beds of hollyhocks whose big flowers swayed in the wind. The overcast and raining sky darkened the courtyard and dining alcove. Jason lit a candle and took their orders. Each had a bowl of New Mexico green chile stew. Janet had her stew vegan; Tafoya had the meat version. With her pan-seared trout, Janet ordered a dry, white wine. Tafoya ordered the house red wine with his filet mignon, medium-rare. The dining room remained quiet and uncrowded, allowing them to talk without raising their voices. It continued to rain, and gradually the evening sunlight faded. Courtyard lights illuminated the hollyhocks; the candle from the table flickered softly as Janet and Tafoya talked of their growing up, first employments, his experience in Afghanistan, and her field work in the forest. She came to know him as Tulona and a public servant, protecting their community. Tafoya began to know her better as Isleta and a dedicated biologist, protecting land and wildlife.

"Each of us, it seems," Janet said, "are guardians of the world. You for the safety of people, me for the forests." Tafoya, in response to the truth of her view, raised his glass of red wine.

"To our work, to our cause, and...," he paused, "to the footraces!" He had wanted to toast to their relationship, but that seemed too sentimental, too early.

Biology specialist Janet Rael and tribal policeman Richard Tafoya clinked their glasses.

"So, you still not running on Saint Francis Day, Richard?" she asked. He replied that he was not going to run. He was going to be on duty. The elders had always excused him from that day's activities, but other kiva and sacred obligations through the year required his time.

Tafoya thought for a moment, then spoke, "You should come to Feast Day. I'll be around taking care of security, but we will see each other. Remember, no phones, or pictures!" he said, laughingly. "Lots of vendor food and sales booths, dances, races, pole climbing, the Black Eyes making fun. You'd have a blast, Janet."

She told him of the Isleta and San Ildefonso Feast Days she attended, and that she would try and make the Saint Francis Feast Day if work permitted. Janet knew she would like to see him at the Pueblo doing his work, observing him from afar, and then, just maybe, share a burrito at lunch.

After their main course, they ordered coffee, declined dessert, and began to taper off their first dinner together. Janet asked him about the case he had followed all the way to the Navajo reservation, a few days before, and to San Luis that morning.

"It's the case of Robert Dihyja, Navajo, born to the Two Rocks-Sit clan. No longer Robert Red Feather," he replied. Proceeding to tell Janet about his findings, she listened closely. He explained to her that they were looking for Dihyja's friend, a long-time roommate, coworker, person of interest, "We call them POI. Not suspect. The friend's name is Andreas Saltwater, also Navajo. After they were laid off at the mining company, they must have moved closer to Ojo Verde because they shared a POB in Questa."

"So, all you have to do is to 'stake out' the POI at the POB? Is that the right way to say it?" Janet chuckled.

"I wish it was that easy, but Andreas closed the POB a few days ago. Dead end there." Tafoya told her about the turquoise belt buckle and the mysterious origin of the mining source for the dendrite turquoise, explaining the rarity of the type. He thought an important key to solving the case was finding the mine that yielded the turquoise. "But, Janet, where to look?"

They continued to talk, but it was getting late; they had been in the alcove eating dinner and talking for two hours. It was time to go. Tafoya gave Jason the non-verbal hand signal for the check: scribbling an imaginary check in thin air.

Jason brought the check and said to Tafoya, "Please tell Romero and his son, 'Hello,' for me, would you?"

Tafoya looked at the check and placed his credit card in the check's billfold, "I will, Jason, thanks. Romero wanted me to tell you, 'Hello,' as well. He said you were going to instruct his son about skiing this winter."

After leaving a good tip to Jason, Janet and Tafoya left the restaurant and walked to the inn lobby. A water fountain was in the center of the lobby, and around the fountain a bench had been constructed where a few bar customers were watching the musicians set up a performance for later in the evening. Tafoya said he would walk Janet back to the parking lot. He was happy the evening had gone so well. He knew he would take another step in her direction sometime soon. How that would happen remained to be seen. But he would.

The rain had stopped and there were puddles of water in the parking lot. Cars were filling up the parking lot for the bar scene and live music.

Tafoya had to work tomorrow, and so did she. He found her red Subaru and stood beside the door as she climbed in.

"Richard, I enjoyed the evening. I hated for it to end."

Tafoya liked her words. He reached in and patted her on her shoulder. Her left hand came up and touched his hand. Her hand lingered for three or four seconds, by Tafoya's time count.

"Me, too, Janet. I promise to call you again so we can go out."

She closed the door to her red Subaru and rolled her window down.

"Richard."

"Yes."

"Do you realize that the Bureau of Land Management is next door to our Forest Service offices?"

"Yes, I do. Why?"

"It is there that people file claims for mining, including turquoise mining."

20

Wednesday, September 19, Day of Saint Januarius, Month of Corn Ripe Moon

At San Miguel, one more rainstorm passed during the night, leaving water puddles and deeper potholes on roads. The rainstorm acted like a power wash to San Miguel, and with morning, the village gleamed. The morning's warmth sent the aroma of mountain conifers flowing rich and sharp into the village. Armando stepped outside the house, inhaling the smell of piñon fire smoke and the forest of wet ponderosa. Zeke bounded out of sight into the woods. The Ortega horses recognized Armando and Zeke, neighing a greeting. One of horses clamped down with its teeth on a steel feed bin hanging down on the rail, raised it, then let it fall, creating a loud clanging noise. "Come down and feed us!" Armando sauntered down to the stalls, put some hay in the feed bin and a small amount of grain. Each horse went to their separate bins and began to chomp breakfast. Luis joined Armando at the corral.

Loretta looked out the kitchen window at her husband and only son. She was tired already. Armando complained about arthritis and aching joints. They were in their seventies, after all. The doctors down in Taos, below Ojo Verde, had prescribed medicines. High blood pressure medicine for the both of them, cholesterol-lowering drugs for Armando. Loretta wondered how it would all end? Heart attack, stroke, accident, gradual decline into decrepitude? And, wondering *how* brought Loretta to think, *where* will it all end? Here in San Miguel, a nursing home, assisted living? She was thinking not only of herself, but Armando. She cut short her ruminating intentionally, for it was a suffering process, and the Catholic church taught, "Take no thought for the morrow, for the morrow...." Armando and Luis came back inside and helped wash and put away the breakfast dishes. Loretta went outside and stood on the porch, clutching her apron and calling Zeke back to the house.

After finishing the dishes, Luis said he was going to the Pueblo to instruct Lion Walks Night on farriering. Armando told them he needed to go into the woodcutting area of the National Forest above Lama to gather and cut firewood. "I want our firewood pile to be big enough to get us through the winter. It's already good size, but we need more. I want it higher than the roof!" Loretta always worried when he cut wood in the forest because he used the chainsaw. Armando took an axe, but the chainsaw had to be fired up. Other woodcutters would be up in the forest in case he had an accident, but that gave little comfort to Loretta.

"Say a prayer before you start that monster, Armando," Loretta implored.

Luis loaded his sorrel gelding horse, Buck, into the trailer to take to the Pueblo. Buck was bomb-proof—the perfect horse to give farrier lessons. Luis drove to the Pueblo and parked near the old wall and corrals. Luis saw Lion with a group of men near the middle of the plaza digging with long shovels. They were digging a large round hole, about three or four feet in diameter, down six to eight feet. He knew they were digging a hole to set the pole for Saint Francis Feast Day ceremonies.

The Tulona had cut a tall ponderosa in the mountains and stripped its bark. The digging of the hole could have been done with mechanical drilling equipment, but that was forbidden. The Tulona believed they must put their flesh to the digging. Their muscles were the machine; their muscles were the diesel. They applied their bodies, not mechanical devices, to digging and pole climbing. The pole climber cut the food and mutton hanging from the top of the pole, not a person in a lift-bucket. To put a combustible engine and steel auger to dig the hole for the sacred event profaned it. Digging with their hands bound the Tulona together.

Luis was aware of the traditional ways. You would not have motorcycle races on Feast Day, now, would you? No, you run barefoot to connect with the earth, he thought. Luis had always wanted to be closer to Lion Walks Night's kiva knowledge, but he knew it was never to be. Lion saw Luis looking at their barehanded digging, and waved him over.

Several elders stood apart from the men working. Cacique Bustamente saw the labor of the Tulona men as community process in miniature. Bustamente surveyed the plaza, noticing onlookers to the digging and people at their tasks. He knew that those that looked on the digging remembered the day the work was done, the pole erected. The Tulona would feel compelled to attend the pole climbing that was the consequence of young men sweating for them on this day. This one act of communal work radiated a connection, like a stone thrown in a pond radiates ripples to the shoreline.

"These things must be preserved," Bustamente said, aloud.

"What is that you say, Grandfather?" asked a boy standing close.

Cacique Bustamente looked down and saw a boy, about nine years old, that had overheard his words. Bustamente turned to face him and gently said, "This digging, this work, this doing, this pole climbing for the people must be preserved."

He paused, and put his hand on the shoulder of the boy, "One day I want to see you climb to the top of the pole and lower down the food for the Pueblo people and say a prayer."

"I will try, Grandfather," the boy said earnestly.

The arc of Bustamente changed and he was buried in the San Francisco del Monte Catholic Church's graveyard for he was faithful in his own way and the young boy that stood beside him that day and earnestly said he would try did climb the pole on a Feast Day in light snow flurries and prayed and shivered and held on for life and cut down food and when he slid down the pole to his kiva brothers they bore him on their shoulders and paraded him all around the admiring and cheering crowd of tourists snow-looks-likes Black Eyes Puebloans and the boy now man thought of the day his Grandfather looked down upon him and asked him to try as he was borne around the plaza on the shoulders of his brothers he saw a vision of unending files of Grandfathers and Grandmothers and the People looking at him going back in time and into an uncertain Puebloan future.

Lion Walks Night and Luis turned away from the digging and walked to the corral by the old wall. Lion suggested that they take Buck and the trailer down to the common pasture corral and work under the arbor. "There's more space to work in the corral, and we will be away from the plaza." Luis unloaded the gelding and used a slip knot to tie Buck to a corral post. Lion told him that he had been reading up on farriering from some books he had purchased at Coe's Bookshop, but he knew reading was one thing, doing another.

Luis told Lion that the lesson would be short today, but it was very important to get it right. The first lesson was to raise and control each foot of the horse—not bind or harshly bend—but control the foot. Luis had brought along another pair of short-working chaps that covered the thighs, not the legs below the knees. He had Lion put them on. The chaps were stained with sweat, medicines, and liniments. Luis thought of the last time he was with Lion when they were working on Jess, Star, and Hija, and that he had gone, wearing work chaps, with Luis to see Dezba, Ben's new daughter. That made him think of Flowers Dancing, Quail Looks Away's sister.

Luis showed Lion how to lift the foot of the horse by squeezing on the lower tendon of the leg, next to the hoof. "Begin with the left front foot, work your way to the left back hoof, then right back hoof, then finally the right front hoof." He showed him how to put the leg and hoof between his legs, facing rearward, and how to extend the rear leg backward so as to confine the movement of the hindleg, as one trimmed and filed the hooves. Buck was bomb-proof and dozed with his head down as Luis made Lion go through the drill.

"Try to always have a hand on your horse's flanks or shoulders, so as not to startle the horse as you move around to each leg," Luis cautioned.

Luis instructed Lion how important it was to begin working with the horse's feet at an early age, even on the day they are born. "I use a small hammer on the foals the day they are born, gently tapping their feet, so they get used to humans messing with their hooves." They worked on bomb-proof Buck for an hour. At noontime Luis stopped the lessons. They loaded Buck in the trailer and drove to the old wall next to the plaza, finding a cottonwood tree to park the trailer under, so Buck would be in shade as they lunched at Luis's home. The hole for the feast pole had been completely dug, and several *vigas* had been laid across the hole to prevent animals and children from falling in.

Lion's *madre* fixed burritos for the two of them with plenty of red chile sauce and iced tea from the gallon jug. As Luis started to leave, he asked Lion if Flowers Dancing was visiting Quail.

"No, Flowers Dancing went back to Española," Lion answered. Lion saw a look of disappointment on his friend's face. "You like her, don't you, Ortega?" Lion chuckled. He already knew the answer. He saw Luis' attraction to Flowers Dancing on the day Ortega held Dezba. He also saw Flowers Dancing looking at Ortega, holding Dezba on his stained chaps under the skylight at Ben and Quail's home.

Ortega smiled and said nothing about his feelings regarding Flowers Dancing. As Ortega walked out the door onto the plaza to go back to San Miguel, Lion Walks Night shouted, "But Flowers Dancing will be back for Feast Day and footraces, bro!"

Tribal policeman Richard Tafoya arose early in the morning, had coffee, dressed in uniform, and started on the Dihyja case with renewed energy. He had three objectives for the day. Call the Saltwater family out near Tohatchi to see if Andreas Saltwater was known to them, gather up the turquoise belt buckle from evidence and have Tony Rodarte of The Silver Concho pry the stones from the bezel to verify the "B" and "L", and pay a visit to the Bureau of Land Management office to see if they had any record of an Andreas Saltwater or Robert Dihyja filing a claim. He called Sergeant Romero on the cell phone to ask him if he would call the Saltwaters at Tohatchi and find out about kinship relations to Andreas. Romero answered affirmatively and would call him back or enter new information online.

Tafoya turned his vehicle into the sheriff's office substation parking lot across from the Forest Service, but did not see Janet's red Subaru. The BLM was east of the Forest Service headquarters. He turned his patrol car around and drove across the street to the BLM headquarters to see what time they opened. The sign outside read, "8:00 a.m. to 4:00 p.m." He next looked at the Forest Service headquarters sign and saw that they had the same business hours. Satisfying his curiosity, Tafoya drove across the street to the sheriff's office and parked his patrol car. His cell phone rang. It was Romero.

"That was fast, Sergeant," Tafoya exclaimed.

"I talked to Rhonda Saltwater, the matriarch of the family and one of the elders of the clan. I noted the clan's name. Just a second," Romero set the phone down. Tafoya heard a rustle of paper. Romero came back on the landline. "Here it is, the Near the Mountain clan. I don't know if that means anything, but what does mean something is that Rhonda and her family know Andreas Saltwater. He is the son of Roger Saltwater, grandson of Niesmith Saltwater."

"When has she seen him last?" Tafoya quickly asked.

"I'm afraid she hasn't seen him recently. She said maybe two, three years ago. And, that was only briefly. He was still living out at San Luis." Tafoya and Romero knew the significance of Rhonda's information. Andreas Saltwater was the son of Roger Saltwater who despised Santiago Majerus. Andreas would have heard the story of Niesmith Saltwater, the Navajo medicine man who rejected his son's pleadings to be taught his father's chantways and curing ceremonials, favoring Majerus over his own son.

Sergeant Romero continued. "All three of these people, Andreas, Robert, and Majerus are connected in some way. Majerus is a medicine man, steeped in Navajo ceremonialism. Andreas's father loathed Majerus and held a grudge against his own father, Niesmith. A cousin of mine is full Navajo, and I remember how skittish he was of dead people and so-called ghosts. I remember his telling me of how, in the old days, if a Navajo died in a hogan the family would move out of the hogan, and let it fall into ruin. There was a cleansing ceremony for the hogan. But that's not what I'm driving at here. Listen to me, Tafoya."

Tafoya listened carefully to Romero. "Let's say Andreas was either the murderer or was at the scene of the killing of Robert. He transported Robert in the old Ford pickup with the Culebra logo to a spot across from Majerus, the man his father hated. One reason he might do that was to get the ghost of Robert Dihyja to haunt Majerus. The ghost would go across the road to Majerus and screw up his life, just like Majerus messed up his father's life."

Tafoya replied. "It's possible, Sergeant. One problem with that theory is that Andreas, if he was scared of ghosts and touching dead bodies, was handling dead Robert and touching him a lot! Maybe Andreas wasn't trying to infect Majerus with the dead body, but do something else."

"That would be true, too, Richard," Romero said. "Robert's body was carefully placed on the ground, not just dumped. His red bandanna was straightened on his head. So, there's some other motivation here that we don't know about."

"We've got to find Andreas. We've got to find the kill spot, Romero." Tafoya said.

Tafoya checked the turquoise belt buckle of Robert Dihyja out of the sheriff's evidence room. "Yes, I know the rules of the chain of evidence." He had already called Tony Rodarte at The Silver Concho. He agreed to take the turquoise out of the bezels and examine the underside of the turquoise for the letters, "B" and "L."

Tafoya knocked on The Silver Concho front door. The steel door protecting the front door had been opened, an adobe brick propping it, but the inner door was still locked. Rodarte came to the door and let Tafoya in. He locked the front door back. He had cleared a large workbench with focused lighting and a magnifying scope for close work. He had a 35mm Nikon camera positioned on a desk tripod to take pictures.

"I wanted to get some photographs of this dendrite turquoise, Richard. The dendrite is rare, and the color of the stone is uncommon. I want it for my files. Maybe one day the tribal police will give me permission to use the photos in a book?"

Using the photos in a new book about turquoise sounded like a good idea, but Tafoya wanted the Tulona Tribal Police to get a favorable mention. "Sure, but get permission from us first before you use them."

Rodarte mounted the buckle on a small vise attached to the table. He placed cloth squares around the silver buckle to prevent scratching. Taking photographs as he proceeded, he lifted the stones from the bezel. Using a felt cloth for polishing, he turned the stones over to examine the underside. He continued to photograph. He placed a stone under the magnifying scope.

"Yes, there's the 'L,'" he said as the let Tafoya look through the scope.

Tafoya peered and saw the "L," acknowledging the carefully incised letter.

"Look closer under the 'L,'" Rodarte directed.

Tafoya adjusted the magnifying scope and saw the numbers, "593." He looked at Rodarte, and Rodarte shrugged his shoulders, indicating he did not understand the significance. Tafoya wondered aloud if that had anything to do with the lapidary or some jeweler's code? Rodarte said he knew of no hallmark or lapidary using numbers for identification.

"We do know from Yazzie, who set the stones, had asked Dihyja what the 'B' and 'L' stood for, and that was 'Blue Lady'. Dihyja had mumbled something else about a lady of fortune," Tafoya said. "So, now we know five-nine-three is under the Lady, but for what reason?"

Rodarte interrupted. "I had a guy in here the other day that wanted me to autograph my book he had purchased from Coe's Bookshop, and he had me write, 'To Andreas, Best wishes with the Blue Lady.' And, of course, I signed my name. Do you think...?"

"Yes, there's a relationship, for sure," Tafoya said. "Coincidences abound in investigations, Tony, and some of them have no daylight between them. What else did he say? And, do you have any security tape from that day?"

"The tapes self-erase after forty-eight hours. Sorry, Richard."

Tafoya pulled up the photograph of Andreas Saltwater on his cell phone, and Rodarte verified it was the man who talked about the Blue Lady.

"That's the guy. He talked a lot about turquoise mining. Seemed knowledgable, skilled. He asked about the La Osa Falls caves."

Tafoya took down the information and asked Rodarte to examine the underside of the other stone.

Underneath the "B" were three more numbers, "918."

Rodarte took more photographs, front and back of the gemstones, and reset them exactly as they had been set originally. While at Rodarte's, Tafoya called Yazzie about the numbers. Yazzie had not carved the numbers, only the letters. Some other jeweler, or Dihyja, had carved the numbers. Tafoya placed the buckle back in the evidence bag, perplexed about the numbers "593" and "918," but excited about new connections falling in place. The La Osa Falls caves needed examining, requiring at least an afternoon of work. There were three waterfall areas and small caverns around each of them. Tafoya's next stop would be the BLM, next to the Forest Service and Janet's office. Maybe she would be available for a quick lunch.

He noticed as he drove by the Forest Service that Janet's red Subaru was gone, so a quick lunch with her was out of the question. After he checked in the evidence bag, he walked to the tribal police room and wrote up what he had discovered. As he was writing up the report, the numbers, "593" and "918," puzzled him again. Where had he come across numbers like that? Two three-digit numbers pushed together, forming one six-digit number. Where had he seen this kind of metric before?

Armando Ortega wiped the sweat from his face with an orange bandanna. Zeke, his companion for the day, puttered around and chewed sticks. The mid-afternoon sun had begun its decline to the west, beyond Pedernal Mountain. He had finished using the chainsaw and welcomed the quiet of the woods. Armando threw the last cut of logs in the back of his pickup, the stack reaching above the closed tailgate and beneath the back window. A blue jay flitted limb to limb above him, flying off on some errand to alarm other creatures. But during the day, the jay kept returning to Armando and Zeke, seeking their company.

Armando felt healthy, the blood flowing strongly in his arms. From his exertions, he saw his arteries well-formed in his forearms and hands. Armando projected ahead that before supper he would unload the wood onto the woodpile, storing it far enough under the woodshed to remain dry. Splitting and forming the logs with an axe awaited his future, but that would give him more exercise and, hopefully, good health. He loaded up his chainsaw and galvanized-steel gasoline container in the bed of the pickup, securing them with black tie-down straps. He whistled for Zeke, who jumped willingly into the front seat. He started his pickup and carefully, slowly, drove down the forest road. The heavy load pushed him. He coasted, barely using the engine.

Rather than drive SH 522 southward to San Miguel, Ortega decided to travel the Old Taos Road. The Old Taos Road, FR 493, took him by the old store and saloon. He would see new things and observe the drought conditions of the late summer season.

"Surely, this dry weather has got to break with more rains," he uttered under his breath.

The pickup steered better with a heavy load. As Armando slowed down to safely make a curve, he came upon the old saloon and store. The building had been kept reasonably painted and patched over the years. The mural of the whiskey bottle was beginning to fade and needed repainting. Over the past couple of years, Armando had noticed two pickups parked in back, but he had not seen the tenants. Slowing down for the curve, he looked over at the old saloon and saw a man loading cardboard boxes. Through the pickup's open door, he saw men's clothes had been thrown onto the backseat.

Looks like the guy is moving, Armando speculated. The man looked at Armando. Armando waved, but the man ignored him. Given the need for privacy that so many residents in backcountry held onto, Armando was not insulted. He drove on. He looked back in his rearview mirror and saw the man slam the rear door and go back into saloon.

Andreas Saltwater had seen Armando and his pickup full of wood. Saltwater was intent on vacating the old store and saloon. With camping gear loaded up, and the dendrite turquoise locked in a storage trunk in the back seat of his pickup under the clothes, he pondered his next move. He left behind a cache of raw turquoise buried a hundred yards back in the forest behind the saloon, returning later after he resettled. Saltwater's storage trunk of turquoise contained the most valuable raw turquoise they had chiseled from the Blue Lady—the dentrite.

"Good! Now, is it Questa or the camping ground?" Salwater said aloud. He started his pickup and drove to turn either north or south onto FR 493. Pausing, he turned north, toward Questa.

Luis Ortega arrived at the house in San Miguel a few minutes after his father. He unloaded Buck, pitched him some hay, and assisted his father unloading wood from the Columbine-Hondo woodcut area. Loretta came out of the house and told them that their cousins had called from Cimarron about the sheep they had pastured with them.

"Is everything all right?" Armando asked, alarmed that something had gone wrong. He realized he was still on edge from chainsaw work. The machine made him dicey.

"Yes, Armando, all is fine. They had rain yesterday, like we did, and the water tanks filled. They wanted to tell us there was going to be a *matanza* at the Trujillos in Cimarron, and we were invited."

"When is it?" Luis asked.

Luis liked *matanza*. It was a community festival, dating back to early Spanish days. It was ritual, but had not been conducted for a long time. Today, the essential reason for the *matanza* being conducted was community socializing, rather than its original purpose of providing meat for families during the winter months when there was no refrigeration. At the present, with local grocers and refrigeration, fresh meat was available anytime of the year. For Luis, the *matanza* meant meeting people and dancing to music. He thought that if he and Flowers Dancing became friendlier, he would take her to the Cimarron festival.

"They said a month or two after the Saint Francis Feast Day at the Tulona Pueblo," Loretta answered.

Laughing, Armando said, "Oh, I see. They probably also asked if we would contribute a lamb or two for the feast. They asked far enough in advance, didn't they?"

Loretta told him that she had granted one lamb for the *matanza*, since one-half of the flock was hers. Armando concurred with her decision and added that the next time they talked with the cousins, he would add a lamb of his own.

"There hasn't been a *matanza* we've been invited to in ten years. I wonder what is going on with the Trujillos to do this?" Armando said.

"Is one of them running for political office?" Luis said, and laughed.

21

Thursday, September 20, Day of Saint Andrew Kim Taegon, Month of Corn Ripe Moon

Early Thursday morning, Sergeant Romero and Officer Tafoya met at the Tulona police station. They agreed that Romero would attend the Tribal Council meeting that morning to hash out security details about the upcoming Feast Day on October 4, two weeks away. Tafoya was supposed to have the day off, but he declined to take it. He wanted to drill down further in the Dihyja investigation. The numbers, "593" and "918," on the back of the dendrite turquoise belt buckle, puzzled Tafoya. Romero had not come up with any solutions to the numbers, although he had rearranged the numbers in a dozen ways on his legal pad.

"Enough with the numbers for now!" Romero said. "Let's consider a couple of other things. Why hasn't Andreas come forward to volunteer information about Dihyja? They were friends, roommates, worked together. I'll tell you why. Andreas is hiding something. He has a guilty conscience. He knows if he shows his head on this case, we will have a lot of questions, and he doesn't want to provide answers. He's hiding something, and it's not good."

"I agree, Tony," Tafoya said. "We've got to find Andreas. I'm still fixated on the numbers and I feel they will reveal something, but I'm not sure what."

Tafoya rose from his chair and walked to the front window, looking out on Tulona Plaza. It was shortly before eight o'clock, and not much was stirring in the Pueblo. The sun had risen above the mountains, no shadows on the mesas toward the Tusas. The weather forecast for the day predicted warm temperatures in the eighties with clear sky, light winds from the south. Tafoya saw Ben Lovato amble over to a neighbor's house. He heard the school bus brake in back of the station to transport children and teenagers to Ojo Verde and the Pueblo primary school farther down the road. Tafoya noticed the Feast Day pole had been stabilized in the ground; long nautical-thick ropes dangled from two short *vigas* crisscrossed at the top. The pole was yellow, shiny, stripped of bark.

"That's a slick pole to climb this year, Romero."

Romero looked up from his doodling and saw the pole. He reminisced about pole climbing in the past, mentioning the year that the Black Eyes had to raise a wooden ladder up against pole to give a boost to the climber.

"I remember that year," Tafoya said. "My father was one of the Black Eyes that day."

Tafoya went back to the breakroom to get himself and Romero another cup of coffee. As he sat Romero's coffee cup down on his desk, Romero said, "We have an upload from the state police out in Gallup about Dihyja's college transcript."

"Oh, anything interesting?" Tafoya asked.

"Have a look for yourself, Richard," Romero said, turning the monitor toward Tafoya.

Tafoya adjusted the large monitor so he could read standing up. Dihyja had gone to the community college run by the University of New Mexico in Gallup. Dihyja's course load over a two-year period included the normal load of history, English, mathematics, some business courses. His grades were Bs and Cs; an A in history stood out. Dihyja also had taken a summer course in archaeology field school that was on the junior-senior level.

"Look at this, Romero. He took a field school course in archaeology. That must have been by special permission because it's upper level. That was his last six hours of coursework in Gallup; he earned two Bs." Romero looked at the transcript, remarking that Dihyja should have stayed with his studies and avoided Ojo Verde. Tafoya wondered where the field school was held. It must have been near Gallup since he was living with his family. Tafoya pulled out his notebook and made a note about the field school.

After finishing his coffee, Tafoya informed Romero he was going to drive up to La Osa Falls and examine the caves. Rodarte at The Silver Concho had told him the day before that Saltwater had quizzed him about turquoise in the caves. La Osa was not that far away, and he would only be at the site for a couple of hours.

"There's a cell signal up there at La Osa. Check your phone when you get up there, in case I need you, Tafoya," Romero ordered.

Tafoya drove the Explorer patrol car that had all-terrain tires and four-wheel drive. He drove out of the plaza onto Abalone Road, past the Tulona Mountain Casino, and entered traffic on US 64. At the yellow blinking light, he turned east toward Arroyo Luz and La Osa Falls. As he drove through the village of Arroyo Luz, he noticed a good breakfast crowd at the Calico Cow. He drove past Santiago Majerus's long lot home and the *descanso* that had been set up for Dihyja alongside the road. Some new plastic flowers had been laid at the cross.

The La Osa Road branched off to the north from Arroyo Luz toward the falls and caves. The road was paved for a half-mile, then devolved into a well-maintained dirt road. The elevation was around 7,500 feet, and the cool mountain air had attracted expensive homesites and corporate retreats. Continuing on past the homes, the road became rough. Tafoya shifted into four-wheel drive, continuing on a number of switchbacks, taking him up to the first of the three waterfalls and caves. Tafoya was able to park within a hundred yards of the first two falls and caves. The view out toward the west was spectacular. He saw the Tusas Mountains and the Rio Grande Gorge. Farther away, the Jemez Mountains rose in a blue, faraway haze. He looked at his cell phone; he had four bars of strength.

Although the forest was lush and green, the drought had slackened La Osa's waterflow. Tafoya stepped carefully down the trail to the first waterfall, its cave behind. He walked under twenty-foot ceilings and saw pictographs higher up on the walls that included circles, crosses, shaman figures. Most of the pictographs had been vandalized. He walked back to areas that had been chiseled away, but showed no recent mining. Campfires had been built recently; charcoal littered the ground. Tafoya was surprised there was little trash. He counted one plastic water bottle and two cigarette butts.

Leaving the first falls, Tafoya stepped down the trail to the second falls. It was a smaller cave. He looked carefully at a newly chipped-away area at the rear. He scraped away loose dirt and uncovered black-on-white potsherds. He picked up a handful of chipped rock, put it in a plastic baggie, and shoved the baggie in his knapsack. He turned his flashlight on the ceiling and saw a couple of pictographs that replicated the first cave, except there were no shaman figures. Tafoya unholstered his cell phone and took photographs of the cave as he had done at the first cavern. At the spot where he had found the potsherds, he smoothed the dirt back over the black-on-white remains.

Tafoya walked back to his vehicle. The third La Osa waterfall and cave compelled him to drive back down two switchbacks, and then turn onto a rough road and park the vehicle. The trail to the third falls appeared to have been little used. Leaves, twigs, and branches lay on the trail, indicating few visitors. The third cave of La Osa was the largest. No water fell over the ledge, but there were signs of moisture on the walls.

The ceiling was twenty feet high and the interior went back fifty feet. Three short tunnels of five to ten feet angled off from the main cavern. The pictographs in the cave were closer to the floor. The pictographs were geometric like in the other caves.

Tafoya flashed his light into each of the three tunnels. There was only one tunnel tall enough to stand in; the other two tunnels required him to crawl in on his hands and knees. Shining his light into the smaller tunnels, he saw no activity, mining or animal. The larger tunnel harbored blown-in debris. He took photographs. His cell phone was down to forty percent power. Tafoya sighed and thought his efforts at La Osa essentially worthless, other than to eliminate investigative tangents to Saltwater and Dihyja.

As Tafoya walked out of the third cave, he stopped, turned around, and looked at where he had been. He saw a narrow gulch on the left side of the entrance to the cave, rising upward with juniper trees obscuring the way. He noticed that dirt in front of the junipers had been disturbed, and a tree branch twisted awry—possibly by a large animal. Tafoya, having come this far, decided to investigate. He walked over to the disturbed dirt, and with his arm pushed the juniper branches to one side. The disturbed path became a discernible trail. He walked back twenty feet, discovering a smaller cave that angled away from the trail toward the third falls. The cave was ten feet high, and looked to be, as he shined his flashlight all around, ten or fifteen feet long. He stepped into the cave entrance, abruptly stopped, and stared at the cave floor.

Seeping out from the ground was a dark-stained, blackish blotch. The area of saturation was an oval of three or four feet. A putrid, organic, dead smell rose up. Tafoya side-stepped the blotch. He shined his light on the wall and saw fresh chiseling, and underneath on the floor of the cave, he saw a geology hammer. Beside it, a sharp, pointed chisel bore dark bloodstains on its surface. A large shaman figure had been pecked on the wall, an ancient petroglyph, intact, not vandalized. He took photographs and backed out of the cave carefully. He looked down at his cell phone and saw he had two bars of signal strength. He scrolled up a familiar number from his contact list and activated the number.

"Romero. I've found the kill site."

Within an hour, law enforcement arrived on the scene: Taos County Sheriff's Department, New Mexico State Police, and Sergeant Romero of Tulona Tribal Police Department with additional officers. The F.B.I. in Albuquerque relayed, "We are on the way." The forensic team of the sheriff's department took charge of data collection. Tulona WarChief

Juan Concha drove an off-road vehicle to ferry equipment and evidence to and from the scene. The warchief objected loudly to the cutting of the brush and trees that hid and sheltered the entry to the scene.

"Don't prune those trees to get in there. Let me show you what to do."

Concha took rope and baling twine and encircled the brush and trees. Then he pulled the rope, anchoring brush and trees to larger trees nearby. "See? I made you a clear path and saved the trees." Although La Osa caves were under private land protection, Concha said he and his kinsmen would patrol the area until snows came and forced hikers away.

"This used to be ceremonial ground, years ago, in a faraway time," the warchief said.

Diane Parker, F.B.I. Special Agent in charge, arrived before dusk. With a large entourage in tow, she examined the site and nearby cave, issuing orders for gathering evidence and taking photographs. Generators provided power for klieg lights and equipment.

Tafoya said, under his breath, to Romero, "I'm sure she is putting together a powerpoint presentation in her head right now to brief her superiors back in Albuquerque."

Parker heard a quick briefing from the on-site team. She asked, how and why did they know to come to La Osa? The deputy sheriff nodded his head in the direction of Tafoya. Tafoya gave her the rationale for his La Osa investigation.

"I got a lead from Tony Rodarte at The Silver Concho in Ojo Verde. Andreas Saltwater had come in to his shop and talked about La Osa turquoise. Saltwater was a close friend and roommate of Dihyja. I thought the falls and caves needed investigating, if only to eliminate them as a concern. So, that's how we got here today, Agent Parker."

"Well done, Tafoya, well done!" Parker said. Tafoya nodded, looked at Romero who quickly looked up in the trees for any sign of wildlife that would distract him from the awkward exchange.

The cadre of investigators worked together with the sheriff's department commanding the scene. After several hours, members of the collection team signed off and went back to Ojo Verde. Sergeant Romero returned to the Pueblo, but Tafoya remained at the site until the sheriff's department forensic team concluded their work at eleven o'clock. He then hitched a ride back to his vehicle with WarChief Concha who drove the ATV.

"So, what do you think happened at La Osa, Tafoya?" the warchief asked.

"The forensic team will do the bloodwork and fingerprints and give us the science, but this, I think, is true. Dihyja was killed at La Osa Falls cave. It's Saltwater that plunged the chisel into Dihyja. He dragged or carried the body to his pickup. Loading Dihyja into the pickup bed, he drove back down La Osa Road to the Arroyo Luz intersection. At that point, Saltwater directly crossed Arroyo Luz Road, opened the broken gate, and drove to a spot down the fence line on the reservation where he dumped the body."

"But, cousin, why didn't Saltwater leave the body at the cave? He left everything else, chisel, hammer, gleanings of rock."

Tafoya and Concha gripped their siderails, as they went over a bump in the road. "I don't know, Concha. It's very strange, but I intend to find Saltwater and make him tell me."

The warchief steered carefully around another bump in the road and said, "You know as well as I do, cousin, those caves at La Osa have always been power spots. Power spots for good medicine, power spots for witchcraft as well. I'm glad we Tulona abandoned the caves long ago." WarChief Concha and Tafoya bumped fists in agreement.

"Let us go home, cousin," Concha said.

22

Friday, September 21, Day of Saint Matthew, Month of Corn Ripe Moon

Aspen trees continued to turn, and larger swatches of yellow and red swiped the mountains' dark green conifers. Cold mornings always occurred, but temperatures were lowering into Quiet Time, and more blue-white smoke rose from stove pipes and chimneys. The turning of aspens for Jason Taylor, who waited tables at Tablita's, meant an influx of tourists to see the colors—more tourists, more tips toward his season pass and ski equipment; Ben Lovato and Lion Walks Night planned for ceremony on Saint Francis Feast Day; tribal policemen Tafoya and Romero worried about security for the vespers and Feast Day, as their kinsmen gathered aspen and cottonwood branches from the mountains; G. Armstrong Coe looked at the changing of aspens as vistas he wished to paint; and the Ortegas saw the yellow slashes of aspen from another angle—it meant checking their wall calendar for dates to buy and store hay for sheep and horses.

The people of New Mexico's northern Rio Grande lived with the land, the beautiful territory alongside the sacred mountains of cold, high country. The Month of Corn Ripe Moon was drawing to a close. The Month of Leaves Falling Moon was coming, a time when leaves fell in abundance, exposing sky and allowing Wind Old Woman to blow forcefully through bare trees, altering destinies in the cold, high country. All residents were bent and tasked by the weather, the wind—like every other thing, organic and inorganic, on the face of the earth.

Tulona policeman Tafoya arose early and, after dressing in uniform, drove into Ojo Verde to Maria's Café for a breakfast burrito, orange juice, and coffee. By phone, he checked in with Sergeant Romero, informing him he was going by the BLM office to inquire about mining claims under the names of Saltwater and Dihyja. Not knowing how the BLM kept records, he might be there two minutes, or two hours. As Tafoya drove away from the Maria's Café, he looked up at Tulona Mountain for patches of yellow and red; he saw yellow, mainly, and drove on. When he turned into the BLM parking lot, he glanced over at the Forest Service parking lot, expecting to see Janet's red Subaru. No car, no Janet. Tafoya parked his patrol car facing outward and walked into the BLM office headquarters.

After stating his business, and emphasizing his inquiry involved a murder case, he was shown promptly to the office of BLM record keeping. It was a large office, staffed by three people, large filing cabinets set against the walls, and work tables with topographic and geological maps spread around. A large Smokey the Bear poster, with the fire-danger needle set at "Low", had been permanently affixed to the wall. Tafoya was greeted by an older woman in her fifties with gray hair cut short, wearing a BLM uniform. Her name was Bessie Talbot; she shook his hand firmly, asking him to have a seat in a chair beside her desk. Tafoya was accustomed to working with maps, but this office was an uber-ultra map place. It reminded him of his military tour in Afghanistan, when they received briefings before a mission with map coordinates, time and distance analyses, objectives, order of battle. He was glad that part of his life was over.

"What can I do for you, Officer Tafoya?" Bessie said. She had sky-blue eyes; the whites of her eyes were as clear as clouds. Healthy eyes, good person, sober for decades. Tafoya explained the rudiments of the case, asking if anyone had filed a mining claim under the name of either Andreas Saltwater or Robert Dihyja within the area.

"Let me look." Bessie drew out her keyboard from under the desktop and typed in Andreas Saltwater. "No, nothing under any Saltwater. Let's try the other name. No, nothing under Dihyja either. Let me scroll through similar names." She scrolled, shook her head, "No," and frowned.

Tafoya began to stand up but Bessie said, "Wait a minute, Officer. We have another record base to search. It's an inquiry record. A record of people that ask information, but do not continue to file the paperwork to get a claim. It takes a minimum ten-thousand-dollar bond deposit, or more, to get the claim, and not many people, other than a corporation or syndicate, have that kind of money."

Bessie clicked another link on her keyboard, fetching another database. She looked down at her notepad and typed in the name, Andreas Saltwater.

"Got him! And Dihyja, too. They came in last year, August twelfth, to inquire about filing a claim. One of our filing clerks at the front counter gave them information about the filing process. It says here in her notes they already had a name, Blue Lady, picked out for the mining claim. But when she told them about the bond deposit they had to make, they looked shocked and declined to go any further in the process. Dihyja remarked that maybe they could get a syndicate out of Santa Fe and file the claim. His partner, Saltwater, became frustrated at that suggestion. They never went any further on the claim. The filing clerk entered detailed notes."

"Did they say where they wanted to file?"

"Yes, somewhere in the Carson National Forest."

"Well, that sure narrows it down," Tafoya said.

Tafoya asked for a copy of the inquiry record; Bessie printed off the one-page record. He told her he was appreciative of her help, and she replied she wished she could have been more specific on the location. "I know, Officer, the National Forest is a big place. One-and-a-half-million acres. Sorry."

Tafoya concluded that at least there was additional corroboration the Blue Lady was a mine. Plus, evidence surfaced of conflict between Dihyja and Saltwater over bringing in outside capital. That's good, and that's more than I knew when I started this morning, he thought. Exiting BLM, Tafoya looked over to see if Janet's red Subaru was parked under the Forest Service solar-panel carport. The red Subaru was nowhere to be seen.

Tafoya turned north on Paseo del Pueblo, his destination being Coe's Bookshop. He hoped Coe opened earlier than ten o'clock. As he turned northward, a block behind him, Janet wheeled into the Forest Service headquarters. She saw a patrol car, but could not tell if Tafoya was behind the wheel. Once she stopped under the solar-panel carport, she wrote a text message to Tafoya, "Thinking about you. Hope all is well. I see the aspens! Later." Janet paused for a moment after writing the text. Should I hit, "Send", or "Delete"?

She wondered if sending a text would turn Tafoya off? Why am I hesitant? Am I hesitating because I don't want to scare him away? She shook her head, this is nonsense! I'm thirty years old. If sending a text message offends him, then we have a problem. I'm sending the text!

Janet pushed, "Send," into internet ether. Pocketing her cell phone, she walked into the Forest Service headquarters, vowing not to look at her cell phone for at least an hour. She turned off her ringer sound, settling behind the front counter after pouring herself a cup of coffee. She did not last "not-looking" for an hour. She looked down at her phone after five minutes and saw a text from Tafoya.

"Been thinking about you, too, Janet. We need to see the aspens up close—together."

As Tafoya walked into the Coe Bookshop, a cat followed directly behind him. From behind the counter, Coe said, "That's all right. The cat belongs here about as much as I do these days. What can I help you with, Officer?" Tafoya explained to Coe he wanted to show him a picture of a Person of Interest in the Robert Dihyja case, and see if he had ever seen the man. On his cell phone, Tafoya showed Coe a photograph of Andreas Saltwater. Tafoya withheld the fact that Tony Rodarte of The Silver Concho had told him that Saltwater had purchased his book at Coe's.

Coe looked closely at the photograph. "Yes, I've seen him before. Strange dude. Somewhat unfriendly, paid in cash, no receipt."

"Why do you remember him so well, Mr. Coe?"

"He was on a mission for geology, mining, books on turquoise. Usually, people that come in here are browsers. Some customers shop with focus, nearly all are friendly. But this guy wasn't. That's why he stands out. He was in here only a week or so ago."

Tafoya learned further from Coe, "Saltwater did not like Fenster." Coe added he saw Saltwater pull into traffic, headed north on Paseo de Pueblo, driving an old, dark-colored Ford four-wheel drive with new tires. The contrast of old pickup with new tires caught his attention. Coe could not remember if there was a logo on the side of the pickup, but he didn't think so. That opened the possibility, Tafoya surmised, that Saltwater had scrubbed the logo to hide the identity of the pickup. After thanking Coe for cooperating, and giving a scratch to the purring Fenster, Tafoya drove to the tribal police station.

Across from the police station stood the Tulona Feast Day pole, fifty feet tall, stripped of bark. The pole in the middle of the Pueblo Plaza seemed foreboding, impossible to climb. Tafoya uttered a prayer for Feast Day and the Black Eyes. He entered the station; Sergeant Romero was at the front desk, going over the data collection and analysis from the third cave at La Osa. Tafoya went to his office and began to do the same. The F.B.I. laboratory in Albuquerque had begun work early in the morning, and results were being posted hourly.

After the noon hour, Santiago Majerus decided to go to Arroyo Hondo and buy groceries at the small store. The business had been in operation for decades at the crossroads of SH 522 and the old road to Tres Piedras. The old road, now designated B-007, descended to the Rio Grande, crossed the river via the John Dunn Bridge, then ascended in switchbacks to the top of the mesa, then heading west-northwest in a straight line to Tres Piedras. The B-007 was renamed Montosa Road on top of the mesa. When he was younger, Santiago had swum at the bridge site over the Rio Grande, its water cold, fast-flowing. Farther southward in the big river was Manby Springs, a hot spring, at the river's edge.

The small store at the crossroads was Hondo Seco Market and Spirits, selling liquor, wine, beer, and groceries. Flush on the southside of the Hondo Seco Market was a saloon and dancehall. Majerus had more good memories than bad at the dancehall. He had taken his girlfriend from Questa to the dancehall a few times, and after they had broken up, he had come to have a few beers and dance with the single women on Saturday nights. Ojo Verde had its places of Saturday night revelries, but he preferred the smaller community socials at Arroyo Hondo.

Majerus pushed a small shopping cart along the three aisles, picking up coffee, bread, canned peaches, fresh tomatoes, and chili peppers. He was looking over the fresh meat in the butcher's section for ground chuck, when an unfamiliar voice spoke behind him.

"Did he ever teach you the Big Godway, Mr. Majerus of Arroyo Luz?" The voice was hoarse, a kind of brittle, rattling tone that bespoke dark stories. Stories that must remain untold.

Majerus slowly turned around and saw a man he did not know, but had facial features that seemed familiar. He did not understand what the man had said.

"What did you say?"

"I said, 'Did he ever teach you the Big Godway,'" Again, the voice broke hoarsely.

Majerus clearly understood the words, but not the context, not even remotely.

"I'm getting groceries and I have no idea what you're talking about. Excuse me." Majerus turned back around, nervously continuing down the aisle to finish his list and get away. He would pick up fresh meat, elsewhere.

The stranger spoke again, "My name is Andreas Saltwater, born to the Bead People, born for the Black Streak Wood People. My father was Roger Saltwater, and my grandfather was Niesmith Saltwater, the man that taught you the Red Antway, but would not teach my father."

Majerus stopped, turned slowly around, and looked at Andreas. The familiarity in the man's face he had seen earlier, now refocused in seeing his Navajo teacher's facial features in Andreas Saltwater. This was a bad situation. Tafoya had called him on Wednesday, informing him that Andreas Saltwater, the grandson of Niesmith Saltwater, was probably living nearby and was associated with Robert Dihyja who had been dumped across from his home three weeks before. Now, he was face-to-face with him. The store attendant heard part of the exchange between the two men, and she came out from behind the counter, leaning over to peer down the aisle.

Majerus gave her the hand signal to call the authorities. Being between Questa and Ojo Verde, and knowing the behavior of people in an isolated area could run aggressive, the store attendant needed no further prompting. She grabbed her cell phone and walked out the front door, dialing 911, as she stood in front of the saloon. They would respond immediately with the Taos County Sheriff's Department and the Tulona Tribal Police; the tribal police would get there first.

"What do you want of me?" Majerus asked, wishing he had gone into Ojo Verde to get groceries.

"You are too late to give me or my father anything. You should never have come to Tooh' Haltsooi and learned the Red Antway. Bad medicine began with you."

Majerus stood still and made no effort to reply.

"Make the ghost rest!" Saltwater spoke forcefully, taking a step toward Majerus.

With neither pistol nor knife, Majerus stood aside from his grocery cart. He pushed his hat back on his head. Then in a powerful repositioning of his body, he put his right arm straight out, palm opened, fingers spread out in a halting gesture. His left arm he crooked as if shaking a hand, then pointing like a bison-horn knife, he confronted Saltwater. Thus, facing his enemy, he assumed the posture of power to repel evil that Niesmith Saltwater, his Red Antway teacher, had taught him. Would this work against Niesmith's grandson?

Slayer of enemy gods, help me, Majerus prayed silently.

Saltwater stopped, as if frozen by an invisible force. He turned around and stalked out of the store and past the clerk who darted inside. Majerus ran to the door. He saw Saltwater get in an old Ford pickup with new tires and drive eastward, burning rubber across SH 522, in the direction of the mountains and countless roads, where he would be impossible to find. Majerus watched as the pickp disappeared over a hill.

Yes, Andreas, your grandfather taught me Big Godway, Majerus thought.

Majerus heard a siren coming from the direction of Ojo Verde. Over the rise of the hill, he saw the familiar green color and black stripes of the Tulona tribal police car. But Andreas was already out of sight, lost to discovery. Majerus stood still in front of Hondo Seco Market and Spirits. He saw cottonwoods alongside Rio Hondo, hearing faintly the rattle of their leaves, as magpies glided down onto sandy shoals. He inhaled, letting his breath out slowly. Majerus sighed, deeply again, resigned to what lay before him.

"My enemy is here."

23

Saturday, September 22, Day of Saint Lorenzo Ruiz, Month of Corn Ripe Moon

On Saturday morning, more information came in from the Albuquerque F.B.I. field office and forensic lab regarding the third cave at La Osa. Blood samples on the cave floor and chisel were definitely that of Robert Dihyja. The sharp chisel found at the scene conformed to Dihyja's fatal wound in his left side. Two sets of boot prints had been found, one being the Red Feather boots Dihyja wore; the other set of boot prints were from a different individual. The fingerprints on the chisel were of two individuals, Dihyja and another unidentified person. Dihyja's prints were faint on the chisel, but the other prints were clear and superimposed over the fingerprint whorls of Robert Dihyja.

The F.B.I. report further concluded that Dihyja did not commit suicide by stabbing himself in his side. The angle of entry was more from the posterior of the body than the anterior. It was impossible for him to stab himself from the posterior angle, or even fall on the chisel from that angle. Another person stabbed him from the side. Whether the person had stood in front of him and stabbed him, or surprised him from the side was undetermined. The F.B.I. concluded that the chisel at La Osa was a common, non-machine tool used in geology work. The chisel had recently been sharpened.

As to chips and rocks found at La Osa, the turquoise was moderate quality and had no dendrite qualities like the belt buckle. The turquoise from the crime scene and the belt buckle of Dihyja were of two separate mining sites. The geology hammer found at the scene had fingerprints of both Dihyja and the unidentified individual. A global search for identifying the second individual's fingerprints turned up no matches in the databases.

Tafoya and Romero studied the F.B.I. report. "It says here that the unidentified fingerprints were associated with the blood on the chisel," Romero said.

"Yeah, that's good evidence connecting the two people. I'm still at a loss to explain why Dihyja was carried to Majerus's place, but I'm sure we will find out if we can capture Saltwater," Tafoya said. "We missed a chance yesterday, but we know he is still around here and has ghosts on his brain."

Romero agreed. He replied it was time that they got onto other things, such as investigate an attempted break-in at the tobacco shop and market on the edge of the reservation. "There'll probably not be much we can do with tobacco thieves, but at least it will get us away from the Dihyja case for a while."

"Yes, and away from the ghost," Tafoya said, hitting the snooze key on his keyboard, putting his computer to sleep.

Later that Saturday night, Tafoya backed his police vehicle under the carport at his house on the reservation. He had talked with Janet earlier about chasing Saltwater, and she had told him about her field survey that day along the Rio Fernando near Taos. "We found evidence of beaver in the river, Richard!" she told him excitedly. Tafoya was on call for the night. He double-checked power in his cell phone and raised the landline phone from its cradle to hear the dial tone. He had enough cell phone power; the dial tone hummed. Tafoya stepped outside for a few minutes before he went to bed. He saw the lights of Ojo Verde to the southwest and, even farther in the distance, the twinkling lights of Los Alamos, the atomic city of World War II, now the nuclear laboratory run by the U.S. government and the University of California. Above him, the stars shined bright. He had refused to set up any outside lighting at his home, so the Milky Way and the Night People appeared in full glory, twinkling and dancing.

Tafoya's cell phone ringing woke him up at two forty-five. It was Romero. He was driving up from Ojo Verde to the Tulona station. They had received information on where Andreas Saltwater was living, and they needed to draw up an operational plan. Tafoya said he would meet Romero and the sheriff's deputies at the station. Tafoya put on his tactical, dark-green uniform, preparing for serious business. When he emerged from his home, the air was chilly, but his field coat was insulated with Hale-Tex, and he was warm. He drove fast to the Tulona station; Romero was already there. Sheriff's department and New Mexico trooper vehicles were parked outside, and all the station lights blazed. He looked over at his mother's house on the Winter side. All was peaceful, but Tafoya realized his future might not be so quiet. An owl hooted in the cottonwoods beside Rio Tulona.

In the station's conference room, law enforcement personnel from the Taos County Sheriff's Department, New Mexico State Police, and Tulona Tribal Police huddled with a liaison officer from the Forest Service. Tafoya made a mental note to tell Janet to try and become a liaison with law enforcement. She would be good at it with her skills of observation, and even, perhaps, her pilot license could be used. He wondered if she had a commercial license. Two pots of coffee had been brewed, and all assembled clutched coffee mugs and Yeti cups to sip and, hopefully, gain traction and energy for the work ahead. At the head of the conference table sat Romero and Deputy Sheriff Chris Cordova. Cordova stood up to brief the team. He read from a yellow legal pad.

Good, no powerpoint, Tafoya thought.

Cordova began, "I'll be leading the planning of operations, but I want input from everyone. First, let me explain how we got this information. The tribal police and the sheriff's department had put out several BOLOs on Saltwater and his vehicle. We finally got a reliable hit. Last Wednesday, the nineteenth, the sheriff's department in Taos got a phone call from a Felix Ruiz of Questa. Felix owns the Old Taos Trail Saloon and store on the road between Questa, Ojo Verde, and Taos. You know the place, I'm sure. The road is Forest Road four-nine-three. I've got hard-copy map handouts. I've also opened a page on our computer channels that have this information and map links. Anyhow, Felix Ruiz called the sheriff's department on Wednesday, and the officer at the desk took down his statement. Ruiz had seen a picture of Saltwater as being wanted for quesitoning on the bulletin board of the Questa Post Office. Ruiz said that he had been renting out the Old Taos Trail Saloon on Forest Road four-nine-three to Saltwater and Dihyja for a couple of years."

"Why are just finding out about Felix tonight, early on Sunday morning? He called on Wednesday, four days ago," a state trooper asked abruptly.

Cordova shrugged. "When Felix called, the officer at the desk and our department were handling two traffic accidents, one on the road to Española, the other on the road to Sipapu; two different shootings in the county; and, on top of that, we were short-staffed that afternoon. The statement was taken and put in wrong basket. This morning, after midnight, when things had slowed down from last night, I was going through the pile of paperwork in the invoice basket and found the statement. I called Mr. Ruiz, who was sound asleep, and got confirmation about his statement at two o'clock this morning. He's is going to meet us at San Miguel Lady of Sorrows chapel. I'll call him when we get this all planned out."

Over the next hour, the team put together a basic plan of

apprehending Saltwater. The final elements of the operation would come together once they met with Felix Ruiz at San Miguel. He would be able to tell them the floorplan of the Old Taos Trail Saloon and other details. A deputy sheriff had driven by the saloon and noticed there were no lights on in the saloon, but there was an outbuilding, perhaps a barn or chicken house, that had lights on.

At the San Miguel Lady of Sorrows chapel parking lot, where they assembled at four forty-five, Ruiz informed them that another tenant had rented the barn and lived in back of the saloon.

"That explains the lights on in the barn," Tafoya said.

The renter was a Viet Nam War veteran, living by himself. Cordova stated that the team needed to make sure if there was any gunfire, the Viet Nam vet must not get caught in the crossfire. How they would handle a panic attack, if that occurred, would depend on the moment. Cordova and the team planned to break down the saloon door in a no-knock entry.

Thirty minutes before daybreak, the roads were blockaded off around the saloon, and each team member were at their positions. Ruiz had complained about breaking down the door, "Isn't there some way to avoid that?" Then, Ruiz fumbled around for a key to the door in his glove compartment, found it, and gave it to Cordova. The team now had another option, instead of splintering wood.

Cordova said Ruiz could file a claim with the Taos County Sheriff's Office, if the door was smashed, because there were no guarantees in an operation like this, "Especially at daybreak in the National Forest at an old saloon on a backcountry road." Ruiz winced, but understood.

As the operation unfolded, tribal policemen Tafoya and Romero said they wanted to cover the back of the saloon and the outbuilding housing the war vet as a tenant. "Not to be prideful, but we Tulonas know how to go silently in the forest. We've been doing it since we were boys. Right, Romero?" said Tafoya, simply as a matter of fact.

Romero agreed, as he inserted his communication earpiece in his left ear. Cordova would be giving the orders and second-by-second updates, if necessary.

Tafoya and Romero entered the forest a hundred yards north of the saloon store and found their way through trees and undercover brush, scaring up a couple of deer as they did. They placed themselves between the barn and the saloon store. Inside the barn window, the light was still on.

"We are in place," radioed Tafoya, after they stopped.

Deputy Sheriff Cordova and two officers silently made their way to the front door. The porch had a portico overhang and a paved-stone entrance. Ruiz had told them there was a large front room with a kitchen and two hallways branching off to bedrooms and storage rooms. He had no idea where Saltwater might be sleeping.

Cordova shined a pencil light on the front door latch and lock. He tried the latch. The door was unlocked. He opened it slightly. Nodding to his officers, he opened the door wider and shined his flashlight all around the front room. No Saltwater there.

Time to make themselves known.

"Sheriff's Department! Down on the floor!" They flipped on all the lights and carefully and went down the halls, "Sheriff's Department! Down on the Floor!" Shouting frequently, "Sheriff's Department!" they cleared every room. No Saltwater.

Law enforcement vehicles pulled into the driveway. Tafoya and Romero found the Viet Nam vet asleep on his cot, carefully waking him up and informing him they were looking for Saltwater. He had not seen him in several days. "Dihyja? Haven't seen him for a couple of weeks." The vet stirred himself and went outside where the team had assembled. He liked the excitement.

"This is fun," he said. The officers eventually gave him a look-see inside their vehicles. "Wow," was all he could say.

Inside the Old Taos Trail Saloon store, their search turned up discarded clothes, canned goods, unwashed dishes and pans, a few old letters of no consequence, and receipts for electricity and propane. Ruiz entered the saloon after it was cleared and showed the officers where the secret compartment was in the kitchen. "Bootleg whiskey was stashed here, a very unique place" Ruiz said. A portion of the cabinet on hinges swung away from the wall. Then, one pried several sturdy planks from the floor. A three-foot-deep stonewall compartment lay beneath the planks. Shelving had been constructed to store the bottles. Steps were affixed to one side.

Tafoya stepped down into the stone compartment and shined his light around. He squatted down to check every shelf. "No booze here," he said laughing. "But look at this." Lying underneath the bottom shelf, next to the wall, out of plain sight, was a mother rock of turquoise, about four inches long, shaped like a pickle wedge. It had been accidently dropped or fallen out of a bag or pack. Gloves on, Tafoya picked it up carefully. Even in its raw state, the flecks of turquoise were brilliant and blue in color.

"Ah, the Blue Lady mine."

Once it had become full daylight, a more thorough search was conducted. Inside one of the outbuildings, a Ford pickup with a Culebra Mining Company logo was discovered. The VIN number matched up with

Robert Dihyja's registration. Andreas Saltwater's pickup was nowhere around, but tire tracks found around the barn matched up with those found where Dihyja was dumped, and they were new Goodyear tires. Dihyja's tires were threadbare. A tow vehicle was called; Dihyja's truck was hauled away, the keys in the ignition. The photographer from the Taos County Sheriff's Department took pictures of the scene, including some artful photographs of the whiskey mosaic on the side of the saloon store. The Viet Nam vet did not mind being photographed. In fact, he insisted that the photographer take a picture of him beside the whiskey mosaic.

"What excitement for a Sunday morning!" he exclaimed.

Tafoya and Romero were not about to let the event conclude at the Old Taos Trail Saloon store. The state police and sheriff's department left the scene, but they remained behind. They chatted up the vet, and once they were satisfied the vet had given them all the information about Saltwater and Dihyja, they thanked him, and told him to go on and brew his coffee, make his breakfast. Smiling broadly, the vet walked away, a skip in his step.

From the backyard of the saloon and the barn corral, Tafoya and Romero ambled separately back into the woods, carefully scanning the ground. Walking in rough concentric circles away from the saloon, they scanned for a hundred yards. They came across old farm implements, several rubbish piles, fencing posts and staves. The Old Taos Trail Saloon store went back in time for over a hundred and fifty years. A trail from the saloon led back up into the mountains. Lobo Peak lay to the east; Flag Mountain rose to the north of Lobo. Returning back down the trail toward the saloon, Tafoya veered off the path, and squatted down to scan where they had come from—back in the direction of the saloon. Then he saw the cache.

The brush cover on the ground had not naturally fallen, but had been intentionally arranged. A critter had dug partially into the hole and thrown up dirt. "Romero, come here. Bring that shovel we saw in the barn." From the cache, they extracted the box of turquoise that Saltwater had left behind. A cursory exam indicated it was like the turquoise sliver they had recovered from the saloon's secret compartment.

"Easiest prospecting, we will ever do, Romero," Tafoya joked, as they headed back to Ojo Verde and the evidence room.

Ben Lovato, Medicine Wind, had arisen from bed shortly before daybreak to help Quail with Dezba who needed her diaper changed and milk for breakfast. Once his daughter was comforted, he went outside.

The sun had not yet risen, but it was getting light, but not so much light that the brightest stars and planets disappeared. All the Tulona police station lights were on. Only one police vehicle was parked in front of the office. Pulling his light blanket around his body, Ben walked over to the station. Did someone at the Pueblo need help? Was there trouble that needed him to intervene? Last night was a Saturday night, and young Tulonas had been known to come in late, drunk, and rowdy. Just last month, a grandfather had tied his grandson to an arbor post when he had come in drunk, and had not untied him until the next morning when he threw a pail of water on him and gave him stern lecturing. No one had interfered with the grandfather's discipline. The grandson, shamed and self-conscious, sobered up, and was made to muck corrals for a week as punishment. So far, the arbor-post discipline stuck hard with the grandson.

Ben heard no commotion like that in the night. He walked over to the station. The officer on duty explained that there was an ongoing operation up near Lama; otherwise, all was peaceful in the Pueblo. Satisfied, Ben walked out of the station and crossed the bridge to the Winter House side of the Pueblo. The racetrack for Saint Francis Feast Day ran east and west in front of the Winter House; at the west end of the racetrack, a platform, with a bower for Pueblo dignitaries and the priest, was being decorated with cottonwood and aspen branches. The decorating had just begun and would be completed by October 3, the day before races and pole climbing. Ben leaned against the large post that formed the frame of the bower and looked eastward toward sunrise. The Rio Cottonwood flowed clear and steady from the mountains. Leaning with his back against the bower post, Ben saw the canyon from where water flowed from Earth Cloud Lake, miles away, and three thousand feet higher from where he rested. The racetrack followed the northside of the river for a quarter mile past the old wall.

Magpies flew onto the racetrack. They walked around like soldiers, stiff-legged and at attention, as if something serious was going to break out any minute. Another group of magpies were in the trees, chattering and fussing. Ben was always amazed at the walkability of magpies, akin to Spanish doves that walked the same way, saying, "We are like humans, too. We walk. We are bi-pedal, like humans."

Medicine Wind listened to how magpies talked, back and forth; he understood them. Just as quickly as they had flown to the ground, the magpies abruptly flew back to the cottonwood trees along the stream. As the flock flew upward, one of the magpies lost a feather, a large black and white tail or wing feather. Ben stirred from his leaning post and walked over to the feather on the Tulona racetrack. He did not pick it up. He looked at it, then crouched down to look at it closer.

The magpie feather was short, maybe four inches. The horn of the feather had stuck in the racetrack; the feather tilted upward, firm in the racetrack at an angle. All around the feather, magpie bird tracks had pressed into the soft earth. Medicine Wind stared at the feather, puzzled, squinting his eyes, trying to see...finally, he asked.

"What is this, Grandfather? What is magpie telling me?"

After a time, Ben stood up. He looked east as the first rays of the sun graced his face; he heard magpie say,

"Begin with the sun and all else shall follow."

Bending down, Ben lifted the magpie feather from the racetrack and placed it in his left pocket. The bell of Mission San Francisco del Monte rang, the rhythm slow. There was but one large bell; it was bronze and not a recording. On the way back to his home, Ben looked at the faithful walking to church, the women with their heads covered, the few men dressed for Mass on Sunday morning. Ben walked over to the pole that had been set in place in the middle of the plaza. He stood apart from the pole, staring at the crossbeams at the top. He wondered who would succeed in climbing to the top and untie the sheep and fruit and harvest for the people below. The climber would be young; the ordeal was not for an old man. The climb was a story in miniature of Puebloan life. Of all life really, he thought to himself.

Turning away from the pole, he walked past the corral and continued down the road toward Ojo Verde and the common pasture that held his horses, Star and Jess. The horses grazed peacefully at the other end of the pasture from where he stood, but several of them noticed Ben from far off and jerked their heads up. The alpha mare of the remuda, a sorrel of good confirmation, turned toward him, squaring her shoulders in an offensive posture to him. She stood transfixed, and after about thirty seconds, affirming Ben was not threat, lowered her head and resumed grazing.

"Ai. The horse chief is on guard!" Ben said, approvingly. Several crows had flown over to the remuda and were eating insects that the horses had stirred up. The paved road that ran alongside the west boundary of the pasture had little vehicle traffic. Ben saw smoke coming from the chimneys of several art studios aligned along the road going into Ojo Verde. The Month of Corn Ripe Moon was ending soon, and the Month of Leaves Falling Moon ushered in fewer tourists, but more time for painting, crafting, and jewelry-making among the Tulona artists. The hunting season opened soon, and fresh deer meat would be on the stoves and grills of the Tulona. Casting one last look at the remuda, Ben turned and starting walking back to the Pueblo.

Time to clean deer rifles and sharpen knives, he promised himself.

Andreas Saltwater drove back from the Blue Lady, past the Old Taos Trail Saloon near Lamy, and saw the yellow crime scene tape encircling the saloon. Not stopping, but speeding up, he continued up the road to a campground near Questa, parking his truck at the most remote camping spot in the forest. He had more to extract from the Blue Lady mine and the Saint Francis Feast Day to attend, and then, "I'm outa here," he said aloud.

24

Thursday, October 4, Day of Saint Francis of Assisi, Month of Leaves Falling Moon

On Tulona Feast Day, the early morning chill was sharp; chill enough to question the reason why a person arose so early in the morning. For the Tulona racers, who dressed in loincloths and body paint, they paid little attention to the chill. Shortly before sunrise, a hundred Tulona males grouped around the far west end of the racecourse, in front of Winter House, and began to dance and sing. Whoops and shrill cries emanated from the troupe. The drumming was quick and staccato, sharp like the air. The affect upon the spectators was fundamentally different from any other kind of music or beat—stuunning, transcendental, unexplainable in words.

For the dancers, the drumming was earth-bound, star-bound, and sun-strong—compelling the body, rhythmically beyond words. Anglo, Hispano, and Tulona onlookers lined the southside of the racetrack, within the boundaries of the old walls of the Pueblo. On the other side of the plaza, market booths were still closed, but sales people were hastily arranging their wares, preparing to open later in the morning. On top of Winter House, three stories high, Tulona women wrapped in colorful blankets stood straight and looked down on the dancers. Yellow, red, blue southwestern designs stood out from the blankets. Standing on roofs earned a special view and privilege to the residents and invited guests of Winter and Summer Houses. Older Tulonas carefully climbed ladders to the second and third stories to see the race.

The dancing began at the bower end, the far west end of the racetrack, and moved east along Winter House homes to the old wall. After the completion of each dance, the participants smiled and behaved haply. Then, at the east end of the Winter House, the dancing halted, and the Tulona dancers, now racers, solemnly walked to the far east end of the racetrack, beyond the eyes of onlookers on the plaza. Beyond the old wall, at the far east of the racetrack, Tulona relatives and guests gathered at the starting line as the sun broke over the mountains. The Tulona on the Winter House rooftops shaded their eyes from the sun to see the race begin.

The Ortegas had come early to see all of the day's ceremonies, and visit each and every sales booth. Luis Ortega looked up on the roofs for Flowers Dancing and Quail Looks Away. He saw them on the first story of Winter House near the bower where the priest and his entourage sat underneath aspen and cottonwood branches. Luis moved to the front line of onlookers crowded along the racetrack, so he could see Lion Looks Away running. He would look for Ben Lovato, but Lion was his first concern. Luis shivered slightly from the chill of the air, but mainly from knowing the fact that racers ran barefooted. He saw stones on the racetrack.

"Take care, Lion, be careful...the Lord be with you," Luis said, as he silently crossed himself for the sake of Lion. Why run barefooted? he grimaced.

Tribal policeman Tafoya had serious matters before him. Yes, the ceremonies were important for his kinsmen and the Pueblo, but he was looking for Andreas Saltwater. Tulona Feast Day was the most-heavily attended Feast Day, next to the Taos Feast Day, among the Eastern Pueblos. Romero was on the lookout along with other law enforcement officers, but Tafoya and Romero had a more intense desire to catch Saltwater. It involved Saltwater callously dumping Dihyja on reservation land. They had spent a hundred hours on the Saltwater-Dihyja case, and they intended to resolve the case—soon. Tulona Feast Day would be an event Saltwater might attend, suspecting he could be lost in the crowd.

Tafoya had invited Janet Rael to come to Feast Day to eat with him and his family at lunchtime. He would take off from duty for thirty minutes and have lunch with his family and introduce Janet to them. Janet was bringing a girlfriend with her from work at the Forest Service.

People were walking from parking lots a half mile away from the Pueblo. The horses had been moved to the far western pasture, allowing room for the cars. Several horses walked up to the fence, next to the cars, staring curiously at the people and cars. A few children ran to the fence line and rubbed the noses of the gentlest horses. Star and Jess were the most attentive to the people, and the excitement unfolding in front of them. The children favored Star and Jess, and pulled clumps of grass to feed them. Some parents scolded their children for getting too close. The sorrel alpha horse, the mare, stood back from the fence line, quietly chomping grass, but remaining alert for trouble by keeping her head always pointed in the direction of the humans. She was remuda warchief; no matter she was not the largest horse, just the most powerful.

Tafoya and Romero had the description of Saltwater as tall, dark-brown eyes, medium-dark complexion, scar under his right eye, muscular, commonly dressed in work clothes, perhaps Navajo embellishment, long hair tied in chignon. Aside from the scar under his right eye, dozens of men fit his description. Tafoya presumed, and he knew there was danger in presumption, that Saltwater would be alone, a solitary figure. He further reasoned that he would saunter among the sales booths, especially those selling jewelry. Navajo silversmiths and jewelers predominated the sales, but jewelry booths from Santo Domingo, San Juan, and Santa Clara were also represented.

The two Tulona tribal policemen had a general plan to mix with the crowd of onlookers and patrol the sales booths. Tafoya brought his binoculars and had a particular spot on the second story of Winter House, a location that he could scan the crowd without being seen. His cousin occupied a home with a screen door facing the plaza; Tafoya could stand behind the screen door, and no one would see him. One drawback was that he had to climb down a ladder on the side of the Winter House and, momentarily, lose sight of the plaza crowd. He and Romero would stay in radio contact; another channel would be open to other law enforcement officers so they could assist, if Saltwater was spotted. The other problem would be identifying the scar underneath Saltwater's right eye from so far away using the binoculars. Therefore, to Tafoya, patrolling the crowd and sales booths might be the most rewarding in catching Saltwater, not the Winter House spy nest.

As planned, Tafoya and Romero arrived early for Feast Day. They stood around the arbor, next to the racetrack, and heard the drum and dancers. They could not see the dancers as the crowd was lined four to five people deep, but they heard the shouts and singing.

"Look at that Anglo carrying a thermos," said Romero. "You think he's drinking this early in the morning?" Tafoya looked at the Anglo carefully.

"It's just coffee, Officers," said the Anglo, noticing their stares. "I've gotta wake up and stay warm," he said laughingly. Tafoya and Romero nodded in agreement, but kept an eye on him, on and off, untill he moved on to the sales booths.

The Tulona racers walked to the far end of the racetrack, beyond the old wall, along the Rio Tulona, to the large grove of cottonwoods where the starting place began. The racers were of ages from ten to fifty, the majority in their twenties and thirties. Ben Lovato and Lion Walks Night were among the fittest of the troupe, Lion being a few years younger than Ben. From the earth, red ochre paint covered their upper torsos, white ochre their lower legs. Arm bands, with ribbons and hawk feathers streaming and floating with the wind, imparted strength and color to the runners. Eagle-down tufts were tied to their long dark hair, and a few of the runners wore moccasins because of bruised feet. Most were barefoot. Ben Lovato Medicine Wind wore one deerskin armband on his left arm, the deer having been killed and afterwards prayed over with pollen applied to its nostrils. Attached to the deerskin, he wore one feather, the magpie feather he had been gifted from the racetrack a few days before.

The earth came forth, adorned with color and runners. The sun shined, the waters flowed, and plants and animals emerged, and on this day of Race and Pole Climbing, the web of life at Tulona Pueblo was singing, dancing, drumming, climbing, eating, laughing, crying, and talking. The incomprehensible-spirit-that-moves-in-all-things was doing just that at Tulona Pueblo: Moving.

Andreas Saltwater parked his mud-covered truck at the parking lot beyond the Summer House before lunchtime. He had driven the backroads to Feast Day, avoiding most cars and pickups that came up the paved road from Ojo Verde to park over by the common pasture. Saltwater wanted to see the pole climbing, but he mainly wanted to see the jewelry sales booths of the Navajo and Zuni. One particular Zuni craftsman had fashioned his belt buckle from Blue Lady turquoise. In his backpack, Saltwater carried a few pieces of the Blue Lady turquoise and he wanted the craftsman to polish the stones in preparation for jewelry, perhaps a distinctive bolo tie for himself. He had returned to the Taos Trail Saloon on the road to Questa, discovering his turquoise cache in the woods had been looted. That angered him, but he cooled down, thinking that he still had the Blue Lady mine, and the only other person that knew her location was dead.

Luis Ortega found his way to the front of the crowd lining the racetrack in front of Winter House, adjacent to the aspen and cottonwood bower where some council members and the priest sat in the shade. The bower platform was eight feet off the ground and allowed the honored guests to peer down the racetrack. The priest had put sun screen lotion on his face. The lotion looked like the white ochre paint on the dancers and runners. Luis wondered, from a distance, if the priest had put on face paint or lotion, concluding it must be white ochre paint, in honor of the Puebloans' Feast Day. It would block the sun, nevertheless, he thought.

Luis saw that the aspen bower was not all yellow in color. Several limbs of aspen were red.

He looked up on the roof and saw Quail Looks Away, Dezba, and Flowers Dancing. They were standing, facing the east end of the racetrack. Quail wore a brilliant yellow blanket of Indigenous symbols. The symbols appeared to be Pacific Northwest, Kwakiutl, perhaps. Flowers Dancing wore a blue blanket with Zuni symbols. The tableau of Quail and Flowers Dancing and all the other women on rooftops seemed ancient in form and behavior. I have seen paintings and photographs of this, Luis thought to himself, but this is now, and real, in the present. How much more powerful. Then, suddenly, the women straightened up.

"Ulllaaaa, ulllaaa, ulllaaa," they wailed.

It was a high-pitched, wavering vocal sound. The waver was piercing, and as Luis looked down the race track, he saw runners coming fast. As they heard the ululations of their kinsmen, they ran faster, beneath the high-pitched trilling of the women. They tagged their team members who began to speed eastward from the bower to the rising sun. Luis looked for Lion, but he was not in sight.

The crowd did not cheer, but remained quiet. The only sounds were the ululations, a few Tulona whooping, and the elders brushing the runners with aspen branches, softly uttering a Tulona prayer. Being at the front of the crowd, Luis heard something else. He heard the feet of the runners hitting the ground, feet-placed-strongly-on-the-earth, in loud rhythm of racing.

"Run fast," Luis said, under his breath. His words were to no particular runner or team, but for all runners.

As the runners went out of sight to the east, ululations ceased. No one was permitted to cross the race track during the contest-ordeal. A dog was shooed off the track. Then, the ululations began again as two other runners appeared from the east. Luis saw Ben and Lion, running side by side.

The strain was evident on Lion's face, almost agonizing. Ben ran evenly with Lion, and as they came alongside Winter House, Luis looked up and saw Quail holding Dezba close to her breast, talking to her, pointing at Ben.

"There is your father and your cousin running with all their heart. Look, Dezba, you remember this!"

Neither Ben nor Lion looked at Quail in her brilliant yellow blanket. The elders waved aspen branches at the runners, softly murmuring prayers....

"Oooo, ahhh," the crowd voiced, as Ben and Lion swept by, running almost in unison with Lion barely in front. Then, Luis saw Ben run by him. He saw the magpie feather floating from the deerskin armband, circling Ben's arm. "Ulllaaaa!" Luis felt heat rising in his head, a glowing, not from the sun, but from running vicariously, within the totality of an ancient ceremony.

Who won the race was not the question. In fact, there was no question as Luis understood the race as an outsider to the Tulona. Perhaps the winning troupe's side allowed their elder to be governor for a year, but he did not know for sure. Luis understood that the Tulona ceremonies remained secret; the racing of Tulonas on Feast Day was part of their behavior he would never understand nor be entitled to know. He had run with Lion in high school and that formed their friendship—and that was good enough for this day. Ben and Lion slowly walked back, along the track in front of the houses, toward the east end of the racetrack. Their feet were tender from the small stones they had run swiftly upon; yet, they did not limp. Their faces reflected solemnity, not fatigue. As they walked by the crowd, they did not look at the crowd, but their faces were downturned to the track they had run upon, as if in worship. The elders they passed by, gently stroking their back with aspen branches, uttering prayers.... Ben raised his face to Quail and Dezba. Quail's breast swelled with pride, or was it a silent grief within she did not want to express.

Saltwater looked at jewelry. The Santo Domingo Pueblo craftsmen fashioned exquisite turquoise chokers. He looked at one choker priced at $100, another choker in an adjacent display case priced at $2,000. Saltwater knew the difference: the $100 choker was plastic; the $2,000 necklace was natural turquoise. It was beautiful, but not like the dendrite turquoise of his Blue Lady mine.

Sergeant Romero had patrolled the crowd around the races earlier that morning. He ordered a few people, Tulona, Anglo, and Hispano, to put away their phones, or he would confiscate them. They were talking on the phones, not taking pictures. Despite large signs at the old wall entrances of the Pueblo warning visitors to not use their phones on Feast Day, a few did so anyway. Romero did look the other way, however, when he knew the person was taking an urgent call to pick up an older kinsman or decrepit friend at the parking lot a half mile away.

He looked carefully at solitary men with their hair tied in a chignon. None had the tell-tale sign of a scar under the right eye. By late morning, after the races, Romero walked across the bridge to the Summer House side of the Pueblo where food stands were located and ordered a Navajo breakfast burrito and lemonade. At the most-visited food stand, he brought out his cell phone and pulled up a picture of Andreas Saltwater, asking, "Have you seen this man this morning? We need to talk to him."

The servers said, "No," they had not, asking what he was wanted for?

"The Tulona Police are looking to question him about a possible murder a few weeks ago. If you see him, contact law enforcement, immediately!" By mentioning murder, Romero deliberately upped the seriousness of contacting law enforcement, adding an edge to the vendors' commercial transactions on Feast Day. The food booth server comped him his burrito and lemonade. He walked over to the shade of the cottonwood alongside the stream and joined two state troopers who were also eating breakfast burritos.

Saltwater ambled over to the Zuni sales booth, looking closely at cluster-style conchos, rings, fetishes, and arm bracelets. He particularly liked the sandcasting method of wrist bracelets and buckles. "Where's Tommy?" Saltwater asked. Tommy was the Zuni craftsman that had polished the Blue Lady turquoise stones to perfection.

"I'm here," Tommy said, as he emerged from behind a sunshade curtain. The day was warming up. Saltwater slipped his daypack off his shoulder and gave Tommy three large pieces of turquoise and mother matrix. Tommy was to polish and refine the turquoise at his lapidary at the Zuni Reservation.

"Is this the dendrite turquoise, Andreas?" Tommy asked.

"Yes, same source, same mine. The Blue Lady, as I call it."

"Where is Robert, I haven't seen him in a while?"

"Oh, he went back to Gallup to visit his mother. She was sick, and I think he intended to stay in Gallup until his mother recovered," Saltwater lied.

Tommy nodded at Saltwater's explanation. He asked Saltwater if he could take his commission of refining the dendrite turquoise by keeping two or three pieces of the refined Blue Lady? At first, Saltwater demurred, but then accepted the trade only if he selected the pieces to apply in paying the commission. They agreed and shook hands. Tommy said he could have the turquoise ground and polished in a month. Saltwater replied he would come out to Tommy's lapidary on the Zuni reservation in a month to pick up the gemstones.

As Saltwater walked away from Tommy's sales booth, he wondered if he could set up his own lapidary and refine his own Blue Lady. Then the turquoise is always under my control, he thought.

Saltwater was hungry, but he did not want sales-booth food from the Summer House side. As was customary on Feast Day, he wanted to take his chances of being invited to a Pueblo household for a quick meal. For the Puebloans, this was Feast Day—a generous day for sharing. The general protocol was that a Pueblo family might invite visitors into their home; the person invited would eat, but not linger at the table. Saltwater walked by several homes; no invitations extended. He reasoned that because he was alone, he was not invited. Just when he was about to give up and go to a food booth, an older woman invited him in for a quick lunch of green chile stew and fry bread.

"Welcome, come in and have some stew. I'm Deer Rain Looking, and this is my daughter, Quail Looks Away, and my granddaughter, Dezba or Blue Flowers Springing. Isn't this such a nice Feast Day, friend?"

Tafoya scanned the crowd through his binoculars. His cousin's screen door on the second floor of Winter House had a negligible effect on the image reflected through the spy glass. He looked at his watch: twelve noon. Time to go to the church courtyard in the plaza to meet Janet and her girlfriend and escort them to a Feast Day lunch at his mother's house. Tafoya had already scanned through the binoculars and saw them in the vicinity of the church, shopping at a Zuni sales booth. Janet's girlfriend looked familiar; he peered closer. It was Bessie Talbot, cartographer at Bureau of Land Management, next door to the Forest Service where Janet worked. That's coincidental. Wonder how they met. Tafoya scanned one more time with the binoculars. No Saltwater.

People were buying tacos and barbeque and hamburgers with soft drinks and sitting on the edge of Rio Tulona, in the shade of cottonwoods, eating. Others found chairs at tables provided by the food booths. Tafoya saw the Tulona runners that had raced and danced eating lunch. For dessert, they were enjoying candies and chocolate bars thrown to them, after they completed their dancing and running. The aspen leaves on the bower were being removed. He made sure his mother collected red aspen branches for her home, for his house. The bower branches were of particular significance since he and Janet had begun their personal conversations about the turning of the aspens. He would give Janet a red aspen branch to display in her apartment.

Tafoya was about to end his binocular scan, when he saw a solitary male, with long hair tied in a chignon and broad-brimmed hat, walk in front of several houses. Tafoya looked at him closely. He was invited into a home with three other people, so, apparently, he did not appear frightening to his hosts. "Which home did he go into?" Tafoya whispered under his breath. Under a porch blocking his view, there were entrances to two or three homes. Which home? The house the man entered was on the Summer House side, across the bridge where Janet was waiting. Tafoya put down his binoculars, opened the screen door, and climbed down the ladder to the ground on the side of the adobe house.

Tafoya swiftly made his way through the crowd to the bridge. He greeted Janet with a half-hug. She introduced Bessie, and they laughed at the fact that all three knew each other. Janet had told Bessie she was coming to meet Tafoya at the Pueblo, and Bessie confided to Janet that Tafoya and she had searched databases for individuals filing mining claims. "We were successful," Bessie said. The three of them started walking to Tafoya's mother's house. Tafoya stopped.

"Wait here just a minute," he said, as they came by the portico where he thought the solitary, chignon-hair man had gone in to eat. "I need to check on something, and then we'll go to my mother's. It won't take long. I'm famished," he added.

Tafoya found that two of the three homes under the portico had been serving food to invited guests. The Quail Looks Away family he questioned said they had just served a man who had his hair up in a chignon, and he was quite courteous.

"He ate quickly and moved on, just a few minutes ago."

Tafoya asked them if he had a scar under his right eye, and they couldn't say yes or no. He showed them a photograph on his cell phone, and Quail's mother, Deer Rain Looking, replied, "No, I don't think that was him. Can't say for sure as we were busy serving up stew. Do you want some?" Quail was just as uncertain, so Tafoya thanked them for their cooperation and returned to Janet and Bessie. He radioed Romero, on the open channel, that he had seen a solitary man that might have fit Saltwater's description, but the hosts for the lunch couldn't verify the identity.

"Let's be on the lookout for this guy," Romero said.

"I agree. I'm here near the bridge and about to go in to have a quick lunch with mother. I'm meeting Janet. I shouldn't be more than thirty minutes. I'll eat and visit and be back out for duty before the Black Eyes come out whooping and yelling on the roof."

"I hope it goes well for you, Richard. Mother meeting girlfriend for the first time can go sour. But I know it'll go well for you. Best of luck," Romero said, seriously.

"Thanks, Sergeant. I am nervous." Tafoya thought to himself, I have no idea how this is going to go down. Aiii!

Tafoya's anxiety lasted only fifteen seconds when Janet met his mother. Bessie was an icebreaker for the meeting. Tafoya's father joked and flirted with all of them, as Tafoya looked on dumbstruck, a loss for words. Janet was respectful and admired the food dishes his mother had cooked. By the time Tafoya had to go back on duty, Janet and his mother were trading recipes, trying to trace common family lineages between the Isleta of Janet and the Tulona of Tafoyas. When Tafoya announced, "I've got to get back on duty," Janet rose to give him a hug.

His mother walked him to the door, as the others returned to conversing and could not hear what she quietly said.

"I really like Janet, my son. My grandchildren will be beautiful."

Santiago Majerus and Johnny Sisneros walked the half mile from the south parking lot to the Tulona Pueblo. They entered the Pueblo Plaza, immediately turning to the right, crossing the bridge to the food booths. The races had already been run. Sisneros had driven in his old Dodge pickup from Arroyo Luz; Majerus was happy being a passenger, not the driver.

"I wish we could've parked closer. But, I'm okay. I'm sure there's no handicapped parking section near the Pueblo," Majerus laughingly said.

They bought beef tacos with a double helping of lettuce and shredded cabbage. Their Dr Peppers washed down the hot green chile sauce they spread over their tacos. Once they were full of tacos, they ordered sopapillas with honey and butter to sweeten their meal. Afterwards, they crossed the bridge to the Winter House side and looked at the sales booths of jewelry. Majerus paid close attention to Navajo craftsmen and exchanged news and lineages since he was Navajo, "Born to Bitterwater clan, born for The Yellow People clan."

"It's easier being non-Navajo when you meet people, Santiago," Sisneros teased Majerus. "All I do is say, 'I'm Johnny Sisneros, and I live in Arroyo Luz.' That usually starts a conversation about our family names, where we came from, and if we were part of the twelve families that stayed behind at the Pueblo Revolt!"

Luis Ortega, after he had witnessed the races and seen Lion Walks Night run, met up with his father, Armando, to look at the sales booths of leather crafts. Luis bought a tooled-leather belt that had rain cloud and Four Corners designs. Armando looked at the leather products, but purchased a pair of earrings for Loretta. The earrings were Zuni silver feathers with a small piece of turquoise on each ring. After viewing a few more booths, including Hopi pottery, Luis and Armando walked over by Ben Lovato's house, and were invited in by Deer Rain Looking for green chile stew and fry bread. Luis was happy that Flowers Dancing was present, serving food. Quail Looks Away was assisting her mother, but Dezba demanded most of her attention. Another man who had been invited in with them, wearing a broad-brimmed hat and hair put in a chignon, sat down beside them at the table, ate his stew and left quickly.

"Other than take his hat off, he wasn't very courteous or talkative, was he, Father?"

"No, he wasn't, Luis," Armando replied. "He looked familiar to me. I've seen him before. That hat he wore jiggles my memory. I didn't get a chance to introduce myself before he ate, said his 'thanks' and walked out. He was Navajo with that hair style."

Luis struck up a conversation with Flowers Dancing. Deer Rain Looking told Luis and Armando that they did not have to finish quickly and go. They could stay longer which pleased Luis; Flowers Dancing liked Luis's attention. Armando looked at Deer Rain Looking and rolled his eyes. She understood the gesture and nodded in the direction of Luis and Flowers Dancing, implying, yes, there are sparks.

Coe and Priscilla had decided to attend Feast Day. They put on their walking shoes and started hiking from the south parking lot before lunchtime. Priscilla glanced over at the horses lounging at the fence line, near where they parked their car.

"Wait a minute, darling, I want to go over and see the horses," she said, as Coe shrugged and slipped on a small backpack with water bottles.

As she briefly rubbed the foreheads of Star and Jess, Coe hoisted two portable L.L. Bean chairs over his shoulder. He knew that Feast Day with racing and pole climbing was not a performance where grandstands and benches were erected.

Priscilla returned and sighed, "I wish we had land for horses, Coe. I miss the horses I used to have back in California when I was a teenager."

"You're too old to ride, Prissy," Coe responded.

"You don't need to tell me that," Priscilla countered. "I know I'm too old to ride a fast horse, but a gentle horse, I think I can manage. Besides, you know the old Indian saying."

"Prissy, there are thousands of old Indian sayings. Which one do you mean?"

"A horse needs to be with a person when they are old and near their end."

"Jeez, Prissy, that's depressing! Besides, you are not nearing the end, nor am I."

"Horses live a long time, Coe." Did that mean, Coe pondered, that Prissy thought her end was near.... What is going on here?

Coe let it go, handed her the backpack with water bottles, while he carried the portable chairs. A golf-cart shuttle gave them a ride to the entrance. Coe and Prissy bought tacos and lemonade from the Navajo vendor, settling under the shade of a tarp that had been erected next to the food services. They looked across Tulona stream and saw jewelry vendors covering up their wares with white sheets. Each vendor left out on top of the sheets several inexpensive but good-quality pins, necklaces, rings.

"Why are they covering up their wares? It's not going to rain, Coe," Priscilla said.

"Oh, you remember why, Prissy. The Black Eyes are going to be coming out soon, and the vendors need to give them gifts. If they don't cover up their stuff, the Black Eyes will pick what they darn well like," Coe answered.

"Oh, that's right," Priscilla exclaimed.

"Maybe we better get you that horse, Prissy, since you are getting so forgetful," Coe teased.

The Feast Day crowd grew in number, surpassing any size that Tafoya and Romero remembered. Romero's quick-and-dirty estimate was 1,500 people; Tafoya agreed. They walked nonchalantly from the pole, to the sales booths, to the food venue on the Summer House side of the Pueblo, greeting people and ordering a few in the crowd to put their phones away. No one was taking pictures; they were merely checking texts or emails.

Around one o'clock, the crowd suddenly hushed.

"Ooooo, look!" the people shouted, turning in direction of the Winter House side of the plaza.

The Tulona Black Eyes had silently risen up on the roofs of Winter House; their black and white striped bodies with cornhusks on their head, sharply outlined by the clear blue sky and mountains, gave them an other-world, out-of-place, eerie appearance, like, "They should not be here! Something terrible is going to happen!"

"Yiiiii! Yiiiii! Aiiii!" they shouted, yelled, jumped up and down.

They pumped their fists and arms in the air; raucously, the Black Eyes thrust their pelvises erotically. They seemed to be a threatening, upsetting element to Feast Day. To those attending Feast Day for the first time, many did not understand the theatrics of these strange figures on top of the houses. Whether Anglo, Hispano, or Native, wide-eyed children clutched their parents' arms and legs. Anthropologists had explained in technical terms that the Black Eyes were a release from conventional conduct, the reverse of the normal. The clowning society at Tulona had a social permit to act in opposites, up is down, insulting rather than friendly, disrespectful.

Being Tulona, Tafoya and Romero knew the Black Eyes had more purpose than entertainment. As the Black Eyes climbed down from the Winter House and began to walk about the sales booths and collect gifts, Tafoya and Romero continued to circulate and look for Saltwater. Two of the Black Eyes came up to Romero, and in a mocking search, made him hold up his hands while they patted him down for weapons without touching him. Romero laughed. The crowd gave wide berth to the Black Eyes as they tromped up and down the sales aisles. They stopped by Tulona houses and asked for, and received, food. They came out of houses wearing horns they had taken off the walls of the rooms, returning the horns after burlesquing with them. Tafoya kept scanning the crowd for Saltwater—unsuccessfully. Somehow, the wide-brimmed hat, chignon-styled solitary male had gone home or disappeared in the narrow lanes between the houses. Laughter rose up frequently as the Black Eyes took cigarettes from the pockets of bystanders. After dunking a few young Tulonas in Cottonwood River, the Black Eyes withdrew from the plaza.

Tafoya spotted Janet and Bessie on the edge of the crowd that had begun to circle around the pole, leaving a large, bare area around the pole. He walked over to where they were standing.

"Are you enjoying yourselves?" Tafoya asked.

"Oh, very much, Richard," Janet answered; Bessie concured. "The Black Eyes came by your mother's house, but, fortunately, didn't come in. I was scared of them." Janet shivered.

"Don't be afraid of them, Janet, they won't hurt you. They are all in fun today. Besides, you get sick, maybe one of them can heal you."

"Oh, really, Richard. I thought they were just clowns."

"They are much more than that. Most people only know of them on Feast Day, or at some other event when they burlesque. They manage certain hunts and are warlike scouts with medicine powers. Big-power guys, they are." Janet nodded.

Tafoya was on duty today as a Tulona tribal policeman. Next year, he would apply black charcoal and white ochre and attach corn stalks to his head for Feast Day. It would be his turn next year to burlesque. If Janet remained close to him, and his mother would be sure of that, he thought, I will tell her I am a Black Eye.

Wind Old Woman and the force that created whorls in fingertips blew stronger through Tulona Plaza. Dust stirred up and people closed their eyes when Wind Old Woman blew through. At the front of the crowd surrounding the pole, Coe folded out his portable chair and walked to the back of the crowd to stretch his legs. Prissy remained seated, chatting with another woman. Coe walked over to one of the Zuni sales booths and looked at turquoise bracelets and rings, pricing a cuff bracelet with a large piece of blue-green turquoise embedded in sterling silver, priced at $700. The letter of authenticity stated the jeweler and the provenance of the turquoise as King's Manassa, out of the now-closed Colorado mine. He liked it, but decided against purchase, even after the Zuni salesman came down fifty dollars. Coe noticed that credit cards were accepted, and the transaction completed by small devices attached to sales people's smartphones.

He shook his head, "Imagine, here on Tulona Plaza, on Feast Day, there is internet, wireless transactions, credit cards."

Coe walked back to the crowd, sitting and standing around the pole, and excused his way to where Prissy was sitting. He stood for a moment. Next to him, he struck up a conversation with a man who was Hopi, from Second Mesa, the village of Soogoopavi. They chitchatted, then turned serious.

"I know only one word of Hopi," Coe said. "It's *Koyaanisqatsi*, life out of balance. It was a film I saw years ago."

"Yes, *Koyaanisqatsi*, misery, anguish in society. Interesting you remembered," the Hopi said, contemplatively.

The conversation lulled for a moment, then, the Hopi asked Coe, "Who do you think will win, Nature or Machine?"

On the east side of the crowd surrounding the pole, a Black Eye emerged and ordered the crowd spread apart to make a path for other Black Eyes to follow.

Coe and the Hopi stood together, looking at the Black Eye scratch tracks in the dirt, leading to the pole upon which a butchered sheep, melons, squash, and other edibles were hanging, fifty feet off the ground. Coe and the Hopi were facing northeast; Coe saw high cirrus clouds over Lucero and Flag Mountains in the distance. He carefully crafted his reply to the Hopi from Soogoopavi.

"In the short run, I think Machine will dominate, but in the long run, Nature will win," Coe answered. "With cell phones and the automobile and the contrails in the skies overhead," he said, pointing to crisscrossing airplane contrails over Tulona Peak, "I am afraid Machine is polluting and diverting attention from Nature and life. Here we are on Saint Francis Feast Day witnessing races and pole climbing that go back decades, even centuries, and people have to be told to put their cell phones away. The Machine has us in its grip—for now." Coe gritted his teeth and, under his breath, cursed.

The Hopi nodded his head in agreement, uttering no words, silent, looking at the approaching Black Eyes hunters coming in from the east, finding game tracks in the dirt, and following them to the pole. With tiny, toy bows and arrows, they shot their arrows upward to the hanging sheep and food at the top of the pole. The Tulona Black Eyes whooped loudly and groaned when their arrows only flew ten or fifteen feet in the air, and then fell back on the hunters. The crowd laughed at the burlesque; but beneath the laughter, serious faces, solemn faces saw that a Tulona was going to climb the pole and, if he slipped, injury or death would occur. Unease, beneath the clowning, settled on the crowd as the Black Eyes hoisted one, then another, then another on the pole, only having climbers go up a few feet, lose their grip and strength, then sliding back down the pole. Coe and the Hopi stood together and each, in their own way, hoped and prayed for a successful climb.

Tafoya glanced occasionally at the Black Eyes attempting to climb the pole, but his focus was on ambling in and out of the crowd on the edges, looking for Saltwater. Sergeant Romero did the same. Could the solitary, chignon-haired man have departed Feast Day? Tafoya looked over at Janet who was under the portico of his mother's house with his kinsmen. All were staring at the Black Eyes trying to climb the pole. Tafoya changed his direction and went over to the cottonwood trees near the stream where people had congregated under the shade. A few yards away, under a red willow tree, he saw Majerus and his neighbor, Johnny Sisneros, staring intently at the Black Eyes, who were now talking heatedly among themselves at the base of the pole. Tafoya caught Majerus's eye and nodded in recognition. Majerus acknowledged by touching his hat.

The Black Eyes, intent on making a successful climb and getting food at the top of the pole, created a human ladder. The stoutest man stood erect at the base of the pole, and then on top of his shoulders another man climbed and stood still, while another climbed on top of him, until there were four men, standing one on top of the other, each grasping the ponderosa. A fifth Tulona, climbed on top of each person, then gripped the pole with his arms and legs and shinnied carefully up the pole to the crossbars at the top. Very carefully, he untied and lowered the sheep and food to his kinsmen below. Prissy, still seated in her chair, turned to Coe in back of her and said, in alarm, "He is shaking, Coe, quivering." The crowd stared, transfixed, at the hunter-climber at the top. Many people could not look and turned away, shaking their head, crossing their fingers.

The Tulona hunter-climber adjusted himself, so that he had the pole between his legs and sat on the crossbars; he faced north, the direction of cold and fierce winter wind. He sat there, gripping the pole and crossbar with his strong legs. He opened his arms toward the north like in a crucifixion, holding himself firmly with his legs, and raised his face toward the mountains. In puzzlement, many in the crowd cocked their heads. What is he doing now? they seemed to say.

The Tulona knew what he was doing. He no longer shook, nor shivered.

He was praying....

Tafoya watched him descend from the pole into the arms of his kinsmen. A gentle tug on his sleeve diverted his attention.

"Aren't you the policeman that was at Arroyo Hondo several days ago, looking for that Saltwater guy?" Tafoya turned to face a young woman who looked familiar.

"Yes, I was there. What can I do for you?"

"Well, I saw him a while ago, over by the sales booths. I know it was him. I won't forget his face there in the store. I was the clerk who called nine-one-one."

"Are you sure it was him?" Tafoya pressed.

"I'm sure. I shambled by him, intentionally, to confirm it was him. He had the scar under his right eye."

Tafoya radioed Romero and other law enforcement officers on site, that there was positive identification of Saltwater made thirty minutes before in the sales booth area. The Arroyo Hondo clerk told him she had become interested in the Black Eyes and pole climbing, and there were no officers around her, until he showed up under the cottonwoods. He was the first officer she had encountered after seeing Saltwater. "I'm sorry I didn't report it sooner," she said.

The main exits out of the Tulona Pueblo were covered by either the sheriff's department or the New Mexico state troopers. Tafoya and the officers knew, however, that there were dozens of ancillary roads in and out of the reservation they could not monitor, but they had to be alert at the main roads, regardless.

Within two hours, most cars and pickups left the reservation; Saltwater had escaped. Tafoya and Romero were exasperated and downhearted. During the day, law enforcement officers had checked license plates of pickups that matched the description of Saltwater's, but no hit was made. "More than likely, he has switched his plates with plates that are stolen," Romero concluded.

The day had been long for Tafoya. His surveillance concluded, he invited Janet and Bessie to walk with him over to the Tulona police headquarters station for a cup of coffee and to show them the facilities. After showing them the facilities, he made a fresh pot of coffee, and they sat down at the conference table. "I hope the coffee doesn't keep us up past our bedtimes," Tafoya joked. They talked about the pole climbing and all the good food and companionship; then the conversation turned to Saltwater and the Dihyja case. Tafoya talked mainly about Saltwater, but then told the story about going out to Tohatchi and discovering Dihyja's identity. As he was discussing Yazzie's part in making the turquoise belt buckle, he brought up on the computer screen the numbers underneath the "B" and the "L" on the turquoise.

"Dihyja had those letters and numbers etched intentionally. We don't know who the lapidary jeweler was that refined and polished the turquoise...or etched the numbers," Tafoya admitted.

"The 'B' and 'L' stood for the Blue Lady mine, not a girlfriend," Bessie said. "That came out in the logbook notes when they first came in to register a claim, which they never got around to doing. Remember that part, Richard?"

Tafoya thought a moment. "Yeah, that's right. Tony Rodarte at The Silver Concho heard it from Saltwater as well. The Blue Lady is a mine, not a girlfriend. But the numbers...," he trailed off. "Here, let me put them up on the whiteboard."

He scribbled on the whiteboard: B 918 L 593. "If we drop the 'B' and the 'L,' we have nine-one-eight, five-nine-three."

"Maybe something to do with mine location?" Janet queried.

"Well, there're not latitude or longitude. I can tell you that for sure," Bessie said, authoritatively.

Tafoya rubbed the magic marker against his temple. Fortunately, he had placed the cap back on the magic marker. "Nine-one-eight, five-nine-three," he repeated again, slowly. He went over to the computer and scrolled back to Dihyja's educational background at the college in Gallup.

"He took a six-hour course in archaeological field school. That includes a lot of mapwork—a lot of it."

"But those numbers are not latitude and longitude, Officer Tafoya," Bessie said again.

Then things started coming together for Tafoya.

"That's right, Bessie, they aren't latitude, longitude coordinates. I think they are Military Grid Coordinates. I used a version of this system in Afghanistan for artillery observation. Those numbers are for the mine, not an enemy position. It would be read this way, 'nine-one-eight easting, five-nine-three northing.' Find the right topographical map that Dihyja used, like in his archaeological field work, draw the grid from the edge markers, and you can pinpoint the location down to a hundred-meter square grid. Dihyja wanted a clue left for the Blue Lady mine."

"So, Richard," Janet said excitedly, "get the right topo map, apply your numbers to it, and we will have found the Blue Lady?"

"That's correct, Janet. We used various scales of maps to pinpoint locations in Afghanistan, but in the case of archaeological survey, topo maps are the standard," Tafoya reasoned.

"We got maps, maps, and more maps," Bessie of the BLM interjected.

Tafoya said nothing, looking first at Bessie, then at Janet, and back up at the whiteboard. He tapped the table in front of him with the magic marker. He smiled, knowingly.

"See you in the morning, Bessie," Tafoya said, pumping his fist in the air.

"I want to be there with you in the morning, Richard," Janet said, enthusiastically.

25

Friday, October 5, Day of Saint Maria Faustina Kowalska, Month of Leaves Falling Moon

Before he drove to Bessie Talbot's at the BLM, Tafoya went to the station at the Pueblo and reread the case file on Saltwater and Dihyja. The day after Feast Day at the Pueblo was busy. Sales booths were being broken down and loaded on trailers. Zuni, Navajo, and Pueblo craftsmen had vacated their booths, having loaded their jewelry and crafts into travel trunks the night before. The climbing pole stood starkly in the middle of the plaza.

Although Tafoya had read the case file a hundred times before, he combed the files again for information that would point to the location of the Blue Lady mine in the sprawling National Forest. The mine loomed significant—it attracted Saltwater, and he was still, probably, mining its turquoise. Tafoya pondered, was there anything in the case file to help him pinpoint the mine's location on the maps and apply the metric, "918593"? Where had Saltwater been seen in the Ojo Verde area? He had been seen at Tulona Pueblo on Feast Day, the Old Taos Trail Saloon where he had lived with Dihyja, The Silver Concho, Coe's Bookshop, and the Hondo Seco Market—five locations. In a global, spatial sense, where had he been roaming unhindered?

On a fresh yellow-tablet page, Tafoya sketched the five locations, placing them, map-like, in association with one another; the locations clustered together. Saltwater's known whereabouts had always been *north* of Ojo Verde, never south of the village. The sighting of Saltwater at the Hondo Seco Market placed him in the northern Questa Ranger District of the National Forest. Tafoya reasoned that the Blue Lady turquoise mine must lie in the northern half of Carson. Tafoya logged out of the case file and tucked his hardcopy notes in the file folder in his desk. He unholstered his cell phone. Time to find 918 easting, 593 northing on the proper map. He texted Janet.

“Good morning, Janet! Meet me at BLM at 8:30.” He received an immediate reply.

“Morning, Richard! C u there!”

Tafoya left a note on Romero’s desk that he was going to the BLM on the Saltwater case, and that he would check back in by phone or radio when he finished. As an afterthought, Tafoya added to the note that he might be gone all morning. He hoped Romero did not come up with some additional work detail for him.

Stepping outside the station, Tafoya encountered a deeper chill in the air. It was October after all. He looked up at Tulona and Lucero Peaks and saw cumulus clouds two-thirds of the way up the mountains; toward the north, a spreading cloudbank of cobalt-blue altostratus indicated chilly weather for the rest of the day—and not much sun.

At least we got through Feast Day with good weather, he said to himself. He started his vehicle and drove off, waving to Romero who was coming up the road to the station.

“I left a note on your desk,” Tafoya radioed. “I’m headed to the BLM in Ojo Verde.”

“Acknowledge, okay. Be safe, Richard,” Romero replied back.

Good! No extra detail, Tafoya thought.

At the BLM headquarters when he arrived, Janet and Bessie were waiting for him at the front desk. After getting fresh coffee in the breakroom, they went into the large map room where Bessie had already commandeered a long table for spreading maps, long rulers, compasses, and magnifying glasses. Other instruments lay about. Sharpened pencils and graph paper were set out. The map room had a scent of something old, something new. Tafoya was reminded of his geography classroom in high school, where Mr. Hughes had pull-down maps all over the front of the classroom and filing cabinets stuffed with maps and worksheets for every student, not just for group activity.

The coffee was exceptionally good. “What is this brew?” Tafoya asked Bessie.

“Yes, it is really delicious, Bessie, where did you get it?” Janet added. She was dressed in her Forest Service uniform with a dark-green quilted coat that went below her waist. She wore a kaki watch cap that fit snuggly over her dark hair. Her hiking boats were clean and showed a light polish.

“We buy the coffee at a place in Española called Mundo Java. We all contribute more money to the coffee-money jar to buy either French Roast or a Sumatra Roast. After we make two pots of either brew, we switch to a cheaper roast for the rest of the day,” Bessie said, proudly.

“I’ll be over early every morning, Bessie,” Janet said, laughingly. “Where’s the money-jar?”

Tafoya explained to Bessie that Saltwater had been seen, or his Culebra logo pickup had been spotted, in several places. He listed them. Janet said nothing, but something flashed in her mind, The Culebra logo...where have I seen that? She let it go, but the thought persisted. Bessie had the topographical map index spread out on the table, listing all the topo maps in northern New Mexico. Bessie pointed out that there were three topographical quadrangles in the index, relating to the search. She pointed at a large map with an old wooden pointer-stick that must have been used during World War II at Los Alamos, Tafoya thought.

"The Lama-Taos Trail Saloon salient lies in the Questa quadrangle, and the Hondo Seco Market location is, obviously, within the Arroyo Hondo topo map confines. Let me get those out of the filing cabinet." Bessie went over to the filing cabinet and rifled through the maps. She brought back the Questa and Arroyo Hondo maps and laid them flat on the table.

"What were the Military Grid Coordinates again, Richard?" Bessie asked.

"Nine-one-eight easting, five-nine-three northing," Janet answered, not giving Tafoya a chance to respond.

Bessie checked blue coordinate slashes on the edges of the topo maps. "The nine-one-eight easting does not fit—not even close for either Questa or Arroyo Hondo. But the five-nine-three northing does show a congruency. We need to look farther west to make the fit." Bessie turned back to the filing cabinets, saying she was going to pull the Burned Mountain, Mule Canyon, and Canon Plaza quads.

"I got it!" Janet said aloud.

"Got what?" Tafoya asked, startled.

"I remember now! I was returning from a biological field count a couple or three weeks ago, and I stopped in at the Narrow Gauge Café in Tres Piedras. Let me see that photo again of Saltwater, Richard." On his cell phone, Tafoya brought up the photo of Saltwater's driver license and showed it to Janet.

"That's him, Richard! He's the man who held the door open for me when I left the café. I'm sure that's him. His pickup had the Culebra logo on it. I noticed tools in the back of the truck, but what made the impression was that he followed me all the way back to the yellow blinking light. I turned south. He turned north. I had begun to worry when I left the café that he was following me for not-so-good reasons. But when he turned north at the blinking light in Ojo Verde, I forgot about him. It was Saltwater in the Culebra-logo pickup. I definitely remember."

"I'll get the Tres Piedras quad as well," Bessie said, turning quickly back to the filing cabinets. She returned with the Burned Mountain, Mule Canyon, Canon Plaza, and Tres Piedras quads. Laying them on the table, they began to scan the maps.

Janet perused the coordinates on the edge of the Tres Piedras quad. "The five-nine-three northing shows a match, but not the easting," Janet reported.

"The same for Mule Canyon and Canon Plaza. There're a little off on the five-nine-three northing," Bessie added.

Bessie and Janet looked at Tafoya who had taken a pencil and circled the 910 easting coordinate tick on the bottom of the Burned Mountain quad. Carefully, he had circled the 590 tick on the west side margin of the quad.

Tafoya stood back from the map table. He stared at the Burned Mountain quad.

"The Blue Lady mine is here. If Dihyja's turquoise numbers are accurate, it's here on the Burned Mountain quad. Let's draw the grid to pinpoint the location," Tafoya said.

Bessie, being experienced in drawing precise grids, drew a tighter grid pattern to pinpoint "918593." It took her a minute; then, they all bent closer to see the location, pinpointed within the tighter grid. An "X" marked the spot.

Bessie spoke, "The Blue Lady lives on the south side of Burned Mountain, about three-tenths of a mile from the top of the peak. The elevation is high at nine thousand eight hundred feet, but the approach to the Blue Lady from the east is a sloping ascent, not a steep cliff face. You won't need technical gear. It's about a half mile from FR 918. Burned Mountain water tank is nearby."

Tafoya and Janet leaned in closer. Janet used a magnifying glass to enhance the details of the site of the Blue Lady mine. She saw the area was south and west of the Hopewell Ridge. The Bone Ranch lay two miles southwest of the Blue Lady, and the Sullivan Park and El Vallecito Ranch lay farther to the south by three miles.

"Grazing permits for sheep are sold for the area," Janet said, "but the Bone and El Vallecito Ranches run cattle. I was out there less than a month ago with a Tres Piedras biology specialist. Burned Mountain and the surrounds are New Mexico's backcountry...good hunting area, too."

Tafoya looked at the quad, carefully thinking his next step.

"Google me the distance and time to Burned Mountain from Ojo Verde, please, Bessie."

Bessie sat down at the computer and googled the distance and time: "Fifty-three miles, estimated time to get to Burned Mountain from

Ojo Verde is one hour, thirteen minutes." She quickly made some other keystrokes on her desktop computer. "By the records I have online, there have been no mining claims filed within five miles of the Blue Lady. Farther up toward Hopewell Lake, as you come off of US 64 onto FR 918, there was a lot of mining activity last century, but all the veins played out, and it became too expensive to process."

Janet and Bessie looked at Tafoya who was sitting down, sipping Mundo Java coffee. They sat down around the map table, pondering what they had uncovered. Tafoya looked at his watch again: 9:17 a.m.

"Do you think Saltwater is out at Blue Lady today in this cold weather?" Janet asked.

"I wouldn't think so, Janet," Tafoya answered, "but we can't say for sure. Yesterday, he was at Feast Day, so he is still in the area." He paused, then said, "Tell you what, let's go out to Burned Mountain. We can be out there before lunch, and it isn't far from FR 918 to hike to the mine. I may be pushing too much on this, but, Janet, do you think we could go in your government vehicle with the Forest Service logo? That way, we wouldn't look suspicious. Going out there in a Tulona tribal police vehicle might scare him away, if he is even there. Given the terrain, we might even drive off-road and get closer to the site. What do you say?"

Janet called her supervisor and received permission to take their best four-wheel-drive vehicle. "Write a report when you get back about the status of whatever fauna you see and the grass cover and water tanks," her supervisor ordered.

Tafoya advised Sergeant Romero of his intention, informing him he was leaving the patrol car at the tribal police substation in Ojo Verde. He was taking the hard-case field laptop out of the police vehicle and porting it with him. Bessie wanted to go, but realized she needed to stay and work at the BLM headquarters. Besides, her cold-weather gear was at home.

Tafoya and Janet stopped by the Bolero Food Mart in Ojo Verde and bought snacks and soft drinks. They called ahead to the Narrow Gauge Café in Tres Piedras and ordered four burritos to go, stating they would pick them up in about forty-five minutes on the way to Burned Mountain.

For safety measures, Tafoya also took along additional firepower from the substation: a tactical twelve-gauge shotgun and extra ammunition for his Sig Sauer pistol. "Not that we will need all this Janet, but I rather be over-armed than under-powered." He took the military-grade laptop from his vehicle and power cables for his police radio, as well.

Leaving Ojo Verde, they turned west at the yellow blinking light outside of Ojo Verde at 10:18 a.m., heading toward the Tusas and Burned Mountain.

Luis Ortega, earlier that morning, stood up from his parent's breakfast table and placed his dirty dishes in the kitchen sink. "I'll take care of the dishes, Luis," his father said, "you go on out to the Tusas and check the grazing lease. We may be able to take the flock out there before the first November snow." Luis's mother told him to be careful, drive safely.

Luis gave her a kiss on her cheek; she blushed. Going out to the corral, Luis decided to take Buck to the grazing lease. Hitching up the trailer and saddling Buck in the stable, he loaded him in the trailer and threw a horse blanket over his saddle and flanks to ward off the chill. Buck liked adventure and had gone eagerly into the front trailer stall; Luis loosely tied the halter rope to the rail.

"You may not even get out of the trailer, Buck, but I know you like to travel." Luis often loaded Buck into the trailer to cart him around as he ran errands in Ojo Verde. Zeke jumped inside the pickup cab and sat upright in the passenger's seat, ready to help and eager to please Luis.

Janet drove the Forest Service vehicle as required by the rules. She sped up to 70 m.p.h., five miles over the speed limit. "You're not going to stop me and give me a ticket for speeding, are you, Richard?" she joked.

"No, Janet, but the New Mexico state trooper might. You can probably talk your way out of it. Besides, I'll tell them we are on a mission together."

They stopped at the Narrow Gauge Café in Tres Piedras and picked up their burritos, storing them in a soft-sided cold case that Janet had loaded with frozen packs. Passing the Tres Piedras ranger station on her right as they left the village, she honked the horn at anyone who was on duty that morning. She picked up the comm, raised the ranger station on radio, and stated she and Tafoya were headed for Burned Mountain to assess the effect of increasing cold temperatures on the sector. "I will apprise you when we leave Burned Mountain."

As they departed Tres Piedras, they rose in altitude on US 64. The semi-arid desert immediately fell away to forests of ponderosa and spruce. The overcast sky dampened the green hues of the forest to darker colors. Along the highway, blue spruces brightened the forest like Christmas trees. US 64 wound its way higher and higher. Groves of white-barked aspen with blackened stripes and gashes quaked with yellow leaves, and occasionally, red leaves. US 64's next major town beyond Tres Piedras was Tierra Amarilla, but they were going to turn off toward the west-southwest at Hopewell Lake Campground. Janet turned at FR 42B that took them by the campground. Campers, RVs, and tents were parked and erected in numbered spots.

Since the fire danger was minimal, campers lit fires that blazed in specialized firepits. Janet turned on FR 91B that angled due south from the campground and into mountainous terrain. Several mountains rose steeply along FR 91B. The GPS on Janet's vehicle indicated their location. The road was passable for only four-wheel-drive vehicles. As she turned a corner, Burned Mountain loomed in front of them.

"There it is," Janet pointed out.

Janet drove along the northside of Burned Mountain. The road circled the mountain on the east side. They looked for an off-road lane.

"Usually there's an off-road path to water tanks in the forest. Ah, there it is." The off-road path was rutted, but within two hundred yards they found the tank and stopped.

"If Robert Dihyja etched those military coordinates for the mine, the mine lies about a quarter mile into the woods and against the face of those cliffs exposed to the south," Tafoya said. They got out of the Forest Service vehicle and stretched. It was cold, the sky overcast.

Tafoya retrieved his binoculars from his field pack and scanned the area. At the water tank, he looked eastward across FR 91B. On the other side of the road, there was a cleared pasture with no fallen timber. The large pasture sloped downward from Burned Mountain. At the far edge of the pasture, he saw a pickup and horse trailer with a horse inside. A man with his black and white dog was walking in the mountain pasture toward the far edge of the forest. They were over a half mile away, ambling nonchalantly.

Turning away from the horse trailer and stockman, Tafoya became more attentive to his surroundings. He saw tire tracks that went up to the edge of the woods in the direction of the possible mine, but there were no vehicles to be seen. In and around the Burned Mountain water tank, there were no signs of campfires, rock shelters, or former campsites. He scanned the ground. "I see deer droppings, nothing else. You're right, Janet, this is backcountry."

He looked at his field watch: 1:13 p.m. The sun had not shown through the clouds all day, and the outside air temperature on the Forest Service vehicle had read thirty-nine degrees. Fortunately, the prevailing wind was upsloping, not tumbling down the mountain. Tafoya tried his police radio; he had no luck in raising the base station.

"No repeaters out here, Janet?" She answered him that they were in a dead spot for radio repeaters, but if they returned to the Hopewell Campground, they could make a connection.

"We have two other options for communication out this far in the backcountry, Richard."

"Oh, what are they, Janet?"

"On the Forest Service vehicle, we have a high frequency transmitter, like in ham radio. If they have their scanners turned on, Tres Piedras ranger station and even Ojo Verde can pick us up." Janet went back to the vehicle, started the engine, and tried to raise the base station on high frequency. "Darn it, I can't get them. They should have their scanners on. Or maybe they are away from the desk."

"What's the other option?" Tafoya asked.

"Smoke signals, says one Isleta to a Tulona," she grinned. They both laughed as they checked their cell phones for a signal. No signal there either. Rather than eat their burritos before they searched for the Blue Lady, they agreed to eat lunch when they returned. Each grabbed an energy bar and ate it to stave off the empty stomach.

They walked due west from the water tank for two-tenths of a mile, coming upon a cleared area of trees where talus rock had eroded down from the cliffs. The cliff face had direct exposure to the south, which was a necessary geological dynamic for creating turquoise, owing to the heating of the granite during the day to melt ice and snow for the mixing of chemicals.

Tafoya and Janet stood and looked at the face of the cliff that had several deep crevices. Trees blocked seeing into the depths of the crevices. They split up, each of them going into a different crevice, to check for mining activity.

It took only twenty minutes before Janet shouted, "Richard, I've found something!"

Dead trees covered the entrance to the mining crevice. The approach into the crevice was narrow, passable for a narrow wheelbarrow, but nothing wider. As you walked back into the chasm, the gap widened into a cavern exposed all the way up to the top of the cliff. Fifty feet into the crevice were stone mauls and gleanings from chiseling into the sides of the cave. Wooden levers remained stuck in some cracks. There were dozens of holes dug, tunneling back fifteen or more feet. The cavern widened as you walked back. Heavy mauls lay covered partially in silt.

Janet and Tafoya shined their flashlights onto the sides of the wall and in the tunnels. A few chiseled petroglyphs of shamans, geometric designs, had been carved. They focused their flashlights on a petroglyph, about five feet off the floor of the cave, that was ten feet horizontally in length. It was a wavy snake with a forked tongue and horns—the plumed serpent. They stared at the art, hundreds of years old.

"Here we have evidence of the Aztlán connection, the plumed serpent, Janet," Tafoya said. "Some of this turquoise probably found its way to Moctezuma." Janet walked up to the petroglyph, and with her fingers traced the head of the serpent.

"Careful, Janet, he may bite." Tafoya looked around. He found modern metal chisels and hammers, indicating recent activity. Then he abruptly halted.

"What do we have here?" he said. Tafoya found a khaki field bag on the floor near recent chiseling. Carefully unclasping the strap, he pulled out a bundle of dynamite, fuses intact. There were two other bundles inside. He carefully put them back in the pack and set it aside. "This is not good."

Tafoya picked up samples of turquoise matrix and two stone mauls, placing them back down after examining them. He took out his cell phone and snapped pictures of the mine, including the plumed serpent. "Let's get on back to our vehicle and call this in. I don't know who is going to have jurisdiction on this site—BLM, Carson, F.B.I., Taos County. But somebody can get rich, if they finish this mine out."

Carefully picking their way back down the talus slope, Tafoya said, "Janet, I want to check out this next crevice. I won't be long."

"I'll meet you at the truck. Burritos await us!" Janet said happily, as she started back to the truck, walking through the grove of trees toward the water tank. As she emerged from the trees near the tank, she saw the dark Ford pickup with wooden side rails on the bed; the same truck she had seen at Tres Piedras. The pickup of Andreas Saltwater. At first, she did not see him, but Saltwater walked out from behind her Forest Service vehicle. He acknowledged her with an awkward, upward nod of his head.

He must have been looking inside the vehicle. Did Tafoya cover up the shotgun in the back floorboard? flashed through her mind. She thought he had.

Janet continued walking toward Saltwater. She raised her hand in a sign of greeting and said loudly, hoping her voice would carry back to Tafoya, "Hello, there!" Saltwater did not respond, but continued walking toward her. She saw no weapon at his side or in his front waistline. It was cold, and he had a heavy coat on, so he might have a pistol underneath, concealed and loaded. As he came closer, the scar under his right eye became more apparent. Yes, this is Saltwater, she thought, and inwardly shivered, but contained herself.

"What are you doing up here?" he asked gruffly.

Janet pointed at the Department of Agriculture National Forest logo on her watch cap, and for emphasis, pointed and tapped at the logo on her coat. She wished the logo read, Forest Ranger, but she had to go with what she had. "I'm conducting a field survey at the moment." She paused, to let her responses, verbal and non-verbally soak in. Again, she made sure her voice was louder than conversational.

"Ummph," he responded.

"The water level in the tank is where it should be after the monsoon rains around here," Janet added, as a matter of information. Fear was mounting inside her. But I will not panic.

"What are you doing up here on a cold, sunless day?" she asked firmly.

Saltwater opened his mouth to speak, then closed it. Janet stood still, waiting for an answer.

"I'm, uh...I'm checking out places to hunt around here. This looked pretty wild and unsettled back in here. You been back up the mountain there?"

"No, I'm not much of a mountain hiker." Janet answered. She thought of the high frequency transmitter in her vehicle. She and Tafoya need reinforcements. She had to radio for help.

"Well, you have a good day, sir," Janet said, "I've got to get back to Tres Piedras and write up a report." She quickly walked past Saltwater.

"Yeah, okay," was all he said, turning to watch her walk to her vehicle.

Janet opened the door to the vehicle and climbed in. She started the engine and grabbed the microphone on the HF radio, "Tres Piedras, Tres Piedras, Tres Piedras! This is Carson one fifteen, do you copy?" All she got was static on the receiver. She repeated her transmission...still no response. Saltwater had turned around and was walking toward the grove, and, presumably, to the Blue Lady mine—and Tafoya.

Tafoya had said he would not be long coming back. What should she do? Drive off and find a signal to bring help? What if Tafoya had not heard her voice? Would Saltwater surprise Tafoya on the path to the cliffs and disable him?

Just then, Janet looked out her windshield and saw Tafoya way off the path to the cliffs, behind a large ponderosa; Saltwater could not see him. Tafoya gave her hand signals to, "Stay put," spreading his arms, palms down, and motioning downward with his arms, as if, "Slow down, or stay put." She stayed in the vehicle.

Luis Ortega, from across the road, three-quarters of a mile away, adjusted the focus on his binoculars to comprehend the scene at the base of Burned Mountain. "That's not looking good," he whispered to himself. Luis had finished his reconnaissance of the Ortega grazing lease, concluding that a flock of sheep could be pastured for the rest of October.

A few minutes before, as Luis looked around with his binoculars, he saw a Ford pickup pull up and park near the Forest Service vehicle. He saw a man get out of the pickup and try the doors on the official vehicle. They were locked. The man looked carefully into each of the windows of the vehicle. From the forest grove, Luis saw a woman Forest Service agent emerge and raise her hand in greeting the man. They conversed for a moment.

As they were talking, Luis noticed a movement in the grove from where the female Forest Service employee emerged. He changed his focus to the movement in the forest. It was not a wild animal; it was a policeman wearing a heavy coat and watch cap. What law enforcement agency he belonged to, he could not tell, but he was moving carefully. The man in the Ford pickup and the woman Forest Service officer broke off their conversation. She got back in her vehicle while the policeman off to the side of the picture was motioning to her, "Stay put," it seemed.

"Something's wrong over there," he concluded. Luis opened the gate to the horse trailer; he unloaded Buck who was already saddled and put bridle and bit on him. He went to his pickup and belted his .357 magnum, Rueger Vaquero, to his waist. He checked that every chamber was loaded and swung into the saddle, directing Buck straight across the meadow to the problem under Burned Mountain.

Tafoya hid behind the tree, while he furtively glanced at Saltwater coming toward the Blue Lady. He wanted to put himself between Saltwater and Janet in her vehicle. Undoubtedly, Saltwater was heading toward the Blue Lady mine. He would allow Saltwater to pass him by; then he would fall in behind him, follow him to the open area below the talus slope of the mine, stop Saltwater and cuff him. He would march him back down to the water tank, and hold him there while Janet drove up toward the Hopewell Campground to get a radio signal and call for help.

There's not a lot of moving parts to my plan. It should work, Tafoya thought.

When Tafoya looked again for Saltwater, walking up the slope to Blue Lady, he did not see him! Tafoya looked quickly on either side of the tree, avoiding exposing himself, but, still, no Saltwater. He held his breath and listened carefully. He heard the sound of the wind in the trees, and that was all. I've lost him. Tafoya did not move. He stayed behind the ponderosa, listening intently, hearing nothing; then he carefully began to back off from the slope of the mountain and go back down to Janet. Hopefully, Saltwater had moved up to the mining crevice. Tafoya was wrong.

Saltwater had returned to his pickup, and had coaxed Janet out of her vehicle. She was looking at her front tire. Saltwater was pointing to something.

This has gone on long enough, Tafoya thought.

"Hands up! Tribal Police! Janet! Move away! Hands up! Tribal Police!"

Saltwater raised his hands, and then grabbed Janet around her neck. She tried to break his chokehold, but could not. Saltwater reached under his coat and brought out a revolver.

"Don't struggle, I'll shoot her!" Saltwater yelled. "Put your pistol down, Officer! Right now! I'll hurt her, if you don't do what I say!"

Tafoya backed off, put his pistol down. "Kick that pistol into the water tank!" Tafoya hesitated. Saltwater slugged Janet on her head with the barrel of his gun, opening up a gash that began to bleed.

"Do as I say, or I'll pop her again!"

Tafoya did as he was told, keeping his eyes on Saltwater. I shouldn't have brought her out here, Tafoya thought, chastising himself. He thought about the shotgun in back of Janet's vehicle.

"It's okay, Richard. I'm not hurt that bad," Janet shouted.

Tafoya began cajoling. "Listen Saltwater, this is over. Don't make this worse for yourself. Put your gun down and let her go! It's over! You probably didn't mean to kill Dihyja. It was an accident."

"Shut up!" Saltwater screamed. "It was no accident. We had been arguing for days about the Blue Lady. He wanted corporate backing on the mine. When he said he had made contact with a syndicate out of Santa Fe, and they wanted to talk to me...I-I-I lost it...stuck him with the chisel...up there at La Osa. We had been partners for years, and he was bringing in someone else!" Janet twisted, but could not break Saltwater's hold.

Tafoya talked quickly. "That was unpremeditated murder, Saltwater. You can get less time for that. Give it up and let her go! It's over!"

Tafoya was focused intently on Saltwater. What one is conscious of when under great stress narrows to a pinpoint. The same was true of Saltwater. He was thinking of Tafoya and how to get out of the mess he was in. The woman he had a chokehold on was squirming. She was stout.

Suddenly, a black and white flash streaked in front of him. It was a dog. He loosened his hold on Janet. As taught in self-defense, she dropped straight down from his loosened grasp and rolled toward Tafoya.

"What the...?" Saltwater yelled. A twelve-hundred-pound horse was barreling down on him.

Buck recognized Janet in distress. She had freed him from barbed wire and soothed him, helped him, and now she was being hurt by a two-legged one. Buck flared his nostrils, pinned his ears back, bared his teeth, and furiously charged Janet's attacker.

Before Saltwater could finish his sentence, Buck ran over Saltwater.

Saltwater screamed and tumbled away, losing his pistol. Luis had spurred Buck to gallop over Saltwater, but Buck had reasons of his own to attack without spurring. Luis had quietly come up from the road and then, just as quietly, spurred Buck into action. Zeke had run out ahead of Buck and Luis, diverting Saltwater's attention away from charging Buck.

Saltwater scrambled out of the way, stumbled to his feet, and ran up into the forest grove toward the Blue Lady. Still bleeding from the gash on the side of her head, Janet ran to her vehicle, opened the door, and pitched the shotgun to Tafoya. Luis dismounted from Buck.

"Stay here Janet," Tafoya said.

"No, Richard. I'm going with you. I'll keep up."

"I really wish...," then, Tafoya let it drop. "Let's go get Saltwater!"

They walked quietly through the forest grove to the bare section of ground that lay in front of the talus rock and Blue Lady mine. Saltwater quickly found his way into the crevice where the mine was located.

"He can't get out of there. The cliffs are too high in there for him to climb out of," Tafoya said. Then he thought of the dynamite. There were three bundle-sticks with fuses; Saltwater could light them and throw them out of the entrance. "Hold off. Let's think about this," Tafoya cautioned. He decided to talk him into surrender.

"Saltwater! Listen to me. There's no way out of there. Other law enforcement personnel are going to be here soon," Tafoya lied. "Give yourself up."

Saltwater threw rocks out of the mine. They landed yards away from where Luis, Janet, and Tafoya stood. "That's not much of an offensive strategy—throwing rocks," Luis chuckled, as he fired a shot in response.

"Luis, hold your fire!" Tafoya said, his ears ringing from the pistol shot.

"Sorry about that shot, Saltwater. I want you to give yourself up and come down peacefully. I'm a Tulona tribal policeman and I'll make sure you are taken care of safely. I'll help you."

Saltwater did not respond.

"Do you hear me?" Tafoya shouted.

No verbal response came from Saltwater, but a few rocks were tossed out, bouncing down the talus slope.

Tafoya waited. Then he spoke again. "Andreas, why did you leave Robert on the reservation across from Majerus?"

The wind, fortunately, still rose upward to the conifer forests above the clefts, a relatively warming wind. A quick break in the altostratus clouds illuminated a large sunny swath around the four of them. A rustle of rocks below them turned their heads downslope. Buck was walking up to the standoff ensemble, wanting to be a part of the remuda and action. "Whoa!" commanded Luis; Buck stopped in his tracks and waited. Zeke trotted back to Buck, sat on his haunches and waited with him. The clouds passed rapidly over Burned Mountain and closed the aperture for the sun. Quickly, the air turned colder.

Saltwater answered Tafoya's question. "I came off the road from La Osa and the gate was open on the reservation. I drove through the gate and turned right along the fence line to Majerus's place. I laid Robert, born to Two Rocks-Sit, across from Majerus to make the ghost go into Majerus's life." Saltwater stammered, "I-I-I don't know...I thought Majerus would take care of Robert's dead body, Navajo-style."

Luis bowed and shook his head from side-to-side. "Terrible and stupid and senseless." He crossed himself faintly.

Saltwater continued. "Majerus received the teaching of my grandfather on The Red Antway and the Godway songs. Those songs should have gone to my father, not him! I wanted Robert's ghost to screw up Majerus's life like he messed up my father's...but Robert was my *compadre*, my friend, and I wanted his spirit to rest.... Majerus could do that for him. But Robert's ghost kept coming to me in dreams and in the wind.... Agghhh," howled Saltwater.

"Let's back up a little bit," Tafoya said. "He's losing it."

Saltwater had low light in the mine, but enough to see and fetch the khaki bag of explosives. He pulled out a bundle of dynamite. He walked to the entrance of the mine, still hiding in the mining cleft from Tafoya and the others. From his field pouch under his coat, he fumbled through his tools and pulled out a lighter. Saltwater stood at the entrance to the cave.

"I've got a question for you," Saltwater shouted. "How did you know the mine was here at Burned Mountain?

"Robert etched the location under the Blue Lady turquoise on his belt buckle," Janet shouted. "He left a trail to the Blue Lady." Janet had put a bandanna around her head and pulled the watch cap snugly over her gash and bloody hair. She looked at Tafoya; he nodded affirmatively.

Saltwater was silent. Then, above the wind, they heard him wail.

"*I was Andreas Saltwater, son of Roger Saltwater. I was born to the Bead People, born for the Black Streak Wood People. Now I am going to meet the Night People, those above me. Hey, yea, yea, hey-o, hey-o, Ho!*"

Saltwater stopped singing. He bent down to the floor of the mine, picked up two small slivers of Blue Lady turquoise, placed her in his mouth, lit the fuse to the dynamite and walked back into the darkened recess of the mine. He stood under the plumed serpent petroglyph.

Tafoya, Janet, Luis, Buck, and Zeke rushed down from the talus slope when the explosion went off. They were far enough away from the force of the explosion to avoid the impact as they ran into the grove. Within the cavern, the walls collapsed from the top of the cliff down into the cave. Rocks and boulders spilled out of the cave's entrance and tumbled down the slope. Then, the whole side of the cliff collapsed on itself, like a mudslide suddenly loosed from the mountain. Grayish dust rose upwards as the side of the cliff settled into a chaos of stone and timber. Echoes of the explosion reverberated about Burned Mountain and the foothills. The Blue Lady had imploded. Saltwater was dead.

Luis rode Buck, with Zeke running alongside, across FR 91B to his pickup and trailer. He loaded Buck and headed back to San Miguel. He left behind his phone number and address with Tafoya for the authorities to contact him. Janet retrieved the first-aid kit out of the Forest Service truck and winced when Tafoya cleaned the wound. On the HF band, she had contacted Tres Piedras ranger atation, and they had alerted the Taos County Sheriff's Department who were sending officers. The ranger station said there had been a brief solar flare that knocked out communications. They were also sending National Forest personnel to assist.

Tafoya had the Tres Piedras ranger station patch him through to Romero. Romero said he would inform the F.B.I., and Parker will want a written report as soon as possible. "I'll bet she wants more than just a written report, Janet," Tafoya lamented, as he ended the conversation with his sergeant.

In less than an hour, the Taos County Sheriff's Department, the Rio Arriba County Sheriff's Office from Tierra Amarilla, the National Forest team out of Tres Piedras, and the New Mexico State Police descended on Burned Mountain and what was left of the cliffside. Janet's field supervisor wanted the Forest Service to be mentioned in the news reports as important links in finding Andreas Saltwater and solving the case. The F.B.I. had decided to helicopter in to the Hopewell Campground, arriving just before Tafoya and Janet were to leave for Ojo Verde. A New Mexico state trooper vehicle brought the F.B.I. team, headed by Diane Parker, to the Burned Mountain water tank, where she insisted on hiking back up to the remnants of the Blue Lady.

Tafoya told Deputy Sheriff Cordova to inform Special Agent Parker that he would write a full report the next day, plus a powerpoint presentation, and send it by email for her perusal. He and Janet were exhausted and needed rest. Tafoya and Janet climbed into the Forest Service vehicle, quietly leaving the scene with dozens of vehicles screening their exit. Parker would not be happy with their early departure. Her problem, thought Tafoya.

Janet drove the vehicle as required by the rules. When they reached US 64 and turned southeast to return to Ojo Verde via Tres Piedras, they were relieved to be on smooth pavement. The sun dipped below the cumulus clouds in the west, so that its rays slanted onto the Taos Mountains and Tulona Peak in the far distance, creating a brilliant glow to the trees. Tafoya turned and looked at Janet as she drove under the speed limit. She was beautiful, he thought, even with the bandage sticking out from under her watch cap.

He reached over and put his hand on her shoulder. She lifted her hand and patted his, leaving it there for a few seconds.

"Like your ancestors before you, you were brave in the face of your enemies today, Janet." Tafoya said.

She looked at him. "You know of that saying, Richard? My Isleta grandfather gave me those words."

"Yes, a Mescalero cousin of mine used to say it all the time. '*Bi da a naka enda,*' was how he said it, most powerfully."

Janet thought of the strange congruence of Mescalero, Isleta, Tulona, and how she and Tafoya faced Saltwater, the enemy, this day. She drove on for a mile or two, without talking, thinking deeply.... Then she turned to Tafoya.

"Back up there on Burned Mountain, I would never have left you, even if you had waved me away, Richard," she said.

Tafoya turned to her, not knowing what to say.

"Richard," she said again, looking straight ahead, driving down the highway.

"Yes," he said, completely off balance by now.

"You're not going to make that powerpoint for Parker, are you?"

AFTERWORD

Death at La Osa unfolds over thirty-six days, from late August to the first week in October. Set in contemporary northern New Mexico about the Taos area, a fictive Pueblo and village are created, Tulona Pueblo and Ojo Verde. *Death at La Osa* is, on one level, a murder mystery and a search for a turquoise mine. The architecture for the novel pivots on pueblo ceremonialism and ordinary daily chores of law enforcement, sheepherding, horse maintenance, waiting tables, and bookshop tending. The environment and weather affect social and economic interchanges. High mountain altitudes, desert mesas, National Forests, and sharp changes in weather from desert heat to snow and rain are ever-present factors in the novel.

On a second level, the novel concerns social interaction of three cultures in northern New Mexico: Pueblo, Hispano, and Anglo. Tribal policeman Richard Tafoya seeks to solve a murder of an unidentified man on the Tulona reservation. Numerous characters assist his investigation, but Forest Service biology specialist Janet Rael (Isleta Pueblo) becomes essential in his search for the killer and discovery of the turquoise mine. Tafoya and Rael grow romantically closer in their relationship. Armando Ortega and his wife, Loretta, along with their son, Luis, are Churro sheepherders residing north of the Tulona Pueblo. Luis is a horseman and teaches farriering to a friend at the Pueblo. Armando and Loretta are experiencing the not-so-gentle aches of old age. From the Anglo perspective, G. Armstrong Coe is a bookshop owner who migrated to Ojo Verde with his wife from California. Coe, over the years of his residency, becomes closer to Cacique Bustamente of the Tulona Pueblo and begins to understand tensions between Pueblo and Anglo culture.

During the thirty-six-day period, two Pueblo ceremonies figure large in the novel, both occurring on Feast Day at the Tulona Pueblo—the annual footraces and pole climbing. At the dangerous pole climbing ceremony, a visiting Hopi of Second Mesa asks Coe, "Who do you think will win? Nature or the Machine?" This somewhat incongruous question on Feast Day and Coe's answer punctuates one of the oldest stories in human history—the loss of the Garden and humanity's attempt to regain the Garden and be redeemed. *Death at La Osa* is a novel about that redemption and reconnection. Some of the characters find the unity; others see it, but lose it. A turquoise mine is discovered, but at what cost to the two men who stumbled upon it?

Death at La Osa reflects the twenty-first century adaptation of Pueblo, Hispano, and Anglo-American cultures to small village and Pueblo life in northern New Mexico. Each culture has tensions and compromises with the other. Set in motion by the Spanish Coronado-Oñate *entradas* and the Anglo-American onslaught of the 1840s, conflict and compromise still rolls unabated. Spanish law, the *encomienda* system of labor control and tutelage, the Catholic Church, Manifest Destiny, paternalism, tangential consequences of capitalism and land hunger, and the emergence of touristification and museumification of Pueblos are powerful forces that challenge freedom and adaptation in contemporary times. Cultural anthropology and archaeology are scientific fields informing *Death at La Osa*'s architecture and plot flow. Gender roles, both fluid and static; ritual behavior; religious transformation; shamanistic practices; magical thinking; and Pueblo group organization within the novel have artistic formation derivative of anthropology.

Death at La Osa is based upon my teaching history and anthropology. My major sources include my personal field notes in observation, site survey, and excavation; my work at Ghost Ranch, New Mexico, at field school; and published work of ethnologists, archaeologists, and historians. I taught Native American history, the anthropology of religion, and courses in U.S. history, world civilization, and humanities. Conducting anthropological field trips to the area of the novel and requiring student field research in the anthropology of religion informed much of this book. Anthropological and historical materials used in this novel are not intended to meet scholarly standards. My interaction with Indigenous friends gave me insight into Pueblo culture, as well as visits to the backcountry of Pueblo reservations. Mountaineering in northern New Mexico gave me unforgettable views of vast landscapes and challenging trails that I apply in writing the novel.

Seeking to describe humanity within a flourishing and personalizing culture propelled me to write *Death at La Osa*. The Pueblo ceremonialism I have witnessed illustrate how human communities honor, respect, and make sacred the earth upon which we walk. I am convinced writing about nature and its sacred spaces will change minds and undergird respect for nature. I may be wrong, but I do not think I am. Hispano and Anglo cultures arrived later and brought different adaptations to northern New Mexico, and all three cultures succumbed to the land, weather, and change of seasons. There are infinite permutations of interactive behavior to nature within the area I write about, and, unfortunately, not all of the adaptations are flourishing and personalizing. To write about these things is reverentially inspiring. A reading of this novel I hope inspires reconnection to each other and nature, so that the Other ceases, if only for a time, to be.

LITERATURE

Death at La Osa is the old story of humanity being thrown out of the Garden, subsequent degeneration, and redemption. Returning to the Garden is the oceanic background set in northern New Mexico involving the tri-cultures of the Puebloan, Hispano, and Anglo.

In storytelling, what this novel illustrates is the daily effort to regain the Garden. To be plain, the Garden is *here*, not lost, and the "regaining of the Garden" is not the spatial reconquest of real estate, but rather the mindful and emotional reconnection of one's Self to Nature and the Other. What was lost is not the Garden somewhere out there, but the Garden in one's body that connects to all motions, other bodies, or, the incomprehensible-spirit-that-moves-in-all-things.

Death at La Osa is, on one level, a murder mystery and a search for a turquoise mine. Those two factors keep the story moving to uncover the killer's identity. On a second level, the novel pivots and moves on Pueblo ceremonialism and ordinary, daily activities. Overarching are the landforms of desert mesas and mountains with the sharpness of weather changes in northern New Mexico, i.e., the Garden-outside.

Even so, exile spoils paradise, pain arises. Logging trucks bring cut ponderosa down from the forests, their engines roaring along the Paseo del Norte, rattling Tablita Restaurant windows, intruding on the life of Ojo Verde in materialistic, capitalistic ways. Jealousy and anger mar backcountry cliffsides in search of turquoise, the blue tears of heaven. The accumulation of wealth spoils the symmetry of friendships and communities, while social deviancy of alcoholism and mental disorder make the daily police blotter list. Despite the congruency of being close to nature in a beautiful setting, naturalism in all its blood and lust intrudes. I place the novel in mainly a classic romantic, transcendental classification, but with degenerative events spoiling the view—realism within the Ojo Verde-Tulona Pueblo communities.

In my writing, I find composing occasionally in the stream-of-consciousness mode is effective. I think it carries, artistically and emotionally, the fluid mental thoughts of a character from page to reader in a direct manner. But I see it, furthermore, as a literary construct to display ecstatic states of characters, i.e., dancing, singing, hallucinations, glossolalia. When Bustamente's boy-to-man climbs the pole in the future, his fluid mental state, I think, is best described in a Joycean style. I telescope the boy's arc of maturity to the day he climbs the pole and is honored by his peers. In a vision, he sees the unending lines of elders watching the ceremony through time. Pueblo future, like all communities, is uncertain.

HISTORY

Tulona Pueblo and Ojo Verde are figments of my imagination, but they arise out of the prehistoric and historic evidence of the upper Rio Grande—north of El Paso—particularly the area around Española and Taos. The geographic location of *Death at La Osa* encompasses the Eastern Pueblos of New Mexico, from Isleta south of Albuquerque to the northernmost Taos Pueblo. The Tulona Pueblo is imaginary, but it is a composite of the 19 Pueblos of New Mexico, particularly the Tiwa-speaking peoples—Isleta, Sandia, Picuris, and Taos Pueblos.

The Coronado expedition in 1540 entered New Spain, known as New Mexico and Arizona today. While Coronado camped at Zuni, a subaltern, Captain Hernando de Alvarado, lead a party of twenty soldiers with a guide and explored the area west of Coronado to the area of present-day Albuquerque, visiting Pueblo villages as far north as Taos. Over the next 480 years—close to five centuries—the eighty villages or Pueblos adapted, succumbed, rebelled, or disappeared in the diffusion of Spanish conquest, the brief Mexican political control, and Anglo-American dominance after the Mexican-American War of 1846-48.

Following Coronado's *entrada* in 1540, the next salient point in the history surrounding northern New Mexico was Juan de Oñate's huge permanent settlement in 1598, consisting of 400 men, some with families. Eventually camping at Caypa, renamed San Juan, the Spanish settled the area, remaining intact until the Pueblo Revolt in 1680. With Spanish conquest, tutelage, and dominance, cultural diffusions occurred, including Catholicism, Spanish law, political lords, radical concepts of land ownership, and the reckoning of time. An objectification of flora, fauna, and landforms by the European, Mexican, and American cultures influenced, but did not destroy, the Puebloan view of the world as animistic—Mother Earth, Father Sky, the sacredness of the seven directions, spirits in all things.

European ideas of discovery and conquest, superiority of culture, and reform gave rise to the Black Legend of the Spanish. The antithesis of the Black Legend was the White Legend, seen in Ben Lovato Medicine Wind's use of metal and horse—both introduced by the Spanish and adopted quickly by Indigenous communities. Attempts were made to wipe out kiva culture and force acceptance of the Spanish *fe*—the Catholic faith. The three pillars of Spanish authority were the *ley, rey,* and *fe*: law, king, and faith. Kiva culture prevailed, remaining robust today.

The historical record may have begun in 1540, but Indigenous oral histories go back further. If you converse with the Puebloan or other Native people, many begin their history with the emergence of Turtle Island, a fertile, mythical, creation narrative. Oral narratives and archaeological material attest of migrations from the North and the interior Mexico. In *Death at La Osa*, Quail Looks Away mentions Bustamente's talk of the ancient-present—what was past is here, now. She is puzzled as to the concept and wishes to talk more with Bustamente about just what "ancient-present" means. What is introduced is the teaching of present-mindedness, "All we have is the present, the now!" In other words, the historical past is not past. William Faulkner wrote, "History is not dead; it isn't even past." *Death at La Osa* is an elegy to the memories of storytelling among the Tulona Pueblo, sat down in the high and cold country of northern New Mexico. But Euro-American history, as a professional intellectual activity, does not deal with the consciousness-phenomenology of ancient-present; that is primarily the purview of anthropology and psychology.

Discovery and conquest by the Spanish and Americans deprived the Pueblos of land and the education of their children in traditional ways. The Pueblo Revolt of 1680 under the leadership of Po-Pay violently expelled all but twelve families of the Spanish to El Paso. A reconquest of the Pueblos succeeded in 1692 under De Vargas, resulting eventually in a softer approach to Pueblo culture, but periodic small-scale revolts continued. Intermarriages and liaisons appeared from the very beginning of Spanish intrusion. In *Death at La Osa*, the emotional and sexual attraction is seen in the relationship of Luis Ortega (Hispano) to Flowers Dancing (Tulona).

The Spanish were paramount in ending the Comanche raiding of Pueblo settlements by the killing of Chief Cuerno Verde (Green Horn) in 1779, near the Arkansas River, closing the raids from the east, but not the west and north. The Navajo, Apache, and Ute remained threats to the Pueblos for decades after New Mexico governor Juan Bautista de Anza's defeat of the Comanche in 1779. Even so, among the tribes, peaceful trade continued. In 1821, the Spanish were overthrown by revolution in Mexico.

Mexican-appointed governors maintained traditional relationships with New Mexicans. Except in name, much looked the same to northern New Mexicans until the Mexican-American War ended in 1848. Americans, especially Texans, began to drift into New Mexico and more seismic changes occurred.

The American government thought Indigenous Pueblos (and other tribes) backward and uncivilized, needing education and resettlement. Back behind this "compassionate" policy lay "land hunger in the guise of civilization." Indigenous culture was repressed, the children of the Pueblos and other tribes were forced from their families and homes, sent to Indian schools where they had their hair cut, clothes changed, and were required to speak English, not Tiwi, Navajo, or Native tongues. Not until the administration of Franklin Roosevelt and the Indian Reorganization Act of 1934, did the policy of Indigenous culture suppression begin to lift. Central to this policy change was the sociologist, John Collier.

Collier introduced the Indian Reorganization Act of 1934, reversing decades of forceful assimilation of the Indian in favor of emphasizing Indigenous self-determination and return of communal land. Indians could live under their own tribal customs. This reversed a policy, articulated as late as 1926, by the Indian Bureau to curb Pueblo religious rites.

The Taos Pueblo Indians in 1974 achieved a restoration of Blue Lake, their symbolic source of life. More than symbolic, the water outflow from Blue Lake, Rio Pueblo de Taos, provides drinking and irrigation water for the Pueblo. Once a year, Taos Pueblo Indians return to Blue Lake for their ceremonial rites. *Death at La Osa*'s second scene involves Ben Lovato Medicine Wind returning from Earth Cloud Lake, a correspondent sacred place akin to Blue Lake. Over the next couple of days, Ben follows the twenty-seven-mile trail back to Tulona Pueblo, encountering Jason Taylor, an Anglo that took the wrong road toward the ceremonial grounds. Wally Covington, like John Collier in history, had been turned back at the first campground because of Pueblo opposition to Anglos venturing onto their sacred space.

In terms of historical context, *Death at La Osa* reflects the twenty-first century adaptation of Pueblo, Hispano, and Anglo-American cultures to small-town, wage-earning, tourist-oriented, and rural life in northern New Mexico. Each culture has tensions and compromises with one another, originating with the Spanish Coronado-Oñate *entradas* and the Anglo-American entry in the 1840s. Conflict and accommodation still roll unabated. Manifest Destiny, paternalism, tangential consequences of capitalism and land hunger, and the emergence of touristification and museumification of Pueblos are powerful forces that challenge and impel concordance among the tri-cultures.

ANTHROPOLOGY

Cultural anthropology and archaeology are scientific fields informing *Death at La Osa*'s architecture and plot flow. Gender roles, both fluid and static; ritual behavior; religious transformation; shamanistic practices; magical thinking; and Pueblo group organization within the novel have artistic formation derivative of anthropology.

My long-range intent is to write a cycle of novels encompassing one complete year, anchored by tribal ceremonies and Puebloan thought. As the first novel of the year's cycle, *Death at La Osa* features foot races, pole climbing, and appearances of the Black Eyes or sacred clowns on Feast Day. Taos Pueblo, to the south of fictious Tulona Pueblo, has San Geronimo Feast Day. Their practices on Feast Day are correspondent to Tulona's ceremonies with similar activities. San Geronimo and Saint Francis Feast Days reflect Spanish cultural diffusion among tribes.

The sources of anthropological data used in *Death at La Osa* are three: my personal notes of field observation; my work at Ghost Ranch, New Mexico, at field school; and published work of ethnologists and archaeologists. Particularly, I am indebted to E. C. Parsons (Taos, Isleta, Zuni Pueblos), Washington Matthews (Diné), Vera Laski (Ohkay Owingeh Pueblo), Leland Wyman (Diné), Alfonso Ortiz (Tewa), and Sylvia Rodriquez's work on "Ethnic Reconstruction in Contemporary Taos."

In *Death at La Osa*, the maintenance of tribal solidarity and social cohesion figure large. In the novel, Tulona men are digging by hand a hole for the fifty-foot pole that will be climbed on Feast Day. The labor is arduous; no mechanical means are employed to dig or set the pole. A young Tulona boy overhears Bustamente say, "These things [digging of the hole by Tulona] must be preserved." Bustamente explains common toil and the ceremony of pole climbing build the unity of the Tulona Pueblo people. The young boy takes the wisdom, applies it to heart, and climbs a pole in the future; a vision of his connects the past, present, and future.

Gender-specific roles within Tulona society are fixed, but changing. Two female characters reflect changing behavior and relations with males within *Death at La Osa.* Most notable, U.S. Forest Service biology specialist Janet Rael starts strong in the novel, and finishes even more prominent in the final chapters. Rael is from the Isleta Pueblo. Tribal policeman Richard Tafoya and Rael are attracted to each other, and their relationship intensifies slowly, but inevitably, as the novel progresses. Biology specialist Rael is a licensed pilot, a tireless field worker, and she is courageous. At confusing moments, she sees through the chaos. Her memory is incredible. A striking moment occurs when she says to Tafoya that she could fly her plane and rescue him, if necessary, out on the Navajo Reservation. Though spoken in jest, she is serious, and Tafoya believes her. Rael becomes more significant and has the personality and character to take control and influence the outcome of events.

A second character, Quail Looks Away, has had to assume roles fixed by tribal custom. She is only allowed to "help" within the Blue Stone kiva, and domestic chores fall under her responsibility—carring water, preparing meals. In *Death at La Osa*, however, she desires excitement and rides Star after birthing Dezba five days before. She is inquisitive beyond the customary role, wanting answers to time concepts within Pueblo esoterica that only Cacique Bustamente can impart. She shows an aptitude for understanding Pueblo cosmology that could break the mold of all-male spiritual leaders.

Another source of ceremonial significance is the burlesque of the sacred clowns. The Black Eyes behavior on Feast Day has been interpreted anthropologically as playful, joking, and opposite of normal behavior. It is a time of insulting and rude behavior, far from the accustomed Pueblo congeniality. Beneath their sacred clown roles, the Black Eyes are healers and will anoint children and adults with Rio Tulona clear waters on Feast Day. Rio Tulona is more than a source of drinking water and irrigation for the Tulona; it is sacred water.

Santiago Majerus, the Navajo Red Antway singer, looms significantly in the novel. Some Tulona see him as a Sleep Maker, a witch. He represents a character that strides several cultural adaptations as Navajo medicine man and a Tulona owner of irrigated land in a Hispano community. Majerus's adaptive behavior in *Death at La Osa* is illustrative of people that must live within different cultures. Majerus's Navajo and Pueblo heritage prevent him from romantic happiness with a Hispano woman, a rejection he never forgot.

Jason Taylor, the restaurant server and ski aficionado, along with G. Armstrong Coe, represents the migratory person that seeks the playground aspect of Ojo Verde, its environment and climate. Jason migrated for the ski valley; Coe and his wife came for the climate, landscape, and exoticism of the Tulona Pueblo. Both Jason and Coe depend on the tourist trade: Jason waits tables for tourists, and Coe sells books to visitors and locals. The work of Sylvia Rodriquez and John J. Bodine examine the impact of migrants and amenity residents on Taos that I apply in writing about Ojo Verde and Tulona Pueblo. Their ethnological observations are invaluable in writing *Death at La Osa.*

As a final figure in cultural conflict in tri-ethnic Ojo Verde, Luis Ortega teaches Lion Walks Night the skill of farriering and helps him in purchasing a horse. Ortega is attracted to Flowers Dancing, a sister to Quail Looks Away. He thinks his Hispano background might inhibit a relationship, but it does not. Luis remains close to his family in sheep tending and assisting his parents in old age.

Death at La Osa, in anthropological terms, is a novel illustrating cultural conflict and adaptation in gender roles and economic interplay, the importance of communal ritual through traditional ceremonies, and the power of emotional and sexual attraction to overcome cultural divisions. The emotional component breaks barriers and establishes bonds that lead to economic exchanges and new family connections. In the best-case scenario, trade and emotional contact make friends and alliances; in the worst case, raids and wars ensue. These are fertile dynamics compelling anthropological research and the writing of fiction.

ADDITIONAL READING

Bodine, John J. "A Tri-Ethnic Trap: The Spanish in Taos." In *Spanish-Speaking People in the United States.* Proceedings of the 1968 Annual Spring Meeting of the American Ethnological Society. Seattle: University of Washington Press, 1968. A brief but insightful inquiry into the Anglo belief that Taos is a kind of utopia, the selling of "ethnicity" to tourists, and the Spanish loss and gain of "prestige and status deprivation" in the community. Despite its 1960s origin, Bodine's observations remain current.

Bullard, Robert D. *Confronting Environmental Racism: Voices from the Grassroots.* Boston: South End Press, 1993. An anthology of articles regarding environmental crisis impacting communities of color. Laura Pulido's article on Ganados del Valle's sustainability effort and the grazing conflict in Wildlife Management Areas near Chama, New Mexico, influenced the sheepherding aspects of *Death at La Osa.*

Indian Pueblo Cultural Center: Gateway to the 19 Pueblos of New Mexico. The cultural center is located in Albuquerque. The website, www.indianpueblo.org, has links to the New Mexico Pueblos. Not all Pueblos have websites.

Matthews, Washington. *Navaho Legends*. Forgotten Books, 2012. Originally published, Boston: Houghton, Mifflin, and Company, 1897, for American Folklore Society. Washington Matthews was a medical doctor on the Navajo Reservation. He became fluent in Navajo and wrote extensively on the chantways of Navajo medicine men, including the Night Chant and Mountainway. This book is a composite of his work.

New Mexico Historical Review. Online archives, 1926-present. A quarterly review of historical articles on New Mexico history that includes book reviews and primary source material. A University of New Mexico publication.

Northern Rio Grande National Heritage Area and Center. A heritage center that is broad-based in function for Taos, Rio Arriba, and Santa Fe counties. Focuses on Spanish and Indigenous culture of the northern Rio Grande. A sizeable effort is made to publicize artists of the area as well as land use. The physical center of the organization is in Alcalde, New Mexico, where the Juan de Oñate statute was located. The statute has been completely removed—not merely a foot—as a result of pressures from various groups in 2020. See www.riograndenha.org.

Ortiz, Alfonso. *The Tewa World: Space, Time, Being, and Becoming in a Pueblo Society.* Chicago: University of Chicago Press, 1969. Ortiz was born into the Okay Owingeh Pueblo and became a professor of anthropology at the University of New Mexico. A detailed book delving into the six categories of Tewa human and spiritual existence. Includes references to principal directional points and sacred landforms in the Tewa world as well.

Parsons, Elsie Clews. *Pueblo Indian Religion.* 2 vols. Bison Books ed. Lincoln: University of Nebraska Press, 1996. Originally published, University of Chicago, 1939. The extensive work on Pueblo religion of a sociologist turned anthropologist. Includes references to all New Mexico Pueblos as well as the Hopi. Sections on variations and diffusion from non-Pueblo tribes included. Detailed, copious, and rich with comparisons and contrasts.

Pogue, Joseph E. *The Turquoise: A Study of its History, Mineralogy, Geology, Ethnology, Archaeology, Mythology, Folklore, and Technology.* Vol. XII, Part II. Washington: National Academy of Sciences, 1915. Extensive study of turquoise from its mineralogy to folklore across the world with geographic specificity, including the Southwest. Pogue's work is considered a culturally significant work and "part of the knowledge base of civilization."

Rodríquez, Sylvia. "Ethnic Reconstruction in Contemporary Taos." *Journal of the Southwest* 32, No. 4 (Winter 1990): 541-555. A scholarly article on the impact of "touristification" on Indigenous and Hispano communities in Taos. The idea of maintaining and sustaining "ethnic forms for entertainment" is rigorously treated. The impact of the ski valley and tourism on watersheds is analyzed.

______, "The Taos Fiesta: Invented Tradition and the Infrapolitics of Symbolic Reclamation." *Journal of the Southwest* 39, No. 1 (Spring 1997): 33-57. An ethnological article on the Taos summer fiesta from the 1930s to the 1990s, starting with elite Anglo dominance to a Hispano fiesta council directing events. Traditions were invented encompassing the bohemian art colony and Puebloans to attract tourists, then evolved to a reclamation of symbolic forms emphasizing Hispano themes.

Sanchez, Joseph P., Robert L. Spude, and Art Gomez. *New Mexico A History.* Norman: University of Oklahoma Press, 2013. An up-to-date survey and readable narrative of New Mexico history. Covers the period from prehistory to the impact of recent political activists and casino business on tribal lands. A good, general bibliography provided.

Silko, Leslie Marmon. *Ceremony.* New York: Penguin Books, 1986. Originally published, New York: Viking Press, 1977. A novel of depth and personal expression that soars. Larry McMurtry and N. Scott Momaday regard it as more than a novel; it is a "telling" in Momaday's review. Silko is from Laguna Pueblo. She writes resonantly about the earth, sky, weather, and the people who must attend to the natural world—first, foremost, and be achingly in it.

The Taos News. Online archives, 1960–present. This is a primary source of weekly news for Taos and vicinity since its founding in 1959. Prior to that, Taos County and region had *El Crepuscúlo de la Libertad*, a journal published by Padre Antonio Josė Martinėz in the 1830s, as well as *El Heraldo de Taos, The Taos Cressett, La Revista de Taos*, and other titles in the nineteenth and twentieth centuries.

Trujillo, Michael L. *Land of Disenchantment: Latina/o Identities and Transformations in Northern New Mexico.* Albuquerque: University of New Mexico Press, 2009. This is an ethnographic study of the Española Valley. Written from a perspective to "tarry with the negative," Trujillo shows the vibrant and conflicting cultures of northern New Mexico. Personal identity for the Latina/o is analyzed deeply and from unusual lenses, such as the typology of joke telling and "remembering and dismembering." Warning! Trujillo's work may be disturbing to some readers! My advice—read it.

ACKNOWLEDGEMENTS

I wish to acknowledge information derived from the anthropological and ethnological work of E. C. Parsons, Washington Matthews, Vera Laski, Leland Wyman, Alfonso Ortiz, Marvin Harris, Merton Leland Miller, John J. Bodine, George L. Trager, and Sylvia Rodríguez. Among my teachers, I am indebted to Dorothy McIntosh, Mrs. Sidney Hughes, Lola Best Covey, Joseph Milton Nance, Herbert H. Lang, Henry A. Bullock, Ken Stevens, William Beezley, and Donald Worcester. To write about turquoise from mine extraction to a finished product, I relied upon the art and skill of Lyle Wright and Larry Martinez. Patricia L. Quintana provided detail on shepherding, horsemanship, and idiomatic expressions relative to northern New Mexico as well as insights into Ganados del Valle, a sustainable agricultural development organization in the mountain village of Los Ojos in Rio Arriba County. My Puebloan friends who care for elders, sing, photograph, paint, sculpt, and craft bison-horn knives enriched and inspired my writing.

In law enforcement operations and constitutional issues, I owe a debt of gratitude to Greg Gullion; Selden Hale; Amarillo Police Department; New Mexico State Police; and the young, unknown-to-me, Taos Pueblo tribal policeman I saw at breakfast one cold morning at El Taoseño Restaurant on Paseo del Sur. What I imagined *his* day would be like, and his life thereafter, initiated this novel. Among other restaurants that influenced my writing are Taos' Doc Martin's and La Doña Luz, Santa Fe's La Casa Sena, Fort Worth's Pacific Table and The Tavern, and Brownwood's Cactus Café and Schwartz Eat Shop. Brown's Bookstore in Amarillo and the Taos Book Shop offered me more than the printed page; they were places of quiet, doors opening new worlds.

The USDA Forest Service Camino Real Ranger District in Peñasco has provided maps, clear trails, and advice for camping and mountaineering along Rio Santa Barbara and Truchas Peaks. The writings of Marion E. Gridley, Frank Waters, Tony Hillerman, Anne Hillerman, Arthur W.

Upfield, Dan Brown, Peter Matthiessen, James Salter, Patrick Leigh Fermor, Annie Dillard, Jim Harrison, Alan Furst, Norman O. Brown, Leslie Marmon Silko, Rudolfo Anaya, and N. Scott Momaday have always been on my bookshelf for style, different lenses, and inspiration.

I am especially grateful to Carl Condit, Director of Operations, and James Clois Smith Jr., Editor, of Sunstone Press, Santa Fe, for publishing and guiding *Death at La Osa* to publication. Carl and James have made collaboration to a finished product smooth and without bumps in the road.

I appreciate the promptings of Tom Bell, Clay Wiegand, Tracy Roeder, Claudia Stravato, Chris Clark, Dusty Blu Cooksey, and Duane Hale to write beyond academia. To my daughter, Wendy Needham, and her husband, Charlie, thank you for encouraging my writing and providing space in Taos to write undisturbed. My wife, Brenda, supported and critiqued my writing efforts, and I am truly grateful for her keen insights.

Finally, I wish to acknowledge my students through the years. We kept each other company to raise our level of confusion and clarity about the world and each other, while we learned the language of the field.

READERS GUIDE

1. In *Death at La Osa,* most chapters begin with the name of the day and date of the week, the Catholic saint of the day, and the Indigenous ascription of the month. What do these three naming categories say about "cultural" time?

2. The three cultures—Puebloan, Hispano, Anglo—in the book blend and conflict. Where do they intersect? Where do they separate?

3. Tribal policeman Richard Tafoya and Forest Service officer Janet Rael eventually work together on the Dihyja murder case. What reasons prompt Janet to work on the case beyond the growing emotional attachment each had for the other?

4. What was the precipitating cause for Saltwater to murder Dihyja? What were the deeper causes of his act?

5. *La osa*, translated from Spanish to English, is "female bear." Why was *la osa* used as a primary name in the novel, and not *el oso*, a male bear?

6. G. Armstrong Coe and Jason Taylor settled in Ojo Verde for much the same reasons. What were they? How were their reasons different?

7. Quail Looks Away puts her newborn on Luis Ortega's lap. Why did she do that? And why did Lion Looks Away want Luis to see the newborn?

8. Cacique Bustamente and the young boy watch the digging of the hole for the pole climbing on Feast Day. Why is communal activity important to the Tulona Pueblo? Or to any people?

9. Why did WarChief Juan Concha rope the tree off from investigators tromping to *La Osa* cave? Why not just cut the branches off as the deputies started to do?

10. On race day and pole climbing, how did the Puebloans, Hispanos, and Anglos view the two ceremonies differently? What were their different reasons for coming to Feast Day in the first place?

11. The murder case was stymied in the beginning with the identity of the victim, identity of the killer, location of the kill site, and motive. Why is Tafoya's trip to Sheep Springs so significant in gaining momentum in the case?

12. At the pole climbing, the Hopi from Second Mesa asked Coe, "Who do you think will win? Nature or the Machine?" How would you answer the question?

13. Santiago Majerus represents a link with the Navajo Andreas Saltwater, the Tulona tribal policeman Tafoya, and the *acequia* culture of the Hispano in New Mexico through his family heritage. How has Majerus found contentment in his latter days with his varied life and adaptations?

14. Horses play subsidiary and significant roles in *Death at La Osa.* They are to be ridden, of course, but what other activities do horses play in the novel—particularly Buck?

15. Ben Lovato stuck his head in sagebrush blossoms as he had seen coyotes do. What does this say about Puebloans' relationship with nature? Is there a contrast with what others might do or say upon seeing the coyote stick their head in sage?

16. Is *Death at La Osa* a murder mystery set in nature, or a novel of nature set in a murder mystery?

www.ingramcontent.com/pod-product-compliance
Lightning Source LLC
Chambersburg PA
CBHW010746310726
48980CB00004B/377

* 9 7 8 1 6 3 2 9 3 4 7 7 2 *